Mike filled them in on every detail that had taken place in the White House and the Pentagon. He pulled no bones about the seriousness of the mission they were about to go on. These men liked the straight word; not the crap other commanders often pulled ... These were Mike's own. Hand picked. Absolutely trustworthy and willing to live or die with him, not for him. That was undoubtedly the main reason for their success. Absolutely dedicated, without fear, or inbred jealousy. Trust. He had it in them and they in him. Almost unique in the army. Nearly everywhere else, it's the old man wants this, higher headquarters directs that. Not here. They were a team. The COBRA team. And by God, as long as he was in command, it would never change. All equals, sharing the same danger ... Unsung, unheralded, and largely unknown, their exploits and actions, if revealed, would have provided top news copy for the nation. Perhaps one day, that might be possible.

THE COBRA TEAM

ROBIN MOORE

&

EDWARD E. MAYER

POPHAM PRESS

CHARTER
NEW YORK

A Division of Charter Communications Inc.
A GROSSET & DUNLAP COMPANY
51 Madison Avenue
New York, New York 10010

THE COBRA TEAM

Copyright © 1978 by Robin Moore

All rights reserved. No part of this book may be reproduced in any form or by any means, except for the inclusion of brief quotations in a review, without permission in writing from the publisher.

All characters in this book are fictitious. Any resemblance to actual persons, living or dead, is purely coincidental.

A Popham Press Book.

First Charter Printing June 1981
Published simultaneously in Canada
Manufactured in the United States of America

2 4 6 8 0 9 7 5 3 1

To those who serve

PART ONE

Chapter 1

MOSCOW WAS REELING under a late winter storm. The bitterly cold wind whipped large snowflakes in every direction as General Boris Kartsalov began walking from the parking area on the west side of the grime-covered walls surrounding the Kremlin.

Pulling his parka snug against his chest, Kartsalov looked up at the Hotel Metropole's time and temperature clock. Two forty-five and 18 degrees below zero. Good Lord, he thought, this cold and Spring. He knew Moscow was cold, at times almost unbearable, when he accepted General Llanmuth's offer to move from his command on the sunny shores of the Black Sea to Moscow, and take over as Chief of Soviet Rocket Forces. But he hadn't dreamed the cold would last month after month.

The thought of facing Premier Krenchev in fifteen minutes made it more unpleasant. How he disliked that man! Domineering, impetuous, and even worse, a self-proclaimed rocket expert.

As he passed through the huge grilled iron gate under the archway leading to the Premier's office and saw row after row of official state automobiles parked inside, Boris was reminded again of Krenchev's contemptuous attitude toward senior military officers of the motherland. Unlike other high government officials, Boris and his fellow Red Army generals were not allowed to drive their Russian-made Fiats into the Kremlin.

This privilege, as Premier Krenchev had announced soon after taking office, was reserved for members of the Politburo and his senior staff. Generals and their ilk, he emphasized, would park in the large area on the west side of the Kremlin which was used once a year for the annual May Day parade. When several generals requested they be given a parking space within the Kremlin grounds, Krenchev had mockingly suggested to his staff that they find a parking area even more remote, in order, as he put it, to give his generals a bit more exercise and thus keep them in better physical condition. His own corpulence, pronounced by a bulky, rotund frame and a protruding stomach, made his sarcastic comments about the overweight Soviet Army officers more ironic.

Except for days like this, with the biting cold penetrating every exposed area of the face, Boris really enjoyed the long walk. Seldom now did he have the opportunity to spend long, lazy afternoons walking in the Moscow parks. Since his appointment as commander-in-chief of Soviet Rocket Forces, he had little time with his wife, Nina, and their grandchildren. Instead, he was intensely busy responding to many demands put on him by his old friend, General Sorge Llanmuth, chief of the Soviet General Staff and Deputy Defense Minister, and Premier Krenchev's almost impossible orders for a more rapid expansion of the rocket forces.

As he entered the door leading to the waiting room outside the Premier's office, Captain Stagnull, the office aide, took his parka and fur cap and said, "Sir, General Llanmuth and the others are waiting in the briefing room. Your equipment arrived earlier and it has been set up as you directed. The Premier will be along in a few minutes."

"Thank you, Captain. We'll be ready for the Premier whenever he is free."

Boris moved into the briefing room. General Llanmuth turned toward him as he entered. "Good afternoon, Comrade Kartsalov. I'm sure you must hate me on a day like this. I read in this morning's *Pravda* that the temperature at the Black Sea resorts was expected to reach 80 today. But be patient: before long Moscow will be pleasant."

Boris laughed. If it weren't for Sorge's occasional sense of humor and their long friendship dating back to their days together at the military academy, his job would have been unbearable. As it was, he knew his old friend often took the brunt of Krenchev's fury without passing it down the chain of command. For this he was grateful.

"Are you going to make any remarks before I brief the Premier on our gadget?" Boris asked.

"Yes. I'm going to try and dissuade him again from going along with this wild scheme of his. But if he's adamant, I'll have you present our foolproof system."

Their discussion was interrupted by Captain Stagnull's announcement, "Gentlemen, The Premier of the Soviet Union, the Honorable Elonson Krenchev."

That stupid bastard, Boris thought. He's getting more and more like royalty, putting on autocratic airs, aping even the kind of address given the President of the United States. The revolution to make us all equal had faded for Krenchev, he thought. It was Comrade Stalin, Comrade Molotov, but not with Krenchev. He had to be the Honorable Premier of the Soviet Union. What a mockery of socialist and fraternal ideals the pompous ass made. His thoughts were interrupted by Llanmuth taking the podium, who with a nod acknowledging the presence of the Premier, began very deliberately and in measured tones.

"Comrade Krenchev, before we begin briefing our technical instrumentation package for the nuclear weapons destined for Cuba, I would like you to reconsider the decision to arm Castro with intermediate range ballistic missiles. I feel, and I know my fellow generals share the view, that you are playing with fire.

"The United States, if it should learn that nuclear weapons are being put into Cuba, probably will be forced to take immediate and drastic action. As I have told you repeatedly, we are inferior to them militarily in every way. We could not stand up to their military might for more than a few weeks. The introduction of nuclear weapons ninety miles from the U.S. mainland is tantamount to issuing the Americans a challenge which they cannot ignore and we are not now prepared to accept.

"In ten or fifteen years things may be different, but not now." Sorge continued, "You have often stated how unpredictable Castro is at times. Can we afford to put our security and future in his hands? Comrade Krenchev, I strongly recommend that you reconsider your earlier decision and not give Castro nuclear weapons. Conventional weapons, yes. But nuclear weapons are too dangerous."

"General Llanmuth," Premier Krenchev said sharply, "I've listened to these arguments before. The Americans, even if they found out, would do nothing. You recall how I cowed their President Ketner when we met in Vienna. He's a young kid afraid of his own shadow. I know. I sized him up in Vienna. He's immature, indecisive, and weak. You must remember, he was elected by a whisker, a whisker. He doesn't have the support he would need to take any meaningful action. You generals are all alike, thinking the Americans are ten feet tall. I'll stand up to any of them. They don't scare me a bit. Now let's get on with the technical briefing; I don't want any further rehash of old arguments you've made before."

"Very well. General Kartsalov will explain our technical instrumentation package."

Kartsalov moved forward, somewhat ill at ease. The Premier had reacted arbitrarily, he thought as he began.

"Comrade Krenchev, we have designed a system for our nuclear weapons being shipped to Cuba which I believe will meet your requirements. The captain will point out the various parts of the system as I describe them. Captain, uncover the equipment on the table, please."

Kartsalov continued. "This is the nuclear warhead for the intermediate range ballistic missile. It is over three feet long and has a diameter of eighteen inches. Its weight, without the instrumentation package, is seventy-eight pounds; with, eighty-one pounds. The firing mechanism for the weapon is located where Captain Menlohov is pointing—it's the small recessed chamber. This is the area we have designed to house the specially configured instrumentation package.

"Premier Krenchev, you stated you wanted a timing device which could be pre-set here before the nuclear weapons are shipped to Cuba, and which would automatically detonate the weapons should Castro, in one of his unpredictable moods, attempt to renege on your arrangements. This instrumentation package will prevent the unilateral use of these warheads by Cuba in the event Castro attempts to abrogate our support and orders us out. If he refuses to return our nuclear weapons, this package enables us to automatically detonate a weapon at a pre-set time.

"Captain Menlohov, will you display the mechanism. You can see, Comrade Premier, the mechanism is not much larger than a cigar box. However, you may be sure that it is powerful enough to detonate the weapon and destroy nearly everything within a radius of four to five miles of the point of impact. Some fallout would result. The General Staff recommends pre-setting each weapon before it is shipped to detonate in exactly one hundred and fifty days. On this basis if Castro behaves, we can transmit a code to Cuba and reset the detonating mechanism for another period of time.

"The system is nearly foolproof because the exact code must be put into the minicomputer which will advance or retract the detonator plunger when it has moved the exact distance pre-set in the mechanism.

Even Castro cannot change the timing. Only Soviet personnel are able to and they first must be given the code. The code for each weapon will be kept here in Moscow in the military operations center.

"A week or two before the one hundred and fifty days are up, orders will be sent to the Soviet military representative in Havana to move to the missile site to reset the weapon by inserting a new code. A list of all weapons by serial number, their location in Cuba, the code expiration date, and a suspense system to remind us to transmit a code change will be kept here."

Boris was pleased. So far not a single question. The Premier seemed fascinated by it all. Moving around to the far side of the table and holding a piece of paper in his hand, Boris continued.

"We have added another device which I now would like to demonstrate. For this purpose, we have placed a small blasting cap in the device to simulate an actual explosion. I do not want to frighten you, Comrade Krenchev, so be prepared for a small detonation as I explain this function.

"Assume this piece of paper I am holding is a message sent from our operations center here in Moscow to the Soviet advisory group in Cuba. It will contain the new code and the serial number of the weapon, which is shown here on this model." Boris pointed out the serial number consisting of numbers and letters located at the bottom of the firing chamber alongside the Russian insignia painted in deep black in the center of the warhead.

He continued, "After verifying that the serial number contained in the message and the weapon are one and the same, the code is inserted by depressing each of the appropriate keys. For example, the code in this case is YP9H48G961. The keys are depressed in that sequence. As each letter or number is recorded, this small red light will glow indicating that the letter or number has been entered into the computer."

"Let me do that," the Premier said.

"Certainly," Boris replied.

The Premier rose from his seat and moved to the small table on which the nuclear weapon was displayed. He fingered it gently.

"No need to worry about it exploding, Comrade Krenchev. It's only a mock-up," Boris intoned.

"I know that," the Premier retorted sharply. "I know all about Soviet weapons. You must remember, General, I was once a lieutenant in a rocket battalion."

"I thought you were a political commissar when you were in the service," Boris said quietly.

"That was my official title. I was really in charge. None of the officers knew a damn thing about these weapons. Only Comrade Krenchev. Even in those days all the men thought I should be in command. They often told me so."

Boris smiled. Krenchev had served with a mortar battalion in World War I and was convinced that mortars of that era were the forerunners of the present day high technology rockets.

"General, this looks too simple," Krenchev said as he fingered the small console. "It's almost like a small electronic calculator I have on my desk except this one has letters in addition to numbers."

"That's exactly what it is," explained Boris. "A small calculator which transmits a code to the minicomputer. It is a simple instrument. It's the code that's difficult. It must be in the exact sequence of numbers and letters. The system is similar to the codes we use in communications between battalions and regiments. According to our security people, these codes are not easy to break."

General Llanmuth, who had been sitting quietly while Kartsalov was explaining the detailed code system, finally interrupted. "Boris, show the Premier the warning device you have built into the system."

"Yes, sir. Comrade Krenchev, we'll let you put the code into the machine. For this demonstration, the code we have selected will be good for ten minutes. As I explained earlier, we can pre-set the timer for any number of minutes, days, and up to six months in the minicomputer."

Premier Krenchev slowly punched each letter and number in the sequence shown on the message. As he depressed each key, the small red light of the receiver glowed brightly, indicating the number and letter being inserted. "There," he said as he punched the last number, "that ought to do it. Now what?"

"See this small glass covered rectangular box here?" Boris continued. "Thirty minutes before the automatic detonation of the weapon, the box will glow a brilliant red and display a crossbones and skull and a written warning of danger. At the same time a loud, intermittent noise will be heard from this device we have installed." Boris pointed out to the Premier each part as he described it.

"What's the purpose of that device?" the Premier asked sharply.

"Sir, we thought that if we ever had to use this system against Castro, we wanted to give the crews manning the weapons a chance to escape before the missile exploded. We feel confident that if they hear the warning signal and see the warning light, they will put some distance between themselves and the weapon."

"If we reach that stage with Castro, I don't give a damn!" Krenchev replied heatedly.

"Sir, some of our own troops might still be there," Boris explained.

"All right, but cut the time to five minutes warning. Can you do that?"

"Yes, we can, but thirty minutes would give our personnel more time."

"General Kartsalov, I said five minutes. If we lose a Soviet soldier or two, what's the difference. However, I'll compromise about the time. Make it ten minutes exactly. That will give everyone time to clear out except the idiots, and we can get along without them."

The Premier started to walk back to his easy chair at the end of the conference table when he turned and said, "What if Castro figures out what we have built into the weapon and tries to disarm it by taking it apart piece by piece?"

"Comrade, we have considered that possibility and have installed a disturbance device in the warhead. If any attempt is made to take it apart without first inserting the exact code, it will detonate immediately. We must have our advisors warn the Cubans never to tamper with these warheads. Only Soviet rocket trained personnel who have access to the code are qualified to disassemble them. Any Cuban who tries will learn that it is a one way trip to heaven, or wherever they go."

Suddenly an intermittent wail of a siren came from the warhead on the table. The glass rectangular box glowed a brilliant red. A skull and crossbones appeared in a vivid outline. Below, the warning message; DANGER, EVACUATE AREA IMMEDIATELY, EXPLOSION IMMINENT in large black letters contrasted sharply with the brilliant red. The siren sounded louder and more shrill.

Boris had to shout to overcome the noise of the beeper. "Comrade Krenchev, that is the alerting alarm signal and warning message. If you do not deactivate the nuclear weapon with a code at this time, it will go off in minutes and blow you to bits unless you can put three to four miles between you and the weapon. However, as I mentioned earlier, in this demonstration we are using a small blasting cap to simulate a nuclear explosion."

The eerie sound of the siren was beginning to get on Krenchev's nerves. As the alarm became louder and louder, Krenchev covered his ears with the palms of his hands. Finally, the sharp crack of the exploding blasting cap reverberated through the room. Then, suddenly, there was a deadly silence.

"Comrade Krenchev," Boris explained in a calm

voice, "that's how the system will work when it is operational, except the final explosion will demolish everything within several miles. Do you have any questions?"

"As usual, General Kartsalov, you have done your homework well. I'm satisfied the system will work; it should protect our interests should Castro start behaving irrationally. Now a final question for you, General Llanmuth," Krenchev continued, "how soon can these devices be manufactured and installed, and when can we start shipping the warheads?"

"We can manufacture and install the device on one weapon in about two weeks. And one more every two weeks thereafter. We should be ready to ship the first weapon in about a month. Do you agree, Boris?"

"If that's your decision, Comrade Krenchev, then we can have the modifications made and the warheads ready for shipment in the time mentioned," Boris replied.

"Goddammit," Krenchev said emotionally, "the decision has been made. Get on with the program. You generals are all too timid. That's why I'm Premier. I make decisions. No vacillation on my part. Set the timers for exactly one hundred and fifty days and have Admiral Yonsolas get the missiles shipped to Cuba as soon as possible. We'll fly the warheads there as soon as they are ready. Won't Ketner be surprised to wake up one morning and find the United States hostage to Soviet nuclear weapons which cover that country day and night! I can hardly wait for that day to come. It will be a glorious achievement in our long struggle with the prima capitalists of the world. Canada, West Germany, Japan will all topple like dominoes when the United States capitulates. That is all, Comrades. Dismissed." The Premier rose abruptly and left the room. The two generals stood silent, each reluctant to speak. Finally Sorge could hold his emotions no longer. "Boris, is he mad?"

"He's either mad or stupid," Boris replied. "I suspect

the latter. But what can we do?"

"Nothing except follow orders, I guess," Sorge said in disgust. "I'll have Admiral Yonsolas pick up the missiles as soon as you have them ready for shipment. We'll ship the nuclear warheads by air. Be sure and have the timing devices set for one hundred and fifty days. At least that is a plus for Krenchev, thinking of a foolproof system in the event Castro misbehaves."

"Okay, we'll get the modifications started immediately. It won't take us long. However," Boris continued, "with luck, Krenchev may slip on one of our icy streets and rejuggle his befuddled mind."

Putting on his parka and fur cap, Boris started the long walk back to his Fiat. Maybe the fresh cold air would clear his doubts about Krenchev's foolish adventure. If only there were some way they could change heads of state like the practice followed by most Western nations. For once he envied the system of government in Great Britain, France, and the United States. When they had an intolerable leader they could get rid of him. Perhaps one day the Russian people would be able to institute a similar system. But Boris despaired of its happening in his lifetime, if at all. That was the Communist dogma. He dared not challenge it.

Chapter 2

THE TREES ALONG the George Washington Parkway were alive with color. Summer was a lovely time in northern Virginia. However, Robert Ketner was nearly oblivious of the colorful surroundings. Only the majestic Potomac River cascading over the large rock formations on the near side of the river caught his eye as his car sped toward Key Bridge. He wondered what crisis caused him to be summoned to an early, urgent meeting at the White House on a Sunday morning.

When he left the President yesterday afternoon there was no indication of trouble. He and the President had even indulged in banter about the chances of the Washington Redskins getting to the Super Bowl.

The Skins were about to open their training camp at Carlisle and the sportswriters were already touting the strength of the "over-the-hill gang" with the acquisition of several well-seasoned tight ends, a quarterback who had won the Heisman trophy several years before, and the signing of the lengendary Tom Brooks as their coach.

Certainly their conversation about the escapades of Senator Brown, which had been spread across the front pages of Saturday's *Washington Post*, could not have prompted the meeting. Brown in the past few weeks had been repeatedly the subject of news reports and gossip alleging that he kept young women on his payroll who could neither type nor file, but who, according to the senator, had no equals in meeting and greeting his constituents and taking care of their every need.

The Lincoln Continental hesitated only briefly before being waved through the East gate of the White House grounds. Bob Ketner literally sprang from the car as it pulled up to the White House entrance. He glanced at his watch. Two minutes to eight. Exactly thirty-five minutes from the time he had answered the phone in his suburban home in McLean and heard his brother's voice telling him to get his butt out of bed and meet with him at the White House as soon as he could get there.

As he hurried up the steps leading to the front entrance, the doors opened and George Holmes, the long time White House doorkeeper, in his sonorous barroom voice boomed out, "A good morning to you, Mr. Ketner, the President is waiting for you in his office." As long as he could remember, George hadn't varied his greeting since the very first day he had set foot in the White House years before.

As he knocked softly on the Oval Office door, a rather gruff "Come on in, it sure as hell took you long enough to get here" came from behind the closed door.

Bob Ketner pushed open the door and quickly looked around. Except for the President pacing back and forth behind his desk, no one else was present.

"Good morning, Mr. President. Where the hell is the fire?" Bob Ketner knew he could needle his brother like no other cabinet officer would dare.

"Hold your horses, Bobby," the President shot right back. "After all, you have no one to blame but yourself for being called in this morning. Remember, you pleaded with me to let you have the job as my National Security Advisor, even on a temporary basis you said, when Harrison Walliford resigned in a huff several weeks ago. But you're not alone in having your Sunday morning lay-in disturbed. I've also invited Ben Taylor and John Askins to join us. They should be here any minute. I want their views, as well as yours, on a major problem I'm facing. While we're waiting, have a cup of coffee; it's on the house."

As Bob Ketner poured his coffee from the silver carafe on the President's desk, Benedict Taylor and John Askins arrived. Taylor, the ramrod-straight chairman of the Joint Chiefs of Staff was resplendent in his uniform bedecked with ribbons that seemed to cover the available space on the front of his well-tailored blouse.

He had always liked Taylor. They had been friends from their very first meeting in Europe some years before when Taylor, a handsome young general with a distinguished record of army service, then commanded U.S. Forces in Berlin. Bob Ketner had visited the beleaguered city as a congressional staffer. He felt a bit responsible for Taylor's appointment to the prestigious chief's position after recommending him to the President, shortly after the inauguration.

On the other hand, John Askins simply baffled him. The longtime director of the Central Intelligence Agency was still an enigma in many ways. Quiet, unobtrusive, always extremely formal, and absolutely certain of his great expertise in the intelligence business. He had not been able to adjust well to the President's informal and often casual way of deciding the great issues facing the nation. However, the President had refused Askins every time he suggested resigning in favor of the appointment of a new intelligence director who might be more compatible with the cabinet and the President's personal staff.

Bob Ketner took his usual seat and looked at his brother still pacing nervously back and forth behind his desk. He could see the faintest suggestion of fatigue and weariness in the President. The dark circles under his eyes were a telltale sign that he had spent a sleepless night.

The President sat down abruptly in his wingback

chair facing the fireplace and gazed at the sunlight streaking in the window. His face was grim as he turned and opened the conversation. "Gentlemen, I'm sure you're wondering what the hell has happened that I'd get Bobby out of bed, have Ben give up his golf game with the Air Force Chief of Staff, and keep John from his early morning walk along the C & O Canal. As a matter of fact, I had very little sleep during the past twelve hours. Late last night, I received a call from a close confidant whose identity I must protect. He told me that the Cuban community around Miami was rampant with rumors that the Soviets were introducing intermediate range ballistic missiles armed with nuclear warheads into Cuba.

"Then, an hour or two after getting back to sleep, I had another call. This one from the Secretary of State. He had had an unplanned midnight visit by the ambassador from one of the Iron Curtain countries who informed him, on a highly confidential basis, that he was concerned about certain actions the Soviets were taking regarding Cuba and strongly recommended, almost implored, that we increase our surveillance of Cuba at once. Finally, Senator Kern called me at about 5:30 this morning to advise me that he had reliable information the Soviets were moving nuclear weapons into Cuba. He reminded me that he had passed this same information to me over a month ago. He noted that I had apparently taken no action. Accordingly, he wanted me to know that he felt free to express his deep concerns and apprehensions about these developments later on today when he is to appear on "Face the Nation." I asked him for his source on his latest information. He declined to share it with me at this time, but Ken was positive his information was absolutely reliable."

The President hesitated for only a moment before continuing. "There is a possibility that Senator Kern's source and my informant are one and the same, but I doubt it. Think it over. More than a month ago, based on the earlier reports, including Ken Kern's private conversations with me, I gave the three of you carte blanche to use any and all resources available to the government to determine the truth about these rumors.

"Ben, you keep telling me that air reconnaissance over Cuba has been intense and has produced nothing of significance. John, you repeatedly have insisted that it is all rumor being spread by certain elements within the Cuban community in Florida. And Bobby, you tell me the FBI is not involved and has no responsibility in the matter."

The President turned his chair slightly to the right and looked directly at Bob Ketner. "Bobby, we've known Ken Kern for a long time. Even though we're from different political parties, he is an honorable man and a loyal and devoted American. He is convinced that the Soviets are arming Castro with nuclear weapons aimed right at us. Ken and I may differ politically but we have always been together on security issues. I respect his judgment. Thus, when the ambassador of an iron curtain country, who happens to be a close personal friend of the Secretary of State, tells us to increase our surveillance of Cuba immediately, I'm concerned that our intelligence collection effort is missing something really important."

With an inquisitive look on his face and looking first at Ben Taylor, then at John Askins, he continued: "Do either of you have any suggestions or recommendations on what we might do that hasn't been done up to now?" Glancing quickly at Bob Ketner and Ben Taylor to confirm that he was expected to reply first, John Askins rose from his chair and faced the President.

"For God's sake, John, sit down. I'm asking for suggestions, not a formal briefing." From his voice, it was apparent that the President was irked.

"Mr. President," John began, "we have polled every source we have to determine the validity of these reports. As you know, we have a large number of informants within the Cuban community in Florida, and an extensive agent network in Cuba.

"We keep getting reports out of the Florida Cuban community every day passing along this type of information. But we have not a bit of substantiation. We have rated most of these reports F6, which you will recall is the lowest rating assigned in the intelligence field and translates into the source being completely unreliable, and the information false."

"What do you hear from your agents in Cuba?" the President asked quietly.

"Much of the same. If we took their reports at face value, Cuba would have sunk by now if only a quarter of the reports of Soviet equipment being introduced were true. I'm absolutely certain our information is accurate. Ken Kern, and the others, are using rumors to embarrass you and your administration. I'd be happy to poll our sources again but I would expect nothing new from them except possibly to blow their cover and expose them, which would be frightful. Indeed, a cardinal sin in the intelligence business."

Bob Ketner glanced at the President who was biting his lower lip and making an obvious effort to control his anger. Finally, after a long silence, the President looked directly at John and said, "You're telling me that all you can do is more of the same; nothing more. I take these reports seriously. I will do so until I get some substantial evidence that proves them false. Your only capability, if I understand you correctly, is to conduct a poll of your informants and get another report from your agents. Have you fellows out there at Langley lost all of your visionary intelligence concepts that are constantly being shown on TV and written up in the press? If so, we're in deeper trouble than I thought."

John Askins leaned forward in his chair as if to rebut the President's statement but decided that silence was a more appropriate stand. With the President in this frame of mind, nothing he could say would improve his position, or that of the agency. He'd bide his time and wait for a more opportune moment when he and the President were alone. Dammit, he thought, he wouldn't have his agents and informants concoct stories and reports just to satisfy the whim of the President.

"Ben, how about the Joint Chiefs? What can the military services offer?"

"Mr. President, every square foot of Cuba has been photographed without results. To be honest with you, the photography has been broad in coverage. We have taken low-level detailed photography of only a few likely looking sites. Obviously, if we had any idea where these weapons might be stored or emplaced, we could direct low-level, high-resolution photo missions against the appropriate targets to verify any weapons in storage, or being installed.

"Your instructions were to limit our coverage to high altitudes, to avoid being shot down. The only exception was to be against areas of a suspicious nature which showed up in high altitude photography. During the past month we have flown eight low-level missions and have found nothing more exciting than goatherds, pig farms, an apparently unauthorized nudist camp, or possibly an office party that got out of hand. John tells me that his agents on the ground are reluctant to stray far from their homes or places of business. In my opinion, that makes them almost totally ineffective."

"Ben, I direct my agents and informants. I'll judge their performance. Don't tell me how to run intelligence affairs." John Askins' voice was trembling as he glared at Ben Taylor.

"Sorry, John, but that's how I see it. In sum, Mr. President, without agents on the ground who can pinpoint more precisely the locations of possible weapon sites, I feel our photography efforts will not be of much value. I have a recommendation. While sitting here and listening, and perhaps talking too much, the thought occurred to me that this might be the time to consider committing our COBRA Team."

"COBRA Team! What the hell is that?"

"That, Mr. President, is a small, highly trained, tightly disciplined team we have hidden in the army for use on only the most critical missions affecting the security of our nation. I thought for sure that you had been briefed on their capability before. Bob, wasn't that your understanding?"

The President looked at Bob Ketner with a wry smile. "Bobby, have you been holding out on me again?"

"Yes, Mr. President." Bob Ketner continued. "If anyone is to blame, I am. General Taylor briefed me on the COBRA Team shortly after you assumed office. I had intended to inform you at an appropriate time should we ever be faced with a situation where they might be needed. After listening to John's tale about his informants and agents, and Ben's problems with photography, it might be worth considering the use of the COBRA Team. Incidentally, only half a dozen or so key personnel in the government know about this team. Am I right on that, Ben?"

"That's correct," Ben replied. "Besides the four other members of the Joint Chiefs of Staff, only the chief of the Special Operations Division on the Joint Staff and a couple of key officers on the army staff are aware of this outfit. Oh, yes. The Special Forces commander at Fort Bragg, where the team is stationed, is also privy to their special status. Of course John knows about it. His agency supports the team with special equipment. John, as far as I know, only you and your chief of Clandestine Services are aware of this arrangement."

"That's right, Ben. Bill Neilson and I know the details of the COBRA Team. Others who support it think it's just another Special Forces detachment among the many they support at Fort Bragg."

It was obvious to Bob Ketner that the President was interested in the COBRA Team. He had begun to smile. Leaning back in his chair and lighting his pipe, he appeared deep in thought. Finally he spoke. "Before you continue, Ben, what is the background of this team? Who started it? Why? When? And how might we use it now?"

"Mr. President, the requirement for a COBRA team dates back to World War II. You may remember that during that war, intelligence sources reported the Germans were working on a heavy water plant in Norway which our scientists were convinced was to be used in building an atomic bomb. President Roosevelt and Winston Churchill were so concerned that Hitler might beat us in developing an atomic capability that they ordered the heavy water facility destroyed. It was located in the side of a high mountain in Norway, immune from allied air attack.

"The Combined Chiefs of Staff recommended the formation of a small team of Americans, Brits, and Norwegians-in-exile to attack the site and destroy the equipment manufacturing the heavy water. Their recommendations were approved. While organizing the team, it was found that it took a special breed of men to undertake that type of mission. The fact that they succeeded was due almost entirely to their superior physical condition, extensive training and some highly specialized equipment developed solely for the operation.

"After the plant was destroyed by the raiding force, consideration was given to disbanding the team and having the men return to routine military duty. Fortunately, wiser heads prevailed, and the team was kept intact and continued a strenuous training program. It wasn't long before they were called upon to mount an operation into Germany to capture an antitank missile armed with an infrared homing device which had been invented by the Germans, and was being used with deadly accuracy against allied tanks and trucks.

"Through a very ingenious plan, the team not only captured the antitank missile but brought out with them the principal Germans in charge of the entire infrared program, including Dr. Rudolph Von Guessling. Along with Von Guessling, the team evacuated key members of his organization. This team of infrared experts provided the basic technical knowhow and leadership for our own very successful infrared program.

"Based on such experiences and several others like them, a decision was made after the war ended to keep a highly trained special operations team within our military forces. That decision turned out to be the forerunner of our present day COBRA Team."

"Ben, that's simply great!" The President was elated as he continued. "Who commands the team now? What's his experience?"

"Colonel Mike 'Dagger' Donovan, a U.S. Special Forces officer commands the outfit. And is he qualified? During World War II, as a twenty-three year old captain detailed to the Office of Strategic Services, the old OSS, he was selected as a member of the team that destroyed the heavy water plant. It was during the raid that he acquired the nickname 'Dagger'. I can't remember all the details but as I recall the story, Donovan had taken out one guard when he was jumped from behind by another wielding a dagger. As the guard was about to thrust the dagger into Donovan's back, he whirled and with an arm movement taught in commando school, turned the dagger away from him and into the guard's own body.

"Later he was second in command of the team that went into Germany and brought out Von Guessling and his group. During the 1950's he commanded several small actions, but none matched his World War II exploits in importance. However, an operation of his late in 1959 is well-known to you and the public. Donovan proposed, planned and executed digging the tunnel into East Berlin to tap the Soviet headquarters building housing their main communications system.

"You may remember that this operation continued for several years and the intelligence take from the communications taps was invaluable. Donovan's participation in this project has never been publicly announced, even though President Eisenhower awarded him a Distinguished Service Medal for the part he played in getting the operation established."

General Taylor hesitated briefly, then went on. "Ironically, Donovan is well-known to the Russians, not for his special operations exploits, but for an incident involving Premier Krenchev and the diplomatic community in Moscow. It happened during Donovan's assignment to Moscow as an assistant military attaché. Krenchev was hosting a large garden party attended by the Kremlin brass and most of the ambassadors and attachés posted to Moscow.

"It seems that after several hours of heavy drinking by all, Krenchev was making one of his long-winded speeches which seemed to go on and on. After damning the world in general and capitalists in particular, Mr. Krenchev concluded his speech by saying that if anyone had any doubts about Soviet superiority and what he had said, may he drown in vodka. Whereupon Colonel Donovan, by then slightly inebriated himself, picked up a half-empty bottle of vodka and poured it over Krenchev's head. Needless to say, Donovan was out of the country the next day, the ambassador expressed U.S. apologies, and Krenchev demanded the court-martial of Donovan."

Ben Taylor looked at the President who was trying to restrain his laughter, before continuing.

"There were strong recommendations from State that Donovan be dismissed from the service. However, after reviewing the entire affair, the Secretary of the Army decided to have Donovan reprimanded and again assigned back to the COBRA Team he left to take on the attaché assignment.

"Krenchev railed at our failure to court-martial Donovan. He has remarked several times since then that

Donovan one day would get his comeuppance from the Soviets, one way or another. To keep Donovan's unique assignment as the COBRA Team leader secret, he occupies the position as commander of the 7th Special Forces Group, an airborne colonel's job.

"Within a Special Forces Group there are thirty-six or forty-eight detachments, each with twelve highly trained men. The COBRA Team is one of these detachments, specifically Detachment 7A12. With this arrangement, Donovan can accompany the COBRA Team anywhere without attracting undue attention, as all the teams within his group are frequently on the move for various jobs. Donovan occasionally accompanies other detachments as well. We feel his cover and that of the COBRA Team is nearly foolproof. History bears us out. For the nearly fifteen years that the team has been in existence, their special status and arrangement has never been compromised."

"Ben, how would you use the COBRA Team now?"

"Mr. President, we might consider putting them into Cuba to make an on-the-spot deliberate ground reconnaissance of suspected areas of possible Soviet missile sites. COBRA Team members, through the use of CIA-provided make-up kits, can be made to look somewhat like Cubans. At least at a distance it would be hard to tell the difference.

"Team members speak Spanish fluently, as well as one other language, as a minimum. Some have a staggering language capability. Donovan, for example, is fluent in six languages that I know of. However, before giving you any firm recommendation, I'd want to consult with Donovan personally to get his assessment of such a mission, the number of men he would need, his views of the risks involved, and length of time it would take to get the team ready, should you decide this was a viable alternative to pursue.

"I believe that Donovan and the team could determine once and for all what the Soviets are up to in Cuba. Mr. President, I recommend you consider this option."

The President sat silently for several seconds. Turning his chair slowly toward the west window, he appeared deep in thought. Bob Ketner looked at his brother, wondering what was going through his mind. Finally, the President turned his chair and faced Ben. "I'd like to give this more thought. If Donovan and his men were caught by Castro, the fat would be in the fire and the lives of every team member in extreme jeopardy. That's putting it too mildly—that would be the end of them. Castro would line them up against a wall and shoot them as spies. I could hardly blame him. Hell, they would be spies! I'd like to talk to Donovan personally and get his reaction. In fact, I couldn't ask any man to undertake such a dangerous mission unless he met two conditions. First, he must volunteer for such an assignment, and, second, have no immediate family ties."

"Mr. President, to answer your second condition first, neither Donovan nor any of his men have any close dependents. That's one of the requirements we imposed several years ago. They are almost like a foreign legion. No ties, no strings, all guts. Donovan himself was married but his wife died in a tragic automobile accident during the late 1940's and he has never remarried. As far as volunteering for such an assignment, I think you will find that every man selected will do exactly that. A precondition for assignment to the COBRA Team is to volunteer for any mission our government decides is necessary. However, I think Colonel Donovan is the man to talk to and get his opinion firsthand. When would you like to see him?"

"As soon as possible."

"Good, I'll have him here this afternoon at four if that's convenient," Ben replied.

"How do you know he can be here by four? You haven't even talked to him."

General Taylor picked up the red phone on the President's desk which was connected directly to the Pentagon. "Operator, this is General Taylor. Get me Colonel Donovan, commander of the 7th Special Forces Group at Fort Bragg, please."

Chapter 3

THE SHARP, PERSISTENT ring of the telephone woke Mike Donovan from a sound sleep. He rubbed his eyes and glanced at the clock atop his bureau. Eight forty-five. Who was calling at that time on a Sunday morning! Still half asleep, he picked up the phone and grumbled, "Colonel Donovan here."

"Sir, this is the national military command center in the Pentagon. Please stand by. The chairman of the Joint Chiefs of Staff would like to speak with you."

Still holding the telephone in one hand, Donovan scrambled out of bed and reached for the notebook and pencil on his night stand when he heard the chairman's voice.

"Dagger, this is General Taylor. Hope I'm not interrupting anything but it's urgent I see you as soon as possible. I'll have a T-39 at Pope Air Force Base at one this afternoon to pick you up. Bud Sharp will meet you at Andrews. Plan on spending at least tonight in Washington, and wear your civvies."

"Yes, sir. Could I ask what's up, General?"

"I'll let you know after you get here. In the meanwhile you might have your executive officer get your group together for a small exercise south of the border. Incidentally, the tail number of the T-39 will be 463. Will plan on seeing you later this afternoon for sure!"

"Yes, sir, I'll be ready."

After a quick shower and shave, Donovan picked up the phone and dialed Ed Sweet, his executive officer.

Sweet's wife answered.

"Pat, this is Dagger. Hate to bother you this early but could I speak to Ed for a moment? By the way, that was a great party you had last night. Stayed out too late, though."

"We always enjoy your company, Dagger. I think you and Donna make a wonderful couple. Here's Ed."

"What's up, Colonel?" Ed's voice sounded much like his own, dry. No doubt from too many cigarettes and the plentiful supply of scotch the night before.

"Ed, I've got to go to Washington early this afternoon. I'd like to meet with you at eleven, if that's convenient. The operations room in our headquarters. Contact Marc Mayberry and have him there too."

"Anyone else?"

"Not for now, Ed. I'll fill you in then on what I know. Which isn't much."

Still yawning, he hung up the phone and walked into his kitchen. His bedroom and living room were fine. But the kitchen was nothing more than a small alcove. He turned on the hot water and made himself a cup of instant coffee. Awful stuff, he thought as he took the first sip. No time to perk the real thing. He buttered an English muffin. But his mind kept returning to the chairman's call.

South of the border. Where? Costa Rica! Come on, Donovan, get with it. Cuba! Hell yes, Cuba. The papers had been filled with stories of Soviet efforts underway there. Nuke weapons and all, according to some of the articles he'd been reading. However, Marc Mayberry, his crack intelligence sergeant, had never been able to find a single intelligence assessment which did anything more than allude to reports from unreliable sources to that effect. It had to be Cuba. Nothing of any significance seemed to be going on anywhere else.

He wondered why Bud Sharp hadn't called him earlier and given him some warning that the chairman would be in touch. That wasn't like Bud. As chief of the Special Operations Division, he was Dagger's contact in the Pentagon for everything involving his team. In fact, his only direct contact.

Still thinking of the chairman's call, he slipped on the trousers to his very best suit. A gray flannel twill he'd had made in London during a visit there the month before. He packed underwear, socks and a clean shirt in his well-traveled attaché case. Slipping on his tie and coat, he headed for his Jaguar parked in the rear of the apartment.

The clear fresh North Carolina air was like a shot in the arm as he drove down Honeycut Road enroute to his headquarters on Smoke Bomb hill. Fort Bragg was a beautiful old army post and he always enjoyed the sunny days of summer. It got hot and muggy there, but not till late August.

He wheeled his car sharply into the parking lot. Only Tom Benton's battered old Ford occupied one of the reserved parking spaces directly in front of his headquarters. No doubt he was Officer of the Day. As Mike walked into his headquarters building, a cheery "Good morning, sir" broke his train of thought.

"Morning, Lieutenant Benton. Any coffee?"

"Yes, sir, Colonel. The mess hall sent up a fresh pot about a half hour ago. I'll get you a cup."

"Fine, Tom."

He walked into his office and glanced at several notes his adjutant had left him the afternoon before. Nothing much. Call Jim Slade. The medics need to see you for a tetanus booster shot. Finance called, they need a new withholding statement if you want to increase your income tax deductions.

Without looking up he took the cup of coffee Lieutenant Benton handed him. The last note intrigued him. Call Diane as soon as possible. He put that note into his pocket and with the fresh cup of coffee in hand he walked down the hall to his operations room. As he twirled the dials of the massive door back and forth, he remarked to Benton, "When Ed Sweet and Sergeant Mayberry arrive, have them come right in. They will be along shortly."

"Yes, sir. Is there anything else I can do for you?" Lieutenant Benton was all of twenty-three and his high-pitched voice reflected every year of his short life.

"No, Tom. Go about your duties. Colonel Sweet, Sergeant Mayberry and I will be here for about an hour or so. See that we're not disturbed."

Lieutenant Benton excused himself and returned to his desk just inside the front entrance to the headquarters. Being 7th Special Forces Group Officer of the Day was an important assignment to him. After all, he was in charge of the group when all the other officers were off duty. He didn't mind the duty one bit. He fantasized one crisis after another, making on-the-spot command decisions which invariably brought great credit upon himself, the United States Army, and the United States of America. Yes, sir, he was ready for any challenge, any crisis.

Graduating from West Point at 21, he already had two years of service under his belt, and the last year in the Special Forces really convinced him that he was ready for anything. Excitement, daring suspense, last-minute rescues. He conceived one situation after another, imagining his special forces team in every possible danger and invariably at the last minute, he would provide a brilliant solution or ploy and save their hides. Yes, he was ready. Lieutenant Benton's daydreams were interrupted by the arrival of Lt. Col. Ed Sweet and Sergeant Mayberry.

"Good morning, Lieutenant Benton. I see Colonel Donovan is already here."

"Yes, sir, Colonel Sweet. He's waiting for you and Sergeant Mayberry in the operations room."

When Ed Sweet and Marc Mayberry entered the operations room, Donovan was examining a map which was spread out in the middle of the conference table. He looked up briefly, nodded to Marc Mayberry, and moved around to the large map board which displayed the entire Western Hemisphere.

"Ed, I got a call from the Chairman of the Joint Chiefs of Staff just before I called you. He ordered one of the small executive jets into Pope to take me to Washington. Wants to see me this afternoon. I didn't get much to go on except his reference to south of the border. I assume he must mean Cuba. Sergeant Mayberry, have you noticed anything unusual in the latest intelligence reports?"

"No, sir, Colonel. Only occasional reports that the Soviet Military Advisory Group in Cuba is training the Cuban army on some rather large missiles. Nothing more definite than that."

"That's about how I understood the situation. Ed, I'd like to have you and Mayberry take a good look at all the recent intelligence and pinpoint any locations in Cuba where such missile training has been observed, or where any possible sightings of missiles have been reported. Then take a good look at the coastline nearby and locate the best landing sites should we be ordered in. Also, check our data and locate likely areas for drop zones should we consider going in by parachute. My inclination would be to go in by submarine if at all possible. I like the extra security an entry by sub provides. Incidentally, find out where the Grayback is located. Commander Terry with SEAL Team 2 at Little Creek should be able to tell you. Tell him we're thinking of running an amphibious exercise within the next week and we'd like to know where we could go aboard."

"Okay. Do you want me to alert anyone else?"

"Not now. I'll give you a call from the Pentagon as soon as I find out anything definite. I may be letting my imagination run away with me. For all I know, the chairman may want us to go to Acapulco and put on a demonstration for visiting dignitaries. But I doubt it. I don't think he'd call me so early on a Sunday morning to arrange an administrative exercise. Having Bud Sharp meeting me at Andrews reinforces my view that something is up. On second thought, in addition to checking on the sub, call the Air Commandos at Eglin and find out how many C-130's they have operational. Also check to see if Keith Himes is still there. We may need a good weather man, and he's tops."

"Fine, Colonel. We'll also dig out all the aerial photographs of Cuba we have on hand. They might come in handy if we do some crash planning."

The conversation was interrupted by the ringing of the gray telephone in the far corner of the room. "I'll get it, it must be Bud Sharp. He'd be the only one calling on the secure line today."

"Donovan here," he spoke in military tone as he picked up the receiver.

"Dagger, this is Bud Sharp. The chairman called me about an hour ago to get my ass down to the Pentagon right away. Just finished a meeting with him and he told me you would be coming up this afternoon. I'm to pick you up at Andrews at two-fifteen and have you at the White House by four to meet with the President."

"The President!" Dagger's voice betrayed the tension which had been growing in him ever since the first call. "Have you any idea what's up?"

"No, I was hoping you could tell me something. Or are you going to hold out on me too?" Sharp's voice was pleading.

"Bud, the only thing I know is the chairman called and wants to see me. Said he'd have a plane pick me up at Pope at one o'clock. He then mentioned the possibility of a little exercise south of the border. Ed Sweet and I are trying to G2 that comment and feel the only place that has anything going on is Cuba. I didn't know till now that I'd be meeting with the President."

"I'm to see the chairman again in about fifteen minutes. Then I'll take off for Andrews to pick you up. If I find out anything more, I'll fill you in on the drive back to town. Have a good flight."

Mike Donovan frowned as he looked at his executive officer. "Bud told me I'm meeting with the President at four. That means a decision might be imminent on some type of covert operation. You better get Roger Landsdale, Tiger Tangier and Danny Thompson alerted. And take a look at me. The chairman said to wear civvies. Is this light gray flannel suit appropriate for the White House?"

Ed Sweet was laughing as he told Dagger he looked great. Then as an afterthought he added, "At least Donna thought you looked cute last night."

"Okay, wise guy. Twelve-twenty already. I've got to get going. The plane will be landing at Pope any minute." Gulping another quick cup of coffee, he headed for his Jaguar. He heard Lieutenant Benton's "Have a good day, sir" only faintly. He was too engrossed in his thoughts to reply.

As Donovan approached the Post Chapel, traffic slowed him down. Boy, would he catch it tomorrow. His group chaplain, Captain Dancer, conducted the service this Sunday and Mike always made a point of attending when his own padre was holding forth. He chuckled. He could imagine Dancer's comment, "You're a sinner, Colonel, the top sinner."

John Adams, the post commander, and his family passed by in their car and waved. The Adams kids really liked him. But Dagger knew it was his Jaguar that really got their attention. He pulled into visitor parking at Pope. Attaché case in hand, he walked into base operations. A young airman was behind the counter reading the Sunday edition of the *Fayetteville Observer*. As Donovan reached the counter the airman put the paper down, snapped to attention and with a broad smile on his face asked, "Could I help you, sir?"

"I'm Colonel Donovan. A T-39 is to pick me up here at one."

"Yes, sir. The pilot called the tower a few minutes ago. He's on time and requested we have you manifested by the time he gets here. He doesn't intend to shut down his engines. If you fill out this manifest and let me see your ID card, we'll have you ready. Any baggage?"

"No, only this attaché case which I'll carry on board."

As he completed the manifest, Donovan slipped his ID card from his wallet and handed it to the airman.

"Thank you, sir, and here's your ID. The plane is on final approach now. I'll escort you out to the ramp as soon as he's taxied in. We've got to wait until he comes to a complete stop. It's against air force regulations to be on the ramp while the plane is in motion. If you will have a seat, I'll call you as soon as the plane has arrived." Without waiting for a response, he picked up the *Observer* and continued reading.

Mike looked at the young airman. He admired the youngsters the air force was bringing in. Crew-cut, clear-skinned, and with a slight trace of a whisker or two beginning to show. Rank didn't faze them. Do your thing, then get back to your personal pursuits. He'd often wished the caliber of the army's newest recruits could stack up to the air force's. That seemed to be wishful thinking. Not too many men today wanted to slog along at Mach .002 in the infantry, when they could fly at Mach 2 in a sleek air force jet. He glanced out the window and saw a plane touching down at the far end of the runway. The young airman, without any outward indication that he had noticed the plane's arrival, abruptly put down the paper and turned to Colonel Donovan.

"Sir, your plane has landed. If you will follow me, I'll lead you to the ramp."

As they arrived at the nearside of the ramp, the T-39 applied its brakes and came to a halt, engines still running. Donovan glanced up at the tail number: A374 463.

"That's it," he exclaimed.

The door of the plane opened and the retractable steps lowered. Mike Donovan bounced up the steps two at a time. As he entered the plane a lieutenant in air force blue thrust out his hand.

"Colonel Donovan, I'm Lieutenant Kendrick, your pilot. Welcome aboard. This is Sergeant Ainsworth, our crew chief. She'll show you to your seat."

Mike Donovan did a double take. Sergeant Ainsworth was not a grizzled old crew chief like the ones he was accustomed to working with in the Air Commando C-130's. This sergeant was a stunning blonde, who thrust out her hand and said, "I'm your hostess. You can have your choice of seats. As soon as we're airborne, I'll be offering you a drink, sandwich, or whatever else strikes your fancy."

Colonel Mike 'Dagger' Donovan had ridden on many a T-39 before, but never one like this. Plush in every way. Rugs at least an inch thick. Interior a light blue. Four heavy upholstered seats, two on either side. A white linen cloth covered the small table between the seats. Indirect lighting accented the harmony of the interior appointments. Then for the first time he noticed the seal of the President of the United States and the embossed gold lettering underneath: PRESIDENTIAL FLIGHT DETACHMENT.

He took a seat on the right side of the plane and fastened his seat belt. Sergeant Ainsworth, with a quizzical smile at Mike as though asking for permission to be seated, took the seat directly across from him. She was fastening her seat belt as the plane began to taxi. It halted momentarily as it turned and entered the runway at the near side of the field. Mike could hear the engines increase their power as the plane hurtled down the long runway. They were quickly airborne.

He looked across the table at Sergeant Ainsworth. Her eyes met his. She smiled. "Colonel, a drink? Sandwich?"

"Sounds great. How about beer and a sandwich?"

"Fine. We have ham and cheese on rye, turkey, and egg salad sandwiches. What's your poison?" Donovan laughed. This gal had a sense of humor. He looked at her again. She was really beautiful. Blonde, trim, above average height, but much above average in looks. Donovan was still looking her over when her crisp question brought him back to reality. "What kind of sandwich, sir?"

"Ham and cheese on rye. I'd better skip the beer, though. Make that black coffee instead."

The idea of a beer really appealed to him but since he was about to meet the President of the United States, he let his better judgment overrule his desire for a foamy brew. One thing he didn't want was to reek of beer when he met John Ketner for the first time.

"Here you are, sir." Sergeant Ainsworth carefully placed the cup of hot coffee on the table and served the sandwich. She handed him a napkin which Donovan noticed had a small presidential seal embroidered in gold in its center. He was struck by her lovely hands—long, slender fingers with just a touch of polish to set off perfectly manicured nails. He wanted to reach out and touch her hand but restrained himself. Instead, he looked at her and smiled.

She returned his smile. "Sir, if you don't mind, I'll have a cup of coffee while you tackle your lunch." He watched her as she sat down. The blue uniform showed every graceful curve of her body to advantage. He munched at his sandwich and remarked, "This is really good."

"Glad you like it. Made it myself." Her voice was tantalizing. "Incidentally, Colonel, you've set some kind of first today."

"How's that?" he inquired.

"To the best of my knowledge, we've never had a colonel on this plane as a passenger before. The plane is reserved for use by members of the cabinet, senior officials on the President's staff, and only occasionally an admiral or general. Never a colonel. But I might add," she continued, "it's a pleasure having you aboard."

"Thanks very much." Mike Donovan chose his next words carefully. "By the way, you're a very beautiful girl. Gorgeous is a better word, beautiful doesn't do you justice."

"Oh, thank you," she replied. Mike could see a faint blush forming on her cheeks.

"Have you been in the air force long?" he asked.

"No, as a matter of fact, I haven't. I'm in the Air Force Reserve. I'm a student at the Georgetown School of Law and on active duty for a month between semesters. It's a very good arrangement for me. I earn enough to help pay my tuition—and have a chance to meet some nice men. Unfortunately, they all seem to be married. How about you, Colonel? Do you have a wife and several kids back in North Carolina? Or are you going to tell me you're single like most of the others I meet?"

"As a matter of act, I'm a longtime widower," he replied.

"Really! That's a new line for me. For some reason I've never met a man your age who wasn't single, divorced, or permanently separated from a wife who didn't understand him."

"Miss Ainsworth, I can assure you that I'm not married, have no steady girl friend, and haven't the time to get romantically involved with any gal." Donovan bit his tongue. Why the hell did he have to tell her that?

"Are you going to be in Washington long?"

"No, only overnight."

She looked at him again. Tall, muscular build, maybe thirty-three, thirty-four. No, they didn't make colonels that young in the army. Late thirties, she guessed. The tanned face and crystal blue eyes intrigued her. His wavy brown hair was a bit ruffled. Damn, he was an interesting-looking man. She could tell that his suit was custom tailored. His white shirt and lightly striped brown tie contrasted nicely with his gray flannel suit.

"Any plans for the evening?" she asked quietly.

"None planned. Any ideas?"

"There are some really nice restaurants in the city. Any type of food you like. Chinese, Mexican, seafood, it's here."

"Would you join me?" he asked casually.

"I'd love to. I'm off duty as soon as we get back and don't have another flight until Tuesday morning. Any particular time?"

"How about eight o'clock? I'm sure to have finished my meeting by then."

"Great. Here's my telephone number and address. Do you want me to pick you up anywhere? I've got a Volks."

"I'm staying at the Key Bridge Marriott. Don't want to put you out, though. I'll grab a cab."

"That's just around the corner from me. I've a townhouse in Georgetown, on Thirty-Fourth Street Northwest. I'll pick you up about eight. By the way, my name is Susan."

"I'm Mike Donovan and delighted you'd let me ride your plane." She laughed as she took his outstretched hand in hers, gave his a slight squeeze, and with a smile said, "I'm looking forward to this evening."

Mike Donovan felt a surge of excitement flow through his veins as she held his hand for a moment longer than the casual handshake he expected. The dull sound of a bell and the lighting of the 'Fasten Your Seat Belt' sign broke the spell of the moment. He smiled at her across the table. She returned his smile as she fastened her belt. He would have given anything had they run into a storm and been delayed. Spending time alone with Susan in the small cozy cabin would have been Utopia at its best.

Chapter 4

AFTER A HASTY thank-you to the pilot and another lingering handshake with Susan, Mike Donovan started down the plane's ramp where Bud Sharp was waiting.

"Welcome to Washington. From what I see from here, you must have had an interesting flight." Bud Sharp took another look at the beautiful, shapely blonde standing at the top of the steps.

"Not bad. How's Jean?"

"She's fine and sends her love."

Bud Sharp and Mike Donovan were longtime friends. Bud and his wife, Jean, had always treated Mike as a member of the family. Without fail, Jean would remember Mike's birthday and other special occasions, and treat him to a home-cooked meal. Invariably, Jean would invite a blond, redhead, or brunette beauty to be Mike's dinner partner hoping to entice him into giving marriage another try. And, invariably Mike would lavish his full attention on the chosen lady for the evening, then promptly forget her. Long ago, he had given up explaining to Jean that he'd know when he met the right girl, and, telling her politely, without her help.

"Any baggage, Dagger?"

"No. Only this beat-up attaché case."

"You always travel light, don't you?"

"Sure do. And with good reason. That way you characters can't keep me around too long. I'm convinced you've cooked up something to get me to Washington."

"No, Dagger. This is as much a surprise to me as it is to you."

Bud Sharp unlocked the front door of his car and leaned over to unlock the other door. Mike Donovan got in. For awhile, neither said a word. Finally Bud looked directly at Dagger.

"I had a lengthy session with General Taylor after I called you. It seems that something big may be brewing in Cuba. You know that for months rumors have been circulating that the Soviets are putting in intermediate range ballistic missiles armed with nukes."

Mike Donovan interrupted. "I've read that, but all the intelligence reports I've seen rate the sources as unreliable and the information probably false."

"That's true. Apparently the President has information from a source he considers absolutely reliable. And the pressures on him to do something about it are building up. Today, for example, Senator Kern was on 'Face the Nation,' and really blasted the administration for standing idly by while the Soviets armed Castro to the teeth. Early this morning, the President had General Taylor and John Askins on the carpet for failing to get hard evidence about what's happening. Solid information would clear the air. Apparently, aerial photography over Cuba has produced nothing, and CIA's agent network hasn't been productive. The President was especially disillusioned about the CIA's performance, according to Taylor."

"John Askins is an old friend of mine," Mike responded. "Remember, he was Chief of Station in Bonn when I was Director of Special Warfare in Europe. He's no slouch and I suspect if his agents can't find out whether the Soviets are introducing nuclear weapons, it well may be because there aren't any. By the way, am I being too bold to ask what my role might be?"

"Dagger," Bud replied, "you're not going to like what

I'm about to tell you. As a result of this morning's meeting, General Taylor suggested to the President that he consider sending the COBRA Team into Cuba to make an on-the-spot reconnaissance and get at the truth."

"My God, you don't mean it!" Dagger's voice revealed an uneasiness which Bud detected immediately.

Bud hesitated a moment before continuing. "The President had no prior knowledge of the COBRA Team and was amazed to find out we had such an outfit. To make a long story short, he told Taylor that he wouldn't order anyone into Cuba without a clear understanding by each individual of the great risks involved in such an operation. Taylor explained to the President that you characters are all volunteers, and did whatever was best for the nation. The upshot of the meeting was to have you meet the President face-to-face and tell him that."

"Taylor knows the ground rules for serving in the COBRA Team," Mike said emphatically. "We gave up any right to pick and choose our operations when we signed up for the outfit. The rest of the Special Forces have that privilege, but not the COBRA Team."

"Dagger, as I understand the scenario for this afternoon, the President is going to size you up, then ask you point-blank whether you could mount such an operation, the number of men you would need, and whether you and the men would volunteer, considering the possible outcome. Taylor asked that I also attend the meeting. He feels that should the decision be made this afternoon, we won't have much time to get ready."

"I'll tell you and I'll tell the President. If it's important to the nation, and the President wants us to go, we're as good as on the way."

"I told Taylor that when we discussed the situation late this morning," Bud replied. "However, he's in complete agreement with the President that the final decision is up to you. He isn't about to pressure you either way."

Sharp parked his car near the reflecting pool and he and Dagger started walking toward the East gate to the

White House. Only the chirping of birds could be heard as they walked silently side by side. Both were in deep thought. Bud knew Dagger would never say no. Perhaps this would be his final mission. Lady Luck had been on his side too often. Could it last forever? He doubted it. One detail overlooked, one slip, and it would be all over.

Dagger Donovan's mind had already started planning the operation. Who would he take along? Marc Mayberry for sure. He was the best intelligence man he'd ever known, and his skill as a radio operator was recognized throughout the special forces as perhaps tops. A medic, Roger Landsdale would be the man. Nearest thing to a doctor you could have around.

He remembered his performing an appendectomy on an old Montagnard high in the hills of central Vietnam four years ago. Nothing but a thatched hut, several ammo boxes pushed together for an operating table, and a scalpel. The old man was up and walking around the next day, feeling fine and positive Landsdale was God, Himself. Tiger Tangier would go along for sure. He could do anything. Level-headed and cool as a cucumber. That ought to be enough. No, Danny Thompson, the nominal team leader had to be in that group. Only a junior first lieutenant but more guts and brains than many a colonel that Dagger knew. If anything happened to him, he'd want Danny to take charge. Almost half an A team. Perfect. Every skill needed and no finer men on the face of the earth.

The guard at the East gate was a huge man. Six-six and 250 pounds if he weighed an ounce. "Gentlemen, can I help you?"

"I'm Colonel Sharp and this is Colonel Donovan. I believe we are expected."

The guard looked down at his clipboard, nodded his head. "Your ID's, please."

He examined each one carefully, looked at Sharp's face, then Donovan's, and handed back the cards.

"Straight ahead, gentlemen, enter by the door you see to your immediate front." He opened the gate and let them through, then pushed a small button mounted above the guard shack door. The door to the White House opened as Bud Sharp was reaching for the doorknob. A short, heavy-set black man was waiting. "Follow me, please." He led them through a long corridor and into the large waiting room outside the President's office. "Have a seat, gentlemen. I'll inform the President you have arrived."

Mike Donovan looked around. Nothing much had changed since the last time he had been here to call on the President, the predecessor of the man now occupying the White House. The great seal of the President of the United States centered in the rug caught his eye. The colors were bright and almost overpowering. "New rug," he muttered.

"Mr. President, I've asked Colonel Sharp, the chief of my Special Operations Division to join Colonel Donovan for our meeting. Sharp is my key man in the Pentagon for clandestine operations and would handle the details required to support Donovan should you decide to send in his team. He has all the security clearance required and does much of my legwork. If I am out of town for any reason, I'd like to have Colonel Sharp contact you directly should it be necessary."

"Fine, Ben, I'm looking forward to meeting these officers."

A brief knock at the Oval Office door was followed by a curt announcement, "Mr. President, your visitors have arrived."

"Thank you, Henry. We'll be ready for them in a moment. Offer them a cup of coffee while they're waiting."

"Yes, Mr. President."

Henry's great dignity and formality always pleased the President. Long the Chief White House Usher, he had served the last five Presidents with courtesy and distinction. He was lucky to have him in his administration. Henry had offered his resignation soon after the inauguration. Felt he was getting too old to do justice to the job the President deserved. The President requested he stay on. At sixty-nine, Henry was in far better shape than many of the forty or fifty-year-olds who worked around the White House.

"Ben, if you're ready, I'd like to meet Colonel Donovan now."

Ben Taylor walked into the waiting room outside the Oval Office. "Dagger, I'm glad to see you made it." He shook Donovan's hand.

"It was a great trip, General, I like that style of traveling."

"Thought you might. Dagger, I want you to use your best professional judgment in answering the President's questions. Don't feel intimidated by my presence. Remember, the decision is yours. This way, gentlemen."

"Mr. President, I'd like to have you meet Colonel Mike Donovan. And, this is Colonel Bud Sharp."

"Colonel Donovan, Colonel Sharp, it's a pleasure to meet you. Your reputations have preceded you, I might add." The President's handshake was firm. That pleased Dagger. "I believe that both of you know John Askins, the Director of CIA."

"Good afternoon, Dagger, it's been a long time." John Askins' voice reflected their longstanding friendship.

"Nice seeing you again. And how are things at Langley?" Dagger inquired.

"Fine, busier than ever. I expect our activities will increase a bit more if you get involved in the subject about to be discussed. By the way, Dagger, do you know the Attorney General, Bob Ketner?"

"I'm Bob Ketner, Colonel Donovan. I'm delighted to have you aboard."

"Thank you, sir, I'm honored by being invited."

"Have a seat, gentlemen." The President's voice was sharp and to the point. "I believe we have some important decisions to make."

Dagger looked at the President. He was younger-looking than he had imagined. Certainly years younger than the last President he had met in this room some years before. He liked what he saw. And he was certainly in charge. Every word, every action, appeared to be calculated. It was hard to believe that this was the same man that the papers alleged had been overwhelmed by the Soviet Premier in Vienna a few months before.

"Colonel Donovan," the President began, "General Taylor and John Askins have briefed me on your COBRA Team and your own distinguished record. I'm impressed. As I understand it, Colonel Sharp filled you in on what we are considering at the moment. We may be facing a very serious crisis. However, I don't want to make decisions on innuendo, rumor, and pressure. We need help in getting information which is current, reliable and convincing. It seems as though we have reached the end of our capabilities to acquire intelligence, using conventional means. Apparently, you and your COBRA Team offer an alternative. I asked General Taylor to bring you here today to hear firsthand whether you feel that an operation as proposed by General Taylor might be possible, and, more importantly, whether you would be willing to undertake such a mission."

Dagger gazed at the President. Here was the number one bureaucrat of all asking him for his recommendations. What a change. Most government officials simply directed actions be taken to get the job done, regardless of the circumstances. They usually cared little about how the personnel who had to execute their orders felt. Getting the job done was their only concern.

"Mr. President." Dagger groped for the right words. "If you feel that what you need cannot be obtained in any other way, and the information is vital to our nation's security, my answer is an emphatic yes. And I speak for the entire team. I believe General Taylor can vouch for the fact that at times I have resisted using the COBRA Team for a poorly conceived operation, often based on half-baked ideas and perhaps to satisfy an ego. However, from what I have been told, I feel satisfied that this need is very important. We're prepared to do our best to satisfy those requirements."

"Colonel Donovan," the President said, "your response confirms the pride and confidence I already felt for your team, and you, personally. I'm not asking you to go into Cuba to blow up the country. What we need is good intelligence to pinpoint sites where the Soviets might be locating intermediate range ballistic missiles. If that turns out to be going on, we especially need irrefutable confirmation of their actions by on-the-spot photography of their weapons and sites. This would be a dangerous mission. I've got to consider carefully the possible consequences should you and your team be captured by Castro's security forces. John tells me Cuba is pretty much a closed society. That makes it doubly difficult for you and your men. Incidentally, have you given any consideration to the number of men it would take to do the job?"

"The fewer men, the better. Offhand, four or five would be the maximum number I would consider. More than that makes it extremely difficult to operate clandestinely. Yes, sir, four or five. I'd certainly not want to make a blind infiltration, though," Dagger continued.

"Blind? What do you mean by that, Colonel Donovan?" the President asked.

"Sorry, sir, that's an expression that we use in special operations signifying that we do not want to go into an area without a friendly agent or reception party to meet and assist us on arrival." Dagger looked at John Askins.

"John, do you have a reliable agent-in-country we might use for that purpose?"

"We've got quite a network in operation. However, I'd like to check with my Clandestine Division to determine whom they would recommend for such an assignment. Of course your method and place of infiltration would play an important part in selecting the right agent. Incidentally, we've had pretty good success in introducing and exfiltrating our own agent, a little better than fifty percent."

"Fifty percent?" the President interrupted. "I wouldn't consider such an operation without better odds than that."

"Mr. President," Dagger's voice was firm. "I wouldn't either. I don't know how John has been putting his agents in, or taking them out, but I feel confident we can come up with a plan that would increase our chance of success to ninety-five percent or higher."

"That's more like it." The President was obviously relieved.

"I'd also like to consider introducing a notional team at the same time the COBRA team is put in, that is, if we go in by parachute."

"A notional team! You've lost me again, Colonel Donovan." The President was shaking his head.

"Let me answer that, Dagger." John Askins chimed in. "Mr. President, a notional team is an imaginary team we make the Cubans believe has been sent into their country. Usually the notional team is introduced far from the actual site where the real team is inserted. It ties up their security forces chasing a will-of-the-wisp, while the real team makes its entry. It's a very effective method. For some reason, though, it's no longer in vogue, especially among my personnel. However, I strongly endorse Donovan's idea of using a notional team on this operation."

"John, I hear what you're saying but I still don't understand how a so-called notional team operates. How can you get the Cubans to believe they are looking for the real thing?" The President leaned back in his chair and listened intently as Askins replied.

"We have several methods. One that has been highly successful in the past is very simple. You rig up four or five parachutes with a huge cake of ice weighing about 100 lbs. attached to each chute. You then fly over the area where you want the security forces to think that a team has been brought in. At the right spot, you shove the parachutes out the door. They deploy in the normal fashion.

"Several hours later the ice has melted, leaving nothing on the ground but parachutes which for all practical purposes appear to have been used to infiltrate personnel. The security forces find the abandoned parachutes and come to the logical conclusion that four or five agents are loose within the countryside.

"The longer they look, the more intense the effort to locate the spies or saboteurs they know are in the area. The search area is expanded and additional security forces are brought in to help scour the countryside. Meanwhile, the real entry is taking place far removed from the site of the notional force activity."

"That's ingenious." The President was obviously pleased. "Let's do it if we decide to go with the COBRA Team."

"Mr. President, we've improved on that method." Dagger hated to upstage John Askins but felt it essential that the President not make decisions on his operations unless the recommendation came from him.

"We've refined that procedure to make it even more credible," he said. "It's still very simple. A Cuban-in-exile is selected whom we are confident is a double agent. One, in other words, who outwardly supports the United States but is in fact an agent for the Cuban government. We recruit him for a mission in Cuba, and tell him that he and others are being parachuted in to perform acts of sabotage or other types of operations. He and four or five members of our team are trained together. We then inform the person we have selected that based on an objective evaluation, his performance during training has been outstanding and he has been selected as the team leader.

"Then on a dark night we put them all aboard a C-130 aircraft and fly over the area selected for entry. All lights on the plane are turned off. The team leader stands in the door ready to parachute into Cuba when the plane is over the drop zone. The rest of the team is rigged and standing in line behind the team leader all ready to jump. At the appropriate moment, the leader is given a pat on the back signaling him to jump.

"As he is parachuting earthward, he is confident the others are in the air behind him. As soon as the team leader has jumped, the other members of the team return to their seats and the plane returns to its home base.

"After the team leader has safely landed, he either tries to assemble the team and lead them to Cuban security forces, fully expecting to be rewarded with Castro's medal of honor, or he might attempt to contact Cuban security forces and report the team loose in the area. The Cubans react with a tremendous search effort. The longer they search without success, the more doubtful they are of their turncoat comrade. He often becomes their only victim. And I might add, justice is served both ways."

"Fascinating. Gentlemen, I believe we have a practical alternative to our dilemma. However, I shall withhold final judgment until tomorrow. Colonel Donovan, I'd like to have you sleep on it. Give every possible contingency serious thought. Then, by noon tomorrow, let General Taylor know your decision. I will support it whichever way you decide. However, rest assured that if you decide it's too risky, I'll respect your judgment completely.

"If you decide to take the risk, give me an estimate on how long it will take you to get the team ready. Gentlemen, thank you for meeting with me today. Colonel Donovan, Colonel Sharp, you have been most helpful. Good luck. General Taylor, let me know by early afternoon what you recommend. Good day."

As the group filed out of the Oval Office, Mike

Donovan reflected on the meeting. The commander-in-chief really impressed him. Considerate, probing, demanding, decisive. He liked the man.

"Dagger, sleep on it. Let's you, Bud and I get together in my office tomorrow morning at nine and get down to the finite details which must be considered before making a decision. I'm sure Bud will see to it you get settled for the evening. We've been invited to dinner by the Air Force Chief of Staff or Gladys and I would love to have you spend the evening with us." After a firm handshake, Ben Taylor departed. John Askins and Robert Ketner both wished Dagger well before they left.

"Bud, would you mind dropping me off at the Key Bridge Marriott on your way home?"

"Glad to, Dagger. How about joining us for the buffet at the Fort Myer club? Jean would sure like to see you."

"Thanks, Bud, but I'll take a raincheck. I'm already committed for the evening."

"I'll bet the blonde I saw on the T-39 has some connection."

"Could be," Dagger responded dryly.

"How do you do it, Dagger? You spend an hour with a girl after meeting her for the first time and you've got her wanting to crawl into the sack with you."

"Bud, in this case I wish that was true. She's quite a gal. But I doubt I'll be able to make that kind of progress after treating her to dinner. Not that I would mind. If I had the qualities of seduction which you so generously attribute to me, I wouldn't be spending so many lonesome evenings alone in my bachelor quarters."

As Bud Sharp pulled his car up to the front entrance of Mike's motel, he remarked, "I'll meet you tomorrow morning at nine in the old man's office. Enjoy tonight. It might be your last evening of fun for a long, long time."

Mike closed the door to his motel room and settled

down in a large overstuffed chair for a much-needed break. He gazed out the window overlooking the Tidal basin. Beautiful. Small boats moving back and forth over the clear, blue waters of the Potomac. What an alluring and deceptive scene, he thought. While at this very moment the President was weighing alternatives which could affect everyone in the United States, most Americans were going about in unhurried pursuit of leisure, unaware of the threat of events in nearby Cuba.

He called Ed Sweet at Fort Bragg and gave him an update on the afternoon's session. He chose his words carefully to avoid a breach of security. Then a quick shower and shave. He kicked himself for not bringing another suit. He wanted Susan to think he was a man about town. And he had the suits hanging back in his closet at Bragg that would have given him that appearance. Oh hell. She'd have to take him as is.

A light knock on the door and Susan's voice outside woke Donovan. He came bounding from his chair. He had dozed off and was unaware that it was now quite dark. He flipped on a light as he opened the door. He was still blinking his eyes as he looked at Susan standing in the doorway. With a cigarette dangling from her lips and a coat slung casually over her arm, Susan drawled, "Won't you invite a poor starved girl in?" Donovan broke out in laughter.

"Of course, Madam," he replied in his most serious tone of voice.

His eyes sparkled as he gave her the once-over. She was much more beautiful than he had imagined. A small blonde bang drooped ever so carelessly over her right eyebrow. Her white silk blouse was open at the throat and tauntingly revealed the edges of her well-formed breasts. At a glance he knew she belonged to the liberated group wearing no brassiere. Her skirt was a well-tailored English tweed with a random weave; the matching jacket was slung casually over her right arm. With highheeled shoes Susan looked taller than he had remembered. Mike was convinced he was looking at a stunning model who graced the covers of the most fashionable magazines of the day.

"Please come in. Let me take your jacket."

She tossed it to him as she walked slowly over to the large picture window overlooking Washington and exclaimed, "My, what a beautiful view!" Her voice was soft and yet her tone was enthusiastic.

"Could I offer you a drink?" Mike was still awestruck as he looked at her. The view from the rear was just as imposing as the one from the front.

"I thought you'd never ask. I'd like a martini on the rocks. Make it a double, I feel so relaxed."

Mike dialed room service and placed her order and a double scotch for himself. He could use a double after the day he'd been through. It was only minutes before the waiter came in carrying the drinks on an oversized silver tray. Mike tipped him generously and he left hurriedly.

He handed Susan her double martini. As she took the glass from his hand her fingers touched his. He felt the same excitement he had sensed earlier that afternoon when they had first met.

"To us," he said, as he tipped his glass toward hers. "To us," she repeated, as she clicked her glass lightly against his. She sat down on the far edge of the sofa, seeming to invite him to join her. Instead, Mike took the big overstuffed chair and sat facing her. The reflection from the glass-topped cocktail table between them cast small beads of light over her body. To Mike, she looked like an angel.

The intimate setting really pleased him. He often envied married men in his outfit who went home to their wives and children. But he wouldn't have traded this moment for anything. A leisurely drink, a beautiful girl, a cozy room. What more could anyone ask for? Her perfume had a fragrance that made it all the more perfect.

"Mike, have you given any thought as to where you might want to have dinner?" she said softly.

"No. I'm open to a recommendation."

"Then I'd like to suggest a small restaurant in Georgetown. Bannigans. It's quaint, maybe old-fashioned, but comfortable and really nice. The food is superb. I like the atmosphere. Best of all, no reservations required. It's still not too well known. You can usually get in without much of a wait, if at all."

"Sounds great. Another drink before we go?"

"Fine with me, unless you're in a hurry."

"Not at all." He dialed room service and placed the order. She heard him say, "On second thought, make those doubles." He looked at her to get her approval. She smiled. "That's it. Bring them right up, please."

The knock on the door signaled the arrival of the waiter. He placed the drinks on the cocktail table, took the twenty-dollar bill from Mike's outstretched hand and quietly closed the door behind him.

"Susan, are you a native of Washington?"

"Heavens no! I grew up in Minnesota, attended the University of North Dakota at Grand Forks and received my bachelor's degree in business administration. After graduating, I came to Washington seeking fame and fortune. It didn't take me long to realize that a girl in Washington is not judged by her academic background or skills. Her physical attributes and her attitudes are much more important.

"I had a rude awakening. Like hundreds of others, I became a secretary in one of the thousands of offices that exist in this great bureaucracy we call government. Washington is a very lonely town for a single girl, believe it or not. Plenty of opportunities to participate in every type of party imaginable. From the jet set to swinging singles.

"But there is only one thing most of the men are interested in doing. To take you on a long weekend to Vegas, Bermuda, or the Bahamas. All married, of course, and wanting to get away from a nagging wife they plan to divorce as soon as the proper moment arrives—which never does.

"I also learned that the only women in this city who command equal respect and attention are the professionals. Lawyers, doctors, mathematicians, scientific types. That's why I'm going to law school. I'm not going to be another pawn in the great game of chess that goes on in this city. Mike, I'm talking too much. How about you? Where are you from?"

"It's quite a coincidence. I grew up in North Dakota. A small town north of Bismarck, the state capital. McClusky, the center of the state, and I might add, a nice little community."

"Oh, I know where Bismarck is. I've been there several times. McClusky? Never heard of it."

"I can see why. It's really small." Mike continued. "I joined the army at a tender age. Was lucky enough to get a commission and have kicked around the world ever since. Married right after the war but my wife died in an automobile accident years ago while enroute home to visit her parents. No children and never remarried."

"I'm sorry, Mike."

"It's been a long time ago. Life must go on, even when it's altered by tragedy. Enough of that. Let's talk about us. Do you live alone?"

"Sure do, have this small townhouse a few blocks from Law School. Rent is reasonable, and I can crack the books without putting up with a talkative roommate. I've saved enough from my active duty pay I earn during the summer to get by during the school year. With a little tutoring I do on the side, I make out rather well."

Complete darkness had settled over Washington and the faint twinkling of running lights on the small boats moving up and down the Potomac made a picturesque scene. They sat in silence looking out over the city showing a new beauty when lighted. The Washington monument like a giant obelisk thrust its unique structure skyward. Susan sipped her drink slowly. "Mike, a penny for your thoughts?"

"I wouldn't dare."

"Please tell me."

"You won't feel insulted?"

"No."

"I was thinking how nice it would be if I could kiss you."

"Why don't you try and find out," she replied teasingly.

Mike looked at her. The dim light reflecting from the glass top of the cocktail table seemed to cast a spell over the entire room. Without a word he moved around the table and taking her hand drew her toward him. Her lips met his. He kissed her again and again. Each kiss became more passionate than the one before. He could feel the pounding of her breasts as she clung tightly in his embrace. He brushed away the solitary bang which had been hanging carelessly over her right eyebrow. With his fingers he caressed her ears, her cheeks. He slowly moved his hand until he reached the first button of her blouse. He unbuttoned it slowly. He then caressed her exposed breasts. Then again and again.

Her arms tightened around his neck as she moved her body closer to his. A surge of excitement flowed through his body. He nibbled at the lobes of her ears, another kiss more passionate than before and then, ever so tenderly he kissed each breast. She clung closer and closer, every nerve in her body aflame. She had never felt like this before. Every instinct that she had told her to push him away, but she couldn't. His kisses and caresses thrilled her till every part of her body was alive and throbbing for the great love she knew she could no longer withhold. Her pounding heart seemed to be echoing a staccato against his chest. Silently she took his hand and led him slowly to the king-size bed at the far corner of the room.

The bright sunlight streaming in the bedroom window awoke Mike. He raised his head from his pillow and the light blonde hair tousled in a small curl caught his eye. For a moment he was stunned then remembered. There she was, curled up like a small child hugging her pillow. Her soft white skin contrasted sharply with the heavy dark curtains of the window next to the bed. He leaned over and gently kissed the nape of her neck as he moved his hand down her bare back. She stirred at his touch.

"Rise and shine, beautiful," he said. It awakened her. She turned toward him and, rubbing her eyes, exclaimed, "What time is it, anyway?"

"Quarter of seven, and I've got a nine o'clock appointment with the chairman of the Joint Chiefs of Staff."

Donovan still had a slight taste of scotch in his mouth. What an evening. One he would never forget. He looked at her lying beside him. Her cream white breasts, so young and firm, protruded like two perfectly shaped pears. He kissed each one in turn. Her arms reached out and drew him closer. "Quarter to seven and you have a nine o'clock appointment. Oh, Mike, we have plenty of time." She began to kiss him even more passionately than she had the night before.

They showered together and he teased her by pretending to splash water on her curls. She laughed and jumped out of the shower as she turned the handle all the way to cold. He gasped once as the icy water hit his body. It took him a second to figure out what had happened. Not only was she beautiful, this gal had a real sense of humor. He liked that too, among the other things he had found so desirable. He ordered two continental breakfasts while they dressed. They ate in silence. He looked longingly at her across the table. She smiled. He had his answer. She had enjoyed the evening as much as he had.

As she dropped him off in front of the River Entrance to the Pentagon she leaned over and kissed him on the cheek. She murmured softly, "Will I see you again, Mike?"

"As soon and as often as possible." He leaned over, kissed her lips and whispered, "I love you, Susan." Before she coupld reply, he was walking rapidly up the steps of the Pentagon.

She drove slowly back to Georgetown wondering if she would ever see Mike Donovan again. She certainly hoped so. Or was she only a one-night stand for him? Tears welled in her eyes as she fought back her emotions. She loved Mike too. Why hadn't she told him?

Chapter 5

MIKE DONOVAN FLASHED his ID card at the guard as he turned to the right and down the E Ring corridor of the Pentagon. Majors and lieutenant colonels passed him walking at a fast clip, their papers in hand. Damn, what a place. Action officers everywhere, all going about "coordinating"—getting "concurrences" on staff papers. Hadn't changed a bit since his last tour there some years before. He paused briefly in front of Room 2E868 before entering. He spied Bud Sharp standing in the far corner looking out the window at the endless line of traffic winding its way up the narrow road leading to the River and Mall entrances. A navy Yeoman sitting at the desk outside the inner door leading to General Taylor's office looked up and said, "Could I help you, sir?"

"I'm Colonel Donovan. I believe the chairman is expecting me."

"Yes, sir, he is. Colonel Sharp arrived a few minutes ago."

"Morning, Bud. Glad to see you up and about so bright and early." Mike liked to needle Bud. Often when they were on the phone he would kid him about the soft touch he had in the Pentagon, knowing full well that Bud was putting in twelve to fourteen hours a day.

"A good morning to you too, sir. And did you have a

pleasant evening, dinner and all?" The emphasis on the all came across loud and clear to Mike.

"It was tolerable. On second thought I had a grand time. She's very nice. I hope Jean understood why I turned down your invitation."

"She understood perfectly. After all, she knows you quite well, Dagger." Bud laughed. "So do I, as a matter of fact."

The Yeoman opened the inner door, informed the chairman they had arrived, stood at attention and said, "The general will see you now." He waved them inside.

General Taylor was sitting at his desk with a sheaf of cables in his hands. He looked up, nodded his head to acknowledge their arrival, and said "Have a chair, I'll be with you in a minute."

Mike looked at the huge globe to the rear of the chairman's desk. It had obviously been used recently. That was apparent.

Cuba was boldly outlined and at eye level to the viewer. The bank of telephones astride the console just below the huge globe caught his attention. Red, blue, green, gray, orange and black. Six in all. He knew the red phone was connected to the President. The gray phone was always the secure line. Lord knows where the others led.

To the right above the telephones was the usual command board with its lights listing the nation's military leaders. The Commander-in-Chief; Secretary of Defense; Chariman, Joint Chiefs of Staff; Chief of Staff—Army; Chief of Staff—Air Force; Chief of Naval Operations; and Commandant, Marine Corps. Then a long list of major world-wide commanders. Opposite each name were three equal squares with one illuminated indicating the location of the individual: Office, Home, Other.

He noticed the board reflected the President as being in his office. Mike wondered what was going through his mind. His own thoughts kept returning to Susan. He smiled. What a stroke of luck that the chairman had ordered him to Washington the day before.

General Taylor flipped the last cable in the stack into his out box on the right side of his desk and stood up. He walked around the desk, put out his hand to Mike, and remarked in an off-hand manner that he hoped someone had entertained him the night before. Taking a chair between Mike and Bud, he looked directly at Mike and in an almost inaudible voice asked, "Dagger, what's your decision?" His voice indicated the deep concern the question involved.

Donovan looked at the general. That's why he admired the old man so much. No pussy-footing around. No long staff meetings. No ahs, no buts. No nothing more than "What's your decision?" He left it entirely up to him. No pressure, no beating around the bush, no maybe's. A simple question. And he knew he wanted a simple answer. Just Yes or No.

Mike's mind flashed back to Susan. A simple No would let him see her again tonight, and many more nights thereafter. Dammit, why after all these years did he hesitate? Hadn't he and his men been kept in readiness day after day, month after month, at great expense to the army, for such a moment, and here he was vacillating.

"Dagger, do you need more time?"

"Sorry, General. No, I don't. Considering everything I have learned about the situation, I see no alternative. If we don't find out, and Castro gets nukes, we might never know what hit us. Sir, I agree, the COBRA Team may be the answer. I'm willing to try."

"Dagger, much as I personally dislike having you and your men taking such a great risk, I'm proud of the decision you have made. Nothing else we have tried has been productive. You're our best and last hope. Rest assured that any support you need from our government will be provided without question. Bud, I mean that literally. Give Dagger anything he and his men ask for. Anything. And use my name freely if you run into any bureaucratic haggling over authority or justification. You know the whole gamut of things the characters in this building try and throw at you. Don't let anyone delay or complicate this operation. Walk over them if necessary. I'll back you to the hilt."

"Yes, sir, I'll handle it," Bud replied confidently.

"One other thing, Dagger, how soon can the team be ready?"

"Twenty-four to forty-eight hours, sir. Provided the Grayback is available that soon. I'd sure like to go in by submarine."

"I almost forgot," Bud interrupted apologetically, "Ed Sweet called me last night and asked that I pass on to you that the Grayback is in Florida, and the Air Commandos have four C-130's operational. He tried getting you but had no luck, so he called me instead. I'm sorry I didn't get the word to you earlier."

"Dagger," General Taylor continued, "I'm going to continue my past practices in operations of this type. You do the planning, make the decisions, and whatever you say goes. I've learned a long time ago that you fellows don't need any advice from us old cruds. Much as we'd like to provide it from time to time. You're in a unique business and are the real professionals. You have my complete confidence and support. Go to it. I'm sure you and Bud have plenty to talk over before you return to Bragg. Incidentally, when would you like to go back?"

"Right after lunch, General, I've got plenty to get done there, even though more time in Washington might be more interesting."

"Good. Bud, arrange to have Dagger at Andrews at one-thirty. I'll have a plane standing by for the flight to Pope."

General Taylor stood up, placed his arm around Donovan's shoulder and his "Be careful" conveyed more meaning to Mike than any platitudes he could have uttered.

* * *

Susan Ainsworth had just returned to her townhouse after leaving Mike at the Pentagon's River Entrance. She kicked off her shoes and was having a second cup of coffee, still thinking of the wonderful time she had with Mike when the telephone rang. Hoping it was Mike she waited until the second ring before answering in her most alluring voice, "Susan Ainsworth speaking."

"Susan, this is Captain Smith with the Presidential Flight Detachment. The Secretary of Interior is leaving today for a week's trip out West to inspect Bureau of Reclamation projects and has requested you as part of the crew. He said he was highly impressed with your abilities during his recent trip to Kentucky and wanted you along on this trip. We're scheduled to leave in about two hours. We're taking 783 this trip. I'd appreciate it if you could get the refreshments set up before our departure. I know you weren't scheduled for another flight until tomorrow but we'll make it up to you after our return."

"All right, Captain, I'll be there. But I'm holding you to your promise to give me some time off when I get back. You know I'll give my all for the good old U.S. Air Force, but I do have other interests." She hung up the phone before Smith could reply.

Why couldn't it have been Mike asking her to save the evening for him? Instead, she'd have to face that lecherous Secretary of Interior hour after hour as they flew across the country. During their last trip his eyes had never left her. He watched her every move and while he hadn't come out and directly propositioned her, he'd certainly made enough off-color comments to convince her that the least bit of encouragement and he'd be across the cabin table in record time.

What about Mike? she thought. What if he did call and she wasn't there to answer? She'd call him from out West somewhere. That'd surprise him. Only the per diem she would draw on the trip brought her any sense of comfort. She'd much rather have stayed in Washington hoping for another evening with Mike. She had so many things she wanted to tell him. The very thought of their next date thrilled her.

As she showered, dressed, and drove to Andrews, her daydreams turned more and more to the man she had known only a day, yet really loved. She desperately wanted another chance to prove that to him. She'd call him at her first stop and have him fly to Washington the same day she returned. He was a colonel. He could get away anytime. Then they could pick up where they had left off, followed by dinner at Bannigans. She was happy thinking of a perfect day on her return to Washington.

Bud Sharp led the way down the E Ring, took the first flight of steps going down and moved at a brisk pace to his office located in the basement directly below the chairman's office. Donovan exchanged pleasantries with the officers and men in the Special Operation Division. He had known most of them for years. He winked at Nancy, Bud's attractive secretary, as he followed Sharp into the inner, vaultlike room where some of the most sensitive operations in the entire Defense Department were planned.

His mind temporarily flashed back to Nancy. In the not too distant past they had quite a romance going, but she had finally tired of his infrequent visits and married a quartermaster captain assigned to the Logistics Division of the Army. Poor guy. He thought he had been courting a virgin. If he had only known.

"Dagger, we haven't much time if I've got to get you to Andrews by 1:30. So let's get with it. Have you firmed up your tentative plan and what do you need from me?" Mike realized why he had always admired Bud. He was a second General Taylor. Business first. Then the small talk.

"I've given it considerable thought. Much as I like parachuting and the success we have had getting into denied areas that way, I consider this operation is better suited for a submarine infiltration. All of the team are scuba qualified. I believe by using the Grayback we can get close to shore, keep submerged and use the "lock out" capability the sub has. Maybe a SEAL or two to help us with our gear. We could also spend the last hours aboard the sub going over every detail of our plan. We're going to be short on time anyway."

"I'm inclined to agree with you," Bud replied. "I'll have the sub ready to go by the day after tomorrow. I'll ask Commander Terry to give you the three best men he has on his team. They have all the equipment you might need and will be a big help in getting you in—and out. Marrying up with your assets ashore will be the most difficult part of the entry."

"Don't I know it!"

Bud continued, "Merv Collins from the CIA came in earlier this morning. John Askins sent him. They have several good in-place agents who are experienced in acting as reception parties for agency infiltrations. Askins recommends you consider sites A and B marked on this map. Both are close in and the fathom line is deep enough at high water to keep the sub submerged throughout the operation and yet give you a short run to the beach. They have agents at both sites and will provide them with the necessary identification codes as soon as you make your decision. These sites are not too far from the areas you and I fixed on yesterday and are reasonably close to the reported missile emplacements. That's a plus."

"I see John hasn't wasted any time. He never does. Looking at both locations, I'm inclined to use B. Let's plan on that. I'll get my team to examine it in detail. Otherwise we'll be losing valuable time."

"John has the entire intelligence community working round-the-clock to develop anything which might be helpful to you and the team. Merv Collins and I will fly down to Bragg at the last minute to update you on the latest take and to bring you the most current analyses. In fact, we'll follow you to Florida if the situation warrants and time permits. We'll also bring along the back-up signal operating plans and latest one-time pads you will need to encode your messages." Then Bud added emphatically, "This is one time it's a must that you see your burst transmitters."

"We sure will. I see you haven't let any grass grow under your feet since you got the word yesterday. What time did you get to bed last night?"

"I didn't, as a matter of fact. After having dinner with Jean, I came back here and did some more homework. Expect there will be a bit more of it before the week is over."

"Yes, I'm sure of that. I'm sure glad you're at this end of the business. I feel a lot better knowing you're on top of things. Too many rinky-dinks in our line of work who don't understand there is more to special operations than wearing a Green Beret."

"Isn't that the truth. I really get disgusted hearing all the chairborne commandos sounding off about how they would have done this or that. And you can't convince them otherwise. Trying to talk any sense into them is like pissing into the wind. A sure loser."

"Aptly put, my friend." Dagger laughed. "Two final requests for now. Keith Himes, the weather guy with the Air Commandos at Eglin. I'd sure like to have him at Bragg and Florida. And how about lining up Bunson Burner Cochrane as the pilot of the C-130 that will take us to Florida. I want him on standby during the entire time we're in Cuba with the Fulton skyhook system rigged on the C-130. He's a real expert on that device and you never know when it might come in handy."

"Okay, I'll take care of those actions this afternoon. You can count on it unless I notify you otherwise. How about a sandwich before we take off for Andrews?"

"Sounds great. Could I use your phone a minute? Alone?"

"Be my guest. That will give me time to get the boys cracking on a couple of projects while I'm on my way to Andrews."

Sharp left the inner room and joined the other officers in his division where he assigned various tasks to be done in his absence.

Dagger dialed the usual nine to get an outside line, then carefully dialed Susan's number. He let the phone ring a dozen times or more before finally hanging up in disgust. Damn, I thought she was going right home, he muttered to himself. He reached for a small three-by-five card lying at the end of the table and scribbled a short note. He joined Bud and they made their way up to the executive dining room on the third floor. As they were finishing their lunch, he handed Bud a twenty dollar bill and the note he had written earlier.

"After you get back from Andrews, would you mind stopping at the florist on the concourse and order a dozen red roses sent to this address with this message? If the twenty doesn't cover it, let me know. I'll send you the balance."

"As good as done." Bud took the card and read aloud. "Susan Ainsworth, 6601-34th Street, N. W., Georgetown, with love and thanks for an evening I'll never forget. Mike. Is this serious, Dagger?"

"I hope so. I've never run into a gal quite like her. For the first time since Margie died I have the feeling she may be the one. As you know too well, I've romanced dozens of dames and except for an occasional let-down, they've turned out to be mostly one-night stands. It may be for real this time. If I get back okay, I'm going to find out, and in a hurry."

Mike Donovan leaned back in his seat and closed his eyes, hoping to get a short nap during the one-hour flight back to Pope. If only Susan were aboard. He had so many things he wanted to tell her. On top of it he owed her a dinner at Bannigans. No matter how good that might have been, nothing could match the delightful substitute she had provided. If only more dinner dates turned out the same way.

He thought of Donna who was his dinner partner at Ed and Pat Sweet's party two nights before. Her pretense of not being able to drive, one too many drinks. Would Dagger take her home? Then insisting he come up for a nightcap. Another. Music. Must get into something more comfortable. A sheer negligee clinging to every inch of her body. More music. Another drink, another dance. Her passionate kisses.

The smartest thing he had done all week was to quietly slip out the door while she lay naked in a half-drunken stupor on her queen-size bed and undoubtedly waking up Sunday morning fully convinced that she had finally succeeded in seducing him, after seeing the ruffled pillow and Dagger's tie beside her. In her own smug way she'd tell Pat Sweet what a wonderful, absolutely wonderful time she and Dagger had after leaving their dinner party.

"Fasten your seat belt, sir." Looking across the table he realized he was back with the air force he knew so well. Sergeant McGuillicuddy was the typical crew chief, brusque, and a stickler for every air force regulation ever published. But try doing without them. They were the unsung heroes of every plane crew. Preflight inspections, maintenance, hot coffee, jack of all trades, who did everything but fly the damn planes.

Mike grudgingly admitted that the Susans, as beautiful and likable as they were, could never really do the job that crew chiefs did day after day without too much bitching and grumbling. That sacred and sacrilegious privilege was the private domain of the enlisted men in every service, despite equal rights for women.

Ed Sweet and the COBRA Team members he had tentatively selected for the mission were waiting for him in the operations room. He laughed as each member of the team took turns ribbing him in their typical barracks-room language about his night in the big city. If they only knew. He laughed. These guys ribbing him. With the exception of Ed Sweet, who was happily married, all were known to romance a girl in nearby Fayetteville every night of the week.

Mike filled them in on every detail that had taken place in the White House and the Pentagon. He pulled no bones about the seriousness of the mission they were about to go on. These men liked the straight word; not the crap other commanders often pulled. Telling their men only the skimpiest details and asking them to put their faith in his good judgment.

These were Mike's own. Hand picked. Absolutely trustworthy and willing to live or die with him, not for him. That was undoubtedly the main reason for their success. Absolutely dedicated, without fear, or inbred jealousy. Trust. He had it in them and they in him. Almost unique in the army. Nearly everywhere else, it's the old man wants this, higher headquarters directs that. Not here. They were a team. The COBRA Team. And by God, as long as he was in command, it would never change. All equals, sharing the same danger, and reveling in their successes, but only within the closely knit group that had long ago forsaken the prerogatives and privileges that came with recognition of heroism on battlefields in faraway lands. Unsung, unheralded, and largely unknown, their exploits and actions, if revealed, would have provided top news copy for the nation.

Perhaps one day, that might be possible. But not in the foreseeable future. Their specialized capabilities had to be kept secret. With the world in a constant state of turmoil, no nation dared to send in the sizable expeditionary forces of old. Highly selective, covert, clandestine operations of the type pulled off by the COBRA Team were the only viable options left. The United

States was fortunate that a few men long ago had the wisdom and foresight to keep that kind of capability intact.

Mike Donovan sat quietly as each member of the COBRA Team stood by the operations map and explained his part of the planned operation. Their quiet, confident voices reflected the high degree of professionalism that the team had acquired in its many years of working together. As each detail was unfolded, Mike judged that they had a better than average chance of pulling off the mission.

He glanced again at the large map of Cuba on the war room wall. The reported missile sightings marked in red appeared in clusters around Havana and toward the north and west coasts. The area selected for landing his team from the submarine was only a few miles from a nearby location reported to be a missile complex. That would save time, even though the chance of being detected while landing might be increased. Time was of essence. The President had repeated that several times.

The team couldn't spend days moving overland from a remote, safer landing site to the reported missile locations and still meet the President's requirements for speedy verification. No. They had all agreed to take the risk of putting ashore near the objective area. Anyway, as Marc Mayberry had pointed out, the risk of detection while moving from a faraway, remote site overland was perhaps even greater, considering the distance they would have to travel.

Danny Thompson said, "Sir, that completes the briefing." It jolted Mike Donovan. Somewhere in the middle of the session his mind had wandered back to Susan and the night before.

He'd give anything for an encore. No girl in years had made such an impression on him. He was convinced that she had everything he had been searching for, for so long. Beauty for sure. But her other attributes also appealed to him. Easy grace, pleasant voice, radiant smile, and her naturalness and sincerity made her affection more appealing. Her ambition and apparent determination had also impressed him.

While he mused, the COBRA Team waited patiently for him to respond to Lieutenant Thompson's announcement that the briefing was over. Damn, he thought, had he missed any key points during the briefing which might come back to haunt him later on? "Excuse me, Danny," he said, relieving the apprehension felt by the team.

"Let me take a few minutes and review the sequence of events." As Mike recounted each aspect of the plan, he could tell by the expression on the faces of the men that he had absorbed the detailed plan even though his mind had dwelt on Susan. "That's it, we'll leave for Florida first thing in the morning." He signalled the end of the long eight-hour planning session. The clock above the map showed it was midnight.

Mike hurried back to his bachelor quarters. He was weary. He reached for the telephone and dialed Susan's number. He let the phone ring time and time again before admitting to himself there was to be no answer. Several times during the day, he had called her at the number she had given him with the same results. No answer. Had she been leading him on? He called Washington information twice and was told the last time in an emphatic tone they had no listing for a Susan Ainsworth. He replaced the phone and sat down.

The perplexed look on his face mirrored the thoughts which were racing through his mind. Had he been her patsy? Her one-night stand? Reflecting back on the events of yesterday, he began to think it had all been too easy. Meet girl, a drink or two, a romp in the sack, a tearless goodbye and hope to see you again, and wham. He'd been taken. Cripes, what a fool he was. And after explaining to her in his most subtle way that he wasn't a 3F. He remembered her quick response, "You mean 4F" and his equally quick reply, "No I'm not a 3-F—Find'em, Fuck'em and Forget'em."

It was ironic. Here he thought he was reassuring her that she was someone special, not just a passing fancy, or a target of opportunity, but the girl of his dreams. He felt he'd been conned. And after his years of experience with girls of every nationality, in various cities, hotels and bars, from Europe to Asia, he'd been conned right here in the United States. Damn, was he stupid!

He turned over every word she had said, recalled her every action, and imagined the smile on her face, the soft tone of her voice. All the images led him to believe she had fallen for him. There just had to be a clue. Some word, something she had done should have warned him. He searched his brain. Nothing. Absolutely nothing. Was he slipping? He'd have to do better than that on the operation with the COBRA Team or he would be leading them to an untimely end, all because he had lost his sense of judgment.

It wasn't until hours later that Mike Donovan fell into a deep sleep, mentally and physically exhausted.

Chapter 6

THE WARDROOM OF the Grayback hadn't changed since Mike Donovan's last visit. He felt right at home. This was his 23rd or 24th voyage on the old World War II vintage sub and he loved every square inch of her hulking frame. He was particularly happy to see Jim Knowles still on board as skipper.

Jim and his crew had been hauling Mike and the COBRA Team from one strange place to another for years. The only submarine the U.S. Navy still had in service that was dedicated to support special operations. Jim Knowles and the crew knew that Mike Donovan was responsible for keeping her in the active fleet.

Every year at budget time, navy bureaucrats had her at the top of their list for decommissioning. And every year Mike Donovan would arrange a chat with the Chief of Naval Operations about keeping her in service. The navy hierarchy could never understand why the CNO would overrule their recommendations and with a penciled "Keep her in service," and his initials, undo what they had spent days doing—writing position papers on how much money the navy would save if this old diesel-driven relic of World War II was sold for scrap.

It became almost a game. The staff, ignorant of the true use of the Grayback, and trying to economize and modernize, would develop a variety of cost savings programs. In the venerable diesel submarine, they were absolutely certain they had spotted an overlooked, worthless asset for the modern navy. Their meticulous work then was undone by the CNO's brief, blunt decision to retain her in the active fleet.

Mike Donovan and Jim Knowles had developed strong bonds of personal and professional respect while working together in past operations. Mike gave brief orders to "drop us off here; pick us up there," and Jim's response invariably was "Aye, Aye, sir." No questions.

The CNO had directed the Grayback's skipper to respond to every request given by Donovan unless the safety of his ship or crew was jeopardized. Then, and only then, was he authorized to confirm the order personally with the CNO before execution. Otherwise, Donovan's requests were to be honored.

Commander Knowles, during his earlier years working with Donovan and his team, had often been troubled with some of the weird things that he had been asked to do. But invariably after every operation, the "WELL DONE AND THREE DAYS OF EXTRA LIBERTY AT FIRST PORT" from the CNO reassured him that Donovan could call the shots.

Mike was especially fond of the crew. Never once, after picking him up at some God-forsaken rendezvous point off a hostile shore, had a crew member asked what they had been doing. They were the silent service and he long ago realized how they got the name. Superb conduct in execution of hazardous orders without the usual propaganda announcements on their fine performance. Getting the job done right was more satisfying and rewarding to them. They were the real professionals of the sea.

The briefings the team had received earlier in the day from Bud Sharp and Merv Collins had been particularly helpful. Sharp and Collins had flown to Key West for a last-minute rundown on the situation before the COBRA Team embarked on the Grayback. However, the recognition signals and the sequence of events between the reception party on shore and the team departed from their usual routine. The team was to be met by two agents, taken to a remote location and left there. Another agent would pick them up, and escort them to a small farm in remote jungle country, then depart. Their final agent contact, with the code name of Perfecto, was to join the team at the farm and work with them in their operation.

The passwords and countersigns for each exchange were drilled into them as though they were secondgraders. Bud Sharp kept insisting they repeat them again and again. Any slip-up, he said, might be met with hostile reaction rather than a welcome. The unusual number of contacts and cutouts disturbed Mike. But his faith in John Askins and the way he operated reassured him. The agency had never let him down and the arrangements made on earlier operations had seemed just as weird at the time.

Mike was, however, disturbed by Sharp's return of the twenty dollars just before he left. According to Bud, the Pentagon florist had called and said they had been unable to deliver the flowers to a Miss Susan Ainsworth at the address given. Their delivery attempt had brought no answer to repeated ringing of the doorbell. None of the neighbors knew her. Mike was convinced that he had been had. Even more than the blow to his pride, he fretted about Susan's real motives.

His meeting with Bunson Burner Cochrane had gone well. Bunson Burner had his C-130 and Fulton skyhook all set to go and could respond in minutes to any request. They had picked out several possible locations in the event the team had to call for help. Bunson Burner had also arranged for an F-4 fighter aircraft to pre-drop Fulton kits at Mike's request at any location, day or night, in the event of an emergency.

Keith Himes had arrived and given the team the latest on the weather. His forecast of moderate to heavy seas in the area selected for infiltration was not promising. However, with Commander Terry's SEALS along to help the team ashore Mike felt the plan could stand. The SEALS would make it easier.

The Sea, Air, Land (SEAL) teams of the navy were much like Mike's own highly trained group and their frequent joint exercises really paid off when they faced the real test of an operation instead of the exercise scenarios dreamed up by most planners.

Jim Knowles joined Mike in the wardroom and again they went over the final plans for the night. The sub would reach Point B, the site selected earlier, one hour before landing time. The periscope would be raised. A triangle of briefly lit lights on the shore would signal the 'all clear' and for the mission to continue.

The COBRA Team and two SEALs would be locked out of the submarine; they'd secure the rubber boat, paddle to shore, and after the challenge and countersign had been made with the reception party, the SEALs would return the boat to the sub. The sub would then cruise back out to sea prepared to return on six hours notice to any site designated by Donovan from among those they had carefully selected that morning.

The SEALs would come ashore on Donovan's signal, and return the COBRA Team to the sub. Almost routine. The many rehearsals and training exercises in the past between the COBRA Team, the SEALs and the crew of the Grayback would pay off again. Mike felt confident that he could count on Jim Knowles and his entire crew. He often wondered why the brass in the Pentagon spent hours and days fighting about roles and missions between the services while out in the field, army, navy, and air force operating personnel took all problems in stride. Never once in his memory had an argument developed between the services operating away from the Pentagon as to who had responsibility for this or that. They simply did what had to be done.

Perhaps if the Pentagon commandos would get out of

the puzzle palace occasionally and see how things were carried out, the unification supposed to result from the National Security Act of 1947 might become a reality. Let the brass wage their Pentagon wars; he'd stay out where the real action was taking place.

"Jim, I think I'll hit the sack for a couple of hours. How about giving me a call about midnight? That will give me plenty of time to get the team ready before you maneuver this bucket of bolts into the rendezvous point."

"Sure will, Mike. I'll have the cook fix you steak and eggs about that time. It might be the only hot meal you guys may have for awhile. Use my room. All the others are hot-bunking it. I'll keep my crew away until H-hour. They can catch up on their sleep after I push you guys out the porthole."

Mike walked to Knowles' room and was sound asleep minutes after hitting the bunk.

Jim Knowles shook Mike Donovan several times before he could get his attention. "Time to get ready, Mike." Mike glanced at his watch. Midnight.

"Breakfast will be ready by the time you get down to the wardroom. Then I'd like to go over the plans with you one more time."

"Thanks, Jim. By the way, doesn't the skipper of this tub rate a mattress without lumps?" Mike asked in his most sarcastic voice.

"Not this year, Mike. Haven't you heard? The navy is on a stringent economy program. No new mattresses for the brass. We'll use them another year, the chief of Naval Material has decreed. He'd save the navy enough money to buy another widget that way. And you know, Mike, widgets are important. Skippers and lumpy mattresses can't compete with that kind of logic." Mike laughed. That was Jim Knowles at his best.

As Mike entered the wardroom he saw his entire team busy enjoying steak and eggs and marvelling how the navy fed its men. He joined the group's amusement hearing Marc Mayberry telling the skipper that in the army they had a choice between dehydrated eggs and SOS. As he explained it to Jim Knowles, the SOS, better known as "Shit on a Shingle," was a longstanding army tradition that creamed chipped beef on toast be fed its soldiers for breakfast every morning. Marc went on to add that the navy had given up its rum ration but the army was still making a staff study on the nutritional value of SOS and its relationship to soldier diet and morale.

Mike looked around at his team. All were taking part in the discussion on the relative merits of SOS and the other fringe benefits that went to servicemen. If only some of the beef-raising congressmen from out West could sit in on one of these bull sessions and get the real facts of life, instead of extolling the virtues of having the boys in service get a ration of beef with every meal.

The congressmen from the dairy states pushing cheese, cream, and butter could also learn. And the representatives from the chicken-raising areas who insisted that poultry was the soldier's choice and give'em all they could eat. Donovan remembered too well the bill introduced by a congressman requiring the army to feed its troops C rations at least twice a week, to put large stocks remaining from World War II to use.

The congressman went on to explain that welfare recipients were not used to eating that kind of food, but soldiers were and they loved it. He had it on good authority from his nephew, who had served as an orderly in General Eisenhower's headquarters during World War II, and had often heard the general say, "Two up and one back, and feed'em a hot C ration," and the troops would go anywhere and do anything. What an idiot! If he had only added, "—and they would have gone over the nearest hill," he might have come close to reflecting the true feelings of the fighting doughboys.

Mike called out, "Okay, boys, the fun's over, let's get with it."

At Jim Knowles' invitation Mike peered through the raised periscope. Seeing the dark outline of the coast of Cuba made it clear that the time for action had arrived. As his eyes grew accustomed to the darkness, he was amazed at the detail of the coast the periscope revealed. A small cove with long overhanging tree limbs framing the narrow beach looked like the perfect spot to land. It would provide them a chance to assemble without detection from either side of the coastline extending as far as he could see.

He pointed out the spot to the navy SEALs standing at his side. They nodded agreement. Tom Newhouse, the senior SEAL added, "We'll put you right into the pocket, Captain. Just say the word."

Mike smiled to himself. He'd been working with SEALs for years but he still had to find the first one that would call him Colonel. It was always Captain. As one SEAL had told him once, "Those eagles on your collar mean you're a captain to me. If you army types can't tell one rank from another, then you'd better join the navy and find out what the eagles mean—a captain." After all, they'd claim the navy was the senior service and that Johnny-come-latelies from the army had better start showing some respect for that longstanding navy tradition of an eagle signifying the rank of captain. Why in hell hadn't the army, the air force, and the damn marines developed their own insignia designating a colonel, rather than copying the navy and trying to impose a new name for that rank?

The SEALs knew why. Those simple-minded jerks in those services never had an original thought of their own. So they adopted the navy insignia and just called them something else. On top of that the army was really screwed up. They had 2nd and 1st lieutenants. The navy was a hell of a lot more precise. They had ensigns and lieutenants junior grade, and lieutenants senior grade.

The army called their senior grade lieutenants "captain", and any idiot would know that a captain was the senior rank below flag rank. "Oh well," he had continued, "what the hell could you expect from an outfit that got around by walking and shoving mules by the ass up a mountain trail?"

"Mike, it's twenty-nine past midnight. As soon as you give the word I'll prepare for the lockout." Jim Knowles' voice was crisp and commanding.

"Okay, Jim, as soon as I get the signal that it's all clear, I'll be right up." Mike's voice too was businesslike and authoritative. He kept scanning the coast focusing on the area on either side of the cove. Suddenly three lights flashed on and just as rapidly were extinguished. Held about one foot apart to outline each corner of a triangle, the light signal confirmed that the reception party was waiting and the area clear. God, he hoped they were right.

He was the last man out of the lockout. He felt the warmth of the water as soon as he hit the Caribbean Sea. The SEALs and his team had already positioned the rubber boat when his head broke water. The waterproof bag containing the team's equipment and clothing was hoisted aboard the boat. Three-foot waves tossed the boat from side to side in a calypso style rhythm. The swish of the water as each wave hit the huge rubber pylons framing the boat in its boxlike shape seemed to grow louder as the team silently pushed the boat toward shore.

Mike Donovan kept scanning the coastline as it came clearer and closer in view. Only the wind rustling through the trees and the lapping of the surf against the shore broke the silence of the night. The quarter moon above the horizon cast eerie shadows across the shoreline as the boat and the seven scuba-clad frogmen moved slowly toward the inner part of the cove.

The sandy bottom told Mike that they had arrived. As

he scrambled ashore a sharp "Que Amigos" stopped him dead in his tracks. "El Cambio," he replied instantly in a soft low voice. Out of the dark, dense underbrush two figures emerged almost at once. After a brief handshake with the reception party, the team changed from scuba gear to the lightweight, casual clothes retrieved from the waterproof bags. Within minutes the team had unpacked its radios and other gear, and the SEALs slid silently back into the water pushing the rubber boat seaward with the scuba equipment stashed inside the boat's small interior. It wasn't until the boat began to disappear in the distance that Mike Donovan heaved a sigh of relief. So far, everything was going according to plan. It seemed so easy.

Following the guides through the dense underbrush soon began to tax the team. The high humidity and the hot tropical air were far different from the cool night breezes that prevailed over the training areas of North Carolina. Mike Donovan made a mental note that hereafter he'd have to take his teams to the army training area in the Panama Canal zone more often if they really wanted to get into the proper physical condition to cope with the steaming, hot and humid jungle areas of Latin America. North Carolina and even Florida wouldn't do.

Finally, after what seemed like hours of painstakingly picking their way through every thorny bush that existed on the face of the earth, they came to a small clearing. The first signs of daybreak were approaching, with birdcalls becoming louder and louder.

Now, for the first time, Donovan could clearly see the two Cubans who had met them at the beach. One was rather short, with long sideburns outlining his swarthy face in the dim light of the rapidly approaching dawn. The other, at least six foot one, was a burly, muscular man dressed in faded blue denim with kneehigh boots adding to his appearance of brute strength. The dark stubble of his whiskers against his dark skin reminded Mike of the villains so often depicted in motion pictures.

He was thankful that for once this man was an ally, not an enemy.

As they approached the far end of the clearing, Mike saw two thatched huts. A small stream meandered its way in an erratic pattern along the clearing's edge. Smoke drifted skyward from a small fire at the front of the huts. The smell of coffee and bacon hung in the air. A tug at Mike's elbow caught his attention. The tall Cuban thrust out his hand and, in pidgin English, informed Mike that he and his partner would be leaving. Their mission had been accomplished. Without another word the two men disappeared into the thick jungle.

Just as rapidly and on Mike Donovan's signal, Danny Thompson moved to the far edge of the clearing facing the trail over which they had just moved. Marc Mayberry took up a position to the far right and rear of the thatched huts, Roger Landsdale to the far left and Tiger Tangier crouched low under heavy foliage inside the heavy jungle which provided a full view of the entire clearing.

Donovan approached the thatched huts warily. The early rays of the sun peeking over the high trees surrounding the open clearing cast long shadows along its entire length. As he reached the door of the hut to the right and rear of the smoldering fire, he detected a slight movement within the hut's interior.

He instinctively jumped to the corner of the building and, with pistol drawn, moved slowly toward the door. Without a backward glance he knew that every member of his team had their weapons trained on the hut, ready to fire at any hostile act.

As Mike reached the door he heard a muffled sound. Glancing inside he saw in the far corner a solitary figure lying face down on the floor with legs and arms trussed at the back and tied together with a heavy hemp rope.

"Seven eleven." The shrill cry startled Mike. It was the agent's challenge which Bud Sharp had so meticulously drilled into him the day before. Without hesitation, he responded "Hacienda," the code word for acknowledging the challenge. He bent down, untied the ropes and reached out his hand to help his contact to his feet. As he did, he pulled back instinctively.

He was a she. Long black hair fell to her shoulders as she arose. With a quick thrust of her hand she brushed the falling hair quickly to the side and smiled. "Amigo, I am Perfecto."

Mike Donovan gasped. "Perfecto" was to be his main agent to assist in accomplishing his mission in Cuba. He had not been told it would be a woman. Only that Perfecto was the CIA's most trusted and efficient agent who would provide him with the support and assistance he needed. Not once did Bud Sharp or Merv Collins ever give him a hint that he would be working with a female. This was a new experience for him. In the many operations he had been on all over the world, never once had he been involved with a woman as his principal agent. This was his first surprise of the operation. He hoped it was his last.

Perfecto moved silently to the door and after peering out, quickly walked to the fire. Taking two battered cups from a small box nearby she poured them both a cup of coffee from the cast-iron pot placed on the edge of the coals. As she handed Mike his cup, she smiled. Her dark hair contrasted sharply with the almost pure white skin of her face. She was a Latin. No doubt about that. But her skin and complexion left no doubt in Mike's mind that at least one of her ancestors had plenty of white blood and that was coursing through her veins. Her dark eyes flashed back and forth over the clearing as if expecting someone to arrive. Finally satisfied that they were all alone, she looked up at Mike and said, "Where are the others?"

Mike motioned toward the jungle areas surrounding the clearing. Her eyes again searched the area from side to side. Turning to him she said in almost perfect English, "They are well hidden. If you like, they can come out and have some coffee. I'll fix them something to eat, I'm sure the long walk has made them hungry."

Donovan raised his right hand and with his outstretched finger pointed skyward, moved it rapidly in a circle and then pointed toward the ground. Perfecto watched in amazement as each member of the team came out of the heavy jungle and moved toward the campfire. Not a word had been uttered by this American, yet his men had responded to a wiggle of his finger. After shaking hands with each member of the team, Perfecto poured them all a cup of coffee and motioned them to be seated.

Then first looking at Mike to acknowledge his presence again, she began speaking in a low, sultry voice. When she had received her radio instructions from the CIA to meet with the Americans, and having acknowledged the rather detailed instructions for contacting them, the use of cut-outs, and her eventual rendezvous at a farm, nothing had gone according to plan.

First, her cut-out, Pascal, had drunk too much wine and had gotten into an argument with the local security officials who had him thrown into jail until he sobered up. Then she had to contact Pancho and his friend to have the Americans brought directly to the farm instead of the intermediate cut-out point. Finally, the Cuban lieutenant who commanded the local military detachment operating out of La Isabela had insisted that she keep him company last night. After convincing him that she had a severe headache and leaving him half dressed in his apartment, she had taken her two agents and her sixteen-year-old brother to the farm to show them where she wanted the Americans brought by daylight. The two agents had immediately left for the coast to signal the 'all clear' and to meet the team as it landed.

Earlier this morning her younger brother had tied her up at her request, to give her a plausible alibi should the Cuban security service detect the team's landing and follow her agents to the farm. She had a story all cooked up about being forced to accompany two men to the farm where they had taken advantage of her and as a final result had demanded that she cook them breakfast before they left for their jobs. They would be back by early afternoon to continue the fiesta they had started the night before. To be sure she would remain, they had tied her up in the hut. Fortunately, the Americans had not been followed. She concluded her story by asking what she could do to assist them. Her instructions were to provide whatever help they needed.

Mike explained the broad aspects of his mission. Were the Soviets moving missiles into Cuba and did they have nuclear warheads? If so, could she help them pinpoint exact locations? The team would photograph such sites from long ranges using cameras with telescopic lens. She could be of great help by pointing out known or likely sites. High hills or other vantage points some distance away would be needed where a team member could be hidden with his camera.

Mike asked if she was aware of any such sites now. "Yes," she said. She knew of such sites and had been reporting them to the CIA by her clandestine radio. She was unsure of the type of missiles but did report that missiles about twelve to fifteen feet long were being moved. She, of course, wouldn't know a nuclear missile from any other type of missile. "What do they look like?" she inquired.

Mike went to great length explaining the possible shapes and sizes of nuclear warheads. She kept shaking her head as he finished describing every possible configuration of the most likely warheads the Soviets may have been giving Cuba.

It wasn't until Mike described a small, coffin-like box made of heavy metal that her eyes began to light up. Waving her arms she claimed that she had seen such boxes. But they weren't missiles. They were just funny-looking boxes. Yes, she certainly had seen them with many guards around them. But they weren't missiles.

The missiles she had been reporting were long, about twelve to fifteen feet, with fins at the rear, and a well-rounded end with a small needle-like antenna protruding from the nose.

The Soviet officer in charge of the rocket forces in the nearby village for some time had been asking her for a date. If the team wanted, she would accept and attempt to develop more information from him.

In the meanwhile, this area would be the home base for the team. It was owned by a friend of hers who was in jail in Havana for crimes against the state and she was taking care of it for him. She and her brother used it occasionally to get away from the nearby village where they lived. She was a schoolteacher there, but when school was in recess she did odd jobs around the city. Her brother had been drafted into the Cuban sugar brigade, Castro's program to use youngsters to help cut sugar cane and get Cuba hard currency to carry on programs for the people.

She would now go back into the village, about an hour's walk away. She would return before dark. After dark, she could lead some of the team members to a location where they could see the missile site from a distance. Unless you knew exactly where to look, the team could never find it, as it was hidden near the edges of high jungle and kept well camouflaged.

Most of the missiles had frame huts built around them, and the Americans could look right at them and never realize there were missiles hidden under the thatched walls and roof. The Cubans had been shown how to do this by some North Vietnam advisors who had visited the island a few months ago. The North Vietnamese claimed that they had fooled the Americans for years in Vietnam that way. And when the Americans accidentally bombed one of the huts holding a missile, the Vietnamese would scream to the world that the imperialist devils were bombing poor farmers.

To support their deception they occasionally took

a U.S. pacifist visiting Hanoi to a farming community and showed the bomb craters left by the American bombers, after having made sure that the other missiles nearby had first been moved.

Mike asked Perfecto why she was working for American intelligence. Very simple, she replied. Her father had been murdered by Castro shortly after he came to power. She was half American. Her father was an American businessman who had lived in Cuba for over twenty years and had married her mother shortly after he had arrived in Havana. If he hadn't noticed before, she was half Spanish, half American.

She thrust out her chest and said she might not be an American Marilyn Monroe but no Cuban girl had anything half as nice. Mike and the team joined in laughter as she cupped her breasts to demonstrate that she was well endowed. In fact, moreso than Mike had first noticed. She was really stacked. While she might not qualify as a reigning Miss America, he was certain she could take Miss Cuba honors if Castro ever instituted the decadent American custom of beauty contests.

The more Mike looked her over, the more impressed he was. She was quite a dish. Her real name was Maria Hollingshead but she had taken her mother's name, Rodriguez, after her father's murder. It just didn't pay to have a name like Hollingshead after Castro came to power.

Before leaving, Maria pointed out a fishing area to the rear of the huts where a small stone retaining wall had been built across the creek, forming a small pond. Fishing tackle could be found in the huts. Often, her brother would come out here in late afternoon and fish. She would arrive later and they would have a fish-fry over the campfire. The occasional envelope she received from an agent out of the French embassy contained funds enough for her, her brother and her mother to make ends meet. The pittance she received as a schoolteacher was barely enough to pay her rent, buy the food, and an occasional dress. The revolution frowned on paying public servants more than necessary for bare survival. If a girl wanted anything more than to serve the nation, she could keep a lover—one of the many Cuban or Soviet officers who seemed to be everywhere.

After scribbling a sitrep and a short footnote which he gave to Marc Mayberry to send back to Bragg via radio that afternoon, Mike assigned each member of the team a watch while the others caught up on their sleep. Maria had warned him before leaving that she'd have a plan for their first night out and he'd better be rested. She'd be back before dark and if the boys felt like it, she'd cook any fish they caught.

Mike Donovan found a shady area to the rear of the hut and sat down with his back against a large cypress tree which overhung the small fish-pond. He unfolded his silk map of Cuba and gazed at the light pencil mark Maria had made to indicate their present location.

On the map, Havana was just inches away. The coast only an eighth of an inch. Cripes, how deceiving. Havana was over forty miles to the northeast and yet it would take at least two, maybe three, nights of traveling overland should there by any reason to go there.

According to Merv Collins, the agency suspected that some of the nuclear weapons were coming in by air and only Havana's airfield was large enough to accommodate the huge Soviet transport planes which could be used for such a flight. God, how he hoped he wouldn't have to go to Havana and stake out the airfield. Operating in Cuba was bad enough, but going into the lion's den would be a bit much. But deep in his heart he knew that he'd go if Washington required it.

The warmth of the day and the rippling of the water as it spilled over the rocky retaining wall below his perch lulled Mike Donovan to sleep. The hectic pace he had been on since Sunday when he was first called to Washington was beginning to tell.

* * *

Bud Sharp was alone in his Pentagon office when Yeoman Lovingwell handed him a message which had come in from Bragg. Bunch of mumbo jumbo to him. The message center hadn't decoded the damn thing. They said to deliver it to the Colonel immediately. Had some sort of operational priority.

Sharp signed for the message, dismissed the young sailor and locked his office door as Yeoman Lovingwell departed. He dialed the combination of his safe, and after a second try found that the door wouldn't open when he got back to zero. Dammit, everytime he was in a hurry it took him at least two tries to get that safe combination to work. On his third try it opened.

He removed a one-time pad from the top drawer and pored over the message, slowly writing each word on the legal-size yellow pad on his desk. He liked the security one-time pads provided for clandestine communications but they were a pain at times. After going through the message and deciphering each word group he read the transcribed message on his pad. "Phase one completed as planned. P.S. You forgot the pills for Perfecto."

What the hell did Dagger mean by that? He picked up his gray telephone and dialed Merv Collins at the agency. He read the message to Merv and asked him what was meant by the postscript. Wasn't Perfecto his contact? Collins' reply in the affirmative only increased his curiosity. What kind of pills had they forgotten?

Collins couldn't understand the meaning of the P.S. either. Was Perfecto a diabetic fellow requiring pills, or what? He'd check with his agent handler at the agency and call Bud back. In the meanwhile he suggested that the P.S. be left off the message when sending it up to the chairman of the JCS who would pass it to the President. He agreed with Merv that trying to explain its meaning would only embroil them in endless conversation.

Hurriedly, he rewrote the short message on a piece of plain white paper after a brief lead and title "Dagger reports as of 1000 hours EST" as simply "Phase one completed." Early this morning he had delivered the first situation report to the chairman which he had received from the skipper of the Grayback reporting a successful entry. On a plain white envelope he wrote "Eyes Only" for the chairman, Joint Chiefs of Staff.

Taking the paper on which he had transcribed Dagger's report he placed it in the envelope and walked upstairs to the chairman's office. Colonel Clay Leyton, the chairman's aide-de-camp said, "Go right in, the old man's alone."

Bud knocked on the door and entered when he heard General Taylor call out, "Come on in."

"Sir, I have the first situation report from Dagger." He handed the sealed envelope to the general.

Ben Taylor ripped open the envelope and stared at the brief message. He looked up at Bud. "Is this all?"

"Yes, sir," Bud replied, "except for a brief postscript he added for me."

"Postscript! What kind of postscript?"

"Sir, his P.S. said that I'd forgotten the pills for Perfecto. Frankly, sir, I don't know what he means. I called the agency and they couldn't understand it either. However, the fact that he made it a postscript indicates it has nothing to do with the mission."

"Dammit, Bud, I thought you guys were on the same frequency with all your codes and all. Try and figure out the meaning and get back to me. Both of us have a lot riding on this operation. I don't want to be a party to screwing it up."

"Sir, you just gave me a clue on what the postscript might mean."

"I did what?"

"I think you solved the postscript. May I use your gray phone for a minute?"

"Go right ahead."

Bud Sharp dialed Merv Collins.

"Collins here."

"Merv, again, a quick question. Did you find out anything about Perfecto?"

"Sure have, and listen to this. She is a female, of all things."

"Thanks, Merv."

"Hey, hold on, I've got more."

"Later, Merv. I'll call you back."

Bud broke out laughing. General Taylor looked at him and grinned.

"How about letting me in on the joke?"

"Sir, when you mentioned that you didn't want to be a party to screwing up this operation, it suddenly dawned on me that perhaps Perfecto was a female agent. Neither Merv Collins nor I knew this when we briefed Dagger at Key West on his contact. His P.S. was just a needle about the poor job we did in giving him the details on his agent."

"Okay, Bud, but let's not have any more surprises. I'm seeing the President in about an hour on another matter and I'll pass on Dagger's report—without the postscript."

Susan Ainsworth was tired. The long flight from Washington to Wichita seemed to be forever. Adding to her discomfort was the Secretary of the Interior telling her off-color jokes and wondering if she wouldn't like to spend the evening on the town with him. He'd show her a good time, he promised. No, she lied, she was engaged and her fiance simply wouldn't understand if she went out to dinner with another man. In that case, the Secretary of Interior continued, they could have a candlelight dinner in his hotel room. No prying eyes, no one would ever know. He needed to relax before his big meeting with the midwestern governors tomorrow and Susan could provide him the right tonic and he'd sleep like a baby. It wasn't until she told him for the third time that under no circumstances would she consider any contact with him once she left the plane that he changed the subject.

Now alone in her room at the Holiday Inn adjacent to the airport she dialed long distance and asked to talk to Colonel Mike Donovan at Fort Bragg, North Carolina. No, she told the operator, she didn't know his number but he was the commander of the 7th Special Forces Group. "Just a minute," the operator intoned, "I'll connect you."

"Seventh Special Forces Group. Lieutenant Dooley, duty officer speaking."

"Lieutenant, may I speak to Colonel Donovan, please?"

"Ma'am, Colonel Donovan is not here just now. Would you like to leave a message?"

"Please have him call Susan Ainsworth at the Holiday Inn in Wichita, Kansas. The number is 316 264-1181. I'm in Room 203. I'll be here until noon tomorrow."

"Yes, ma'am, I'll leave the message on his desk."

"Thank you, Lieutenant."

Susan Ainsworth put down the phone slowly. She had missed Mike so much and had a million things to tell him but she wanted especially to ask him to come to Washington to meet her on the day she returned. She freshened up a bit before heading for the dining room for a quick dinner. On the way she stopped at the front desk and informed the clerk she was expecting a long distance call from a Colonel Donovan. Would he please page her in the dining room when it came in?

She was finishing her dinner when Captain Smith and Lieutenant Kelly came by her table, inviting her to join them in seeing the town. She declined with thanks. Until Sunday when she had met Mike Donovan, a highlight of each trip was seeing the sights with the crew. Invariably they would invite her out, pick up the tab and see her safely back to her room. Only occasionally did one of the pilots suggest doing anything more. Most were married and had wives or sweethearts at home. When they took her along she was truly one of the crew. Not a female to be conquered. She liked it that way.

But now, even that seemed improper. She belonged to Mike. She was his alone. And the thought of that thrilled her. On her way back to her room she again informed the desk that she was expecting a call and would be in her room for the rest of the evening.

She showered quickly and turned on the radio, listening to the semiclassical music which filled the air. Finally, she started a letter to Mike in which she poured out her feelings for him, suggesting that he meet her in Washington when she returned from her current trip. She added a P.S. that if the Key Bridge Marriott was booked solid, not to worry. She had plenty of room at her place. She sealed the letter, placed a drop of perfume on the envelope, walked down to the lobby and dropped it in the mailbox after finally getting a recalcitrant stamp machine to take her change for two stamps.

Chapter 7

MARIA RETURNED TO camp before dark, smiling and enthusiastic. On the way to the village, after leaving the team late that morning, she had scouted along a trail which led to a rocky, shrub-covered high hill overlooking a large clearing. According to rumors rampant in the village, a missile site was being developed in the clearing. She hadn't climbed to the top of the hill, for fear of detection. If the team was interested in checking it out, she would lead two or three of them there after dark. It would be a difficult climb as the hill was quite high and from what she had observed, it was covered with dense jungle at least two-thirds of the way to the top.

All the men wanted to go on the first operation. That put Mike on the spot. As the commander he was determined to go on the first mission even though he had misgivings about his own physical condition. He finally selected Danny Thompson, his second in command, and Roger Landsdale, the team medic and jack-of-all-trades, to go with him.

He selected Danny because he was an expert with the camera and if anyone could get a good shot of what was going on, he would. He had instinct and disciplined skill and would never point a camera to reflect the rays of the sun and give away his position. Danny had a near

THE COBRA TEAM

phobia about using the camera correctly. Mike remembered the incident on the Ho Chi Minh trail a few years before, when Mel Gaston and Danny were roadwatchers photographing North Vietnamese soldiers hauling supplies down the trail. Mel, in a careless moment, had let the bright overhead sun strike his camera and from down a valley where a North Vietnamese company was bivouacked, a scouting patrol moved to reconnoiter the area. Only by the grace of God did Danny escape. When he was last seen, Mel was being led away by the North Vietnamese with his hands tied behind his back. Bayonets were applied to his rear as he was forced to climb jagged rock-lined slopes in the Laos panhandle. From that day on, Danny Thompson swore he and he alone would take responsibility for photography when on a mission.

Mike ruled out taking Marc Mayberry as he was needed at base camp to stand by for any instructions coming to the team by radio. Twice a day, ten in the morning and four in the afternoon, was their scheduled radio contact with Fort Bragg and the outside world. Marc was by far best qualified to handle that duty. During an emergency, Marc could contact Fort Bragg at any time. But the fewer radio transmissions they had, the better security for the team.

In the old days, radio transmissions took an inordinate amount of time. Radio direction finders skillfully employed could pinpoint the location of a clandestine transmitter without much trouble. The advent of burst transmission devices allowed a team like Mike's to transmit a two-hundred-word message in less than six seconds, hardly enough time for direction finders to fix the signal and to be able to locate it by triangulation.

Every member of the team had been trained to send and receive messages, but only Marc Mayberry had the technical know-how to fix the blasted things if they had operating difficulty. Tiger Tangier was the team's expert in using the Fulton skyhook system. And Mike Donovan had requested that kits be dropped to the team at a site he had carefully selected that afternoon. He decided Tiger would remain at the base camp to recover the kits.

Mike Donovan paused to catch his breath. For what seemed like hours, the small three-man group had been following Maria through the tangled brush enroute to the observation point she had scouted out earlier. Maria waited patiently. She finally leaned over and whispered in Mike's ear, "Have you rested enough?"

Much as he hated to admit it, Mike was out of shape. Here was this little girl moving up and down the hills as fresh as ever, and he was pooped. Who said women were the weaker sex? He vowed that he'd get himself into better shape and stay fit. Late night parties obviously had been taking their toll, he hadn't realized how much until tonight. He looked over his shoulder to see Danny and Roger standing by waiting for him to move. Neither one appeared to him to be the least bit winded. Cripes, he'd better think about the mission next time and stay at base camp himself. Maybe he was getting too damned old for this type of activity.

More determined than ever, he took Maria's hand and said, "Let's go."

To his surprise she tenderly squeezed his hand and at the same time leaned over and kissed him. Damn it, Donovan, he muttered to himself, is this girl mothering me? What's with all this tenderness? He felt it was more than just sympathy or a friendly reminder to get going. Her gentle, thoughtful caress had lingered too long and seemed a bit possessive. He'd find out at the first opportunity.

They climbed until every breath Mike took seemed to sear his lungs. He was fighting to breathe. Finally Maria turned and, holding out her hand, indicated they were to stop. Motioning them to get down, she carefully picked her way around a large boulder in their immediate path.

He could see her silhouette as she moved cautiously around the base of the large protruding rock. In a moment she returned and motioned the team to follow her. Again she crouched low as she moved around the base of the large rock.

Suddenly Mike could see a large valley starting at the base of the hill stretching for at least a mile downward. He knew as soon as he saw the work parties that Maria had led them to a bonanza. The view also gave him a fast appreciation of how high they had climbed. The rock was at least a thousand feet above the valley floor. No wonder he had almost pooped out.

But what really intrigued him was the variety and pace of the construction activity going on below. Heavy equipment moving back and forth scraping and clearing trees, rocks, and shrubs. Large missile transporters and erectors moved into position and immediately camouflaged. Walls of thatch seemed to grow around them as prefabricated shields were erected. For all practical purposes they soon appeared to be a natural part of the landscape, very much like the thousands of huts which dotted the Cuban countryside.

Mike was also noting and recording the layout of the site with trucks, trailers and sizable stacks of crates and boxes dispersed on the edge of the clearing under jungle cover. Damn, those Cubans were smart. They had left the upper canopy of jungle intact and, viewed from the air, nothing could be detected. Seeing the site, Mike felt sure of that.

No wonder the U.S. photo missions had never turned up such sites! There wasn't a camera made that could penetrate the jungle growth. Except for the oblique view from the ground level, the general appearance of the area would have been the same as much of Cuba; a region of heavy growth with occasional cleared areas for farming and forestry.

Danny Thompson and Roger Landsdale took out their binoculars and began viewing the scene in detail.

Mike followed suit. Through his glasses he made out missile erectors and transporters, fuel trucks and obvious communications vans. He wondered if command and control of these systems was localized to the individual site. What a find. The observation point was ideal. With daylight and the telescopic camera, he was certain they would get detailed, clear pictures which the President had repeatedly mentioned he needed. With luck, Mr. President, you'll have your proof.

But where were the telltale metal boxes in which the nuclear warheads were moved? He scanned the area from one side to another, examining every type of container in view. They had to be somewhere. The missile he was looking at was the Soviet SS-21. He was sure of that. But not a sign of the lead-lined caskets in which nuclear warheads were shipped.

He scanned the site again and again until it came to him. You don't bring in the nuke warheads until the sites are ready for launch. He estimated this one was not yet operational. Perhaps seventy-five percent complete, but not complete. However, the intense effort going on below him with the hundreds of workers convinced him the operational readiness date was not far off. They had to get the pictures now before the site was complete and well camouflaged. This was the vulnerable period.

Satisfied that the observation point would provide Danny and Roger the best location to photograph the missile site and the work in progress, Mike suggested they rest till daylight while he and Maria returned to base camp. He wanted to get a message back to Washington as soon as possible, giving a summary of what they had discovered and requesting a pickup of the film that Danny and Roger would be taking during the day. Maria would return for them after dark to lead them back to the farm.

After a last look at the beehive of activity going on in the valley below, he took Maria's arm and asked that she lead the way on the return trip. Daylight would soon

THE COBRA TEAM 99

be here and he wanted to put some distance between them and the Soviet and Cuban soldiers before then. No telling when one of the troops might start wandering up among the hills looking for berries or fresh fruit. Or to simply goof off, as soldiers do in all armies of the world.

Going downhill seemed much easier to Mike as Maria led the way back to camp. He noticed that she was taking a different trail on the way back, and his confidence in her rose. She was agent-savvy. One of the first principles taught to novices in the agent training course back in the States was never to retrace your route when going to and returning from an objective area. Almost every successful ambush could be traced to a violation of that basic rule.

As Mike followed closely behind Maria's footsteps he began for the first time to feel confident that his team could provide the President proof of exact missile site locations. The Soviet missile was known to use a nuclear warhead. However, without a photograph of a nuclear warhead being mounted on a missile, an essential element of proof would still be lacking. With luck, though, their long-range photography might capture a glimpse of the nuclear warheads which Mike reasoned were bound to be nearby or soon to be on the way to the missile site. Without them, the Soviets would be engaged in an exercise in futility. Mike knew that they didn't waste their time and effort that way.

The sun was high and the hot, humid air of the jungle was again getting to Mike. He paused several times to wipe the sweat from his brow and catch his breath. Maria would lean up against a tree and wait for him to signal his ability to continue. He had known it would be hot in Cuba, but he realized that he had underestimated his ability to adapt to the sudden change of climate from cool North Carolina. He never had experienced such trouble before in adjusting to a change in climate. Vietnam, Laos and Cambodia had been just as hot and miserable.

He was either getting old or in bad physical shape. The latter thought almost killed him. He was the commander of an elite force kept in top physical condition to do anything demanded of them. Was he to be the weak link in their chain?

Sweat poured down his face as he kept moving forward. Maria's occasional glance and smile kept him going. He was beat. Maria watched him more closely. Finally she left the trail they had been following and turned almost ninety degrees west. The going was even tougher. Jungle vines seemed to ensnarl Mike's legs with every move.

Mike watched Maria in utter amazement as she picked her way through every vine and branch which hung over the trail. Almost casually she would brush them aside and slither through. He tried to imitate her system, only to have each branch and vine come smashing back at him as if spring-loaded.

He thought of the team's recent jungle training at Fort Gulick in the Canal Zone. That had been tough. But nothing approaching this. Maybe they took pity on colonels going through the course and had selected trails which were designed especially for the brass. That was it. Dammit, wait till he got back. He'd tear up that training course. From now on, they'd cut their way through the real jungle, not one especially tailored to make the soldiers taking the course think hacking their way through the jungle was easy.

Maria's outstretched arm and raised palm was a signal for Mike to stop. Then almost as if an actress making her debut on stage, she parted the heavy jungle growth in front of her to reveal a beautiful rock-lined pond. Large boulders jutted out into the waters tumbling down a small waterfall on the far edge of the clearing, not fifty feet away.

Mike thrust his hands into the water and splashed it over his forehead, face and neck. Maria looked at him and, with a motion of her arms signifying a diver about to enter the water, silently asked him if he'd like to take a swim. He nodded his head. Without a further word she took off her clothes and laid them carefully on a rock.

Mike gazed in wonder at her sheer beauty. As she stood on the edge of the rock ready to dive into the deep waters of this mountain pool he imagined her as an Inca princess. Her black shoulder-length hair contrasted vividly with her lovely tanned body. Her breasts accented a body perfectly shaped. With a wave to follow her, she dove into the cool waters. Mike quickly undressed and dived in. Almost at once his body lost the heavy sweat which had filled every pore. The water was like a tonic. Only minutes before, he had been convinced he couldn't walk another step and now he felt like he was seventeen, frolicking around in the cool water of a jungle-hidden pool. No wonder Maria had left the trail a short time ago. She was obviously aware of his fatigue and discomfort. She knew the effect a respite in those surroundings would have on him.

She was enjoying the swim herself and occasionally surfaced near him, splashed water on his face, and rapidly submerged. Mike reached out to grab her each time she approached but she was quick to elude him. A splash, and away she'd go, looking over her shoulder and with a tantalizing look seeming to invite him to "catch me if you can."

After a little while Mike felt a tug at his legs and an arm reaching around his neck. His head was pulled under water. Then to his surprise, Maria's lips were on his and she started to kiss him. When he felt he could no longer hold his breath she pushed him upward with her arms still around his neck. Her kisses became more frequent and demanding. She clung to him and water from her hair trickled down his forehead, cheeks and nose. She pressed her body closer and closer until Mike could feel her breasts on his chest. She kissed him again and again. Her hands caressed his wet body as she kept thrusting her body closer.

The cool, clear water had done something for Mike too. Perhaps Maria's passionate kisses had helped. Mike realized that he wanted her as much as she seemed to want him.

Hand in hand, they swam toward shore and climbed up a large flat rock in the shade of an overhanging tree. They made love with all the passion they possessed under a clear blue sky visible through the opening high above them.

As they lay exhausted he wondered how in the world he would cover this in his sitrep which he was due to send to Washington in a few hours. Report everything you see, hear or do, he heard Bud Sharp say over and over. Any bit of information may help. But this. Maybe he ought to report it exactly like it happened. Nobody back in Washington would ever believe a story like that. In Cuba less than twenty-four hours and reporting a Soviet missile site and a seduction. They'd laugh his report right out of the Pentagon. Hell, he'd just ignore it. What they didn't know back there wouldn't hurt'em.

But what if Perfecto reported it? After all she was a CIA agent and had her own reporting channels. Cripes, maybe the agency put her up to seducing him. What the hell was wrong with him? After all, he had just made love two nights before, to the most beautiful girl he had ever known, and was hoping against hope that she would still be waiting for him when he got back. Dammit, he thought, you've got to control your emotions. You were sent to Cuba to seek out sites, not seduce agents.

The trip back to the base camp seemed to take very little time. But what really bothered him was Maria. She said not a word. Occasionally she would smile at him, take his arm and pull him up a small incline, but not a word passed between them on the way back. She had seemed to enjoy every minute of their lovemaking as much as he had, and he had told her how beautiful she was and that he loved her. But women were fickle. What pleased one seemed to turn others off. Maybe he had assumed too much by her kisses and she had had no intention of going beyond that. He'd ask her the first chance he had with her alone.

Tiger Tangier and Marc Mayberry had tried out the fishing pond. Maria soon had their catch sizzling over a hot fire. Mike almost gobbled his food as he ate. Hell, he'd been starved. That's why he had gotten so damn tired walking through the jungle the night before. After all, he hadn't had much sleep and very little to eat since the steak and eggs at midnight on the sub the night before. He'd show her on their next trip out. He wrote out his sitrep and handed it to Marc Mayberry for dispatch. In the shadow of the nearest hut, he sacked out for the afternoon.

It was dark when Mike awoke. It took him a minute or two before realizing where he was and where he had been. He saw Maria, Marc and Tiger sitting around the small campfire which by now was nothing more than a bed of hot ashes. She was the first to speak.

"Mike, we saved you some food." She handed him a plate filled with small cuts of meat. Lamb. What a treat. Also hot beans, a baked potato with its skin still covered with ash and a large cup of steaming hot coffee. He ate silently. Finally she got up and announced that she had to leave to pick up Danny and Roger. She'd go alone and would make better time. She'd be back by midnight. Then she suggested they spend the rest of the night moving to another camp as she was worried about staying here another day. A casual remark by a waitress in the nearest village gave her cause for concern. The waitress had inquired what Maria had found so attractive out in the hills since she was spending so much time there. Mike recognized the implications and agreed to an early move.

It was midnight when Maria, Danny and Roger returned. They were bubbling over with enthusiasm about the pictures they had taken during the day. As Danny described it, they had photographed Soviet and Cuban soldiers removing missiles from long shipping crates and installing them on missile launchers, then erecting a thatched hut around the launcher. Danny was convinced that the simple expedient provided perfect camouflage from detection by air.

Their discussion was cut short by Maria's insistence that they get moving to a new site. Mike detected in her for the first time a degree of nervousness. That seemed to contradict the cool, professional attitude she had exhibited up to now. Loaded down with heavy gear they moved slowly through the jungle, Mike following immediately behind Maria with Danny bringing up the rear.

Just before dawn Maria halted the column which was now spread out in single file about fifty yards behind her. Telling them to remain where they were, she disappeared alone into the heaviest part of the jungle to her immediate front. In less than ten minutes she returned. The smile on her face told Mike that she was pleased at what she had done.

Again she led the way until they came to another small clearing. On the far edge was a huge granite rock overhanging almost two-thirds of the clearing. Trickling over the near edge of the rock was a small waterfall which formed crazy patterns on the small pond just below. This was a nicer place than the one they had just left. While the team hid their gear in the outer edges of the clearing, Maria was busy building a small fire and had coffee brewing in minutes. She soon had pinto beans and small pieces of pork boiling furiously over the fire while a third pot held rice trying to perk its way over the top of the heavy-lidded kettle. The team ate in silence. A day in a hot, humid jungle sapped one's strength. Much like spending too much time in a sauna bath.

Mike laid out the plans for the day. Maria, Marc Mayberry and Tiger Tangier would take off to reconnoiter the route to another suspect area about five miles away, which Maria indicated might be the scene of Soviet missile construction. He and Roger would scout around and pinpoint several areas for use in having the Fulton skyhook pick up the exposed film being taken, and also a location for a supply drop. Even though they needed very little at the time, Mike was conservative and wanted enough supplies to keep them going in the event a resupply drop became too dangerous.

Cuban security was wise to the procedures used by Americans to resupply agents and forces, and the last thing Mike wanted to do was give them any clue that agents were now operating in their backyard. With a final warning to Maria, Marc and Tiger to be back before midnight, he watched them take off through the jungle. He was thankful that he didn't have to make the ten-mile round trip today. Another day of rest and he was sure he'd be up to it. Roaming around the area of their new base camp suited him just fine.

Susan Ainsworth thought she'd try one more time. For weeks she had been calling Colonel Mike Donovan at Fort Bragg only to be told each time they would leave a message informing him of her call. She dialed Fort Bragg again.

"Seventh Special Forces Group. Sergeant Ailes speaking."

"Sergeant. This is Susan Ainsworth. It's important that I talk to Colonel Donovan. Is he there?"

"No, ma'am. As I have told you several times before, your messages have been left on the colonel's desk."

"Has he read them?"

"I don't know, ma'am. All I do is take them and put them on his desk."

"Has he been in lately?"

"Sorry, ma'am. I am not allowed to discuss the colonel's comings and goings. You understand. This is a military organization. What the commander does is not for me to know or question. I'm only the duty clerk and

I'd be happy to leave another message that you have called again."

"Forget it." She slammed down the phone.

Five letters, a dozen telephone calls, and not enough courtesy and decency even to acknowledge she existed. She had given him everything she had. At least he should be man enough to tell her that wasn't enough and to get off his back. Not a word. She remembered their first conversation on the airplane that Sunday over a month ago when she asked him if he had a wife and several kids back in North Carolina. He said he was not married, had no steady girl friend, and really didn't have the time to get romantically involved with any girl. Was he telling her then that this was going to be how it would end? No time to get romantically involved.

She took her pen and on her best engraved stationery began to write. Dear Mike. No, Dear Colonel Donovan. She chose each word carefully. The salutation. The close. Sincerely, respectfully yours. Hell no, she didn't respect him. After much soulsearching she penned in "No doubt another one of your 3F's," signed her name and sealed the envelope. As she put a stamp in the upper right-hand corner she brushed away a tear. Determined not to change her mind or the contents of the letter, she walked rapidly to the nearest mailbox and dropped it in the slot. "There," she muttered, "that's the end."

Summer turned to fall and Mike Donovan wondered how much longer he and the team could take it. After their initial success at locating a missile site, week after week passed without finding another. Then the repeated requests from Washington to check out this location, that location. Cripes, Washington had run his team all over northern Cuba without result. Then suddenly a series of urgent messages that higher authority was getting impatient. Information was needed and needed fast.

Finally in desperation, Mike turned to Maria and asked her to take a trip around northern Cuba, develop contacts and build a relationship with Soviet and Cuban officers to try to acquire data on specific site locations, if they did in fact exist. In frustration, he even told her to seduce them, if necessary, to get information. Her look of utter contempt for him and his suggestion made him feel like a heel. Before he had a chance to apologize and withdraw the suggestion, she shrugged her shoulders and stomped out of camp after telling Danny Thompson to have a guide at a certain spot each Sunday morning at ten o'clock to meet her. Meanwhile, they had better move every few days or she wouldn't accept responsibility for their security.

Mike Donovan could have kicked himself in the ass all the way to Havana. What the hell had gotten into him, anyway? He knew that without Perfecto the team would have been captured long ago. Time after time, she had suddenly halted them on the trail just minutes before a Cuban army patrol passed to their front. Now he had alienated the best agent he had ever worked with. What right had he to offer her services to the officer corps of the Cuban and Soviet armies, anyway? Just because in an unguarded moment they had made love gave him no right to use her as he saw fit. He was disgusted with himself. If there were only some way he could regain her respect and confidence. He wanted that, no matter what. Not only for the good of the team's mission but for his own self-respect. He was using her. She knew it and he knew it.

He was convinced that this was going to be his last mission. With his current frame of mind, he was not only dangerous to himself but to the entire mission. If something didn't happen soon, he was going to request his own evacuation, even though Washington might not want the team withdrawn. Mike Donovan realized for the first time that he was over the hill. He was too old, too set in his ways to change. And change he must, for mere survival if nothing else.

He wiped his brow. Sweat continued to roll down his

face. His bones ached. Then chills gripped his body. He gasped for breath, then he thought he saw three Danny Thompsons looking at him intently. He lost consciousness as he reached out to grasp Danny Thompson's outstretched hand.

PART TWO

Chapter 8

FOR WEEKS THE news had been dominated by stories of Soviet missiles being secretly emplaced in Cuba. Feature writers were having a heyday in explaining the havoc and destruction atomic explosions could cause.

Maps of major cities in the United States were published and exhibited on TV portraying the destruction a single nuclear weapon could inflict on a city. Almost invariably the most prominent building in the city was selected as ground zero and Soviet aiming point. Emanating from those centers of impact, a series of concentric circles described the varying extent of damage. In bold letters, the estimates stood out vividly ranging from destruction, catastrophic damage, major, heavy, severe, moderate, light, and finally, mild damage. Writers and TV commentators grimly discussed casualty levels; not a living soul would survive within the concentric circles labeled catastropic, major or heavy. Less than fifty percent of the population would remain alive if located in the area labeled severe. Moderate damage areas entailed almost sure death if persons were caught in the open. It wasn't until one reached the light and mild areas that any hope remained of being able to survive a nuclear explosion.

Other maps showed the range in miles attributed to

nuclear weapons fired from the vicinity of Havana. Most U.S. metropolitan areas, except those in the far northwestern United States, were within range.

The stories and commentary accompanying the charts explained the hazards of fallout and specific dangers it posed. Arrows demonstrated prevailing winds. Noted scientific authorities were quoted in their predictions of a doomsday landscape to follow a nuclear attack.

Politicians added to the uproar, accusing each other of failing to provide an adequate civil defense program with fallout shelters, emergency food supplies and water, especially for the elderly, the poor, and women and children. The Civil Defense Preparedness Agency was swamped with requests for help. Its director, John Davison, asked people to remain calm. His agency was doing everything humanly possible to upgrade public facilities for use as shelters against any nuclear attack.

Others joined in denouncing cuts made in the armed forces in the face of the new threat posed by the Soviet Union and Cuba.

The President's increasingly frequent press conferences attempting to refute the charges and contain a rising hysteria only provided his critics with more ammunition. Repeated statements that he had no evidence to support the charges that the Soviets were moving atomic weapons into Cuba were dismissed as mere legalisms.

The most outspoken critic, however, was America's number one TV newscaster, Don Grimes. His sonorous voice night after night on network TV reported mounting criticism of the President and added his own. His suggestion that the President consider resigning for the good of country received surprisingly strong editorial support in some of the nation's most influential newspapers.

The utterances of the Soviet Premier lent support to the President's most vociferous critics. The Premier trumpeted about the right of Cuba to defend itself; extolled the power of the Soviet Union and its ability to destroy the imperialist United States at the pull of a lanyard, but repeatedly denied that the Soviets were arming Cuba with nuclear weapons. Soviet weapons and support to Cuba, he said, were strictly defensive.

After all, President Ketner had often expressed his intense dislike for the Cuban dictator, and the Soviets were only providing Castro with a means to defend himself should the President order an attack on Cuba. Cuba was a socialist state, the Premier pointed out, and had every right to expect support and assistance from the first socialist state. What was so different, he asked, between the relationship of Cuba and the Soviet Union, and say West Germany, Turkey, Greece or Italy and the United States? Two could play power politics, Krenchev added.

The *Washington Post* and the *New York Times* editorialized that the President could not lead the nation into war based on rumor, hearsay, and mass hysteria. They suggested he should renew his efforts and get the truth. After all, they reasoned, he had the nation's entire intelligence community responsive to his direct control. Certainly the capabilities of this large and expensive governmental apparatus could determine the facts with respect to developments in Cuba.

David McHenry, a *Washington Post* reporter, bylined a penetrating article on the in-fighting taking place within the administration concerning how best to deal with the Cuban crisis. Quoting informed sources, he said the pattern of actions backstage demonstrated that the President was more interested in politics than in meeting the serious challenge facing the nation.

As proof, he detailed the schedule of presidential activities during the past month. Twenty-two days outside of Washington on political "junkets", including one to Hawaii. He quoted "a high administration source" without specific attribution accusing the President of encouraging Soviet adventurism by continuous cutbacks in key defense programs. If the trend continued, the unidentified government official was quoted as saying, "we had better be prepared to accept second place in the world, as military superiority appears rapidly to be passing to the Soviet Union." This was due, he emphasized, to the President's mistaken view of national priorities, and his emphasis on welfare before defense.

The ABC television network had a one-hour special on the developing situation in Cuba and concluded that the President was taking every possible step to verify the alleged introduction of Soviet nuclear weapons. Based on their preliminary findings, no rational leader would lead the nation into war on the flimsy evidence now in the government's possession.

Congress felt the pressure of events. Letters, telegrams, and telephone calls inundated their offices demanding action. Political loyalties evaporated as members of both parties took turns calling on the President to recognize that a crisis existed and to state the actions he planned or had underway to safeguard the nation against the current threat.

Congressman Harlington's suggestion that the Congress consider impeachment if the administration failed to take decisive action caused an uproar and had more than token support.

Senator Ken Kern, heretofore one of the President's sharpest critics, tried to lessen the rising intensity of the growing congressional debate by calling on the President to appear on nationwide TV to explain personally what the government actually knew of the Cuban situation. Congress would support the President, he emphasized, but only if the nation was kept advised of developments. Congress, he made clear, insisted on being consulted in advance concerning possible courses of action being considered by the President.

Senator Jonathan Smyth was certain that being Senate Majority Leader wasn't all it was cracked up to be.
Fending off the loyal opposition was great sport, something he really enjoyed. But keeping his own party

stalwarts from criticizing the President for his handling of the Cuban crisis was a tough, demanding chore. Since he felt inclined to agree with much of their barbed comments about a "do-nothing" president, Senator Smyth found his current role a great burden. Yet party loyalty demanded that he carry the President's case in Congress regardless of his personal views.

This morning, John Ketner had been vehement in his criticism of the majority leader's performance in the Senate. "Your job," the President said, "is to keep the Senate—at least on our side of the aisle—in line." After all, a large number of them owed their election to riding in on his coattails, the President argued. And he added, "I don't appreciate it one damn bit when they are in the forefront of a rigged effort to pressure me into action without fully considering the risks and consequences to this country which could result from such bravado. And the onus is on you, Jonathan. I'm holding you personally responsible to see that such unwarranted, undisciplined, inopportune, and disloyal criticism is stopped. Show me some of the leadership which you claim for yourself in every press conference you hold. You say leadership is one of your great strengths; all right, Jonathan, I'd like to see it. How about demonstrating your talents in support of my position?"

Jonathan Smyth was still not sure how he had been able to control his temper during that unpleasant meeting with the President early today. While he and the President had never been close friends, he accepted the position as majority leader only after being reassured by his colleagues that he could work out an effective and cordial arrangement with John Ketner, while retaining the freedom of action he valued and followed since he had been sworn in as a United States senator. His subsequent performance had earned him the reputation as the finest and most effective senator in that body during the last decade.

Now a President who was half his age and lacked his

experience in government was castigating him for lack of leadership. For weeks, governors, citizens groups, labor and industrial leaders and bankers had petitioned Congress for some action to the threat posed by Cuba, since the President obviously was unwilling, or incapable, of doing anything effective.

Jonathan Smyth felt hurt. For the past month, and in particular, the last few days, he had been working without rest—and precious little help from the White House—to stifle the increasing restiveness in the Senate, only to be harshly reprimanded. He had made significant progress in getting commitments from many senators to support the President and give him a chance to resolve the issue. His good friend, William Cabot, the minority leader, had joined with him in trying to keep the rebellious Senate in check. Cabot had an obligation, he had gone on to explain, to point out the failures of the administration, but in a temperate manner. But what really galled both Smyth and Cabot were the President's frequent absences from Washington to campaign. The results of his lackluster performance in dealing with the Cuban crisis seemed to them to approach disaster.

The Senate was in heated debate with the introduction of a resolution by Senator Warner demanding that the Senate take the initiative in resolving the Cuban crisis when Jonathan Smyth was called from the floor to take an urgent call from the President.

"Jonathan, Jack Ketner here."

"Yes, Mr. President."

"Please accept my apology for my intemperate and unwarranted remarks this morning. I've been under great strain trying to cope with this situation. To blame my friends and associates for my own failures is wrong. I've been following the debate in the Senate and the House and now with the Warner resolution, I realize the difficult position you and the Speaker face. I need your help and hope I may have it."

"Mr. President, I appreciate and accept your apology.

However, I doubt that there is much more that I can do to keep the Senate off your back with the Warner resolution. I believe we are going to be overwhelmed with demands that we resolve the crisis. People are frightened. They have been subjected to night after night of news depicting the horrors of the nuclear threat only minutes away. To put it bluntly, Mr. President, the judgment is that you are doing little, if anything, to meet the threat."

"Jonathan, I need more time. I am convinced that the actions I have been taking are prudent and the proper course for the nation at this time. However, I appreciate the spot you're in."

"Time, Mr. President, that's the crux of the problem. The people feel, the Senate feels, and I hate to tell you this, but I feel, you have had more than adequate time to come to some firm judgment. It's now time to act. I see no possibility of restraining the Senate any longer. The pressure is just too great. And, the Speaker tells me he has the same problem in the House. I see no alternative but immediate and forceful action on your part. I fear the Congress will be required to step in and take over the responsibility which is rightfully yours."

"If that's the situation and sentiment, and I have no reason to doubt your assessment, then I ask you to announce to the Senate that one week from today, I will request a joint meeting of the Congress where I will lay out in full the actions I have taken to date and what I propose be done in the future. Pending my personal appearance before the Congress, I'm asking you, and I will ask the Speaker of the House for the same consideration, please to exert every effort to delay any further action to resolve the crisis. I need another week, Jonathan, and I'm asking you for your support. I promise you that should I fail to convince you, the Congress and the American people that the course I have been following and will propose has been the proper one, I'll consider resigning."

"Mr. President, I accept those terms. I'll do my very

best to uphold my end of the bargain."

"Thank you, Jonathan. I'll call the Speaker immediately. If he also agrees, I'll announce that decision to the press this afternoon."

John Ketner put down the phone slowly as he began to realize the full impact of the commitment he had just given the Senate Majority Leader. What the hell had possessed him to go that far?

Ken Kern's call a few minutes earlier reporting on the strong sentiment in the Senate possibly to oust him from office had shocked him. He had followed Kern's recommendation to ask for a week's reprieve, but Ken had neither suggested nor intimated that he consider resigning. Only to take the Congress and the people into his confidence and tell them what he knew, what he had been doing, and what he proposed be done. But not resign. He'd never even considered that. Hell, if he couldn't resolve the crisis in another week, he might just as well resign. From what he had been seeing and hearing the last day or two, he could be impeached anyway if something wasn't done, and in a hurry.

The Speaker of the House was even more adamant than Jonathan Smyth. He reminded John Ketner that Congressman Harlington's suggestion that impeachment be considered was widely endorsed as the sense of the House of Representatives. However, if the Senate Majority Leader had accepted the offer of a week's delay, he would reluctantly go along.

John Ketner made one more call. He ordered his appointments secretary to schedule an emergency meeting that afternoon with his key advisors. Get them there, no matter where they might be. But in particular, he wanted Ben Taylor and John Askins to be there.

Bud Sharp peered at the photos again. "Merv, what more can the COBRA Team provide in the way of proof? These pictures seem to tell it all."

Merv Collins leaned back in his huge executive chair

and nodded agreement. "I agree with you, but will the President be satisfied? You know when we have our show-and-tell with him this afternoon, we've got to be sure all bets are covered. John Askins is going to recommend the team be pulled out at once, feeling there is nothing more productive that they can do under the circumstances. I'm inclined to agree with him. Even though the President has been informed of the general nature of Donovan's sitreps, Askins has suggested that we spend the initial few minutes of the briefing this afternoon going over what has happened during the past month before we get into the technical interpretation of the photography."

"That sounds OK to me," Sharp said. "I'm sure General Taylor would have no objection. Incidentally, the Secretary of Defense will be there too and we've got to be sure that we don't say anything that will get his nose out of joint. After all, the President deliberately excluded him at the beginning and now, for the first time, is letting him in on what has been happening. I understand the President will meet with the Secretary of Defense thirty minutes before our scheduled briefing and fill him in on the broad outline of the project, with the details to come during our briefing."

"Bud, I'm surprised." Merv's voice was strained. "I had no idea that the Secretary of Defense hadn't been in this from the start. Knowing his reputation, he won't take this lying down."

"That's politics for you. We've known on the Joint Staff for a long time that the President was not too enamored with the Secretary of Defense. Too often, we'd get requirements laid on directly from the President's national security advisor. In nearly every case, he would go to great pains to caution us not to mention the requirement to personnel in the Secretary's office and to respond directly to him. He'd take responsibility for informing those in government who needed to know. General Taylor, soldier that he is, has often complained of this arrangement but his objections have been overridden time and time again." Bud Sharp rose and shook Merv Collins' hand as he departed, remarking he would see him later that afternoon at the White House.

The drive back from Langley took only twenty minutes. The George Washington Parkway had little traffic at ten in the morning. Bud made a mental note to schedule his trips to CIA at that time of the day. No hassle beating your way through heavy traffic which was so common at most times of the day. As he pulled his car into south parking at the Pentagon, Bud Sharp began to feel that this was the day of decision.

Mike Donovan slowly opened his eyes. The cool icepack on his forehead was a welcome relief from the stifling heat. Then he saw Maria's smiling face. He tried reaching out to her but she patted him to remain motionless. He saw Danny Thompson, Marc Mayberry, Tiger Tangier and Roger Landsdale all standing over him with broad smiles on their faces. He shook his head, then asked, "What the hell happened?"

Danny Thompson was the first to speak. "Colonel, you have been flat on your ass for the past two weeks with a severe case of malaria. This is the first time you have been rational during that entire time. And you can thank Maria for bringing you around. Without her, I'm afraid you would have been the late Colonel Mike Donovan."

"That's right, Colonel, without Maria, you would have joined the men of Custer's last stand by now." Roger Landsdale was serious as he continued. "When you passed out, I was sure you had malaria. Every symptom you had pointed to that. I administered the usual treatment and drugs for malaria and they had no effect on you at all. Then I radioed Bragg, described the symptoms and asked the doctors there for a diagnosis and guidance on what drugs to administer. They came right back. Malaria, and prescribed the same drugs I had been giving you. I asked them again for help. They went to the army's tropical disease center. Same diagnosis; same drugs. I continued giving you the drugs but no progress. Then Maria returned. She took one look at you and said 'jungle fever.' She went to the nearest village for a local drug they use here which I have never seen or heard of before. It worked. From what Maria tells me, you had a type of malaria which is peculiar to the jungles of Cuba. Even in Cuba there is a difference in the malaria contracted in the low-lying swampy areas from that found in the jungle. She's been hovering over you day and night for the last week and for the first time, today, we could see a marked improvement."

Mike Donovan was stunned. Two weeks! He looked up at Maria and smiled. She returned his smile. He raised his hand and she put hers in his. Then he remembered. He looked at her again and said, "Maria, can you ever forgive me?"

"I already have. You were sick and didn't know it and I was stupid not to notice." She bussed him on the cheek and patted his forehead. He took her hand and kissed it tenderly. She smiled at him again and remarked to the rest of the team, "He'll be himself soon. Two or three more days at the most."

"Danny, what about the mission? What's been going on?" Mike's voice was weak but audible.

"It's been going great, again due to Maria. Had three 'Attaboys' from Washington in the last week."

Mike laughed weakly. Attaboys from Washington had been a rarity on this mission. One, to be exact, up to the time of his illness. Short congratulatory messages for a job well done in government circles had become widely known as Attaboys. But before his sudden illness, all he remembered was urgent messages for more information. His "Attaboys for what?" brought a smile to Danny Thompson's face. He asked Mike to save his strength and he'd bring him up to date as to what had transpired during his unauthorized sick leave.

"Colonel, you remember asking Maria to take a trip around northern Cuba. She returned after being gone a week and gave me a map pinpointing eight missile sites including the one we had thoroughly photographed shortly after our arrival. I asked her how she got the information. She told me never to ask that question again. We started checking out the locations and everyone turned out to be a bona fide missile site. We've photographed four of them this past week and got the film for three sites back to Washington. That prompted the Attaboys. We finished photographing the fourth site last night and the film will be picked up tonight. Had a message from Washington today that we were to lay low until further instructions."

"That's great, Danny." Mike Donovan looked at Maria again. Before he could say a word, she touched his mouth with her fingers and said, "You must rest now."

"Maria, how can I ever repay you?" he asked quietly.

"You already have. On the rock by the pool. Remember?" She smiled as she walked quietly to the far end of the camp. She hoped Mike hadn't noticed her tears. A white lie for a sick man wasn't too much to give at a time like this. If only it had been different. But she knew it would never be.

Chapter 9

THE OVAL OFFICE of the White House was a bit more crowded than the last time Bud Sharp had been there. In addition to the President, Jason McNaughton, the Secretary of Defense, was there as well as Simon Lee Oliven III, the highly respected Secretary of State. General Taylor, Bobby Ketner, and Jason Askins were all nervously fidgeting while Merv Collins and Bud Sharp set up the screen and projection equipment. Bud Sharp flicked on the projector and the screen lit up. "All set, Mr. President," he said.

The President summoned his appointments secretary and informed him that under no circumstances was the meeting to be interrupted for anything less than an unprovoked attack against the United States. Stanley Roburn took one look around the room. "Yes, Mr. President, I'll keep everyone out," he said, closing the door behind him.

"Gentlemen, before we proceed," the President began, "I've informed the Secretaries of State and Defense what has been going on. I would like to have you review briefly for their benefit the early reports from the COBRA team. Colonel Sharp, Mr. Collins, you may proceed."

"Mr. President, gentlemen, Merv Collins and I will be giving this briefing together. He will give the technical interpretation of the photography and what it means as he is much more of an expert in that field than I ever hope to be. In early July we put the COBRA team ashore in Cuba from the submarine Grayback to pinpoint and photograph missile sites. A CIA agent, code name 'Perfecto', met the team and has been working with them ever since. According to Colonel Donovan, the team leader, he has established an extremely close working relationship with Perfecto and the team's reports reflect a close association.

"Soon after the COBRA Team arrived in Cuba," Bud continued, "Perfecto led the team to a site thought to be a missile site even though she, yes, Perfecto is a female, had indicated that she wouldn't know a missile from an artillery piece. However, the location turned out to be an actual site where Soviet and Cuban soldiers were emplacing missiles. The team's mission was to pinpoint its exact location and, through the use of cameras equipped with telescopic lenses, to photograph the site in detail, especially missiles, and if possible, to determine the location, numbers and types of nuclear warheads for these missiles. If you will direct your attention to this screen, I'll show some of the photographs taken by the team and Merv Collins will explain and interpret what is being seen."

"Gentlemen." Merv Collins' voice was crisp and authoritative. "This series of movies shows the ongoing construction of the missile complex in the vicinity of El Cuzo some thirty-five miles southwest of Havana. You can see the detail provided by the telescopic lens. Shown here is the SS-21 missile being taken from its shipping container. The missile which we have positively identified is an intermediate range ballistic missile with an effective range of 2,800 miles. It carries a 50 to 100KT nuclear warhead. The missile does not have a conventional warhead; only a nuclear warhead. The recessed section shown here is the chamber into which the nuclear warhead is placed. The particular warhead used

THE COBRA TEAM 125

with this missile is the Mark 47. The other key components of a nuclear missile site are shown in these pictures. This is a launcher erector and this a missile transporter. The fuel tanks are these rather odd-shaped pylon-looking tubes.

"This series of pictures shows the sequence of action. As soon as the missile site has been prepared, the missile launcher is moved into place, and almost immediately the pre-cut thatched hut is erected around it, thus precluding its detection from aerial photography. If you look at these scenes carefully, you will see how cleverly the work around the actual site has been done. The Cubans have cut the lower part of the jungle to make room for storing the vast amount of material associated with missile site while leaving the very top of the jungle foliage intact, providing perfect cover for the site."

"That, Mr. President, is why our aerial reconnaissance has been so unsuccessful in photographing these sites. They have been well hidden," General Taylor remarked apologetically.

"I'll take your word for that, Ben," the President intoned in a matter-of-fact way. "However, if it's that simple to deceive your elaborately built planes and equipment, why the hell does the Pentagon come in year after year for more and more millions to keep buying more and more planes which can't do the job? That's another matter, though, Mr. Collins. Please continue."

"Sir, this series of pictures was taken at a site some twelve miles from the location we have just seen. Its exact location is two and one-half miles southwest of the village of Cayajabos. Again, you will see the familiar items associated with the SS-21 missile. The launcher, the missile erector, the fuel tanks and the large vans holding the communications equipment used for command and control.

"The site is estimated to be approximately 75 percent complete and could become operational with less than two weeks of additional work. We did not find anything new at this site that had not been previously uncovered at the first site shown earlier. However, what we label Site C, located approximately eight miles due south and one mile east of the village of La Isabela, shown on this map, gave us for the first time photography of nuclear warheads.

"In this series of pictures you can see Cuban and Soviet soldiers unleading these coffin-like boxes from a truck. Here is another series of pictures taken a short time later showing the nuclear warhead itself being lifted out of the container and being carried to the transporter for mating with the SS-21 missile. The National Photographic Center has taken these pictures and enlarged them tenfold. Here is what the Mark 47 looks like in closeup."

A loud gasp was heard as the closeup picture of the Mark 47 was flashed on the screen.

A Cuban soldier was lifting one end of the warhead out of the box while a Soviet officer held the other. The center of the warhead had a red star, the Soviet national logo, superimposed over a hammer and sickle painted in bright black paint which contrasted sharply with the silver-colored warhead. The serial number of the weapon was plainly visible below the rectangular glass-enclosed box at the bottom right side of the warhead.

"By the way, Mr. President, we have the names and backgrounds of the Soviet officer and Cuban soldier shown in the picture. Perfecto was able to obtain this information through her contacts." Merv Collins was obviously pleased at being able to provide that detail of intelligence.

"And, Mr. President," John Askins added, "Perfecto is one of our agents, not one of the Defense Intelligence Agency or one recruited by the COBRA team. She belongs to us."

"Thank you, John. I hadn't realized that the ownership of agents was so important in the intelligence business." The President's voice bordered on sarcasm.

"Please continue, Mr. Collins."

"Gentlemen, while this nuclear warhead has been positively identified as the Mark 47, it has an additional feature we have never before seen. If you will look closely at the area just above the serial number you will see a small glass-covered rectangular box.

"To the right is a keyboard which contains letters and numbers very similar to the hand-held calculators we see in everyday use. We have not been able to determine the purpose which the calculator serves nor the significance of the glass-covered rectangular box. However, we surmise it relates to the firing system and may have some connection with a code or timer, but that is pure conjecture at this time. Our experts are studying the matter further and perhaps we can determine its exact use or purpose after more intensive analysis."

John Askins quickly added support to Collins' statement.

"Mr. President, I can assure you our analysts will be able to solve that riddle. We haven't had the time to examine all of the photography in sufficient detail and to develop the detailed analyses needed to reach solid conclusions. You know we have some of the best scientific minds in our employ and I feel confident that additional research will quickly produce an answer."

John Askins' comment was made with obvious pride in expressing the great faith he had in his personnel. "After all," he continued, "the Central Intelligence Agency has carte blanche to tap anyone in the nation to assist it when needed."

And John Askins had built his reputation doing just that. Seldom, if ever, did he acknowledge the contributions made by these faceless and nameless outside consultants. He defended the practice in order to protect their scientific and professional status. If their association with the CIA became public knowledge, a valuable source of expertise might dry up overnight.

Everyone in the room had heard his explanation before, and all agreed with the principle set forth so precisely by John Askins. However, for some reason, the Director of the CIA seemed to want reassurance that his use of outside technical assistance was proper, and indeed, the only way to go.

"Mr. President, we have countless more film and pictures which show the missile equipment and sites," Merv Collins continued. "However, basically everything that you have seen up to now is only repeated in the other scenes. However, if you like, I'll be happy to go through the remaining film."

"Thank you, Mr. Collins, I believe we have seen enough. In fact," the President added, "more than enough. I think the COBRA team has done an absolutely magnificent job. Ben, I want to personally recognize them as soon as possible after they have been withdrawn from Cuba."

"Yes, Mr. President. If I may, sir," General Taylor hesitated a second to choose the exact words he wanted to express, "it has been over a week since the last film arrived from Cuba and Colonel Donovan has asked us twice for any additional information we need, or requests approval to have the team withdrawn."

"Ben, I recognize that and must apologize for delaying this briefing for so long. You know we have an election soon and I was out West doing a bit of campaigning for some of the party stalwarts who are up for reelection. In all honesty, I was also campaigning for some who are not so stalwart, but unfortunately that is the price one must pay when belonging to a political party. They claim it takes all shades to make a cohesive party. I'd surely like to know the idiot who first made that astute observation and get his views after being President for a week. It would be fun to see how cohesive he could make it."

The President continued. "Let's review the bidding once again. Do these pictures prove without a shadow of a doubt that the Soviets are arming Cuba with nuclear intermediate range ballistic missiles? You all know what prompted putting the COBRA Team into Cuba. And, gentlemen, the pressures from Congress, my own party in fact, and the press have been tremendous, all demanding I take action. I have always resisted a precipitous showdown without proof. I think we have it here but I'd like to get your views. Simon, what is your view?"

The Secretary of State was obviously stunned at what he had just seen portrayed on the screen. His voice reflected that concern. "Mr. President, you will recall that it was several months ago that I had a midnight visit from the ambassador of one of the Iron Curtain countries advising me to have our government increase our surveillance of Cuba. When I passed on that bit of information to you I had no idea that things had gone this far. In fact, you may recall, I was one of the doubting Thomases about reported Soviet actions. After all, the Soviet Ambassador has told me repeatedly that his government is providing Cuba with only defensive weapons. Certainly what I have seen today, if it were made public, would convince any man with an open mind that the Soviets are indeed arming Cuba with these tremendously destructive weapons. And there is no way I can foresee how they could explain them away as being for defensive purposes only. In summary, I recommend we call in the Soviet Ambassador and confront him with this proof."

"Thank you, Simon. Jason, your views, please."

Jason McNaughton looked directly at the President. The features on his face revealed an inner anger which he fought to control. His voice showed his impatience with everything he had learned during the past two hours.

"Mr. President, at the expense of upsetting you again, I want to strongly register, in fact, emphatically register my strong disapproval of how this whole affair has been set up. A major military operation undertaken without my knowledge or approval. Then after months I'm finally brought in and a few short minutes later asked for my *official* position in regard to a matter which may have the most serious national consequences. I would be the laughing stock of this nation if it were known that the Defense Department was deeply involved in a covert action against Cuba and the Secretary of Defense was in complete ignorance of what was going on. However, I expressed these views to you privately a few minutes before this briefing began. I want this opportunity to put it on the record, in front of my colleagues. And General Taylor, I wish to inform you of my utter contempt for your action. Withholding such information from me is tantamount to treason. Mr. President, you have my resignation, effective immediately." Without a further word, Jason McNaughton stomped out of the room.

The silence that fell over the Oval Office was ominous. Finally the President broke the spell.

"Gentlemen, before we continue, I want to say that Secretary McNaughton has every right to be upset. And I take full responsibility for what has happened. He has been the Secretary of Defense as my personal choice since the beginning of my administration. By every right, and by law, he is the chief executive of the Department of Defense. Nothing of importance should take place within his area of responsibility without his personal knowledge and approval.

"However, for months I have suspected him of providing the opposition with information which they have been using to good advantage in criticizing my stewardship of the armed forces. A series of articles in the *Armed Forces Journal* during the past few months have been particularly critical of my actions in delaying certain programs proposed by defense, stretching out others, and in general being accused of favoring welfare over our nation's security. It was obvious to me while reading these articles that much of the information had been leaked to the editor of that magazine from high officials in the Department of Defense. In two instances, in particular, the only logical source to me was the Secretary himself.

"In fact, I went so far as to call Benjamin Berry, the editor of the *Journal,* to ask him his source. He happens to be an old friend of mine and usually a strong supporter of my defense policies. However, in this case he laughed at my request. He indicated that he'd be glad to print any rebuttal which I might make, and offered me the going rate of $150.00 a page for anything I submitted. I told him that if he didn't hold his tongue I'd get my friends to cancel their subscriptions to his magazine. He countered by suggesting that I attack it instead. That way he knew the subscriptions would double overnight. Then he reminded me the *Journal* was a spokesman for defense, not a propaganda forum for the administration.

"When we first considered putting in the COBRA team," the President continued, "Jason McNaughton was out of the country. Finally after several weeks of not informing him, I decided that perhaps it would be best if I didn't. The team was already in place and there was nothing he could do about it. Perhaps if he had been brought in when we were first considering the possibility of their use he might have objected, and with valid reasons.

"Once the decision was made, I didn't want to expand the number of people who knew about the team. Protecting the security of the team has been, and will continue to be, my first priority. And knowing Jason as well as I do, I feel confident he will maintain its secrecy. In fact, after he has had a chance to cool off, I'm going to ask him to reconsider his resignation. He's too good a man to lose. But, back to the issue at hand. Ben, do you feel these photographs are adequate proof?"

"Yes, sir, I do. My concern would be how to maintain the secrecy of the team if we were asked to explain how we got the photography."

"Good point, Ben. No matter what, we're going to maintain that secrecy. John, I've saved you for last, and for good reason. You are usually the devil's advocate and please play that role for us now."

John Askins smiled. He was pleased at the President's compliment. He often wondered how the President felt about his performance. At times he seemed to be completely out of step with the administration. But the President kept reassuring him he was doing great.

"Mr. President, I too have been impressed with what I've seen here today. Ben, my congratulations also to the COBRA team. They have been truly magnificent. Mr. President, being the devil's advocate that you allege I am, I wish to express some reservations. The pictures seem to portray missile sites, launchers, weapons.

"However, I must remind you that the Soviets are past masters at deception. You will recall a briefing I gave you a year or so ago showing a vast array of airfields along the Soviet-Chinese border, together with hangars, airplanes galore and tactical fighter aerodromes. And, you remember, it was all a complete phony. The runways surfaced with a light material and painted to perfection which made them appear to be the real thing. Airplanes made of styrofoam which were exact duplicates of the most advanced Soviet fighters. And buildings, fuel dumps, ammo storage depots, all phonies. Yet the average layman would be absolutely certain they were seeing the real thing. Only an expert photo-analyst could tell the difference.

"What I'm suggesting, Mr. President, is that we may be the victim of the biggest hoax ever perpetrated. Even though I feel reasonably satisfied that the photography does, in fact, represent actual missile installations, I would feel much more confident of our position if we could get our hands on one of the Soviet warheads. Confronting the Soviets and the world with an actual warhead of their manufacture would indeed be convincing. Confronting them with photography may create doubt and deep suspicions among our friends that they reflect the real thing, but as proof, I doubt that it would hold up in a court of law."

"Bobby," the President interrupted, "As Attorney General, do you agree with John's view that the film evidence may be legally insufficient?"

"Yes, Mr. President, much as I hate to admit it, I doubt that photography alone could stand up as proof in any international forum. You recall the rhubarb during the last election when one of our most effective senators was smeared through the use of trick photography and went down to resounding defeat. Knowing the Soviets as I do, I doubt that they would ever admit the presence of nuclear weapons in Cuba based on the photography I have just seen. The COBRA Team did a great job, but I have deep reservations that it is sufficient evidence by itself to convict the Soviet Union in the eyes of the world. On the other hand, this evidence, and a Soviet-manufactured nuclear warhead would cinch the case for the prosecution, so to speak."

"Bobby, are you suggesting we go after a warhead?"

"No, Mr. President, what I am saying is that with one, our case would be a thousand-fold stronger."

The President nodded his head slowly as though in agreement. For a moment he turned and gazed out the window. It had finally come to this. But how? Was it possible that the COBRA team could lay their hands on one? And even if they could, how the hell would they get it out of Cuba? "Ben," the President began, "it looks like we're in a box. I cannot in good conscience order the COBRA team to try to get their hands on one of the weapons. It would seem to be sheer suicide. But, is there any possibility they could do it?"

"Mr. President, I don't know." The chairman of the Joint Chiefs of Staff groped for words as he continued. "Donovan and his boys have been in Cuba for months. They are a courageous bunch and would attempt anything we ordered them to do. But in this case, I would need Donovan's personal evaluation of what he thinks his chances of success might be. I would be happy to get a message to him outlining the alternatives and get his on-the-spot appraisal."

"Ben, please do that. But be absolutely certain that his instructions are worded in such a way that they do not constitute an order. I will not risk sacrificing that superb bunch of men to satisfy our perception of what we feel is clinching evidence. I'm prepared to go before the United Nations with what we have. However, I agree that a warhead in our possession would give us the proof to convince anyone. Finally, if Donovan feels that the risks are too great, have the team evacuated as soon as possible. They have done much more than we had ever hoped they would be able to do and I, for one, will be ever grateful for their superb performance. Gentlemen, let's adjourn until we get some word from Donovan. Then I'll make my final decision on what our course of action will be. Thank you again for this very comprehensive briefing."

As they had left the Oval Office, General Taylor told Bud Sharp to draft the message to the COBRA Team following the President's guidance, and bring it to him at the Pentagon before it was sent, within the hour.

Chapter 10

FULLY RECOVERED FROM his bout with malaria, Mike Donovan was still bored. For over a week he'd been waiting word on what more was wanted of the COBRA team, or an order to get out of Cuba. He thought the team had done remarkably well in photographing five different weapon sites. Washington had ordered them to lay low and not go after the other three reported sites unless they gave the word. But still no order to pull out. What the hell was going on back there, anyway? After all, Cuba wasn't a vacation. The longer they stayed, the better chance of being captured. The thought of that possibility sent chills up and down his spine.

Maria's attitude also bothered Mike Donovan. Since that day when they had made love on the rock-lined pool deep in the jungle, she had avoided him except for the brief period when she nursed him back to health from his attack of malaria. She remained aloof, formal in her dealings with him, even though she was responsive to his requests for information. But nothing more. Twice he had tried to hold her hand while on the trail. Each time she had recoiled as though he was a leper not to be touched.

As each day went by with nothing to do but wait, Mike's thoughts turned more and more to Susan

Ainsworth. Was she for real, or had he been taken? He'd find out as soon as he got out of this Godforsaken country. For years, he'd never given most women a second thought, but she was different. He often dreamed of meeting her again at the Key Bridge Marriott, a drink or two, some music, and then showing her how good a lover he really was. She'd never forget him. All he needed was another chance.

He gazed around the small camp they had been in for the past couple of days. The seventh or eighth one—he had lost count—since they first set foot in Cuba. Maria kept insisting they move after spending no more than a week or two in any one place. That gal was not going to take a chance her wards would be scuffed up by Castro's security forces.

The longer Mike Donovan worked with her, the more impressed he was with her almost uncanny ability to anticipate danger. Time after time, she had the team move from one base camp to another just hours before a Cuban army patrol visited the recently abandoned camp in its search for evidence of American spies.

According to Maria, the local Cuban security officer had been getting rumors of possible American spies in his area. And on her own, she had gotten to know the local security officer rather well. Also the Soviet army captain who commanded the rocket troop advisors in the immediate area. Her more frequent dates with both of them had begun to upset Mike, but the information she was able to obtain from these rather talkative professional soldiers was enormous.

The number of missiles at each site, the shipment of warheads, often the exact serial number of each one, the guard details, the methods of transferring weapons from Soviet to Cuban forces, and much, much more. His reports to Washington based on the information she had provided had grown longer and longer. He suspected she had an affair going on with each officer. No other reason, he rationalized, could explain her continued success in acquiring the amount of information she had been able to wring from their lips.

And this worried Mike Donovan. He knew from past experience that agents could be turned around and become double agents by seduction, blackmail, or threat. Maybe she had fallen in love with one or both of them. That could explain her almost detached attitude toward him. Certainly, nothing he had done the day he made love to her on the rock should have turned her against him. She had responded to every passionate embrace, kiss, and touch. He was convinced that she had enjoyed every minute of their rendezvous. Hell, he'd even whispered in her ear how much he loved her. Women were fickle. No matter what you did, or how well, there were times when they didn't appreciate it.

Donovan's thoughts were interrupted by Marc Mayberry. "Sir, you will never believe this." He handed Donovan a message he had just deciphered after having copied the coded words in his radio contact with Fort Bragg a few minutes earlier.

Mike read and reread the message. Were they out of their cotton-picking minds back in Washington? He looked at it again.

> "Highest authority requests your evaluation on the possibility of an operation to secure and bring out a nuclear warhead without Cuban or Soviet forces knowing immediately that a theft has occurred. This is not an order, but a request for your best judgment on whether such an operation is feasible. Include in your response best estimate of chance of success. If answer is negative, stand by for immediate instructions for team evacuation. Reply soonest."

Good God, Mike muttered to himself. Why the hell didn't they say "the President requests . . ." This highest authority bullshit. And hadn't he been taught throughout his service that a request from a higher commander was tantamount to an order. Why start kidding him now. Dammit, either they wanted it done or not.

His "best estimate." Hell, any idiot back in Washington should have been able to tell the President that the operation was at best an attempt in futility and the chances zero. Who the hell did they think had the nuclear weapons? A Cuban boy scout troop? He'd tell them to blow it out their smokestack. And who in the hell had given the idea to the President?

Ben Taylor? He was smarter than that.

Bud Sharp? Never! Bud was a cool, calculating sort. Even a suggestion along those lines would get short shrift from him.

John Askins? He'd bet money it was that bunch from CIA. Look how easily the COBRA team had been getting information from that closed Cuban society, they would say. If they were able to do that without too much trouble, getting a nuclear warhead ought to be just as easy. Yup. It had to be those bastards from Langley who would put the President up to sending that kind of request. No other reason.

Would he have his day in court with them after he got back! He'd tell John Askins to his face what he thought of those fools that worked for him.

And then the added blow. "Without the Cuban or Soviet forces knowing immediately that a weapon had been taken." They must be out of their minds. Get a weapon, take it back to the States, and not have the Cubans or Soviets know a weapon under their control had been snatched. Maybe Houdini could have done it in his day. But the COBRA team? Impossible. He'd tell them just that, and ask for immediate evacuation.

The thought of spending the weekend with Susan was a lot more pleasant than trying to bring off the half-baked idea of getting a Soviet nuclear warhead. That was it. He'd give that stupid suggestion the answer it deserved. After all, they had spent over two months in the jungles of Cuba. There was a limit he could ask his men to put up with. In his opinion, it had already been reached and even exceeded. They had done everything they had been asked to do and done it well. Exposing the team to further danger just didn't make sense.

But why? Why had the President even considered such a request? He was a smart man. And he had shown his concern for the team's safety the day Mike had first met him. Why? That's what bothered him. Why?

Obviously, the President had approved the message. There had to be some compelling reason for even asking the COBRA team to consider taking on such a risky operation. Dammit, Donovan, think! This was no will-of-the-wisp request.

The President must have felt, and felt strongly, that he needed a Soviet nuclear warhead, even at the risk of exposing the COBRA team to the great danger such an operation would entail. At least he'd have to examine the possibilities of pulling it off and making a frank appraisal of the chances of success.

Marc Mayberry said, "Colonel, what are we going to do?" It brought Mike Donovan back to the realities of the moment.

"Marc, I don't know. Get the rest of the team and let's talk it over." Mike Donovan's voice was lower and slower than Marc Mayberry had heard in weeks. Had the old man fully recovered from his bout with malaria or was the long stay in Cuba getting the best of him? As the message was passed around to each member of the team, Mike Donovan began to regain his composure. If they had only been given the mission when first sent to Cuba, or at the very least a week ago! They had been sitting around during the past week doing nothing. Now all of a sudden a new, major operation.

He needed time, badly. You didn't plan an operation like this by the seat of your pants. Detailed planning was needed. Then each step examined for flaws. Then another detail, then another reexamination. Only then could you ever hope for any chance of success. Then rehearsals. How the hell could you rehearse an operation like this in Cuba? Then a deception plan.

Timing, speed, perfect execution. That's what spelled success. Maybe, just maybe, there was a chance. Think, Donovan, think. After all, the army has been paying you well for over twenty years to use you at times like this. Now it is your turn to repay the good life you usually lead. There must be some way it could be pulled off. Some weakness in the Cuban and Soviet security system. Then exploit that weakness.

Maria, yes Maria. Dammit, she'd been playing footsie with the Cuban and Soviet troops. She could help. But how? Laying an ambush would be easy. But that was ruled out.

The Soviets and Cubans were not to know that a weapon had been stolen. That meant a surreptitious method had to be used. But how? And a substitute weapon had to be available for the real thing. Manufacture one. Out here? Impossible. The States. A possibility. They had enough photography that one of the labs ought to be able to make a rather good replica. At least make it possible to pass it off temporarily.

The army had duplicate training weapons that looked like the real thing. That was an idea. Let the army training-aids people build a duplicate. From a picture. Maybe, if given time.

Or one of those big manufacturers that built actual weapons for the services. They should be able to come up with a reasonable facsimile. They had terrific engineers and he'd seen a lot of their work. Yes, he'd need a reasonable copy. Then substitute it for the real thing. At least it might fool the Cubans for awhile.

But getting into a missile site undetected. Too risky. Where were they vulnerable? While they were being moved by truck. After all, hadn't Maria reported that they moved the nukes from the railhead at San Cristobal to the sites by truck?

That was it. Hit the truck enroute. Come on, Donovan. You're coming close to a concept. Hadn't you learned anything in all those previous operations you had been on? The heavy water plant attack in Norway during the big War. The kidnapping of the German rocket scientist right under the noses of the Werhmacht. The operation into Pyongyang, North Korea, the very heart of the enemy during the Korean war, to get at the Chinese general advising the North Koreans.

And the biggest coup of all. Getting an SA 7 Soviet-made Strella missile during the Vietnam War which was so successful in bringing down U.S. aircraft. Within weeks after the COBRA team had gone into North Vietnam and snatched a Strella missile under the control of the Soviet advisors, U.S. experts had built a device for mounting on U.S. aircraft which effectively nullified the danger posed by the Strella.

Donovan, those missions were almost as difficult as the one you are now facing. Take a positive view. Assume the President had asked you for a plan. You'd have at least given it some thought. That's all he's asking for now.

"Mike, any ideas? The team has read the message and we're ready for any instructions you might want to give us." Mike looked at his second in command. Not many like Danny Thompson. No doubts expressed about the message at all. Only "We're ready for any instructions."

If only the army could produce and keep more lieutenants like him. The future security of the nation depended on young, eager, ambitious, and dedicated officers like Danny. Yet, too often they were driven from the service by the constant harping of the politicians about the luxurious life led by the officer corps and all the fringe benefits that went with service life. All the Danny Thompsons had to do was to look at their civilian counterparts who had gotten out of college at about the same time. Stable homes, infrequent moves. A salary almost double what a lieutenant was making, and no twenty-four hour days.

"I've got an idea on just how we might be able to pull it off." Mike Donovan outlined his plan. Only one problem really thwarted him. "How the hell," he asked, "can you get a truck column to stop even temporarily without some obvious action or incident, like a downed tree, a blown bridge, or some other obstacle in their path, without alerting them to possible trouble? How? There must be some way but damned if I can think of it."

He looked at each member of the team in turn for an answer. All shook their heads. Except for Roger Landsdale, the team medic. His grin indicated to Mike that he had an idea.

"Roger, you're smiling about something. Let's hear it."

"Colonel, I know of only one thing that will stop anyone dead in his tracks without any obvious outward threat or event. And I guarantee it."

"Dammit, Roger, how about letting the rest of us in on your secret?"

Grinning broadly, Roger Landsdale reached into the first-aid packet he was wearing at his side and pulled out a bottle and handed it to Mike Donovan. In bold letters the word "LAXATIVES" stood out like a neon light.

Roger could hardly control his laughter, "Colonel, I guarantee that you give any man a couple of tablespoons of this stuff, sooner or later, and I suspect sooner, that man is going to stop anything he might be doing. And, I might add, for a considerable spell. And it doesn't make a damn bit of difference if he's a Cuban, a Russian, or an American. It will affect them all equally." The entire team broke out in laughter as Roger's explanation of his secret weapon was unveiled.

Waiting until the first wave of laughter had subsided, he continued. "Imagine giving the truck drivers and their guards a shot of this stuff just before they took off in their convoy to deliver the weapons to the missile site. I'm certain that somewhere enroute, that column is going to stop on its own initiative and defecate all over the beautiful Cuban landscape regardless of orders to the contrary."

Mike Donovan looked at Roger Landsdale with the same expression a doting father would bestow on his son who had just hit a home run. "Roger, you brilliant SOB, that's it. Incredible! That's the missing link. At least, the big obstacle to getting at the weapon without any outward action on our part to halt the column. Any idea on how soon the stuff takes effect?"

"Not exactly, let's read the label. Uusally some indication on that."

"Results should be felt within 30 to 35 minutes after taking," Mike read aloud from the label.

"How much of this stuff do you have on hand?" Mike's enthusiasm was evident by the manner in which he put the question to Roger.

"That's it, sir, that one teeny weeny little bottle."

Mike Donovan turned to Maria who had been sitting quietly while the plan was discussed. "Maria," he said, "is there any chance you could slip a little of the stuff in this bottle into the food or drink of the Cuban and Soviet soldiers who have the job of moving the nuke weapons to the missile site?"

"Si, Senor—I mean, yes, sir." Maria blushed as she caught herself speaking Spanish. In all the time the team had been in Cuba, she had spoken only English, by her own request. As she explained to Mike the very first day they met, she spoke Spanish every day. She wanted to keep proficient in English and asked that the team speak only English to her, even though she realized that every one of them could speak Spanish. Mike had honored her request on the spot, and frankly, had been delighted. While his Spanish wasn't that bad, he felt more comfortable giving his requests to her in English. She was much more proficient in English that he was in Spanish and in this business any misunderstanding or breakdown in communications was dangerous.

Maria continued, "Both the Soviet and Cuban soldiers like ice cream, chocolate in particular. I could give them each a going-away present as they leave the loading area. They would have to eat it immediately as it melts rather fast in this weather. I'm sure I could arrange to do that without suspicion. You know, I'm on very good terms with both the Soviet and Cuban commanders and they would think that my little gift was out of gratitude for the many favors they have showered on me the past month."

"Great!" Donovan's enthusiasm was more than an expression of approval. It reflected a deep inner satisfaction that somehow, someway, they were getting to a plan that had a reasonable chance of success. "Maria, how many trucks are usually involved when they move these warheads, and how many guards?"

"Usually only a single big truck is used to carry the missile. A jeep or small truck precedes the big truck by about one hundred meters, with a driver and a guard in the cab and two or three men in the rear of the vehicle. Then the big truck with only a driver and a guard in the front and the missile in the rear. The canvas sides and top are tied down to the truck bed. Then another small vehicle brings up the rear, about another hundred meters back, with a driver and guard in front, and two or three soldiers riding in the rear.

"Without exception, they have been moving out every Sunday night right after supper to make their deliveries. By the time they leave, it is usually starting to get dark. From what I gather listening to my Cuban and Soviet friends, the Sunday night departures are cued to shipments which arrive in Cuba from the Soviet Union each week. As I understand it, the missiles and all the equipment arrive by ship. The nuclear warheads are flown in by Soviet aircraft each week, then moved to storage in San Cristobal and from there by truck out to the missile sites."

"Maria, how many of them are carried on each truck?" Mike asked.

"Usually only one, in fact, I have never seen more than one being moved at a time. And always in that coffin-looking metal box."

"Does the box have any type of lock on it?"

"Yes, one Cuban and one Russian-made padlock on each box."

"Good." Mike was clearly pleased with what he had been hearing. While the U.S. armed forces used a similar type metal box to ship its nuclear weapons, they used combination locks and no single individual had the combination to more than one lock. Thus, always two men were needed to unlock any nuclear container. And for good reason. The United States didn't want to take any chances of having a single individual fooling around with nuclear weapons. All it would take was one demented character and all hell could break lose.

But the Soviets were turning their weapons over to the Cubans completely convinced that they could control their use through the Soviet Advisory Group in Cuba. By turning over the weapons to Cuba, the Soviet hierarchy had come to the conclusion that by giving the Cubans control of the weapons, they had a logical, and to them, acceptable rationale for disavowing any association with the missiles should the Cubans take it upon themselves to blackmail the Americans with the threat of nuclear devastation. At the appropriate time, the Soviets could use their Cuban proxies to do their bidding should a showdown between the United States and the Soviet Union become necessary. And Mike Donovan thought that that date might not be far off.

In all, the team had figured, the Soviets were introducing forty nuclear weapons into Cuba. From what they had determined, each site was built for five weapons. So far, five sites had been checked out. All the same. With the remaining three sites they had not visited, a total of eight sites, five weapons to a site. Forty in all. More than enough to cover most of the United States with devastating results. No wonder the President was concerned, and rightly so. He'd have to work fast.

This was Wednesday, the next shipment was due to leave Sunday night. Could Washington respond to his requirements in time? Carefully picking each word, he prepared a message and handed it to Marc Mayberry, "Get this on the air as soon as possible." Three days to prepare the details of a plan down to the last gnat's eyebrow. Was the team up to it? He'd press them and himself to the hilt. This one had to succeed or the past would be prologue. The very thought of failure gave him cold shivers, despite 100 degree weather.

Chapter 11

"BUD, HAS DAGGER lost his mind?" General Taylor was concerned. In over thirty-five years of service he had never read a message like the one he was holding in his hand. He looked at it again.

"Mission risky but possible if following support provided expeditiously. Request thirty-two ounces of laxatives, federal stock number 6505-00-045-7786, packed in plastic containers, not over four ounces per container. Imperative you conduct a test on at least ten men giving each man one to three tablespoons of aforementioned laxative and report exact elapsed time between consumption and first defecation holding it as long as humanly possible without going in one's britches. Essential you report differences in timing and reaction between one, two, and three tablespoons, if any. Urgent you report results soonest. Laxative information essential for mission success, repeat, laxative information essential for mission success."

General Taylor shook his head and exclaimed, "Is this some kind of joke, or has the jungle heat gotten to Dagger?"

"Sir," Bud Sharp was at a loss for words, "I'm as confused as you are, but that's exactly how the message translates. In fact, I was so dumbfounded when I first read the damn thing that I went right back to Dagger and asked him to confirm contents and retransmit message. It came back exactly the same."

General Taylor continued to shake his head in disbelief. "If this is some kind of joke, I'll have Dagger's ass when he comes back. That is, if he has one left after getting a thirty-two-ounce supply of laxatives for five men. How the hell am I going to explain this to the President? I think I'll just let him read the message and see his reaction. That should be worth the price of admission to the White House any day of the week. Even though it's against my better judgment, we'd better comply with Dagger's request. But where the hell can we get volunteers to take laxatives and have guys with stopwatches standing over them to see the exact time they take a shit?" I'll leave the action on that part of the message up to you. Now to deal with the rest of his requests——"

"Require exact duplicate of a Soviet nuclear warhead. Weight, shape, size important, but appearance of replica must lead casual observer to conclusion it is the real thing. Also need master keys for Soviet and Cuban padlocks used to secure containers in which warheads are shipped.

Delivery of replica weapon, keys and laxatives needed no later than during hours of darkness Saturday night. With this support and delivery by time specified, feel confident we have a ninety percent chance of success. Without this support by time specified, request operation terminate and earliest evacuation."

"An exact duplicate of a Soviet nuclear warhead. By Saturday night. Today is Wednesday. Cripes, Dagger isn't going to waste any time. But dammit, he's on the scene and must call the shots as he sees them. He has always been precise before. But this operation is going down in military history. 'Laxatives essential to mission success.' Some historian will spend years trying to figure that one out. Bud, I'd better advise the President of Dagger's response. He's bugged me three times in the last couple of hours to see if we had received any reaction from him." General Taylor picked up the red phone on the console behind his desk.

"Mr. President, Ben Taylor."

"Yes, Ben."

"Donovan has replied to our query. He rates chance of success at ninety percent if we provide him with certain support not later than Saturday night."

"What kind of support?"

"An exact replica of a Soviet warhead."

"Is that possible?"

"I think so, but not from a government source within the time specified."

"What do you mean, not from a government source?"

"It would take too long to get one of our labs to build a duplicate. They would want to pull together a task force and have us submit fifty reams of paper justifying the requirement and authorizing payment for overtime. You know the story."

"What's the alternative?"

"A civilian contract research firm."

"A what?"

"A civilian firm."

"Like Boeing? Lockheed?"

"With plenty of time they'd be fine. But not on a crash basis. Their bureaucracy is almost as bad as the government's. What I had in mind is one of the professional services firms, the think-tank variety. Some of them build prototypes of new equipment and they are generally geared to respond quickly to any request."

"You mean the so-called 'Beltway Bandits'?"

"Yes, Mr. President."

"Any one in particular?"

"I personally know the president of Bradley, Dunsfield and McDaniel. Earl Wilson by name. Perhaps you know him."

"Doesn't ring a bell with me. Sounds like a stockbroker outfit or a law firm to me. What's their background?"

"Bradley, Dunsfield and McDaniel are all Ph.D.s in physics. They were all professors at some university back east, as I remember it. The army kept calling on them for advice and professional assistance. Seems that after a while they were spending more time advising than teaching so they decided to go into business for themselves to provide professional services support to the armed forces. The president, Earl Wilson, has been a friend of mine for years. Used to work with him when I was in the army's nuclear program some years ago and he was with the Sandia Corporation. Fine fellow, fine outfit. They do a lot of work for us and are one of the real comers in the professional services business. They have a small laboratory and can turn out prototype equipment, one of a kind. They are not in the manufacturing end of anything. That's one reason we like to deal with them. They have nothing to sell but the expertise of their people and are not interested in pushing any pet project or piece of hardware. As a result, we can get a completely unbiased and unprejudiced view on any programs we have them study for us."

"Ben, I'll leave that decision to you. Whatever route you want to go suits me fine. You can use my name freely if necessary. This thing has just got to go if all Donovan needs is support from us. By the way, is that all he asked for?"

"The big items. He wants some other support which we're in the process of trying to pull together."

"For instance?"

Ben Taylor hesitated. Should he tell the President or could he waffle it? He decided on the latter.

"Oh, some odds and ends and bits and pieces."

"Ben, you're holding out on me."

"Mr. President, you'd never believe me if I told you."

"Try me."

"Well, he wants us to run a test on some men who have been given a certain laxative and report to him the length of elapsed time between the taking and tne shitting, so to speak, down to the last second. Then he wants a supply of thirty-two ounces of this tonic, I mean laxative, all wrapped up in plastic bottles."

"You're kidding me!"

"No, sir. That's exactly how the request came in."

"O.K., Ben. I've often heard about how the Pentagon gets mired down in muck of its own making, but for the first time I'm beginning to understand what's behind that comment. And by the way, Ben, give Jason McNaughton an update too. You know, of course, that he has withdrawn his resignation."

"Yes, sir. I do. He called and apologized for his outburst and especially the statements he made about me. I accepted his apology and we're having dinner together tonight to go over the differences and misunderstandings that exist between the JCS and his office. The other chiefs are joining us for dinner."

"Fine. I called him after giving him time to cool off. He's too valuable a man to lose. And I'm really to blame for putting him into the position he found himself. I told him that and asked him to reconsider. He did and withdrew his resignation. To make it short, he's back on the team, and I'm very happy to have him. Keep him informed of the progress you are making to fill Donovan's request, especially any problems you may encounter with respect to that special lubricant and the test of its timing. I suppose when this is all over, we'll have to give Cuba some foreign aid with at least several million earmarked for outdoor privies." The President was still laughing when he hung up the phone.

"Bud, stick around a minute. I'm going to call a friend of mine in McLean who runs a professional services company. Want to see if they will build the weapon replica for us. If they can't, we'll have to go to Redstone or Picatinny arsenal and that would take time."

General Taylor took a card from his top desk drawer and dialed a number.

"Earl Wilson."

"Earl, Ben Taylor."

"Yes, General."

"Need a favor and in a hurry."

"Anything you say."

"Still have your small lab to build prototypes?"

"Sure do."

"Good. I can't discuss my requirement over the phone but I'll send Colonel Bud Sharp, one of my division chiefs, out to see you right away. He'll tell you exactly what we need. And we need it by noon Saturday at the latest. Without fail. Will require several of your best-trained nuclear engineers and a machinist or two to put it together, if you follow me. And work around the clock if necessary. I'll add whatever it costs to one of your current contracts but we'll have to do the paperwork later."

"Fine. I'll wait for Bud Sharp. In fact I think I've met him. Believe he's an old friend of one of my vice presidents, Donald Dunwoody."

"You mean Donald of Philippine fame who chased senoritas all over Luzon while the rest of us were fighting Mac's war in the jungle?"

"Same guy."

"I know him. Give him my regards. Lost track of him since he retired."

"He came to work for us when he hung up his uniform."

"Earl, if you run into any problem in complying with the requirement Sharp will give you, especially the time element, give me a call. There can be no slippage. If you can't meet the deadline, I'll have to go elsewhere."

"Ben, if we can't make the deadline, there is no one else who can do it either. I'll stack our engineers and lab against any group in the United States. And thanks for thinking of us."

General Taylor turned to Bud Sharp and told him to get on the way. "Tell Wilson that this is a training aid. Give him enough pictures to see every angle of the weapon. Cut off the extraneous material so there is no indication as to where the pictures might have been taken. And keep it at a top secret level. Finally, you had better get someone going on the laxative test."

"Sir, I took care of that before I came up with the message. Called Ed Sweet, Donovan's executive officer at Fort Bragg, and gave him the requirement. After he got through his first wave of hysteria he said he'd get right on it and report the results by late today. That is, if there was anything left to report. I also called Merv Collins at the agency and he will take care of the request for the master keys. Sees no problem in providing them."

"Do you know where Bradley, Dunsfield and McDaniel are located?"

"Sure do, General. I've been out there several times. General Dunwoody, one of the vice presidents has been involved in several of our study programs and we frequently call on him for help. He's a real pro in our business and a valuable consultant and contact for my office."

"Fine. Give me a progress report later tonight, at my quarters."

"Will do, sir."

Earl Wilson introduced Bud Sharp to the engineers he had assembled in the conference room of the Bradley, Dunsfield and McDaniel Corporation. Sharp in turn introduced Merv Collins who had been called before Sharp left the Pentagon and asked to join him at the meeting in McLean. Sharp explained the immediate requirement and asked Merv Collins to convey the technical details.

It was arranged that Merv would remain with the engineer team throughout their work to provide whatever technical interpretation they needed.

Bud felt a sense of relief when Earl Wilson asked him to notify General Taylor that they would turn out the replica in time. He would personally stake his professional reputation on doing the job Taylor wanted. After all, he told Sharp, their motto was Q^2TC^2 which, translated, meant "providing the requisite quality and quantity of each on a timely basis within controlled costs."

Bud smiled. These professional services companies were much like the army. They had a logo, the army had shoulder patches. They had mottos, like the service. Perhaps he was most struck by their willingness, readiness and "can do" attitude. No wonder these outfits could turn out those high-class professional studies.

By the time Sharp got back to his office in the Pentagon, a message from Fort Bragg was in his 'In' box. He glanced at the subject and broke out laughing for the for the third time that day.

Subject: Results of Defecation Test. In accordance with verbal instructions from the Joint Chiefs of Staff, the Seventh Special Forces Group conducted subject test this date with results as follows:

a. Average elapsed time from swallowing or forced feeding of prescribed tonic to onset of first symptoms: 31 minutes, forty-one and three-tenth seconds.

b. Shortest period: 30 minutes, fifty-eight and four-tenth seconds.

c. Longest period: 32 minutes, four and one-tenth seconds.

d. Differences in dosages both in time and tonnage too insignificant to measure.

e. Minimum period for first relief: eight minutes and two-tenth seconds.

f. Longest period: still in progress.

P.S. Suggest future tests be conducted elsewhere. Post medics in uproar and demanding high-level investigation of possible attempted sabotage by foreign agents. Pending further tests of post water supply, drinking of water from post supply prohibited. Soldiers and dependents have been directed to drink only bottled water or canned beverages until further notice. Advise if any further information is required. Signed Sweet, Acting Commander.

Bud encrypted the pertinent portions of the message and dispatched it to Fort Bragg on a priority basis for onward transmission to the COBRA Team. Then still trying to control his laughter, he called the chairman of the Joint Chiefs of Staff at his quarters at Fort Myer and gave him a report on the progress at McLean and, with tongue in cheek, reported the test results.

General Taylor's laughter over the telephone seemed to rise as each item was read. With a comment that since the Secretary of Defense and the Chiefs of Staff of the Army and Air Force, and the Chief of Naval Operations and the Commandant of the Marine Corps were having dinner with him, he'd take the opportunity to give them the latest update of that highly important operational test. In the meantime, he continued, perhaps they had better save a copy of the report and at a later date send it to the Army Operational Test and Evaluation Agency as a shining example on how to write results of operational testing. The best they had ever been able to do was a twelve page summary covering a test on how a soldier could maintain the cutting edge of his bayonet using a commercial nail file.

Mike Donovan took the message from Marc Mayberry and read it slowly. Average time thirty-one minutes, forty-one and three-tenths seconds. Round it off, thirty-two minutes. He unfolded his map, located the position where the Soviets and Cubans took off with their loaded trucks and, using the average speed of movement as timed and reported earlier by Maria, he measured the distance in hundreds of yards which the column could move in thirty-two minutes.

Finally satisfied that he had the exact position marked on his map he began examining the location in detail.

Beautiful. Jungle almost up to the edge of the road on one side; the other side cleared for hundreds of yards and planted in sugarcane. There wasn't a soldier in the world who would choose the jungle if a cleared sugarcane field was quickly available. Mike Donovan was sure of that.

He'd been in that position too many times himself and had often spent valuable, precious minutes locating a suitable field site for his daily visit to the outdoor privvy. He was sure Cuban and Soviet soldiers weren't a damn bit different. When you had to go, you had to go, but choosing an appropriate location was also an important consideration. Nobody, but nobody, wanted a twig stuck up their ass when they dropped their pants and lowered their buttocks. Soldier, civilian, man or woman. It didn't seem to make any difference. Site selection was an important criteria and by God, he'd bank on it when planning the operation.

Tomorrow, he'd take a couple of the boys and they would make a reconnaissance of the area and pick four or five positions about ten meters apart on the jungle side of the road, all nearer to the point of origin.

No matter what, that would be as far as the truck column could get without stopping. Then depending on when Maria could pass out the goodies as she bade farewell to the troops, the column's distance would be dictated by the effects of the laxative. If she could pass out the ice cream when the trucks were loaded and motors running and ready to go, Mike would bet a month's pay that the spot he selected would be within a hundred yards of the stopped column. Then the COBRA Team would have exactly eight minutes to make the switch.

If the plan worked, he'd recommend Roger Landsdale for the Distinguished Service Medal. His idea was a stroke of genius worthy of that honor. Of course some congressman might raise a stink about awarding an enlisted man such a high award but Mike doubted that the net result would be as great as the one he hoped to create Sunday night.

Donovan was happy that the message confirmed a drop on Saturday night for the special items he had ordered. Bet some eyebrows were raised about his request for the defecation test. Maybe not, though. He had the results in record time and not a comment. He had toyed with the idea of explaining its purpose when he had made the request but decided against it. Cripes, if he started to explain his concepts of operation, he'd never get anything done. He'd get more advice on what not to do and how to do it than he could possibly stomach.

He remembered that years ago he used to send back brief concepts of operation. By the time he got an answer back after apparently endless staffing and, as the message said, "after due deliberation, suggest you consider . . . etc.," he decided the hell with it. Since then, give me the mission and keep the hell out of my way and out of my hair.

His successes proved the wisdom of that decision. Even with the growing tendency for the Pentagon to manage every last aspect of an operation, he'd been successful in keeping them at arm's length, thanks to guys like Bud Sharp and Ben Taylor.

Taylor had often told him he was interested only in results. "You guys do your thing. I'll stay out of your hair and insist the staff do likewise."

Donovan knew that special operations was considered to be a problem to most war planners. They didn't understand it, didn't want to and wouldn't listen to anyone who did, but they delighted in wielding the axe when forces had to be cut. Invariably Special Forces, Navy SEALS, and Air Force Commandos topped the list. Only the chiefs and their operations deputies saved their hides, in fact, their very existence year after year. They knew what the forces did; the others weren't privy to special operations.

In a way, secrecy hurt special operations, but without it the forces could never have pulled off an operation. The Pentagon always talked about tradeoffs. If only some whizz kid could come up with a solution to trading off secret operations for staff support, he'd have the undying gratitude of Mike Donovan and his assorted cohorts in all the services.

But Mike knew that was wishful thinking. Nothing would or could be changed. The nature of the secret work they did was not susceptible to that kind of analysis and to think otherwise was naive.

It was early Friday morning when Bud Sharp received a call at his home in Fairfax that the warhead replica had been completed and was ready for his final O.K. Merv Collins had also been called and was already on the way. The sun was just beginning to peak over the horizon when Bud Sharp wheeled his Pinto into the Bradley, Dunsfield and McDaniel parking lot. At the far corner, he could see Merv Collins' Plymouth Fury.

As he entered the reception area in the lobby, Joe Bradley was waiting for him. After quickly signing in and presenting his ID card to the Burns Security guard on duty, he followed Bradley down two flights of stairs to the laboratory. Joe was one of the founders of the company and had a title of vice president for technical programs. It was obvious to Bud during the initial meeting some forty hours before that Joe was one of the driving forces in the company. A nuclear physicist, he had almost driven Merv Collins up a wall by his penetrating questions about the size, dimensions, capability, etc., of the weapon they had been asked to duplicate.

As Joe ushered Bud into the conference room adjacent to the laboratory, he saw the four or five engineers he had met some hours before. Their haggard faces and heavy stubble of beard told him that they had been at their work since the very first meeting.

Merv Collins was standing to one side deep in conversation with Earl Wilson. Without hesitating, Joe Bradley moved to the podium, and asked that all be seated. Dimming the overhead lights, he flicked on a vu-graph on the left screen. Projected on the screen was one of the pictures of the nuclear weapon that Sharp had provided them during their first meeting on Wednesday. Taking a pointer, Joe Bradley pointed out significant features of the weapon. Each detail was explained: its size, function, color, and shape. On and on he went.

Then flicking on another vu-graph showing a different view of the weapon, he went through the same routine again explaining each part, size, shape and color. Finally, after showing three or four more, all pictures that Sharp had given them earlier, he flicked on a vu-graph showing a scaled drawing which they had prepared outlining the key elements of the weapon, their detailed analysis as to size, weight, shape, function, and color. He went into a brief technical description of each component part, emphasizing and highlighting important conclusions they had drawn during their intensive study of the photography.

Sharp and Collins were both amazed at what this group of scientists had been able to do. Their perceptions were uncanny. No wonder, Bud thought, that this firm had the reputation it had. No guesswork, no bull, just hard cold facts.

Joe Bradley's commentary continued. "Gentlemen, here again on the left screen is the original picture of the weapon I used earlier to show the front view of the warhead. Based on our detailed examination and the scaled model we prepared, I will now show you on the right screen a picture of the replica of the weapon that our lab has built." With obvious pride in his voice, he said, "Here it is."

The right screen was filled with a photograph that pictured a weapon identical in appearance to the one on the left. Bradley, using his pointer, traced every important feature of the weapon displayed on the left screen and indicated its exact likeness to the weapon displayed on the right screen. He went on to explain that during the actual building of the weapon, a series of photographs were taken of the replica and placing that photograph and the original photograph provided by the Pentagon under a stereoscopic magnifying viewer, the identical components were compared on a step-by-step basis to insure almost perfect replication.

"Colonel Sharp, Mr. Collins, here is your weapon." He walked to the right of the stage and lifting a large cardboard box from the center of the table exposed the model they had just finished building some forty minutes before. Bud Sharp glanced at the model on the table, then at the picture on the screen and back again to the table. It was an incredible likeness. Even the red in the Soviet Red Star centered on the weapon appeared to be identical.

Joe Bradley walked over to the model displayed on the table and pointed out the small calculator-type console mounted in the exact position displayed on the original photo. His voice was strained as he spoke. "While we do not know the exact purpose of this letter and number device or the glass enclosed rectangular box shown here, we suspect that it is used to put a code into the weapon, either activating the weapon at a predetermined time or changing the yield of the nuclear explosion. For example, the weapon may be set to produce a kiloton yield ranging from 20 KTs to 100 KTs. As you can see, each time we depress one of the keys, the number or letter appears in the glass enclosed rectangular space. We could deduce that much from a study of the original photographs of the weapons you provided us, Colonel Sharp. But in the limited amount of time we had, we concentrated on replication of the weapon rather than determining the specific purpose of the coding device. Are there any questions?" He looked directly at Sharp and Collins. Bud Sharp's face revealed the great satisfaction at what he had just seen and heard.

"Dr. Bradley—" Bud began.

"Joe, please, you're among friends."

"Joe, to put it mildly, I'm in a state of shock. What you have done in the short period of time since we laid this requirement on you is incredible. I can now understand why General Taylor went to your firm for help. I have never seen anything like this in my life. I'm sure that General Taylor will agree with that assessment. However, I'd like to ask Merv Collins for his comments. He's much more technically oriented than I am. Merv?"

Merv Collins too had become more impressed with each passing minute of the proceedings. While he had remained with the group for several hours after the initial meeting on Wednesday, they had finally suggested he go home and get some sleep. They'd call him if they needed further help. It wasn't until four this morning that he got the call. He knew that his agency had technical experts but was convinced that none could match the performance he had just seen. "Joe, I have no comments but I do have one question. When can you guys start doing some work for my outfit?" That brought forth a roar of laughter.

"Anytime, Merv. Just give us a contract." Joe's response was typical of what he had been giving other agencies for the past couple of years. Every time he and his company had been given the privilege of working on a government contract and had briefed the results, attendees had almost invariably been impressed and popped the same question, "When can you start working for us?"

It was that kind of reception that pleased Dr. Bradley more than anything else and was responsible for the fine reputation his firm had acquired among the many agencies of the government for which they had been doing highly technical work. Dr. Bradley and the other two owners of the company had agreed when they first organized their firm that profit was not their motive—they wanted to make a marked contribution to important programs and national security. If they could do that, they reasoned, they would be successful.

And, it was for that reason, Bud Sharp thought, that Bradley, Dunsfield and McDaniel had achieved their outstanding reputation among key officials in the government. He, for one, would be a strong proponent in their continued use on programs of major importance.

After arranging for the weapon to be delivered to his office in the Pentagon as soon as possible, Bud and Merv had a short conversation in the parking lot before they left to report to their respective bosses. Hardin and Weaver were at their morning's best as Bud sped down the George Washington Parkway.

Those two characters had just what he needed that morning. A sense of humor. Poking fun at the nation's former first Lord of the Admiralty, the Honorable Richard M. Nixon, recently retired, who didn't know the difference between the stern and bow of a ship, and then taking on Congress for changing the title of junkets to "study trips," and vacations to "district work periods." Their subtle humor took his mind off the urgent business which was about to take place. Forty-eight hours more and the COBRA team would pull off the biggest coup in history, or, as he pictured the consequences, a twentieth century reenactment of Nathan Hale. The very thought of that possibility underscored his determination to do his end of the job—perfectly, or else.

WMAL's gloomy weather forecast finally brought his mind back to the problem at hand. A tropical storm was forming between Cuba and Florida and it was being watched closely to see if it would become Hurricane Nancy, the latest of the season.

After parking his Pinto in the Pentagon's South Parking he hurried into the building. A note pinned to his office door and written in large red letters asking him to call Keith Himes as soon as possible caught his attention. He dialed the number and was relieved to hear Himes' voice.

"Keith, Bud Sharp returning your call."

"Bud, hate to be the bearer of bad tidings, but want to

warn you now that the 'must' flight you had scheduled for tomorrow night will at best be marginal. Tropical storm brewing and if its intensity continues to grow, no doubt in my mind that tomorrow night will be scrubbed."

Bud's "Dammit" said it all. After months of hard work and the final payoff only hours away, weather, that unpredictable scourge of mankind, might screw up the works. Not Castro, not him, but the damn weather. What Soviet soldier was fondling his rabbit tail now? Or was he squeezing his worry beads? No matter what, the bastards seem to thrive on luck. Bud's silence was broken by Himes. "Are you still there?"

"Just thinking what alternatives we might have."

"Talked to Bunson Burner Cochrane and his copilot, Ted Tanley. They both agree that if the flight could be moved up to tonight, they might have a chance of getting in before the situation gets any worse."

"Tonight?"

"Yes, sir, tonight a chance; tomorrow night, not a prayer. At least that's our considered judgment."

"O.K., Keith, tell Bunson Burner and Ted to be prepared to fly the mission tonight. I'll get back and confirm as soon as possible."

The steps leading up to the chairman's office from the lower level of the E-Ring corridor seemed longer than ever before. With victory almost in hand, the situation was turning into a murky mess. "Is the chairman in?" Bud demanded of the yeoman standing guard outside General Taylor's office.

"Yes, sir, go right in."

Bud knocked softly on the door before entering. General Taylor was on the phone and only the curved portion of his back was in view as Bud stood silently waiting for the conversation to end. Taylor said, "Then I'll see you and Dr. Bradley in just a bit," terminating the call.

"Morning, Bud," Taylor's voice was exuberant. "That was Earl Wilson. Told me they had finished the job and you were on the way back. Invited them both down to give me a rundown on their baby. From what they say, it must be a winner."

"It is, sir, I was just going to give you a report on my meeting with them this morning, which was great. However, another complication has set in. You remember Donovan's request for delivery no later than tomorrow night. Well, I've just had a call from Florida and a tropical storm is brewing and may turn into a hurricane by tomorrow, making a flight impossible. Even tonight might be marginal, but we'd have to inform Dagger of the change, get the weapon to Florida, and take a chance Dagger could make it to the drop zone in time."

"That's all we need." Taylor's voice, which had just been so exuberant, suddenly changed to dismay. "Can we pull it off tonight?" he asked, almost pleading. His thoughts turned to the President's dilemma. A delay now might prove disastrous with the tremendous pressures being put on him to take action, or else. Several of the nation's leading senators had announced that they might take whatever action necessary to install a leader in the White House who would face up to the hard decisions that needed to be made and in a hurry.

Their patience had worn thin with the vacillation and procrastination shown by the commander-in-chief. The security of the nation took precedence over their loyalty to a President who was too weak or unwilling to risk a showdown with the Soviet Union, they proclaimed from their lofty perch at the other end of Pennsylvania Avenue.

Only reluctantly did they agree to a one week moratorium requested by the President. If his explanation next week to a joint session of Congress concerning the actions he had taken and was taking did not satisfy them as adequate to meet the threat, they would act.

Approvals and endorsements of their position from both sides of the aisle were substantially reinforced by the nation's newspapers and TV commentators. Don

Grimes' commentary on national TV seemed to reflect the nation's mood. "A President," he said, "who had sworn to uphold the constitution had better start doing so, or the people's elected representatives should use their power and responsibility to find one who will."

Ben Taylor wondered how Grimes had ever earned the title "The Nation's Number One Commentator." He had been listening to him for years. All he did was echo the current feelings running through the country. He changed as often as the wind. Only last week he was positive the President was acting too rashly.

"Bud, what must be done to get the flight off tonight?"

"Sir, I'll get a message off to Dagger immediately giving him the change and asking the team to man both the primary and alternate drop zones."

"We can't take a chance of parachuting that weapon into Cuba without absolute assurance the COBRA Team is on the spot to receive it."

"Roger that, sir. We have a procedure that covers such a contingency. The drop will not take place without passage of a prearranged recognition signal between the ground party and the plane's crew. I hate to ask Dagger to man two drop zones but feel it's essential. First, the distance he must travel from his present location may prevent his arrival at the drop area before the plane is scheduled to arrive. Second, manning both drop areas increases our chance of a successful mission should weather close in over one of them. I'll also have to arrange a special mission aircraft to fly the warhead to Florida late this afternoon in order to get it there before the C-130 is scheduled to take off. Also, I might add, we've got to get our secret weapon aboard."

"Secret weapon?"

"The liquid laxative. You know, packed in four-ounce plastic containers."

General Taylor's roar of laughter eased the tension in the room.

"O.K. Bud, get the message off. And arrange for delivery of the baby from Bradley, Dunsfield and McDaniel. Get the thing set up in your secure room downstairs. As soon as Earl Wilson and Dr. Bradley arrive, I'll bring them down and they can give me an explanation of the details that went into building that prize. In the meanwhile, I'm going to call the President and give him a status report. I'll also notify the Secretary of Defense."

As Bud Sharp left the office, Ben Taylor picked up his red telephone. The President answered immediately. He gave the President a complete report on what had happened and the actions he had ordered be taken. As an afterthought, he added that he was about to get a look at the newly manufactured weapon and a detailed explanation from the builders.

"Ben, I want to see the thing myself. Would it be an inconvenience if I joined the briefing?"

"Not at all, sir. We'll need about thirty minutes to get things organized and I want to notify the Secretary of Defense. Either he or I, or both of us, will meet you at the River Entrance."

"That's great. I had an appointment to meet with Senator Smyth and Congressman Harlington at that time, but I'll postpone that meeting. In fact, this gives me a needed break. I don't think I could remain civil with thost two gentlemen for very long. See you in thirty minutes."

Taylor next called the Secretary of Defense who said he'd meet the President and asked that Ben join him at the River Entrance a few minutes before the President's scheduled arrival.

After a hurried call to the Chiefs of Staff of the Army and Air Force, the Chief of Naval Operations and the Commandant of the Marine Corps, Ben called his aide in the outer office and asked that Earl Wilson and Joe Bradley be ushered in. He had kept them waiting and apologized for the delay. Explaining to them what was about to transpire, Taylor excused himself to meet the Secretary of Defense at the River Entrance after asking his aide to take his visitors down to Colonel Sharp's office.

Chapter 12

MIKE DONOVAN REREAD the message and rechecked his map. "Assemble the troops!" he ordered Marc Mayberry. No time to lose. Of all things, weather was about to raise havoc with his operation. For two months the unpredictable weather hadn't made a damn bit of difference to the team's operations. Now of all times, with the showdown near, weather became the key.

The plan had been gone over and over again. The ploy he had set up with Bud Sharp to get the Tactical Air Command to fly fighter aircraft at low altitudes across Cuba at night to condition the Cubans to turn off their truck lights at the sound of a plane was working perfectly. In truck movements they had observed the last two nights, Cuban drivers had turned off their lights at the approach of a plane. Maria confirmed that the Cuban Army, at the suggestion of their Soviet advisors, had passed the word down the chain of command to turn off truck lights at the first sound of an airplane. It had to be an American spy plane, they explained, because the Cuban Air Force was not flying at night.

The message announcing the airdrop tonight didn't upset Donovan nearly as much as the thought of trying to pull off his operation Sunday night without support from the Tactical Air Command. If the weather Sunday night was going to be soupy as the message indicated, his planned night operation might go down the drain and he and the team along with it.

His orders to the team were crisp and to the point. "Danny, Roger, Tiger, you man the primary drop zone. You know the recognition signal. Get the lead out and start moving. It will be touch and go to make it there in time. Marc, Maria and I will take the alternate drop zone. If you can't get back by dawn, cache the drop and hole up for the day. We'll do the same. If weather causes an abort, get back here as fast as possible. I've got to keep Marc with me in case we get any late-minute radio traffic."

The officers and men assigned to the Special Operations Division watched in amazement as they first saw the Army Chief of Staff being escorted into the division's inner sanctum, followed almost at once by the Air Force Chief of Staff and the Chief of Naval Operations.

Only minutes later the Commandant of the Marine Corps came in, breathing heavily. He had been in the middle of a high-level planning session with his staff in nearby Marine Corps headquarters when he received the call from the chairman of the Joint Chiefs of Staff that an emergency meeting had been called. But in Room 1E840, the bowels of the Pentagon. He, like the rest of the Joint Chiefs, had never before met there. He wondered what was up. Ben Taylor was not a jokester. That he knew for sure. But why here?

As he was ushered into the inner sanctum he looked around in awe. A complete operations center. Double screens, electronically operated briefing boards, maps of every description lined the walls. Dotted pins were evident everywhere with small letters and numbers beside them. The designations 601, 715, 908 immediately caught his eye on the larger three-dimension map of Cuba which was displayed on the right front briefing board. A shortwave radio set in the left rear of the room was illuminated. A slight hum indicated it was in an operational mode. Banks of telephones, all in different colors, were located just above it. A teletype machine was to its immediate right with an on-line crypto machine nearby.

General Tom Landry, the youngest commandant in Marine Corps history was impressed. No wonder the special operations boys could do so well. They were away from prying eyes and not bothered by the usual bunch of staff officers all vying for the same map board, telephone and other accessories found in the usual operations center. This one was complete. His own marine, Lt. Colonel George Armstrong McMahon, a member of the Special Operations staff, kept him informed of what was going on in the invisible wars the Pentagon special operations boys handled, but never once did he mention this setup. Just as well. No one would have believed him anyway.

Tom Landry was more perplexed than ever after being introduced to the two civilians from that company in McLean. What the hell were they doing there? His fellow members of the Joint Chiefs were no help; they didn't know either. Colonel Sharp, after introducing them to the two guests, invited them all to sit down and await the arrival of the chairman who would be along shortly. But not a word about the purpose of the meeting.

General Taylor said, "Gentlemen, the President of the United States."

After being introduced to Earl Wilson and Dr. Bradley, the President took a seat in the center of the front row. Seated to his immediate right was the Secretary of Defense. To his left, General Taylor. Generals Peterson, Maxwell and Landry and Admiral James Easly, Chief of Naval Operations, his white uniform in marked contrast to the army green, air force blue and marine corps brown of his counterparts, took seats in the row of chairs behind the President.

General Taylor rose and mounted the small stage. He took a few minutes explaining the purpose of the meeting and concluded by introducing Earl Wilson, president, and Dr. Joe Bradley, vice president of the Bradley, Dunsfield and McDaniel Corporation who would give the briefing.

For the second time that day Bud Sharp listened to Joe Bradley explain the method his company used in constructing a replica of the Soviet nuclear weapon. But for the first time that day, and the first time ever, he had the President of the United States in his inner sanctum together with the nation's top military leaders, the Joint Chiefs of Staff.

A sense of pride and accomplishment brought a faint smile to his face. His operations had always received special attention from the brass, but never before in his memory had he seen such a collection being briefed in his own operations room. He was proud of his men, the outfits they represented and the way they did their job. Day after day, working on some of the most sensitive operations the country had going, not a word from their lips after they closed the vault-like door of the inner sanctum and took their places at their assigned desks outside.

To others in the Pentagon who had occasion to visit that bunch of spooks in the basement, and they always emphasized "the basement," they were an oddball collection of guys who did something or other. Nobody rightly knew what, but it couldn't have been too important or they wouldn't be operating in the basement, which everyone knew in Pentagon parlance was the lowest thing on the totem pole.

"Mr. President, gentlemen, I have explained how we went about designing the replica missile. At this time I'd like to show you our product." Joe Bradley walked to the end of the table and removed the canvas cover which had kept the weapon hidden from view.

Bud Sharp watched the reaction. The President looked at the weapon, back to the screen where the original picture was still displayed, then rapidly to the replica. Ben Taylor muttered, "I'll be damned," in awe. Similar comments came from the other chiefs. The expressions on their faces reflected an appreciation of the magnificent replica not ten feet away.

Almost simultaneously the President and the Secretary of Defense arose and walked to the table, peering at every little detail of the weapon. The President touched it as though touching a child. Taking the palm of his hand he ran across the face of the warhead, then down to the code mechanism. Joe Bradley stood to one side as the chiefs joined the President in examining the weapon.

Finally, Joe Bradley said, "Mr. President, if you like, I can demonstrate the small coding device."

The President's nod gave Joe the spotlight again. In laymen's language he spent a few minutes discussing how the system appeared to work and apologized for not having time to really do the full analysis that was required. He explained again that their focus of attention was on exact replication, as General Taylor had requested. He added as an afterthought that they would enjoy taking on the task of trying to decipher the system completely.

"Mr. President," Taylor's voice was filled with pride. "That's it, unless you have further questions."

"Dr. Bradley, Mr. Wilson, I want to compliment you and the members of your firm who have turned out this absolutely superb replica. I had reservations about General Taylor's proposal a few days ago to turn this over to a civilian contract firm, but after seeing what you have done in such a short time, my confidence in his judgment is confirmed. Sometime in the next couple of weeks, I'd like to have both of you visit me in the White House. General Taylor will make the arrangements. And again, many thanks." After shaking hands with the assembled group he left the room, escorted by the Secretary of Defense. After personally thanking Earl Wilson and Joe Bradley again, he asked that Colonel Sharp escort them outside and return as soon as possible. His final words, "You'll be hearing from me soon," brought smiles to their faces.

The Joint Chiefs were in deep conversation with Ben Taylor when Sharp returned. He asked Bud to join them. Taylor went over the change in plans caused by the oncoming hurricane. Then he reaffirmed the detailed plans that each service member would be responsible for carrying out that night and the planned operation on Sunday. Satisfied that there were no areas which needed further discussion he broke up the meeting by suggesting each member keep him advised of any problem areas they might encounter and also keep Sharp informed. In turn he and Sharp would keep them abreast of developments as they occurred.

Bunson Burner Cochrane was perplexed. The package he was to parachute to the COBRA Team on drop zone Eagle that night was quite large and heavy. He had already been alerted that Sunday night would be evacuation night for Mike Donovan. Then why a resupply drop tonight? Just forty-eight hours before the team was to be pulled out. You didn't do that.

The fewer flights you make over the general area of Cuba where Donovan and his team were operating, the better chance of success for those flights that had to go. For the past month, he had been dropping Fulton skyhook systems to the team and pulling out a package the size of a pound of butter. His plane and crew were valuable too. Unnecessary exposure to a possible shootdown by Castro's troops was just plain foolhardy.

Yet Bud Sharp had impressed him with the importance of tonight's flight. Absolutely essential that the drop be made on drop zone Eagle at precisely the prescribed time. If weather caused an abort on Eagle then the alternate DZ Molly was to be used. Positive recognition with ground elements had to be confirmed before drop.

Bud Sharp had personally delivered the package for

air drop to Cochrane earlier that evening. And his instructions were clear. The drop had to be made tonight. He recognized that the weather wasn't going to be too good, but knowing Bunson Burner and his Air Commando crew, he knew that they could do it. They always had.

And to top it all off, the radio message, a codeword, he was to send back to his base in Florida immediately after the drop had been made. In the past, silence from his plane indicated a successful drop. A codeword was used to reflect an abort, for whatever reason. Sharp had informed him that the highest national authority wanted immediate and absolute confirmation that the drop had taken place and only after positive identification of recognition signals from the ground.

Bunson Burner thought of his long career in special operations. From flying the Hump to resupply "Merrill's Marauders" during the early days of World War II; then on to the United Kingdom where he spent the next year resupplying agents of the Office of Strategic Services operating in German-occuppied France. At the same time he worked with the Free French underground putting their agents in and taking them out. Then the many operations since then working with special forces elements in various parts of the world.

He had known and worked with Donovan for years, and with Bud Sharp for the past four or five. They'd always leveled with him. But asking him to get in this flight tonight under marginal weather conditions to make a resupply drop didn't make sense. After all, he'd been resupplying the team on and off for the past several months and when weather interfered, they had a twenty-four or forty-eight hour weather delay. Same place, same time, but a day or two later. The boys on the ground knew the system, and it precluded risking the highly trained air commandos from flying in weather which grounded other aircraft.

But Cochrane knew that regardless of his views, something important was cooking. And he and his crew were a part of it. In fact, an important part. Without fail, after every operation he and his crew would be summoned to Washington and the Air Force Chief of Staff would compliment them for their superb operational skill, saying he was personally honored and privileged to pin the Distinguished Flying Cross, and at times, the Distinguished Service Cross on their chests. But unfortunately, with no publicity.

National security prevented public recognition of their feats. For now, only the personal pride each man had as a participant in an important operation would be all. One day, he promised, the nation would be informed and join with the air force in the long overdue recognition they so richly deserved for their superb performance at great risk to their lives. But until then, the medal, without a detailed citation would be their only reward. Then the chairman of the Joint Chiefs of Staff would come forward and congratulate each man. Often the Secretary of Defense, and on one or two occasions the President of the United States would be present. But not a word was to be leaked about the awards, the actions which prompted them, or further discussion of the operation after the medal award ceremony was over.

But Bunson Burner Cochrane wouldn't have changed the past for any reward. He loved what he was doing. A part, only a part, of some of the nation's most sensitive covert operations.

And his specially selected group of men felt the same way. They knew what they were often asked to do was above and beyond the average soldier's or airman's call to duty. But they were different. They were air commandos, a different breed that set them apart from the rest of the air force. And they were right well proud of that distinction. Day after day, night after night they trained for any eventuality. The specially configured C-130's they flew were the only real recognition that they had received from the top air force brass that they were indeed different. Exotic terrain following radar which permitted them to fly the nap of the earth, and an all-weather capability, made the C-130's their pride and joy. Short takeoff and landing areas were their mainstay in support of the army Green Berets. No need for those two-mile-long hard-surfaced runways. A short grassy strip eight or nine hundred feet long was often the best they could count on.

But what gave the air commandos their greatest satisfaction was in working with the army's Green Berets. Like a well-oiled piece of machinery, each piece doing its part, they had been able to pull off one successful operation after another. Get the job done was the overriding requirement. No argument about roles and missions at their level. That was for the fatcats back in the Pentagon to fight over.

Out in the field, the air commandos and Green Berets just kept on doing their thing, without regard as to whose bailiwick it fell under. The guys who were the best qualified and most experienced got the nod, often over the eyebrow-raising of some of the officers back on the army and air staff.

"You know," one of the air staff officers would intone occasionally, "Bunson don't let the army get into our business."

And on the floor below, an army staff officer would in a serious vein inform Donovan that getting too cozy with the air force was impeding progress being made on defining the air force and army roles and missions. And sometimes, he went on to say, "Your use of air commandos in traditional army roles is giving the air force ammunition for their views on joint papers," citing Donovan's operations as policy precedent. And after all, what is a better foundation for defining roles and missions than actual employment of forces in the field, the staff position papers went on to explain.

Mike Donovan and Bunson Burner Cochrane had

unique positions. Each commanded special outfits which were not universally accepted within their own services as being worth the cost and effort of maintaining them. They had to fight each year to keep their units from being cut or reduced by overzealous staff officers who considered them "the fat" which could be cut out without any reduction in the combat effectiveness of their service. And recently, only an appeal directly to the Chief of Staff of the Army or Air Force had prevented a drastic reduction for another year or two without jeopardy.

But memories were short. A year or two of idleness—noncommitment, in Pentagon parlance—and the threat was renewed. After all, they hadn't been used recently, and there was no indication that they would be in the foreseeable future. If future events required their special kind of capability, they could be reconstituted, the arguments went on.

Ted Tanley called out, "Burner, we're all set for the takeoff. The drop has been rigged and loaded." His words startled Bunson Burner. More and more lately, he had been wondering about the future of his outfit and its chances of survival. Dammit, he thought, he'd talk to the Chief of Staff of the Air Force after this operation was over and ask him to get the air staff to lay off.

"Thanks, Ted, I want to make a last-minute weather check with Keith Himes. I'll be along in a minute." Bunson Burner walked down a short hallway and turned into the room being used by Keith Himes and his weather detachment. The walls were covered with maps of every description, and weather fronts had just been posted by Himes' sergeant.

"Bunson, hold on a second. I'll be right with you." Keith Himes returned to the telephone he had been using when Cochrane walked in. Bunson examined the weather maps while waiting for Keith to finish his conversation. "Thanks, Miami." Himes terminated the conversation and put down the phone.

"Another update from the weather bureau in Miami. It doesn't look good," he said. "The tropical storm is growing in intensity. Both the primary and alternate drop zones are, at best, marginal as of now. The weather enroute is horrible. Under normal circumstances I'd say scrub the mission. But considering the orders we have, I'd say there is a chance, only a chance, that one of the DZs might be open for a few minutes at a time. Only because the storm is just getting started. By tomorrow morning, it will be fully developed. Here is the route I would recommend you use to get to the target area and avoid as much of the bad weather as possible. Even with this route you are going to be in the thick of the storm soon after takeoff."

Keith traced a suggested route on the flight map Bunson had spread out on the counter. No straight line to the target tonight. It seemed that every ten or fifteen miles the route would do a sharp left or right with a few zigs and zags in between. Thank God he had Scotty Carrington on board as navigator. Scotty had first become a navigator in the Army Air Corps during the early days of World War II. After the air force became a separate service in 1947 he declared he wasn't going to be a second cousin in his own service and went off to flight school. But now and then, he liked to get back to being a navigator to keep his touch.

Normally a first pilot in the air commandos, he specifically asked Bunson to come along as a navigator, since Bunson didn't need another set of pilots besides the two planes and crews he had already picked to support Donovan's group. Cochrane had accepted the offer immediately. Getting an experienced navigator who was also one of his best pilots was a bonus.

"Thanks, Keith." Cochrane went down the hall and joined Ted Tanley as they walked to their C-130 parked at the front entrance to the old rundown operations building being used as their forward special operations base.

And it was rundown. Built in World War II for Army Air Corps use, it had been abandoned when the war ended. Then the Florida National Guard had taken over a part of it for their use. They were happy to have the air commandos and army special forces use a part of it and had set aside an area at the north end of the base to conduct joint training exercises the two outfits did frequently. On the southwest coast of the state, only miles from the Gulf of Mexico, the base was ideally located for operations against Cuba. Little air activity, and flights in and out of the base came off the Gulf side. Nothing unusual about that. Eglin Air Force base far to the north frequently used the Gulf for target practice and training. The base in the south was often used for their touch and go landings and other air training. Air commando use, such as now, made no impression on the small civilian caretaker detachment that took care of the place. Just another group doing its thing.

Cochrane looked at his watch. Ten-fifteen. Another ten minutes and they would be airborne with the drop scheduled at thirty minutes past midnight on Eagle, or thirty minutes later on Molly if Eagle was closed in. As he approached his plane Bunson looked at it lovingly. She'd taken him all over the world. And always back to his point of origin. That was the important thing. Getting in and back.

A few times during the Vietnam War he had a real fight on his hands to get that done. Lucky shots by the Viet Cong had punctured his fuel tanks on two different occasions. Another lucky shot had knocked out an engine. Still later the stabilizer had been put out of action. But in each case he had coaxed old 9842 back to a friendly base or field strip and safety. A quick repair job, and back to service.

Damn, she'd been dependable. And tonight she'd better continue that tradition. Mike Donovan was counting on it, and so was the President of the United States. Bunson Burner Cochrane knew that he'd give it everything he had to make that expectation come true.

Danny Thompson was winded. He, Roger and Tiger had taken off for DZ Eagle as soon as Donovan had given them their orders. The distance on the map looked close. But unfortunately, the map couldn't truly reflect the thick jungle they had to cut their way through to get there. And the weather was more stifling than ever. Heavy rainshowers whipped by high winds didn't help a bit. Fighting the jungle was bad enough, but having to cover your eyes to keep out the driving rain only compounded the problem. And moving in daylight was also dangerous.

Normally, a team going to a drop zone would move during the hours of darkness the night before the scheduled drop, then hole up the following day and take the drop that night. Too many chances that a stray Cuban army patrol might see them moving during daylight. Too many telltale clues left while moving, which couldn't be avoided. Machetes chopping down vines to clear a path through otherwise impenetrable jungle. Footmarks around soft marshy areas. Night covered those telltale signs from view.

But waiting until dark and moving to the drop zone was too late for a twelve-thirty drop. They had to get going as soon as they received the order to have any chance of making it on time. And if they didn't, Bunson Burner and his crew would be exposing themselves to another high-risk operation without hope of success. Positive ground-to-air recognition signals and air-to-ground countersigns were mandatory for this drop.

Danny realized that under no circumstances could this be a blind drop. If the Cubans found a replica of a Soviet nuclear warhead at the end of a parachute, it wouldn't take them long to figure out what the hell was up. They weren't too bright, but even an idiot would have gotten suspicious and alerted the rocket troops that something was amiss. Exactly what, they wouldn't know. But finding a warhead in the middle of the jungle

THE COBRA TEAM 181

would be a sure tipoff to disaster.

Roger Landsdale wiped the sweat and rain from his forehead. Tiger Tangier was still trying to catch his breath when Danny motioned them to resume the struggle through the jungle on the way to the drop zone. Darkness had fallen and the jungle was more forbidding than ever. But a quick check at the rest stop they had just made indicated that they were within a half mile of the small jungle opening selected for tonight's drop. They moved cautiously in single file, the two others following the leader. About every two or three hundred yards the man in the lead would stand aside and let the second man take over to blaze the trail. This was the only way to make fast time. It was a tiresome job being the point man, hacking at the vines and low overhanging branches that formed an almost tightwire net across the route.

Roger was in the lead when suddenly he stopped and motioned the others to halt and silence. Taking Danny Thompson's hand he pointed to a small clearing just ahead.

Danny Thompson almost recoiled. Straight ahead, not over fifty yards away, a Cuban army patrol stood under two tarpaulins stretched between two trees. The men were huddled around a small campfire. Several kettles were hanging from spits fashioned from limbs of bayou trees. The smell of cooking rice was barely discernible in the moisture-laden air. On the right side of the fire a large spit held a leg of lamb being roasted over white coals. Stacked against a tree at one end of the tarpaulin-covered area was an assortment of weapons. Automatic rifles, two machine guns, and a small mortar.

It was obvious from the conversation they overheard that the patrol had holed up there for the night and was egging the cook on to get the food prepared. They had been on the march and they were damn hungry, they told the cook, and he'd better get with it. The fact that the cook had been with the patrol didn't seem to make any difference. When they stopped for the night, it was the cook's job to feed them, and in a hurry.

Tiger Tangier joined Danny and Roger looking at the group so comfortably settled in for the night. The two large tarpaulins gave them plenty of room to move around in and protected them from the driving rain. The smell of the leg of lamb was now stronger and Tiger felt a hunger pang in his stomach. The C ration he had eaten at a stop some miles before was nothing like a pot of fresh-cooked rice and a side order of leg of lamb that the Cuban army patrol was about to have.

Danny Thompson wasn't thinking of food. His thoughts were on the mission. More importantly, the luck of having Roger Landsdale in the lead a few minutes ago. Of all the team, Roger had turned out to be the most trailwise. Under the tutelage of Maria, the entire team had improved in moving through the jungle, but none became quite as expert as Roger.

Two months ago, the team would have walked right into the waiting arms of the Cuban patrol. But not now. They were now a thousand percent better prepared as the result of Maria's nagging insistence that this was the way to do it. And no other way would pass her critical inspection of their almost amateurish method of observing, cutting, waiting, observing, and cutting again. Only then could they be sure, she had repeated time and time again, of being able to avoid stumbling across one of the many Cuban patrols that had recently started operating in their area.

Too many night flights of American reconnaissance planes and those slow lumbering transport planes had convinced the Cubans and their Soviet advisors that there was a good possibility that American agents were somewhere in the jungle. Local commanders, Havana had informed them, had the responsibility of seeking them out and capturing or destroying them on the spot.

According to rumors brought back by Maria from the nearby village, a contest had been started by the Cuban army. For the soldiers who captured or killed an American spy, a month-long trip at state expense to the Soviet Union. And authority to bring back custom free any items they purchased from their fraternal brothers in Moscow. In addition, the rumors went on, the soldiers would be provided female guides during their stay in the Soviet Union who would cater to their every need.

Lt. Raul Beyez, who commanded the patrol being observed by Danny Thompson and his team, had told his commander that, by God, he wanted in on that contest. He'd stay out in the jungle until he was successful. After all, hadn't he tracked down that bunch of Cubans in exile some months ago that the CIA had infiltrated from a submarine at night? And hadn't he saved one from being shot on the spot in order that he could be interrogated and provide the Cuban high command the details on where the force was being trained, the number of men undergoing training, and their mission in Cuba.

His insistence that the reward be made retroactive to cover his previous success, however, fell on deaf ears. Too many others would also have to be rewarded. After all, his commander reminded him, he wasn't the first one to capture American trained spies. To encourage the troops, any captures in the future would receive the free trip, and also the coveted Cuban medal of freedom presented by no less than Fidel Castro, their beloved leader.

Lt. Raul Beyez was no ordinary Cuban lieutenant. He was smart. And his earlier success in intercepting the Cubans in exile being put ashore from a submarine was no fluke. He was at the right spot at the right time by making a detailed study on how Americans infiltrated areas by submarine and the telltale signs to look for which might be a tipoff to such operations.

Now again, he was engaged in study. This time to intercept an airborne infiltration which had apparently become the favorite way for the Americans to get agents into Cuba and keep them supplied.

He poured over maps, charts, and reports. He badgered his intelligence officer for any articles or reports on how the Americans operated clandestinely. From translated Soviet documents he read articles describing how Americans always picked cleared areas for drop zones for parachute infiltration and that agents or assets on the ground would shine flashlights at the oncoming airplane. Then the men would parachute when the plane reached the cleared area marked by the flashlights. To insure that the airplane pilot knew that it was the drop zone he was looking for, the flashlights would be arranged in a pattern signifying a letter or symbol.

The most popular flashlight marking was in the form of a letter H or L, the article went on to say. It was easily recognizable from the air, and three or four men on the ground holding flashlights could mark the area. Americans also liked to make their drops between midnight and dawn, according to the article, because most people were in bed and asleep by midnight, and thus the chances of detection were lower.

Lieutenant Beyez had poured over his maps well. Marking each area where reported airplane sightings had been taking place and tracing the straight lines the slower, more cumbersome airplanes had flown, he deduced a pattern that intersected in about a twenty-mile square.

Over the past several months, according to Cuban intelligence, transport planes had been flying late at night over this particular area. American high speed jets had pretty much crisscrossed the entire northern part of Cuba and no apparent pattern could be detected. But the slower transport-style airplanes which were no doubt bringing spies to Cuba had been pretty much restricted to a particular area which Beyez had meticulously marked on his map.

Visiting quite a number of the small jungle cleared areas with his patrol, he had found some rather large footprints and in one case, a small piece of camouflaged silk which looked as though it might have been snagged from a parachute. The frequent heavy rains had washed out most of the footprints but his sharp discerning eye had picked out several deeply furrowed heelprints which were much too large for the average Cuban.

Then too, hadn't his patrol found a round can marked "C Rations, Beans and Pork" the day before yesterday in a small hole just to the rear of a long-abandoned cabin at a large clearing?

The fact that the hole had been used as a privy was apparent, but the sparkle of the metal from the sun's rays had caught his eye. Then that soft toilet paper mixed in with the other crud. No Cuban out in the jungle would be carrying that kind of toilet paper. All they had available were the old catalogues put out by the Cuban national stores from which they could order Soviet goods.

No, only Fidel Castro would be using the kind of toilet paper he had found, and then perhaps only during a state visit by a high-ranking Soviet official. Otherwise, Castro too would use the catalog. He had said many times that he lived no better than the lowest peasant in Cuba, and Lieutenant Beyez knew that was true. His cousin from Havana said she had seen Castro many times, and he was always dressed in his combat boots and fatigues. Never a suit, white tie, or coat. Just plain old clothes, much like any peasant would wear.

A few nights ago Lieutenant Beyez had his patrol at another open area and about one in the morning had heard an airplane overhead. But it was several miles south of the area where his patrol was spending the night. Moving south the next day he came upon a cleared area which he examined closely and found recent large footprints of three or four people. He was convinced that he was hot on the trail of another success and the trip to Moscow. He'd be a hero. Hell, maybe he'd even get promoted.

Earlier that day Lieutenant Beyez poured over his

maps time and time again. He finally spotted a cleared zone near the outer edge of the square he had been examining in detail. What caught his attention was the fact that there was another cleared area just a half-mile away, further to the north and east. Why not, he asked himself.

He called his patrol together and started it moving to the two sites. Seven men were left at the first site and Sergeant Moguez put in charge after giving him explicit instructions to mark the area by flashlight upon hearing the first sound of an airplane. He outlined the figure L on the ground, had each man take his position and demonstrated how to shine his flashlight at the oncoming airplane when one was heard. Then he positioned four other men armed with machine guns and automatic rifles on the edge of the drop zone with orders to shoot at the first sign of parachutists coming down.

Taking the rest of the patrol he moved to the second site and gave his men the same instructions. At this site they would use the letter H. It took seven of his men to form the outline of that letter. He and Juan Maygues, his senior sergeant, would take up positions at either end of the drop zone and with their automatic rifles would bring down any parachutists that might be dropped from the plane. In the meanwhile while they waited, the cook would prepare a feast. This was being done when Roger Landsdale so suddenly stopped on the trail.

"What do you think, Lieutenant?" Roger Landsdale's whisper could barely be heard by Danny Thompson standing at his side. Gazing out again at the Cuban army patrol he took only an instant to reply. "Let's withdraw."

Slowly they made their way back along the trail they had just come over. Some thirty minutes later Danny stopped the group for an instant to tell them that they had better double time back to base camp and warn Dagger of the patrol. It would be futile to try and get to the DZ and pull off a drop with the Cuban army patrol that close. With the hundred or so pound load they had been advised earlier to expect, it would be impossible to keep ahead of any patrol trying to lug that kind of load. Dagger, Marc and Maria might have better luck at the alternate drop zone. But he wasn't going to push their luck here by trying to take a drop at the primary drop zone. "Let's get moving," he said, ending the stop short.

Bunson Burner had never seen a night like this in a hell of a while. Wind, rain, thunderheads in every direction. The air turbulence was severe and he began to feel an uneasiness in his stomach. He'd been flying for years but rough air still brought him some discomfort. Every year the flight surgeon would ask him if he got air sick during turbulent weather and every time he smiled and said never. Too many good pilots had been grounded for that reason and Bunson Cochrane was not about to join them. He loved his job and flying too damn much to let a little stomach queasiness get him down.

Scotty Carrington's "One seven two degrees heading" coming over the earphones momentarily diverted Bunson's thoughts about air sickness.

"Roger, on one seven two and holding," as he finished turning his C-130 to the new heading.

He peered into the radar scope atop the center of the cockpit. Storm clouds in every direction. The way they were moving across the darkened screen was a reflection of the intensity of the storm. Rain splattered across the cockpit window and only occasionally did a break in the cloud cover below reveal a light or two along the Florida coast. Flying in this weather was absolutely stupid. Foolhardy to an extreme.

He thought of the longtime description of pilots. There were old pilots and there were bold pilots. But no old, bold pilots. And he realized why.

Weather like this was a time to keep the old airplane in the aerodrome and the pilots and crew back at the club, or at home, or snuggled in bed with a one night stand, but not out flying. What the hell was so important in that single bundle tied securely to a parachute and stacked at the rear right door, ready to be pushed out over some opening in the jungle over Cuba?

Besides the big box that Bud Sharp had delivered by high speed jet from Washington late that evening, the small box from Fort Bragg that Ed Sweet had sent down didn't make much sense. No bigger than a shoebox and marked "With best wishes and keep us advised of the results," signed, "The Laxative Boys," it seemed to be stretching the urgent necessity for a resupply drop tonight.

Whatever was in the boxes, Dagger had gotten along without it for over two months and he saw no reason why another day's delay would make a damn bit of difference.

On top of it Bud Sharp had given him a warning order tonight to be prepared to make a "Fulton pickup" on Sunday night with at least three C-130's so they could get the team out at one time without repeated passes over the drop zone. Dagger's men had picked several cleared areas where they would be ready for pickup, two at a time, on one line. Even though they much preferred to have only one body swinging from the end of the Fulton sky pickup set, they could handle two at once. And Bunson agreed he'd rather do it that way than make repeated passes over the same area and keep picking them up one by one. He had alerted the pilots of two other C-130's to get their Fulton gear in shape and standby for a mission come dark on Sunday.

The plane was still being tossed from one side to another as the plane changed headings every time Scotty Carrington finished with his slip stick and called them over the intercom. The fury of the storm seemed to pick up in intensity as they neared the coast of Cuba.

Cochrane looked at his copilot Ted Tanley. "What do you think?"

"Pilot error, Burner."

"Pilot error. What the hell do you mean?"

"General McSweeney."

Cochrane burst out laughing. General McSweeney, the Tactical Air Commander at Langley Air Force Base, had a standing rule. Any pilot who had an accident would report to him in person within twenty-four hours to explain and justify to him why he shouldn't be held liable for the costs involved in the loss or damage to the airplane which had been placed in his trust. Without exception, McSweeney felt, pilot error was to blame for damage to one of his beloved airplanes. And it was up to the pilot to prove otherwise.

Cochrane knew that if anything happened to old 9842, he'd be facing McSweeney on the carpet, come dawn. He could hear McSweeney stating that any pilot who would be out flying in the weather which they were now going through had lost all sense of judgment and not only would he pay for the damages but would henceforth be grounded until a board had evaluated the pilot's future use to the air force in a flying capacity. And from what he had heard, very few ever got by the board, hand picked by McSweeney.

"Guess you're right, Ted. McSweeney would have our collective asses."

"Not mine, Burner. You know the rules. You're the pilot, I'm your copilot. The pilot is in command and responsible. Hell, as far as McSweeney is concerned, I'm just another passenger whose life you endangered along with the airplane."

Cochrane realized Ted was right. As he always was. It was a stroke of luck having him in his squadron anyway. A couple of years ago Dagger had called and informed him that Ted Tanley was coming back from a European tour and was being assigned to some job with a National Guard outfit in Maine. He suggested that he get Ted diverted to the air commandos.

Ted had been working for him in Europe and was a

great guy, and on top of it, could fly. After all, he flew Dagger from Paris, and Stuttgart, to Bad Tolz at the foot of the Alps in southern Bavaria, time and time again so that Dagger could visit the 10th Special Forces Group stationed there and get in a parachute jump with his favorite troops. With a complete deadpan voice, Dagger informed Burner that Ted could often land the plane on the short field at Bad Tolz with only two or three touchdowns before finally bringing it in. In fact, the last couple of times they had gone to Tolz, Ted kept the plane on the strip after the first touchdown which was something of a record for him.

Cochrane hadn't known Tanley before but had heard of him. After wrangling with the air force personnel weenies at Randolph Field, he had Ted assigned to his squadron. And it was one of the best decisions he had ever made. A real trooper, superb pilot, and raring to go day or night, rain or shine. The morale in his squadron had taken a tremendous upswing since Tanley's arrival and he attributed much of the improvement to Tanley's sense of humor and his knack of handling men. Of all his pilots, he was glad to have Ted Tanley as a copilot tonight. Others would have cried about the foul weather and aborted the mission. No one in his right mind would ever do anything but compliment you on aborting a mission on a night like this. But not Ted Tanley. Mission essential, absolutely essential it go. That was enough for him.

Chapter 13

"HEADING ONE EIGHT fiver, airspeed one two fiver." Scotty Carrington's instructions were repeated by Bunson Burner Cochrane. His "Roger that" was loud and clear.

However, Carrington's "Eight minutes to IP" caught Cochrane by surprise. He glanced at his watch. Ten minutes after midnight. If only the weather held for another twenty minutes.

Checking in with his crew chief over the intercom he was pleased to hear that the package was all set for the final shove out the door. When Sergeant Murphy gave that kind of report, Cochrane knew he was ready. Murphy was the squadron's pride and joy. He joined the squadron about a year before from a military airlift wing at Pope Air Force Base. As Murphy explained to Cochrane soon after he arrived, he wanted to be in an outfit with some action. He'd been at Pope for over four years. Every day was the same. Load up a plane of 82d Airborne Division troopers. Take off, fly for thirty minutes, then watch them parachute into Sicily North, a drop zone a few miles away on the Fort Bragg reservation, then back for another load, another paradrop, and back to Pope. Monotonous.

Only occasionally did they go anywhere else. Maybe a battalion or so of the 82d would be flown to Alaska or

Puerto Rico and jump in. But day after day he'd see Green Berets take off in air commando airplanes for Germany, the Far East, Panama, and hell, maybe even Dallas, Texas or Portland, Oregon. He wanted to be in an outfit that was going places so he requested transfer to the air commandos.

Another reason, he confided to Cochrane, was a nagging wife at home and it was nice to get away from her occasionally. What he didn't tell Cochrane, but everyone in the squadron knew, was Murphy's reputation and the nickname "Quick Draw" he had acquired. He got the name by his ability to visit a local bar wherever the air commando squadron was at the time, and within an hour or two had some local beauty enthralled with stories of combat exploits and a short time later in the sack.

The current story making the rounds was his forty-six minute quick draw in Manhattan, Kansas. The air commandos had flown a Green Beret team there for a paradrop on the Fort Riley reservation and after parking the C-130 the crew had gone into Manhattan for a night on the town. Within minutes Quick Draw had a blue-eyed, honey blonde from Kansas State in conversation, some fifteen minutes later in bed, and was back in his motel room all within a space of forty-six minutes. That record was the envy of every enlisted man in the squadron, and some of the officers as well.

What really pleased Cochrane though was Quick Draw's performance as crew chief. He kept 9842 in perfect condition. He also had an uncanny knack of putting Green Berets and their air-dropped supplies right in the middle of a drop zone, regardless of the winds aloft.

A green light at the rear of the airplane activated by the pilot up front was the signal that the plane was over the target and ready for the drop to take place. Quick Draw would position himself in the door and even though the green light went on, he'd hold the jumper or bundle until he had determined the exact moment when the jumper had to exit or the bundle be pushed out the door.

Only after being completely satisfied that the position of the plane was just right in relation to the drop zone would Quick Draw slap the jumper on the back and send him on his way. He handled bundles the same way. When his eyeballs told him it was the perfect time he'd shove it out the door. Pilots used slip sticks, and based on wind conditions at jump altitude, determined the position the plane should be in to put the drop where it was intended to be landed. Often during high winds aloft the plane would be several hundred yards to the left or right of the drop zone. With wind drift, the jumper or bundle should land at the intended point.

How Quick Draw was able to do it eye-balling better than the pilots and their slip sticks was still a mystery to Cochrane but he wouldn't fault success. Murphy's system always seemed to work. Cochrane hoped that tonight would be no different.

Lieutenant Beyez had positioned his men the length of the drop zone. The plane had to come from either end to benefit from the full length of the clearing. He felt certain of that. Dropping the width of the clearing would be stupid. What the pilot wanted to do was to put his parachutists on the drop zone, not in the trees. Using the length of the clearing was the only way to do it, Lieutenant Beyez reasoned.

He repeated his instructions to his men. The plane would be coming from either east southeast or west northwest. When they heard the engines or the hum of the plane, flashlights were to be pointed directly at the plane. As the plane approached, they were to follow it slowly, always keeping the beam pointed at the cockpit. Not until the plane had gone over would they turn off their lights.

He had each man flick on his flashlight momentarily and saw the perfect letter "H" he wanted to portray.

With luck, he might just trap those stupid Yankees into parachuting into his arms, and he'd be on his way to a month's vacation in the Soviet Union and the beautiful girl guides who were waiting there.

Satisfied his men were ready, Beyez returned to the still smouldering campfire and helped himself to another bowl of rice. The heavy rain which had been coming down earlier in the evening had abated and only an occasional raindrop was striking the tarpaulin above his head. The wind had also died down and a dead calm had settled over the camp. An occasional spark from the campfire soothed his thoughts.

He began dreaming of faroff places and the good times he would have. Soon he would start to study the Russian language and learn how to say "You're beautiful" and "I love you so much."

Lieutenant Beyez was at peace with himself. Just sit and wait patiently until he could spring the trap on the imperialist Yankees. Maybe he'd capture one alive and deliver him personally to the Prime Minister. That would be a coup, par excellence, and perhaps get him promoted and an assignment to Havana. He'd like that.

He had been out in the field long enough. The senoritas he had seen on every street corner in Havana on the few occasions that he had been lucky enough to get there were beautiful. First a trip to Moscow, a promotion, then Havana. By God, just let one of those Americans fall into his hands.

Suddenly he heard the hum of an airplane. Springing erect he shouted a warning to his troops. "On your feet! Sergeant Maygues, if there are only a few parachutists, let's capture them alive. If there are many, we'll blast them in the air and try capturing only one or two."

The noise of the airplane became louder. "East southeast, lights on," he shouted. Lieutenant Beyez cocked his automatic rifle and stood waiting.

"Heading two niner one degrees, airspeed one twenty

knots, final leg." Scotty Carrington's voice was confident. Threading his way by zigs and zags through one thunderhead after another, he brought the C-130 to the final leg. Now all he could do was count off the minutes and seconds which should bring them right over DZ Eagle.

If only the weather held for a few minutes more. What had been a mean, rough storm with hurricane winds until a few minutes ago had suddenly given way to a relative calm. Only a few raindrops still splattered against the C-130. Like a drum majorette, he moved his slip stick back and forth to keep time with the drops of rain still striking the aircraft's side. Quickly measuring the distance on the chart spread before him, he made a rapid slide rule calculation and announced over the intercom, "Two minutes to target."

Bunson Burner Cochrane peered into the darkness from his dimmed cockpit. Nothing but the dark outline of the heavy jungle beneath. Since making his final turn to 291 degrees at Scotty's direction, his only job was to keep the C-130 on course at 120 knots and 600 feet altitude.

The terrain-following radar was working beautifully. Set at six hundred feet, the plane automatically adjusted to that height above the ground. Old experienced pilots moaned about some piece of equipment taking over the pilot's responsibility when the air force first introduced terrain-following radar.

But Bunson Burner never entertained any such thought. The terrain-following radar had saved him time and time again during difficult night operations. Without it, he would have flown into a mountain peak or high, hard hill hundreds of missions ago.

For him, terrain-following radar was the best thing the air force had ever come up with for use in night operations which required flying the nap of the earth. It took the guess-work out of knowing when a mountain might be ahead. Before its introduction pilots had to draw exact mission profiles from maps and aerial photographs to be sure that on each leg of the flight, their altitude was high enough to get over any mountain peak or manmade obstacle such as a TV or radio tower, now so prevalent throughout the world. The terrain-following radar had solved all that and made night flying much safer.

"One minute to target." Scotty Carrington's voice reflected his satisfaction at navigating the plane to the exact spot for the planned drop.

Cochrane and Tanley kept peering out the cockpit window. Almost at the same time they spotted a string of dim lights in the distance. Three in a row, parallel to the plane's path. Right.

Suddenly Ted Tanley cried out, "There are two sets of lights. Hell that's an "H". That's not the signal. Bunson, that's last week's code. Tonight's is three lights. First one green, then red, then green."

Bunson Burner Cochrane looked at the lights again. Perfect signal for last week's drop. But tonight's was different. Dammit, did Donovan change his mind and we didn't get the word? After all, Donovan prescribed the codes for both his group and our response.

Sergeant Murphy's voice over the intercom announcing a "go condition" got Cochrane's immediate attention. As the pilot, he had responsibility for ordering the drop. His orders were on positive signal recognition. He looked again at the lights now coming closer and closer into view. Count 'em again. Seven lights. Three on each side and one in the center to form the "H". Without hesitating, he barked his command. "Abort primary load DZ, repeat, abort primary load DZ. Quick Draw, drop alternate load, repeat, drop alternate load. Acknowledge."

Quick Draw's voice came booming over the intercom, "Acknowledged." Then moving rapidly to the open door opposite the one he had been standing in, he resumed watching the lights on the drop zone. Finally with a sudden shove he pushed the alternate load out the door and watched the parachute opening below. "Perfect. Tree landing for sure," he muttered. In the dimly lit cabin no one could see Quick Draw's grim face.

Lieutenant Beyez watched in amazement as a parachute blossomed open below the huge airplane flying overhead. He could barely see the outline of the plane against the dark clouds. The roar of its motors sent chills up and down his body. Thank God it wasn't dropping bombs or his entire patrol would have been wiped out.

Observing only one parachute he yelled, "Hold your fire!" As the parachute came closer to the drop zone it drifted rapidly to the outer edge. Just before plunging into the high trees surrounding the clearing, Lieutenant Beyez could see a man hanging from the parachute harness some distance below the billowing parachute.

"We've done it! we've done it!" he shouted, bringing forth a resounding clamor of excited voices from his patrol. His planning had paid off. He'd trapped those stupid, inept Americans at their own game. Moscow, here we come.

Running rapidly to the edge of the woods he saw a man dangling from the parachute entangled in the jungle growth high above his head. The man swung back and forth below the parachute like a pendulum in a grandfather's clock.

Lieutenant Beyez pointed his automatic rifle at the figure now barely visible high in the trees and shouted "We have you surrounded. If you move, we will shoot you down like a dog."

The figure remained silent. Lieutenant Beyez repeated his order. Still no response. He turned to his sergeant and said, "The bastard must have been knocked out when he hit the trees. Keep him covered while I figure out how we will get him down."

By now all of his men had gathered at the base of the tree and were shining their flashlights at the lone individual still hanging high above them. From the light of the flashlights they could see a holster at his side, a canteen slung from a belt to his right rear and a coil of rope fastened to the left front of his parachute harness.

Beyez knew he was looking at a perfectly equipped parachutist. Only last week he had seen a training film shown by his Soviet advisor on American parachutists and how they always carried a coil of rope in the event they got hung up in trees. All the man had to do was to tie one end of the rope to the parachute harness, slip out of the harness and scoot down the rope hand over hand to the ground. As soon as the man recovered consciousness he'd order him down.

Now all they had to do was wait. He'd take the time to notify the district security officer of his capture. By flashlight he scribbled out his message. "American spy parachuting into Cuba captured by my patrol at 12:30 a.m. Will deliver him personally to you by mid-morning. Patrol desires trip to Moscow as soon as arrangements can be made. Signed Lieutenant Beyez." He handed it to his radio operator and told him to get on the air and send the message immediately. He then turned and glanced up at his captured spy still hanging high in the jungle overhead.

Beyez's broad smile reflected his feeling of victory at last. He knew that Sr. Castro would personally pin a medal on his chest within a day or two and maybe even bid him a fond farewell as he stepped aboard the twice weekly air flight from Havana to Moscow. Cuba didn't have heroes every day. And Castro would recognize that it was Beyez's superior intelligence that led him to place a team on the drop zone with the right light signals.

Beyez knew that the smartest men in Cuban intelligence had been trying to figure out how American spies were being brought into the country and hadn't been able to solve the mystery. But, he had. Castro would recognize Beyez's brilliance when he saw it. Lieutenant Beyez leaned against the tree and lit a cigarette while he waited for his prize above to recover his senses.

No hurry. He'd wait.

Beyez had two of his men remain on guard watching the solitary figure still high above him while he ordered the rest of his men to get some sleep. They'd wait till daylight, then go up after him.

Finishing his cigarette, he stubbed it out on the heel of his boot before placing his poncho on the ground and lay down to get a few hours of rest. Lying on his back he gazed up into the tree and again looked at the spy still dangling from his parachute. His ticket to the best time of his life. Never having left Cuba before, he had visions of all the things he would do in Moscow. Parties, celebrations, girls at his beck and call. And, department stores where you could buy all those luxury goods. Without effort, he turned on his side and was soon fast asleep dreaming of the new Utopia he was about to visit.

Bunson Burner's voice was grim. "Ted, are you thinking what I'm thinking?"

"I'm afraid so. If those bastards have policed up Dagger and his men, I'm going to be the first one to volunteer to blast Cuba off the face of this earth." Tanley's voice showed the strain which had suddenly overcome them both.

"Scotty," Cochrane's voice was firm, "get us to the alternate DZ as scheduled."

"Ted, I'm not holding out much hope. From what I've just seen on Eagle, I'm afraid Dagger and his team have been picked up."

"Sure looks that way."

Scotty Carrington who a few minutes ago had felt a deep pride in having navigated the C-130 right on target was still mystified why Bunson Burner had ordered the abort. He'd seen the lights on the drop zone himself as they flew over. "Bunson, why the abort?" he said quietly into his mike.

"Wrong signal," Cochrane replied.

"Maybe the team decided at the last minute to change

signals and had sent a message but there wasn't enough time to relay it to us. After all," Scotty intoned, "We've seen the wrong signals used before and the drops made. Seems to me that this is just a case of someone failing to pass the word that the signal had been changed."

"Scotty, I'm going to draw you a picture. Five men on this team. Seven flashlights on the ground. One or two assets may be available to assist. Man two drop zones with six or seven people and the most lights you could possibly use would be four. No doubt that's why Dagger specified only three lights and with the color combinations had positive recognition. If the team was on Eagle, they're in the hands of Castro now."

Fly this crate for awhile, Ted. I'm going to write a quick message and put it in our package for the drop on the alternate should it take place."

Hurriedly Cochrane scribbled a note "Dagger, Eagle compromised. Seven lights. Going to alternate." He glanced at the message before putting it into a brown envelope. Dammit, for all he knew Dagger was at the primary DZ. In fact, he normally would be. Quickly he crossed out "Dagger" and replaced it with "Team." Sealing the envelope, he walked to the rear of the aircraft and asked Quick Draw to fasten it securely to the load still tied to the end of the parachute in position at the right door.

Returning to the cockpit, Cochrane slid back into the pilot's seat. "How many more minutes before changing course?"

"Just a couple more," Tanley replied laconically. His thoughts were still on Dagger and his men. There was no officer he respected more than Donovan.

Working with him for over three years in Europe was the most rewarding experience of Ted Tanley's life. He particularly liked the way Dagger operated. He'd give you a clearly stated mission, a time for completion, but not another word until the date and hour the project was due. Donovan was noted for giving his officers complete authority to do their thing. He did not look over their shoulders and attempt to tell them how to do it.

Ted Tanley knew he was getting up tight. It would be another ten minutes before they knew whether the alternate drop zone was also compromised.

The C-130 was now flying the most dangerous part of the flight. After reaching the IP the plane maintained the same heading, air speed and altitude for fifteen to twenty miles regardless of when or where the drop took place.

The air commandos and Green Berets had worked out the procedure several years before based on a sad experience. Before then, the air commandos would fly higher and out of small arms range and at the last minute drop down to jump altitude of about six to eight hundred feet, then pop back up as soon as the drop had been made.

The weakness of that procedure was finally brought home to them by a shocking reality. During maneuvers and exercises the force playing the role of the enemy simply tracked the aircraft and marked the spot where it suddenly dropped down and then almost immediately popped up again.

A U.S. army lieutenant, acting as an enemy intelligence officer, had acquired a reputation based on his uncanny ability to direct enemy forces to the very spot where the Green Berets had parachuted in. For a long time he refused to share his secret with his fellow officers on how he was always right in pinpointing almost the exact area where the team had landed. It was only after a few drinks too many in a local bar one night when he started bragging about his uncanny method that the truth became known.

He took each report of an airplane sighting and marked it on a map. Soon he had the line of flight. Then the reports of low-level planes overhead. Always for a short period. Then high in the sky reports. By quick deduction he assumed that the location over which the low level flights were taking place was the spot where the parachute drops were being made.

As a result of the lieutenant's perception, the air commandos and Green Berets worked out the system now being used. Same direction, altitude and airspeed for fifteen or twenty miles. The enemy might surmise a drop had taken place somewhere along that long route but the exact spot would no longer be confirmed by a stupid set of procedures that no one had ever thought of changing until a lieutenant loaded with martinis had shown the weakness.

Mike Donovan, Marc Mayberry and Maria arrived at Drop Zone Molly several hours before the scheduled time for the drop at one a.m.

Donovan knew that there was little possibility that the drop would be made on DZ Molly. The alternate DZ was used only in an emergency when the primary DZ could not be located because of weather or the presence of enemy forces in its vicinity made it unusable.

So far, the COBRA team had been in Cuba over two months and never had to cancel a drop for that reason. The primary and alternate drop zone procedure had first been put to use in World War II for drops to the French underground. The alternate was used more often as the German Gestapo stepped up efforts to determine when and where drops were being made to resistance groups and, through intensified actions to detect the resistance, began to surround likely drop areas with troops. As a drop was in progress, the Gestapo force would sweep out of hiding and kill or capture underground members waiting on the drop zone to receive personnel or supplies. As the war continued, OSS agents used the alternate DZ more and more to outwit the Gestapo.

Marc Mayberry was busy digging a small hole at the edge of the clearing while Donovan showed Maria the exact spot she was to occupy and the direction to point the flashlight on his order. The flashlights were to be lit at exactly 1:00 a.m. and kept on for two minutes, or until the plane was directly overhead and the recognition signal had been acknowledged and the countersign given. Paradrops of personnel and equipment were thus positively controlled.

The arrival over a drop zone took place within a two minute prescribed period with a series of lights arranged in a certain pattern on the drop zone; a later refinement required specific colors and a positive signal from the plane by several methods, turning lights on and off, or sudden bursts of power to the engines. Only after an elaborate set of procedures was followed, all preplanned as to detail, would a drop be made.

In areas far removed from enemy forces, it would not be unusual for the team on the ground to have voice radio contact with the airplane overhead with spoken words used for recognition and confirmation. But not in Cuba, with security forces operating everywhere and Castro's record of being able to use direction-finding equipment to track down locations of clandestine radios.

Donovan had made the hard decision before they were put into Cuba that no voice radios would be taken along or used. Their non-use, he had determined, would provide his men more security than any possible benefit they might provide.

One minute before scheduled droptime. Donovan checked the positions where Marc and Maria were standing. Perfect. Then reconfirming his earlier orders as to light sequence, he took his position and in a low voice ordered, "Lights on."

Marc, Maria and Donovan raised their flashlights and pointed them toward the horizon at a ten degree heading, the direction from which the C-130 would be approaching.

"Thirty seconds to drop," Scotty Carrington's announcement prompted Bunson Burner to peer more intensely through the cockpit window. A light rain had again begun to fall after the plane had flown for the last fifteen minutes in clear, calm weather at six hundred feet. High above, heavy clouds were still moving back and forth, creating crazy quilt-like patterns.

"Quick Draw, stand by for drop." Cochrane's voice boomed over the intercom.

"Roger, sir."

"Lights on DZ!" brought a smile to Bunson Burner's face. He saw the faint outline of three lights parallel to the plane's line-of-flight. Perfect signal. First one green, middle red, last green.

His "flick the wing-lights twice" had Ted Tanley reach for the knob and with two abrupt movements momentarily flashed the red flying lights on the tip of each wing. Cochrane kept his eyes glued to the three lights on the drop zone. Responding to the plane's signal, the first light changed to red, the second to green, and the third remained green. His "recognition signal observed" brought an audible sigh of relief from Tanley who momentarily had to take his eyes off the drop zone while he manipulated the wing tip lights.

A hundred or so yards short of the drop zone Ted Tanley pushed another button. In the cabin's rear, Quick Draw, who had been peering out the right open door while watching the small red light at eye level on the top and side of the cabin door, smiled as the light turned to green.

He pushed the bundle at his feet closer to the door. Looking down over the drop zone he gave the bundle a tremendous shove and smiled as he saw the parachute deploy above the center of the clearing. As he watched, the lights on the drop zone were suddenly extinguished and the night outside became pitch black as it had been throughout the flight. Quick Draw could see nothing as he glanced back one more time before closing the door. He then walked forward and joined the crew in the cockpit.

* * *

Donovan shouted "Bulls eye!" as the plane roared overhead and he watched the bundle hurling groundward. The sudden billowing of the parachute as it opened seemed to stop its downward progress in mid-air. Then like a proud swan with spread wings hovering above its brood below, the parachute descended slowly with the package held firmly in the shroud lines twenty feet below the canopy floating gracefully toward earth.

The slight thud as the package hit the soft ground some thirty feet from Donovan was barely audible. The parachute, with its load no longer forcing air into the canopy, collapsed around the package.

Marc was the first to reach the package on the ground. Rapidly unsnapping the straps holding it to the parachute harness, he brushed aside the parachute which had settled over the package. With his knife he slashed the ropes tied around the bundle and removed the snap link holding the box lid in place. Shining his flashlight into the box he spied a small package which he handed to Maria. The words "LAXATIVES" on its side made him smile. He handed her another box labeled "Keys and Locks."

A slight wind blew part of the parachute back onto the box. As he pushed it aside, he saw a brown envelope taped to the outside of the box. Reaching down, he focused his flashlight on the envelope and saw the word "Team." He handed the envelope to Donovan as he continued unpacking.

Donovan's loud exclamation brought Marc upright. Without a word Donovan passed the message to Marc who read it by flashlight.

"Oh, my God," he said, breaking the eerie silence on the drop zone.

Maria glanced at Marc, and then at Donovan. Where only a few minutes before, broad smiles had been on their faces, now there was only a look of gloom.

"Trouble?" she asked.

Marc nodded, handing her the message. As she read it

slowly, tears came to her eyes. For what seemed like minutes, a completely unbelieving and shocked group stood silently in the middle of the jungle clearing in deep thought.

"Let's get with it and move," said Donovan. Marc started unpacking again.

Reaching into the box, Marc brought out a folded canvas sack. He spread it on the ground and opened the zipper which ran its full length. Then reaching inside he withdrew two canvas vests which he and Donovan promptly put on. Taking the canvas sack they draped it over the box, tipped it on its side, and closed the zipper. Lifting one end upward they fastened two small straps hanging from Donovan's vest to the heavy rings on the canvas bag. Kneeling, Marc fastened his vest straps to the bag. Then he rose slowly. The canvas bag holding the box was slung between them.

Gathering up the parachute and loose ends, they moved to the side of the clearing where Marc had earlier dug a hole. Depositing the parachute and other odds and ends in the hole, they covered it with the small pile of dirt which had been carefully stacked nearby. Then Maria spread a layer of branches over the freshly dug earth. After covering it with jungle grass they stood to one side and with their flashlights surveyed their efforts. No indication that the earth had been disturbed or any other telltale sign that a drop had ever been made. Then back to the center of the clearing for one last inspection to make sure nothing was left behind.

Maria carefully smoothed the ruffled grass as they backed off into the jungle. Finally satisfied, Dagger gave the order to move out.

When well beyond the jungle clearing, Donovan stopped momentarily to tell Maria to lead them to their alternate site. She acknowledged the order by nodding her head and with a slight change in direction started moving through the jungle.

Donovan's mind was still on the message he had just

received from Cochrane telling him that Drop Zone Eagle had been compromised. He wondered what had happened to Danny's group. Had his order to get the lead out and start moving led them to disregard the normal caution they would have observed enroute and upon reaching the drop zone?

Time and time again he had trained his troops to stop short of a drop zone and observe it for some minutes to make sure they were the only ones around. He had found out from long experience that generally a team that was captured had failed to observe such elementary precautions. And that usually occurred because they were in a hurry.

He'd know by early morning what had happened. If they didn't return then, he feared the worst. Otherwise, if they had avoided capture they would come back to the base camp and not seeing the rest of the team, move without further word to the alternate site for which Dagger was now headed.

Always, the first order of business of any team establishing a base camp was the selection of at least one other area to which the team could rally and where they could regroup should they be discovered and have to make a quick getaway, either while on a mission or while bivouacked in base camp.

The next five or six hours would be the longest Mike Donovan would ever experience. He knew that. The team was his family. Any thought of their being in danger caused the same concern any parent felt for a missing child. Until they were found, his concern for the team would grow.

The group plowed on through the night and the forbidding jungle. Dawn finally arrived and their rate increased.

Donovan and Marc were a funny-looking sight. Like two vaudeville actors playing the part of a horse. In this case the horse was carrying a prized possession, the nuke replica. But it was the only way to carry a heavy load.

Long ago, Mike Donovan had told his 7th Special Forces Group riggers that with every load dropped to his teams, a carrying mechanism of some sort had to be packed with it. Often a simple backpack was all that was needed. At other times, elaborately improvised carrying systems were required.

They had certainly done a good job this time. With the heavy load slung between him and Marc, neither had any difficulty carrying his share. One man carrying the same load would have staggered along at half the speed they were making. And speed was essential.

He was particularly pleased with his riggers. Their principal job was to pack parachutes and repair those torn through use. Not only because of professional pride were they careful in repacking parachutes; Donovan regularly followed an ironclad rule. He would go down to the packing shed the riggers used, select a parachute at random, then designate a packer at random, taking him up in an airplane to jump the newly packed chute. Donovan was sure that as long as he continued that practice, he'd never have to worry about one of his riggers getting careless. They never knew when he'd be down to make his next random selections.

The sun had been up for hours when Maria turned and raised her hand, indicating another stop. Motioning them to remain in place, she moved quietly forward. Brushing aside the last piece of jungle foilage she looked out into the small clearing. Only the sound of jungle birds could be heard.

Glancing quickly from one end of the clearing to the other she finally spied what she was looking for at the very far end. Two rather large tree branches stuck in the ground with a small sharpened branch between them. She whistled twice and waited.

Almost at once three whistles responded. Stepping into the clearing her face broke out into a large smile as she saw Danny, Roger and Tiger step out of the jungle and into the clearing at the far end. After giving them a wave to come on, she returned to the jungle edge and motioned Dagger and Marc to follow her. When Donovan saw the rest of his team, tears came to his eyes.

Excitedly they told him what had happened when they had approached Drop Zone Eagle and saw a Cuban Army patrol in the clearing just a short distance from the intended area of the drop. Donovan complimented them on their actions and told them to get a couple of hours of sleep before they had to make final plans for the big operation tomorrow. While they all admired the beautiful replica of the nuclear warhead which Marc had unpacked, Donovan wrote his operational report and handed it to Marc Mayberry for transmission. He then joined his men for a short nap when Maria insisted on taking the first shift at standing guard.

Chapter 14

PACING BACK AND forth in his operations center deep inside the Pentagon, Bud Sharp was on edge as he waited for a message from the COBRA Team.

Cochrane's flash report after his return to his Florida base was upsetting. He tried to banish the thoughts which kept entering his mind. The COBRA team captured and undergoing torture while being interrogated by Castro's security force. He knew the fate that would await the team. Hot irons placed against their cheeks, chest and genitals. Questions. Confessions. Cigarette stubs being snuffed out against the COBRA team's bodies. Beatings with a rubber hose. Drops of acid on their faces. The threat of more torture until every man confessed.

The inhumane treatment meted out to captured spies had been too well documented to even hope the COBRA team would be treated differently. Castro's statements that he would shoot any American spy on sight only added to Sharp's discomfort.

Surely one member of the team had survived and would get a message out. Every man in the group was a trained radio operator and all he had to do was to get to one of the radios that the COBRA team, as a priority project, had cached around the area for emergency use.

His earlier call to the chairman of the Joint Chiefs of

Staff added to Sharp's woes. Getting General Taylor out of bed at three in the morning to tell him of the possible loss of the team instead of reporting the success of Cochrane's mission, was also unpleasant. Recognizing Sharp's deep concern by the tone of his voice, the chairman's remark that things might get worse before they got better made Sharp more despondent.

Taylor's suggestion to get some sleep hit Sharp hard. The COBRA team might be undergoing torture at that very minute, and Taylor suggested he *get some sleep*. What happened to officers when they made general? Did they lose all feeling for the men they commanded?

He hadn't thought that General Taylor fit that category but his abrupt termination of their conversation certainly left that impression. Maybe, he thought, awakening him at three in the morning was the reason. He probably hadn't fully appreciated the seriousness of Sharp's report.

During the last thirty minutes Ross Latimer had received calls from the Associated Press, United Press International, and Reuters, asking for White House comment on a story moving over news service wires that Cuba had captured a U.S. spy and Cuban Prime Minister Fidel Castro would be putting him on exhibition at noon today during a television extravaganza from Havana.

The story alleged that Cuban security forces had laid a cleverly planned trap and had succeeded in fooling the Americans into delivering spies into their waiting arms in a jungle area west of Havana.

At this very hour, the story continued, Cuban security forces were enroute to Havana to deliver the spies to the Cuban Prime Minister, who would be waiting on the steps of the Ministry of Justice. Once and for all, the Cubans were going to prove to the world that the United States had been putting spies into Cuba in contravention of the United Nations charter.

The Cuban Prime Minister had requested complete TV coverage of the historic event to show all freedom-loving peoples the duplicity of the United States. According to the story, previous allegations by Cuba of U.S. spying had always had been denied. This time Cuba would present the spy in person for all to see and judge for themselves the veracity of the Cuban charges of U.S. espionage and subversion directed against the Castro regime.

Latimer's call to John Askins, Director of the CIA, informing him of the breaking story brought only a brusque reply to check it out with the chairman of the Joint Chiefs of Staff. A call to General Taylor had been fruitless; he was equally evasive and remarked that any comment must come from the President.

In the past, such allegations had been vigorously denied by both Askins and Taylor. A figment of Castro's imagination they had said. Now, not only did they fail to deny the story but both refused Latimer's suggestion of "No comment."

As the President's press secretary, Ross Latimer had never been excluded from intimate knowledge about ongoing activities of the government. From his very first day in office, the President had informed cabinet officers and agency heads that his was going to be an open administration and the press secretary was to be its official spokesman. All officials were to cooperate with the press secretary and provide him the background and detail necessary to respond to media inquiries. The President would keep Latimer informed of his actions and decisions. At no time in the past several months had Latimer been included in a briefing on any ongoing operations in Cuba.

A call from the producer of the "Today" show asking for an official spokesman to be interviewed in their Washington studios at 8:30 that morning on a "special" that the Today show would focus on the Cuban crisis convinced Latimer that he must call the President to alert him of the story and get the administration's position in responding to media queries.

He glanced at the ornate clock hanging on the far wall of his White House office. Five after six. He'd just take a chance that the President was awake by this time. The last thing he wanted to do was hit him with a story of this importance and ask for his comments when first aroused from a deep sleep.

He thought of his own situation. He'd been awakened at 5 a.m. by a call from AP. Sound asleep in his apartment, his instinctive reaction was to say, "Absolutely false." After listening to the AP staffer read the entire story, he refused any official statement until he could get down to his White House office and check it out.

Then the call to Askins and Taylor. If they had been holding out on him, he'd let the President know that he couldn't do his job unless he knew what the hell was going on. He had been caught flat-footed several years before in commenting on a story and finding out later that the Secretary of Defense had withheld information from him. He wasn't about to lose his credibility with the press again by less than honest answers.

He dialed the President's quarters. He felt a sense of relief as he heard the whine of an electric razor and the President's "Good morning."

"Mr. President—" Latimer began. He then outlined what had happened during the last hour or so and the request to appear on the Today show special.

The President's order to respond to all inquiries with a "no comment" baffled him. "That will make it seem," he told the President, "that there might be substance in Castro's allegations. If so, the press would only bore in more deeply."

"O.K., Ross, tell them 'No comment at this time.' The White House will make an announcement later today."

"But Mr. President, if there is any substance to this story, it would be better if we made the announcement ourselves. That would take the edge from Castro's charges and lessen their impact. Waiting for him puts us in the role of having to respond to his charges. I assure you, Mr. President, failure on your part to provide our version or perspective of whatever has happened, or is going to, will be far more effective than making them wait to hear Castro's version and leaving us a chance only to respond."

"Ross, bear with me. I'll explain it all to you later and I think you will agree with what I am doing. But in all honesty, I don't have the information I need at this time to respond to the allegations. I hope to have it soon. That's why I suggest you inform the media we'll have an announcement later today. Good luck."

Ross Latimer was speechless as he heard the President's final words before hanging up. What the hell was going on? The President of the United States stating he didn't have the information he needed to respond to such allegations. If he didn't have the information, who the hell did? And why couldn't the President get it now? He had indicated he might be getting it soon. From whom? When?

A call from the chief operator of the White House switchboard relayed her concern that she couldn't stall calls to him much longer as he had requested earlier. "After all," she continued, "the White House press room is filling rapidly with reporters who know that you are in your office."

"O.K., Anne. Tell all callers that I will make an announcement in the press room at 7:00 a.m. Until then, no further calls will be accepted from the media."

As he concluded that conversation, Kay Summers, his girl Friday, walked into his office and tossed him the morning editions of the *New York Times* and *Washington Post* and needled him. "So what else is new?" Kate Summers was a dedicated professional who at times almost singlehandedly kept his office going and her voice reflected her concern that she had been cut out of a fast developing story. No time to discuss it with her now. After all, she'd never believe he was just as much in the dark.

Glancing at the papers he saw the *Times'* banner headline: "Cuba Claims Capture of American Spy." The story which followed was based on the AP and UPI stories which had been distributed by the wire services earlier. The editor's note that attempts to get White House comment had been unsuccessful in the short time between receipt of the story and publication, which bordered on deception. The innuendo was there that the White House was at fault for failure to include a rebuttal or explanation. In fact, it was being caught in a squeeze by a late-breaking story and the deadline before its presses started rolling. The editor's note was designed to keep the *Times* from later criticism for not including the administration's comment.

Ross Latimer knew this was an old trick of the trade. He had often resorted to the same tactic himself.

The Cuban announcement was also *The Washington Post's* lead story. However, the *Post* acknowledged that time did not permit getting the administration's reaction. However, readers were assured that later editions of the *Post* would carry them.

Ross Latimer could feel the tension in the press room as he entered at exactly 7:00 a.m. and announced, "The White House has no comment at this time to statements from Havana regarding the capture of American spies. Later on today, a statement will be issued."

Barry Sullivan, *The Washington Post*, was on his feet first.

"Ross, is the President aware of Castro's charges and does he agree with your 'no comment' to them?"

"Barry, I will not respond to your question. I repeat, our position at this time is 'no comment.' However, I can assure you that later today we will be putting out a statement."

"In other words," Sullivan responded testily, "you

are confirming Castro's charges but will not give the administration's explanation until later today. I expect after Castro's twelve o'clock press conference. I have only one further question. Is your delay a deliberate act in order to first assess the information and extent of Cuban knowledge of our spy operations after you have had an opportunity to learn first-hand what is going to be said at noon?"

By now, the jammed-packed press room was echoing support of the boring and penetrating questions asked by the famed *Washington Post* reporter. Latimer, as a longtime news reporter himself, could sense the frustration felt by the members of the fourth estate. One of the major news stories of the entire life of the Ketner administration was breaking, and all he could say was "no comment." He could hardly blame them for their reaction. He frankly didn't understand the President's order himself. But he was given no option. Yet, instinctively, he had a feeling that the President knew more than he would let on. His "bear with me this once" seemed to connote that, perhaps, just perhaps, this was a prelude to some major announcement which the President was still trying to formulate. His thoughts were again interrupted by Clay Perkins of the *Los Angeles Times*.

"Ross, you realize the great pressure which has been placed on the President for the last several months regarding his failure to take action on charges that the Soviets are arming Castro with nuclear weapons, and the administration's repeated statements that it has no proof to substantiate such allegations. It has been a continuing subject of national debate. My question is this, did the U.S. government attempt to send spies into Cuba to verify the allegations concerning the introduction of Soviet nuclear weapons and is Castro's announcement that he has captured such spies an indication that even this attempt has been as futile as the others the administration has taken trying to resolve this problem?"

THE COBRA TEAM 217

The question was greeted by applause and catcalls from the assembled press. "Answer the question, Ross," was echoed and re-echoed by the reporters.

Ross Latimer knew he was in a "no-win" situation. Without acknowledging the reporters' demonstration, he said "No comment. I'll post a notice later this morning announcing the time for our next press conference." Turning his back on the reporters, he then left the press room.

The sun was peeking over the horizon when a nudge from Sergeant Numez brought Lieutenant Beyez to his feet. The sergeant handed Beyez a message:

"Congratulations on capture. Two helicopters will arrive your position at eleven this morning to airlift you and your men, and the captured spy, to Punto Brava. From there you will proceed by open jeep in a triumphant parade to Havana where Prime Minister Castro will greet you on the steps of the Justice Ministry at noon. The prisoner will be made to ride on the hood of the first vehicle so the population can see him being taken to Havana. Your men will be given the honor of guarding him. The entire population along the route of march has been alerted and will cheer your men as the motorcade is escorted to the capitol. Prime Minister Castro has ordered television crews to record delivery of the spy and he will make a nationwide speech at that time. You will be guest of honor. The press from all nations represented in Havana will cover your arrival and this historic event. Again, congratulations. I have made preliminary arrangements for the trip to Moscow as soon as the Premier has bestowed the thanks of our nation on you and your brave men. Signed, Respectfully yours, Major Gonzalez, District Security Officer."

Beyez looked up at the spy still dangling in his parachute. Not a sound had come from him since he first parachuted into the trees the night before. Maybe he broke his neck. That would save the Cuban security service from doing it later on.

He looked around at his men now gathered in a small group around him. Who wanted to volunteer to climb up the nearest tree and, using the rope attached to the spy, lower him to the ground after cutting the parachute harness from his body? All hands were raised.

Beyez nodded to Sergeant Numez and said, "You have the honor, being second in command."

Without a further word, four of the men hoisted Sergeant Numez on their shoulders and thrust him skyward. He grabbed the nearest limb high above him and worked his way slowly upward until he reached the spy. He grabbed the revolver and tossed it down to the men waiting below. Then he tied the coiled rope securely around the spy's waist and with his sharp knife cut the shroud lines. Taking the rope he slowly released it, lowering the spy to the arms of the men waiting below.

Beyez watched the man being lowered. Six feet tall, he estimated. Blackened charcoal face. Typical of spies. Steel helmet well down on his head so only the lower portion of his chin was visible. Chinstrap still in position. He surmised that he was dead. Not a movement of any kind as he was being lowered.

Two men grabbed him as his feet touched the ground and held him erect. Beyez removed the chin strap and threw back the man's helmet so that he could see his face.

A white card fluttered to the ground. He picked it up and read the neatly printed message "With the compliments of your fellow-Cubans-in-Exile." He slapped the man's face hoping to get some reaction and only then realized he had been had.

It was not a man, but a mannequin!

John Ketner was reserved as he walked into his Oval Office. An operation which had been going so beautifully now seemed to have turned sour, and perhaps disastrous. The early morning call from Ben Taylor reporting on the night's activities and the possible capture of members of the COBRA team followed by Castro's announcement of capturing American spies was too much of a coincidence to ignore. The two had to be related. But, dammit, according to Taylor, they wouldn't know, until later that morning when the next scheduled radio contact with the COBRA team or any of its men who had escaped capture would be made. Taylor's admonition to stand fast until word was received from the COBRA Team seemed like good advice at the time.

However, John Ketner knew that if Castro exhibited a member of the COBRA team and his administration failed to provide information to the press and the American public, all hell would break loose. However, Taylor's description of the deception tactics employed by the air commandos during the supply effort last night might, just might, be Castro's big "capture." If that turned out to be the case, Castro's embarrassment would well be worth the discomfort his own administration had to endure until noon.

But, still no word out of Havana that the noon's highly ballyhooed extravaganza had been cancelled or postponed. Every passing hour without such an announcement would only confirm the worst. That Castro's forces had indeed captured one or more of the COBRA team, instead of the surprise package parachuted into the jungle by the air commandos.

Regardless, he had to get his senior people together as soon as possible to map out his final strategy. Unless he got the Soviet Union to withdraw its nuclear missiles from Cuba voluntarily, his days in office might be numbered.

Even his arrangements with the Senate Majority Leader and the Speaker of the House for a one-week moratorium on the Cuban crisis had been short-lived. The Senate, during debate yesterday, almost passed a resolution declaring they no longer had confidence in the way he was handling the serious threat to U.S. security. Sentiment for impeachment was even stronger in the House of Representatives.

Today's show from Havana might just tip the balance in favor of his critics. But damned if he wanted to lead the nation into a fullscale nuclear war against the Soviets in which neither side could win. The death and destruction such a holocaust would cause would be living proof of his failure as a statesman and leader. What was needed was a voluntary withdrawal of the missiles by a Soviet initiative.

And the plan already crystalizing in his thoughts might do the trick. If the planned operation to bring out a nuclear warhead succeeded, his own strategy would be strengthened tenfold.

The pictures taken by the COBRA team of nuclear weapons in Cuba were superb, but were they enough to convince a doubting public, let alone the leaders of the Soviet Union? He doubted it.

Ben Taylor, John Askins, Robert Ketner and Colonel Bud Sharp had been waiting outside the President's office for forty-five minutes for the nine o'clock meeting with the President.

The delay was caused by a call received by the President at eight forty-five from Secretary of State Oliven that he was enroute to the White House with the Soviet Ambassador. The ambassador had urgent orders to personally deliver to the President of the United States a protest from the Soviet Union regarding the introduction of U.S. spies into Cuba and a warning that continuation of such practices could lead to the most serious consequences for the United States.

Bud Sharp was on the White House secure phone to Ed Sweet at Fort Bragg when the meeting between the President and the Soviet Ambassador ended.

General Taylor was leaning over Sharp's shoulder

looking at the message Sharp was recording as each word was read to him by Sweet. Taylor's face broke out into a wide grin as the last words of the message were written. Grabbing the message with one hand and beckoning Sharp to follow him with the other, he joined Askins and Bob Ketner as they filed into the Oval Office. As the door was closed, Taylor handed the message to the President.

John Ketner's "Hot Dog!" and his broad smile were in vivid contrast to the grim look he wore only moments before.

"Ben, when did we get this?" the President asked.

"Just now. Colonel Sharp copied it down in the other room while you were meeting with the Soviet Ambassador. It came into Fort Bragg just minutes ago. At my request, I had Sharp call Donovan's executive officer and had him decipher it on the spot and call the contents to us here, using your secure phone in the other room."

The President could see that John Askins and his brother Bobby were perplexed by the conversation. He thrust the message at John Askins who read it silently. Askins handed it to Bob Ketner who yelled, "Holy Cow!" A spontaneous laugh erupted from the others.

John Ketner's face and his every word and action radiated a new-found confidence which replaced the pessimism which he had felt all morning. What a break —and just in the nick of time! He told the group of his meeting with the Soviet Ambassador and how he had to sit silently while a message from Premier Krenchev was read to him denouncing U.S. activities in Cuba, demanding an immediate halt to U.S. actions violating Cuba sovereignty, and finally, threatening severe measures if U.S. adventurism continued against Castro and the Cuban peoples.

The President said he had the greatest difficulty in restraining himself during the unpleasant session. At one time during the meeting, he asked the ambassador pointblank whether the Soviet Union had armed Cuba with intermediate range ballistic missles? The ambassador said that the arms being provided Castro were purely of a defensive nature which in no way threatened the security of the United States.

John Ketner informed the group that he had to make a concerted effort to constrain himself from reaching into his desk drawer and dragging out the photographs taken by the COBRA team. But that wasn't in his game plan and any such action would have been premature. He was setting up the Soviet Union for the grand strategy he had been thinking about for the past twenty-four hours. He wasn't going to risk his longer range goal simply to relish the ambassador's discomfiture.

At the President's request, Colonel Sharp briefed the group on Donovan's planned operation which was to take place the next evening. He also covered the arrangements for the evacuation of the COBRA team from Cuba via submarine immediately after the operation.

The President interrupted. "With or without the nuclear warhead, the team must come out tomorrow night. If the planned operation is a success, it will be another plus for the team, but I can't wait for another time and place to conduct a similar operation if for any reason the one tomorrow night does not go."

Leaning back in his chair and smiling, John Ketner began laying out his grand strategy to the group. At about the same time that the planned operation was to take place tomorrow night he would go on nationwide TV and announce that he had positive proof that Cuba was being armed with Soviet nuclear weapons and would demand an emergency meeting of the United Nations.

Before that forum, he would personally appear and present incontrovertible evidence to the assembled heads of state. He would request their attendance in the interest of world peace. He was going personally to call a number of Western leaders tomorrow and give them as much of his proposed strategy as possible and ask their support.

The President then asked Ben Taylor and John Askins to use every available resource and minute to try and deactivate the nuclear warhead as soon as possible in the event the team was successful in tomorrow night's operation.

If they were successful in deactivating the warhead so as not to pose a danger to delegates to the United Nations, he wanted it flown to New York and held in readiness as a final piece of evidence should the photographs fail to convince those in attendance that the Soviet Union had nuclear weapons in Cuba.

And, he added, he was thinking of a ruse to convince the Soviets that it was indeed one of their warheads. He explained to the group exactly what he had in mind and the importance of getting to the secret of how the bomb was activated.

Bud Sharp smiled. He had planned and executed a good many deception operations himself but none bolder or more imaginative than the one he had just heard the President explain. It would be a real triumph and he secretly prayed that Donovan's operation was a success.

"Ben, John—how good are the technical people you'd put to work examining the warhead? How long do you expect it might take to decipher how it works? I'd like to give you as much time as possible to get the job done. However, you must realize that when I propose an emergency meeting of the United Nations, I can't suggest a date further ahead then it would take to get some of the world's major leaders here. Tuesday or Wednesday would be the outside limit. Could it be done by then?"

John Askins replied that he would provide all the assistance he could, but his own agency had to look to the Defense Department for that kind of help themselves. He would defer to Ben Taylor.

"Ben, it looks like the whole ballgame depends on

you, as most of it has from the beginning." The President's comment reflected a pride in the manner in which the Defense Department had been responsive to his requests from the very beginning of the crisis.

"Mr. President, we'll have our best men standing by to start examining the weapon as soon as it can be made available. However, it may be that the National Security Agency personnel at Fort Meade might be the real key to the problem.

"You remember Dr. Bradley's briefing yesterday and his remarks that they didn't have enough time to study the problem of arming and disarming the weapon through what appeared to be a code system. Rather, they focused their entire effort on building a look alike replica. I have asked him and his group to stand by to assist us in breaking the code and the inner workings of the detonating system. You will recall his description of the small calculator-like device containing both numbers and letters and their suspicion that it was a coding device.

"However, to answer your question on how long it might take is impossible to answer now. Assuming Donovan and his men are successful and the submarine picks them up at the planned time of 0400 a.m. early Monday morning, we won't be able to get our hands on the warhead until late Monday night when the Grayback can get back to port in Florida. Then we must fly it to some location for thorough examination.

"I doubt that we could break the code or dismantle the firing mechanism in the twelve or so hours available if the United Nations were to meet on Tuesday. Even Wednesday noon would only give us an additional twenty-four hours. But we'll do our best."

"Ben, I must respect your judgment in these matters. Yet it seems to me we are losing almost a day while the weapon is enroute to Florida in the submarine. Isn't there some way we could get it back earlier?"

"Mr. President, let me pose that problem to Colonel Sharp. He's been involved in these operations for a long time and might have a suggestion."

"I do, Mr. President." Bud Sharp was confident as he continued. "Once the submarine has picked up the team and moved out to the open sea, we could pick up the weapon by a skyhook operation."

"A what?" The President exclaimed.

"A skyhook pickup." Bud Sharp went on to explain the Fulton system. That's how they had been getting the film out of Cuba containing the pictures that the COBRA team had been taking. A very simple and ingenious system, he explained. A small kit containing a plastic balloon, a nylon rope, a carrying or lifting case or suit, a small bottle of compressed gas, all packed into a waterproof container. The kit could be carried in by a team or parachuted to them later. When they had something to evacuate or move out, they requested a pickup by the air commandos at a specified time and place. Then the team would unpack the kit, tie the nylon rope to the small balloon, and using the container of gas, inflate the balloon. Upon being released, the balloon floated upward one hundred to one hundred fifty feet into the air trailing the nylon rope beneath it. Attached to the other end of the nylon rope on the ground was the package or person to be lifted out.

A specially configured U.S. Air Force C-130 aircraft mounted a set of long antenna arms protruding from the nose of the airplane. The pilot of the plane would fly into the nylon rope which would be caught by the protruding arms. Then by a device activated within the cockpit, a clamp would close, holding the rope tightly while the upper part of the rope and balloon would be automatically cut away and the balloon floated free.

The speed of the aircraft forced the rope underneath the fuselage of the plane. A crew member in the cabin using a fish-hook would bring the rope inside where it would be fastened to a pulley which would then be reeled in, bringing the trailing rope and the attached load into the cabin.

"That sounds like a Rube Goldberg device to me,"

the President said. "But can we rely on it to work? God, I'd hate to lose the weapon in the Atlantic Ocean after all the risk involved in acquiring it."

"It may be a Rube Goldberg device, but it works." Bud Sharp was now more convinced than ever that this was the solution. A flotation collar would be tied to the weapon before attaching it to the Fulton pickup system. In the unlikely event that the system failed, the weapon would fall back into the water where it would remain afloat until the submarine crew could recover it again.

"Finally, sir," Sharp continued, "we could have the C-130 fly directly to the site selected for the technical examination and save more time. For example, if the recovery of the COBRA team takes place as scheduled Monday morning at 0400 a.m. we could have the Fulton pickup made at 6:00 a.m. and have the C-130 here in Washington by 9 or 10 a.m. that same morning, some twelve hours earlier than if we waited for the submarine to dock in Florida, then airship the weapon to its destination. We have been using the Fulton system for several years and have never had a failure."

"You've convinced me," the President said. "Let's do it. Ben, any idea where you want to do the technical examination?"

"Sir, I'd recommend Fort Belvoir, just south of Washington. The Army's Research and Development Command has some great laboratories and the Fort has its own airfield where we could bring in the weapon without elaborate security precautions. Additionally, all the experts are nearby, NSA and CIA for breaking the code. And the foreign technology experts of the army and air force can be brought in here easily.

"I'd also plan on having Dr. Bradley and his associate, Dr. Bernie Dunsfield, join our experts for whatever assistance they could provide. I'm convinced they know as much about the weapon as anyone, and perhaps more by this time. Since speed is of essence, they might make the difference."

"Fine with me, Ben. One last thing, though," the President said. "Have Donovan and his group flown to New York City after they have had a night's rest. I want Colonel Donovan there in the event I have some questions which need to be answered before I go before the United Nations."

A knock at the door of the Oval Office interrupted the President. Ross Latimer poked his head through the door and said he thought the President would like to know that the Associated Press was carrying a news story out of Havana at this very moment announcing that Fidel Castro's noontime show had been temporarily postponed.

"Ross, we're about to break up here. Give me another minute or two till we're finished, then let's get together to go over an announcement we'll make at exactly noon today. Since Castro has the attention of the world's media, I think it would be criminal to have this void unfilled. I plan on doing exactly that." The President smiled at Ross and asked that he close the door.

"Gentlemen, Castro has handed me the perfect opportunity to make my own announcement. And I plan on taking full advantage of his generosity. Your briefings have provided me with everything I need at this time. I know you all have plenty to get done in connection with the final, and I hope, successful operation we've asked the COBRA team to undertake. Keep me advised of any developments. On your way out, please ask Ross Latimer to join me. And have a good day."

It was obvious to Bud Sharp as he filed out the Oval Office behind Ben Taylor that the President was back again in full charge of the Cuban crisis. His speech and every action reflected a newfound confidence which had not been apparent for days.

Chapter 15

CAPTAIN VLADIMIR PETROSKY sat stiffly erect on the passenger's side of his Russian built jeep as he ordered his driver to move out. Exactly 8:00 p.m. He had made his reputation in the Soviet rocket forces for being punctual and the truck convoy tonight was to be no exception. Delivering nuclear warheads was no big thing. After all, he had been doing it the past several months. First to one site; then to another, as the Soviet and Cuban army troops readied the sites for Soviet intermediate range ballistic missiles.

He glanced back to see the truck carrying the warhead was fifty yards distant, followed by another jeep with two security guards, in addition to the Cuban lieutenant riding as tail security on the column. At one time today, his superior, Major Nicholas Chevenko had considered adding additional security to the column but finally gave up when he found that most of his men had taken Sunday liberty and gone off to Havana for the day.

The weekend in particular had been hectic. Yesterday he had orders to help his Cuban counterpart get out the local populace to cheer a Cuban army patrol that had captured an American spy. Then later, as suddenly as the requirement had been placed on him, it was cancelled without explanation. Typical Cuban mentality, he thought. They couldn't make up their minds what they wanted done or when.

Yet some Cubans intrigued him. Late that afternoon he had gone to Maria Rodriguez's apartment for dinner and had a wonderful meal. For the past month, he had been seeing her and finally, she had begun to respond to his advances. The afternoon had gone extremely well. Maria had been especially receptive to his kisses and caresses. Only the press of time to meet his convoy departure schedule had prevented him from taking her all the way. He knew that she wanted that too. She as much as promised him that next time she had an intimate dinner for two, she wanted to schedule his work so that he wouldn't have to run off so early.

He had really become fond of Maria. She was so interested in everything he did. She often came down to his compound and had him show her around and tell her how things worked.

Russian girls weren't like that at all. They expressed no interest in the work the men did in the army. Boring to them, they had told him. They were interested in needlepoint, babies, and listening to Western music on the Voice of America when they knew a Soviet agent wasn't around to report them.

But Maria was different. Even small things intrigued her. Like the knots he used to tie tarpaulins to the trucks.

Peculiar to Russia, he told her. She had him show her how clever he was. Tying knots that he could undo in a jiffy while others had to spend valuable time trying to undo them.

Then her final act of kindness to him tonight. As they left her apartment, she took a bag and filled it full of ice and going to the refrigerator, filled it with goodies. A minute or two before he ordered the departure of the convoy, she shared her surprise with him and his men. Ice cream bars covered with that heavy Swiss chocolate. His favorite, and he knew his men were also appreciative of her kindness.

She gave each man two bars and he talked her out of

an extra one when she had four left over. She also gave his driver an extra one. The Cuban lieutenant and his driver bringing up the rear jeep were the recipients of the last two.

He could hardly wait until he got back to see her again. She appreciated his attention and had told him so. Now it was his turn to show her what a lover he was. He knew he wouldn't fail on that score. He had been complimented too many times by the girls he had been dating since his arrival in Cuba months ago. But not one attracted him as much as Maria. For one thing, she had resisted every one of his demands for the past month and only in the last week had he been able to overcome her shyness, kiss her passionately and often, and caress her beautifully shaped breasts. The other girls he had been going with had usually fallen into his arms after the first kiss on their very first date. But Maria was different and that made him happy.

The headlights on his jeep outlined the twisting road ahead. On the right side nothing but heavy, impassable jungle; on the other, a cleared sugar cane field. The heavy rains of the past twenty-four hours left pools of water standing in the ditches on each side of the road. The tropical storm which had gripped the area for several days had blown over. Tonight was clear and calm.

A slight twinge in his stomach brought his mind back to Maria's dinner party. Too much wine and rum. That Cuban rum in particular was strong and he had drunk his share. He soon had an urge to go but decided he'd hold it until they got to the missile site only four or five miles further up the road.

In the far distance, he saw the faint outline of a star. He watched it for a moment before realizing it was coming directly toward him. Suddenly it dawned on him. Was it one of those American spy planes he had been warned about? If so, his orders were to turn off the headlights on his vehicle and come to a complete stop and remain that way for at least five minutes to make sure other spy planes were not in the area.

He glanced at his watch—thirty minutes after eight. Right on schedule. He looked again at the oncoming light and heard the whining noise of a jet engine. He ordered his driver to halt the vehicle and turn off the lights. The other vehicles followed suit almost immediately. They had been briefed exactly what to do in the event of an American spy plane coming overhead. Follow the actions of the lead vehicle.

The swish of the jet overhead scared Captain Petrosky. Not over fifty feet directly over his position. Had the pilot detected the convoy? He hoped not.

Almost at the same time the plane went overhead he knew he could no longer hold his urge to hit the nearest outdoor privy. With a sudden jump from his jeep, he headed for the open sugar cane field, telling his driver he had to go.

The driver too had been having a queasy feeling for the past minute or two but the swish of the airplane overhead was too much for him. He was scared. He too jumped from the vehicle and with one hand unfastened his belt while with the other, he slipped his trousers down as fast as he could—and just in time.

As Captain Petrosky squatted on the rain-drenched field, he was amazed to see one man after another piling out of their vehicles and almost in unison, drop their breeches and take up a squatting position. God, he murmured to himself, if a single airplane can frighten his men so much that they had to crap, what the hell would happen if they got shot at. He'd have to institute a new program to expose his men to more realistic training which would better condition them to the sound and sight of battle.

While still squatting in his field privy, another jet swished overhead. He looked up at the plane and swore that the cockpit was illuminated and the young face of the American pilot was grinning at him. Damn, he'd really have to get a hold of himself. He was seeing things he knew were impossible.

It was a full ten to fifteen minutes later that he was able to round up the last of his drivers and security guards from the sugarcane field and get the convoy underway again. Fortunately, he thought, the planes perhaps took some pictures but had not fired at them. If they had been brought under fire, he could truthfully report to his superiors that his troops had been caught with their pants down. As it was, he could explain the ten or fifteen minute delayed arrival because of the condition of the roads brought on by the tropical storm a few days ago.

He checked the truck carrying the weapon and found everything in order. The canvas was intact and the covering at the rear was still tied securely with those fancy knots of his.

The COBRA team was in position. Mike Donovan, Marc Mayberry and Tiger Tangier occupied the center position picked out earlier by Dagger. Danny Thompson and Roger Landsdale were in the jungle about a hundred yards further up the road. The baby, as they had christened the replica weapon, was with Donovan's group. Marc Mayberry and Tiger Tangier had on the canvas carrying-case and the weapon was slung between them ready to move out on a moment's notice.

The last two days had been hectic. Going over every detail of the plan, rehearsing on untying and tying knots on a canvas flap which Maria had made for them, similar to the one on the truck which carried the nuclear warhead.

A route reconnaissance to their first and second rallying points was made, should any unforeseen event require their immediate withdrawal and possible separation. Then the incredible speed at which they had to work. Eight minutes and two seconds from outset to first relief, according to the report he had on the tests run at Fort Bragg. He planned a maximum of seven minutes for the operation. He assigned Tiger Tangier the job of timing the operation. Roger Landsdale was to do the same for him and Danny Thompson. After seven minutes had elapsed, they were to withdraw regardless of the state of operation.

Foolish to take chances at this late date. If one of the Cuban or Russian soldiers had a cast-iron stomach, maybe seven minutes was timing it too close, but dammit, he had to run some risk. After all, this wasn't an organization day footrace. It was for real.

Maria was sad as she departed earlier in the day for the village and her rendezvous with Captain Petrosky, the local Russian commander. Fortunately, the box containing the liquid laxative was light. For that, she was thankful. She had made their dinner engagement as late as possible to avoid, as she put it, any possibility they would have enough time after dinner to do much frolicking. She detested the man, she had told the COBRA Team, but she was willing to contribute her all if it was for the good of the team and might eventually lead to Castro's downfall.

She lived for the day that Cuba would again be free. Then she'd show the team Havana in all its glory and the real beauty of Cuba which had been brushed aside by the incessant Communist demands for work, party meetings, five year goals, and double sugar production. But she was really sad because her American friends would be leaving that night.

She had appreciated the offer that Dagger had made earlier to evacuate her brother along with the team later that night. She felt she could do more for the eventual return of Cuba to a freedom-loving democracy as an American agent in Cuba, then join the already overpopulated Cubans in exile in Miami.

Reluctantly, Dagger had agreed with that assessment but told her that if she ever changed her mind, to send a message to her contact requesting evacuation. He would personally make sure it was done. At one of their few moments alone that day, Dagger had asked Maria why she had continued to avoid him, except for official discussions, since the first time they had made love on the rocks many months ago. She refused to answer. He insisted.

Finally, she told him that she would tell him early the next morning as she saw the group off at the coast to return to the submarine. She reminded him that her last act was to proceed from the village after the departure of the convoy and act as the reception party for the SEAL team members coming ashore to help the COBRA Team move the weapon out to sea and to the sub.

Mike Donovan had been nervous before during other operations, but nothing like tonight. Less than six hours before leaving Cuba forever, he hoped, and still sitting deep in the jungle waiting to pull off an operation which was beyond belief.

Everything had to work exactly as scheduled. The convoy depart on time. The delivery of the ice cream bars to all of the men, and that none were allergic to eating chocolate-covered ice cream bars, with laxative added. He grinned in the dark. However, in all of his world travels he had never met a soldier who wouldn't eat ice cream, day or night, winter or summer. He remembered the cold wintry days in Korea and how ice cream delivered through the courtesy of the American Red Cross donut dollies was the most popular item they provided, save one.

Then the tactical air command reconnaissance flights. He had specified the exact time, direction of flight and altitude which he wanted them to fly that night.

Back at Langley, they were wondering what the hell possessed the Joint Chiefs of Staff to order such missions flown. Unnecessary risk of pilot and plane, their commander had wired back. Finally, the Air Force Chief of Staff had gotten on the phone and reiterated the importance of the flight going exactly as scheduled in the direction prescribed, and they had better have the timing down perfect or he'd have somebody's ass the next morning.

General McSweeny shook his head as he issued the order. Had they all gone nuts in Washington, including his own chief of staff? Maybe one day Jerry Maxwell would explain to him some of the screwy orders he had been receiving lately from the air staff. They often bordered on the ludicrous. Yet Jerry Maxwell personally confirmed each one when he had called.

Last month, for example, he had to use some of his best fighter planes to parachute small pacakges to specified areas of Cuba. No explanation, just parachute the damn stuff in at this time, at this place, when the pilot sees this kind of light on the ground.

Then these stupid low level runs over certain roads at night. Like a dry strafing run. But don't shoot back if fired on. Get the hell out of the area. God, what had happened to the air force he had known so well? Order, logic, well-planned mission.

Now, all sudden orders. Do this, do that. Why, he asked? "I'll tell you later," he was told. But still no explanation, and he doubted if he would ever get one. The high altitude reconnaissance flights, he could understand and support. Low level checkouts of suspected missile sites also made sense. But these others. They had slipped a cog somewhere. Oh well, what the hell. He'd be retiring soon and maybe his successor could make some sense of it all.

It seemed to him that perhaps an old army groundpounder was back in charge of air force business, like the days of old when the Army Air Corps had to fight for everything they got because the ground-pounders or current heads who were chiefs of staff in those days didn't understand air power and more than that, didn't know how to use it. It took the air power advocates twenty years to break away from that yoke around their neck. Was there any chance they were going back to it?

If so, retirement to him looked that much more inviting.

The set of headlights far down the road caught the attention of the COBRA Team at the same time. Mike Donovan looked at his watch. 8:24. Right on target.

God, if this continued, the convoy ought to be at his immediate front at the time that the tac air fighter should be zooming across. He complimented himself on computing the road march speed of the convoy and determining their precise position at the exact time he wanted the convoy halted.

When and if this operation was pulled off and they got back to the States intact, he was going to personally ask General Taylor to arrange an invitation for him to address the students at the Army's Command and General Staff College at Fort Leavenworth, Kansas, on the importance and timing of road marches in the conduct of military operations.

He remembered only too well how he and his fellow students used to bitch about the endless exercises they had to go through in planning road marches to the precise minute, when he attended the college. At the time, such training made very little sense to him but the instructors kept drilling home the point. Success on the battlefield depended on such precise planning. Limited roads, they went on to say, precluded all units from moving their motor convoys at a time of their choosing.

Planning to clear a critical intersection at a certain time would let enough convoys move without interruption across the main roads. Patton's famous movement of his Third Army during the Battle of the Bulge during World War II was cited as the classic case on the importance of accurately determining the movement of convoys in battle.

While his little operation tonight did not involve a mass movement, he doubted any convoy movement in military history would be nearly so important as to timing than the one he hoped would begin to unfold in just a few minutes. And on top of it, he thought, what other convoy in military history had depended on a small amount of liquid, federal stock number 6505-00-045-7786 to ensure its success? He was sure there was none, and by God, he wanted to tell those students at Leavenworth that no detail was too small to be considered.

Mike Donovan was the first to hear the sound of the jet.

He looked sharply to his right and in the distance, he could see the wing lights of the approaching plane. The lead jeep of the convoy had just gone by his position when the column of vehicles suddenly stopped and all headlights were extinguished. At about the same time, the jet swished by, close overhead. Absolutely perfect, he muttered to himself.

Then he, Marc Mayberry, and Tiger Tangier watched as one soldier after another piled off their vehicles and headed for the cane field across the road. What timing! The big truck carrying the nuclear warhead was less than twenty feet to his left front.

Motioning Marc and Tiger to follow, he cautiously spread the last remaining jungle cover and stepped out at a crouch. Moving silently to the truck, Marc quickly untied the ropes holding the canvas cover to the body of the truck. Some twenty feet away, Mike Donovan could see three soldiers squatting down and moaning, completely oblivious to what was taking place in the truck they had just left in a hurry.

Silently, Marc and Tangier, using the master keys provided by the CIA, unlocked the padlocks and lifted the lid of the coffin-looking box they found in the center of the truck bed. Then they both reached in and lifted the warhead out of its container and placed it on the floor.

Rapidly, they took their look-alike replica and inserted it into the box in the same position that they had found the real McCoy. They closed the lid, replaced the latch and snapped the padlocks. Placing the weapon in the canvas container, they moved quietly out of the rear door of the truck and, at a crouch, back into the jungle.

Dagger Donovan waited until Marc Mayberry cleared the truck before he began tying the canvas flap back to the truck bed. Was he ever glad that Maria had made them practice tying knots in the dark of night! His fingers nimbly tied each knot, using the peculiar style that Maria had taught them after Captain Petrosky had so kindly shown her how.

With a final tug to check his work, Dagger slipped into the jungle and joined Marc and Tangier for the long march to the rendezvous point and freedom. In only minutes, Roger Landsdale and Danny Thompson fell in beside them.

They had moved several hundred yards deeper into the jungle when they heard the convoy's motors rev up, and start moving. Almost as if a ritual, each member of the team gave each other a fraternal slap on the ass to signify their satisfaction at how things were going.

An hour later, they stopped temporarily at a jungle clearing to put the newly acquired weapon in the same styrofoam box which had been used to airdrop the replica. Then, satisfied that they had removed all evidence of the COBRA Team ever having been in Cuba, they set off for Site F. There they would rendezvous with Maria and the Navy SEALS whom Maria would signal ashore with their rubber boats in tow to assist the COBRA Team in getting out to the submarine, and freedom.

It was three-thirty in the morning when the COBRA Team finally arrived and after a brief exchange of recognition signals joined Maria and the SEALS on the water's edge. Quickly wrapping the boxed weapon in waterproof bags and donning their scuba gear, the team was ready to shove off.

Maria kissed each one of the COBRA Team as she bid them farewell. She waited until last for Dagger. She shook his hand and handed him an envelope, telling him that he should read it after he got back on board the submarine. It would explain her attitude toward him for the past several months. Mike tucked the envelope inside his waterproof bag before joining the rest of the team in the water.

The water was refreshing as Mike Donovan joined the others aboard the rubber boats. Silently, they paddled out to sea.

In what Dagger estimated as about thirty minutes the SEALS halted the boat and dived overboard. In a matter of minutes they surfaced, trailing a rope behind them. They attached the end of the trailing rope to the boats, carefully fastened straps around the box containing the weapon and fixed a snap-link connecting the box to the rope now drifting lazily in the water.

Then Danny Thompson and Tiger Tangier lifted the box over the water's edge where a SEAL grabbed each end and sank silently into the water with the box between them. Minutes later they surfaced again and motioned the team to follow them down, hand over hand, along the rope.

Mike Donovan was the last to go. He looked back at the Cuban coastline now far in the distance. Dawn was about to break and the tree-lined coast looked like an island paradise over the rippling water. He wondered what the future held for Maria, and the Cuban people she loved so much. As Mike entered the Lock Out, he saw in the dim light overhead the shadowy outline of a SEAL pulling at the rope. Finally, he saw the capsized rubber boats being pulled inside, followed by the other SEAL. Then the Lock Out door was closed and the lever placed in lock position. His eyes were now accustomed to the dim light showing through the water overhead and he saw his team and the two SEALS huddled close together.

Mike reflected back on the use of the rope. Army Green Berets prided themselves on being SCUBA trained, but several years ago Commander Terry who commanded the SEAL team almost lost one of the Green Berets at sea. SEALS can swim for hours out to sea and by using underwater compasses and watches, can locate themselves within a fanthom or two of a submerged submarine.

In a training exercise with army Green Berets and navy SEALS, one of the more aggressive Berets insisted he could navigate as well as any SEAL and find the submarine himself. But he couldn't, and after Commander Terry and his men had spent several hours locating one frightened Beret, they decided that henceforth they would find the sub and trail a rope from the Lock Out entrance to the surface which the Green Berets could follow. It was a spur of the moment decision by Terry to provide the field expedient; however, its popularity was so great with the Berets that they insisted on it thereafter.

The sudden swish of air in the Lock Out told Donovan that the pumps had been turned on. In less than a minute, the water had been forced out and the Lock Out became just another room on the Grayback. The clanking of the sea door at Donovan's back was a welcome sound.

As it opened, he saw the skipper of the sub, Jim Knowles, beckoning him to come inside and tempting him with an ice cold can of Coors beer. As each member of the team entered the sub, Jim Knowles gave each one a can of the cold brew and a pat on the back.

Mike Donovan appreciated the small token of affection, fully realizing that Knowles was putting his command of the ship on the line by having beer aboard. But those who didn't know, wouldn't know. Of that he was sure.

While having steak and eggs in the wardroom, Jim handed Dagger two messages. The first one from General Ben Taylor passing on the congratulations of the highest national authority as well as his own for the outstanding professional manner in which the operation was conducted. However, the second paragraph really irked him. It read: "Until the President has appeared before the United Nations on Wednesday, you and members of your team will be kept in isolation and have no contact with others except in the pursuit of official business."

He passed the message to the other members of the team while he read the second one Jim Knowles had handed him. "Upon debarking tonight, get a good night's rest and be prepared to depart for New York City by noon tomorrow. The remainder of the team will accompany you. Airlift has been arranged. Further instructions as to your duties in New York will be forthcoming." Signed Taylor.

Dammit, spend three months in Godforsaken Cuba and then be put into isolation again here in the United States, he muttered under his breath.

"What's the matter, Dagger?" Tiger Tangier had sensed that something had upset him.

Dagger handed him the message. The other team members frowned and grimaced as the full meaning of the order registered on them.

"Boy, that's some gratitude," remarked Roger Landsdale. "After busting our ass and beating the bushes for months, I can't even call my honey chile in Fatalburg that I'll be seeing her soon."

It finally dawned on Jim Knowles that Dagger and the team had no idea of the great events which had taken place in the last forty-eight hours.

He explained the big buildup that had been trumpeted to take place in Havana at noon Saturday, then a sudden postponement, followed by the President's dramatic appearance on nationwide TV last night stating he had positive proof of Soviet nuclear weapons being emplaced in Cuba and he would lay it all out at an emergency meeting of the United Nations on Wednesday.

No doubt the trip Donovan and his men were taking to New York was in some way connected to the

President's appearance that day, but damned if he knew how. He then informed the team that at 5:45 a.m., they would be surfacing to have an air commando plane recover the package the team had brought on board. They were going to use the Fulton skyhook and he and his men had been reading every damn technical manual they could find to see how the thing was done. Sharp had two kits flown down to him the day before yesterday telling him to put them on board but not a damn word on how to employ them. And they never before had used the system. He hoped that perhaps one of Dagger's men knew something about that odd-looking piece of equipment.

"Jim," Dagger began, "since you swabbies have finally admitted there is something you know nothing about, we'll give you a hand. Give Danny Thompson and Tiger Tangier two minutes after you surface and they will have the rig all set up."

"Thank God!" Jim exclaimed. "I had orders that this was the most important operation this ship might ever have to execute and the CNO said that it had better be perfect, or else. I understand that kind of order, I'll have you know."

Mike Donovan and the COBRA Team stood alongside Jim Knowles on the deck of the Grayback watching the approaching C-130 with its Fulton skyhook claws fully extended.

What a strange-looking sight. As the plane flew into the rope, he saw Bunson Burner poke his head out of the side window and wave. At almost the same time, the rope became taut and the prized package they had brought out of Cuba was swished into the air with the flotation collar swinging wildly below. With a final wave to the departing aircraft, they descended into the hull of the submarine which submerged minutes later and headed north to port in Florida.

Quick Draw reeled in the container at the end of the

Chapter 16

GENERAL BYRON PETERSON was getting perturbed. His voice changed from a request to a command as he talked to Major General Charles Somerson, the Commanding General of the Engineer Center at Fort Belvoir, on the telephone.

"Charles, for the last time, I want you to clear out the best laboratory building you have in the Research and Development Command at Belvoir and turn it over to a task group we are going to put out there within the hour. Colonel Bud Sharp of the Joint Staff is on the way there now and will be checking into your headquarters by 7:00 a.m. He will be in complete charge of letting personnel in and out of the laboratory until our special project is completed. It will be off limits to your personnel. Sharp has a list of personnel who will be admitted to the area without question. He will also need a covered truck or van, a small one will do, together with two military policemen, who will pick up a load of material at your airfield from a C-130 which will be arriving there about nine this morning."

"But General Peterson, you must understand that the building you want is within a special access area. We have a lot of Top Secret material we're working on in the lab and I can't permit personnel to enter the facility until I have received verification of their Top Secret clearances and full justification for their visit through security channels. You know that Building 572 contains some of the most sensitive equipment in the entire army."

"Charles, do you want to be the Chief of Engineers one day?"

"You know I do."

"Then dammit, follow my orders. I'm certifying here and now that the personnel Colonel Sharp will grant access to the building are properly cleared and have a need to know. And, remember, all of your employees out of the building by eight. Thereafter, personnel entering or leaving the building will be controlled by Sharp."

"Yes, sir, I understand." As General Somerson acknowledged his orders, he heard the click of a disconnected line as the Army Chief of Staff hung up on him.

For over thirty years, he had drilled into him the importance of security and his responsibilities as a commander of never permitting an individual into a classified facility without first authenticating that the individual had a current security clearance and then only after absolute assurance of a need to know.

Now the Army Chief of Staff himself had as much as ordered him to violate those orders. To top it all off, a colonel, not him, would be calling the shots as to who entered and left the building.

And the final irony of all. He was to provide bunks, sheets, blankets, and the food and coffee the group might want, when they wanted it, around the clock. If he hand't set his sights on being Chief of Engineers soon after graduating at the head of his class at West Point, he'd chuck it all. But that assignment was the ultimate goal of every engineer officer in the army and, by God, he was going to reach that plateau even though he had to occasionally put up with the idiosyncrasies of the top brass. He wouldn't let the assorted bastards get him down.

The chief's job was too damn important to forego.

After all, as the Chief Engineer of the Army, he also would be the nation's foremost builder of dams, locks and other prized projects of the Congress. If he could impress enough congressmen of his superb ability as an engineer, they might request, hell, demand, that he be made the Chief of Staff of the entire army. Then, by God, he'd show the brass how to run things. They would follow published directives on security procedures, or else.

Colonel Max Devlin, General Somerson's chief of staff, was amused. The old man getting all excited about turning over one of his labs to a task group for a couple of days and having the post provide whatever support they needed. No big deal. He told the old man he'd have the building cleared by eight and the rest of the staff would take care of the housekeeping details.

But Somerson's continued harangue about his prerogatives as a senior commander was old hat to him. He put up with it day and night. Frankly, as he had told his staff, let the old man roar and get it off his chest, but get with the program, whatever it is and get it done. He was happy that come next June, he'd hang it up. He'd put up with this sort of chicken shit too damn long. Completing thirty years of service and retirement to Florida next summer was his number one priority. Until then, he'd keep his nose clean and keep dreaming his dreams of a houseboat on the St. James River and lying on deck while dangling his fishing line overboard.

He tried to settle the old man down by telling him to relax and he'd resolve any problem. He knew Sharp, and could handle him easily. He had done so before when he was an upperclassman and Sharp was a plebe at West Point. Sharp had learned then who his superior was and throughout their service, Sharp had often remarked that he owed much of his early training to Devlin's handling of plebes—discipline, adherence to orders, and their rapid execution.

Leadership was his forte, and the cadets had respected

him for instilling in them those attributes which all knew made the officer corps an effective fighting force, and provided the senior leadership to the nation's armed forces.

"Bud, here is the list of personnel who will be assembled at Belvoir to conduct the technical examination." As General Taylor handed Colonel Bud Sharp a single piece of paper, he continued. "The Army Chief of Staff has cleared the use of their major lab building for this purpose. I want you to get out there, get the team organized and meet the C-130 when it arrives at Davison Army Airfield. Fort Belvoir will provide a truck or van to move the weapon from the airfield to the lab building. Also, two military policemen as security.

"I've designated Colonel Jamie Rohrbach of the Air Force's Foreign Technology Division as head of the overall team. However, Dr. Wendy Overby of NSA will be the principal investigator in breaking the warhead's code. Dr. Jim McDonald of CIA, their chief cryptologist, will look out for their interests.

"I've also asked Dr. Joe Bradley and Dr. Bernie Dunsfield of McLean to lend a hand. The President was very impressed with the work they did on building the replica and has approved their continued participation. As soon as all the personnel have arrived, give them a short briefing on the importance of expediting the examination. We've got thirty-six hours to defuse the thing to meet the President's deadline in the event he needs it in New York on Wednesday." He paused, glancing at his notes. "Tell the group that they will be confined until they come up with the answers. Belvoir has been instructed to provide cots and food so the activity can go on around the clock. Don't let the group in on how we acquired the weapon. If they get too inquisitive, tell them we got it from a friend. And finally, I understand Merv Collins will take a photograph of the weapon for the President's use in his briefing at the UN. After you have things well organized at Belvoir, get back here. We have plenty else to do to get ready for the Wednesday showdown in New York."

"Yes, sir, General. I'll give you a call if we run into any problems." Bud Sharp saluted sharply as he left the office of the Chairman of the Joint Chiefs of Staff. He walked rapidly to South Parking, got into his Pinto, and headed south on the Jefferson Davis Highway.

He was surprised at the reception he received from General Somerson. Formal, almost cold, when he reported in to take over temporary use of the building.

It was obvious that Somerson was expecting him but what Sharp was not prepared for was the general's almost total hostility as he went over a list of things needed in the way of support. He was frankly amazed. The Army Chief of Staff had called him earlier that morning stating that General Somerson had been advised of the immediate need for the lab and had been assured that Fort Belvoir was prepared to extend the courtesies of the post. Any support needed would be made available promptly.

Instead of that kind of reception, Somerson was plainly upset by the last minute requirement to reshuffle his personnel and insufficient time to remove classified materials from the building. He was outspoken in his criticism of the lack of consideration shown a commander of a major military installation. However, he had been assured it was important by the Army Chief of Staff and would comply with any reasonable request from Sharp.

When Sharp told him there was no general officer in the group, in response to a question from General Somerson as to who the senior flag rank would be, he became even more discourteous. Bud Sharp was happy to have the initial meeting end and meet Colonel Max Devlin, who would take over responsibility of the building. Time was of the essence. Members of the task group were to report at 8:00 a.m. It was already 7:40.

After exchanging a few pleasantries and promising

they had better get together for lunch soon, Max Devlin showed Bud Sharp around the laboratory facilities. He was proud of what they had done to get the latest testing equipment. The scientists who manned the lab were the best in the business, according to Devlin.

Bud Sharp was impressed. It was a beauty of a setup. Every conceivable testing instrument seemed to be in evidence everywhere. Work benches and lathes filled the far end of the building. Giant hoists and cranes dangled from the center of the ceiling. Small attractive offices were located near the front entrance. Colonel Devlin pointed out the stacks of cots, blankets, and sheets which his staff had delivered earlier that morning. He recognized the importance of the security procedures that Sharp had to follow.

Accordingly, he informed Sharp that he had set aside a small room as a temporary coffee and food bar which he guaranteed would be kept well stocked. It had an entrance door from the building's outside as well as an interior door to the main lab. He gave Sharp a set of keys to the inner door which he suggested be kept locked. His own troops would have a key to the outer door which would be used to replenish food stocks and keep the coffee hot.

He pointed out a yellow pad on a far table. All Sharp had to do was to write down what was needed and when. He'd see that it was provided.

Finally, he gave Sharp his office and home telephone numbers. Call him day or night if any problems arose. He'd take care of them. He remarked that the enclosed van was standing by at Davison Army Airfield and the driver had instructions to take whatever orders Sharp gave him. A two-man MP patrol, jeep mounted, he went on to say, was also at Davison for Sharp's use.

"Max, the arrangements are everything we need," Sharp said, and smiled. "Many thanks. And I hope not to impose on your hospitality any more than necessary. Now, if you will excuse me, I'll stay here and meet the task group members as they arrive." Max saluted sharply, did a prescribed field manual about-face, and rode off in a staff car.

Bud Sharp checked each person into the building as they arrived. Twelve in all. Colonel Jamie Rohrback had two of his civilian scientists in tow. Colonel James Arnett, the Chief of the Army's Foreign Science and Technology Center had Dr. Rufus Hallsford with him. Bud knew him as one of the nation's foremost weapons experts. The third member was Lieutenant Colonel Marcell Halifax of the Army's Harry Diamond Labs who was reputed to be the most knowledgeable individual in the armed forces on fuses and fusing systems.

Dr. Wendy Overby of the National Security Agency was accompanied by Mr. Leslie Overstreet. Dr. Overby informed Bud as she arrived that perhaps she might find it necessary to bring down one other person, a computer specialist. She wasn't sure yet as she and Leslie had never been faced with a problem they hadn't been able to solve, working together.

She had been informed that this was a crash job and would put her heart and soul into it, but she didn't understand why a Dr. Bradley and a Dr. Dunsfield, neither one of whom she knew, had been ordered to assist her. However, General Thompson, the Chief of NSA, had told her that they were to be full participants in the program and she had accepted that on the condition that if events proved that she and Leslie didn't need any help, she'd ask they be disassociated from the project.

After all, she told Sharp, NSA was in the code-breaking business and she doubted any civilian consultants had the background or experience to make much of a contribution.

Bud thanked her for her comments and remarked that he hoped she would be pleasantly surprised with the knowledge and background Drs. Bradley and Dunsfield would bring to the project.

He watched as she walked into the building, with

Leslie at her side. They were an odd-looking pair. Dr. Overby was thirtyish, redheaded, well built and attractive. Leslie Overstreet was about five four, a bit overweight, baby-faced, with just the beginning of a bald spot centered in the middle of his well-groomed hair. Not over twenty-eight or twenty-nine at the most. His dark, thick-lensed glasses, resting on an oversized nose, and well-manicured goatee made Bud Sharp grimace. He was used to neatly dressed, close cropped hair, military types. Some of the civilian oddballs got to him at times.

Dr. Jim McDonald and Merv Collins represented CIA. They arrived simultaneously with Drs. Bradley and Dunsfield. He followed them into the building after instructing the military policeman on duty at the door that no one further would be admitted without his personal approval.

Bud Sharp chose his words carefully. "You have been brought here to examine a Soviet nuclear warhead which we have had the good fortune to have fall into our hands." A murmur of excitement was evident immediately. "As far as we know, it is actively armed so I warn you to exercise extreme caution during your examination. Our immediate task is to defuse it. I repeat, our immediate task is to defuse it. Within thirty-six hours, if possible."

Bud Sharp looked at the distinguished group of scientists sitting before him. All were listening attentively except Leslie Overstreet. He was busily engaged in whispering in the ear of Dr. Wendy Overby who kept nodding her head as if in agreement with whatever he was saying.

Sharp continued. "We are confident that the weapon has a built-in coding device. Dr. Overby, we are looking to you and your associates to break the code as soon as possible." Bud Sharp smiled.

At the mention of her name, Dr. Overby with a wave of her left hand brushed away Leslie Overstreet's conversation and said, "Colonel Sharp, I promise you that it will be done, and long before the thirty-six hours you have alloted us. In fact, Leslie and I have plans for this evening and we don't intend to let a Soviet code keep us from enjoying the affair we have scheduled for tonight."

As she mentioned the word "affair" the others broke out laughing. Realizing her poor choice of words, she came right back. "If you gentlemen would get your minds out of the gutter, you would know that I did not intend to connote a meaning of affair as you visualize it. There are affairs of an artistic nature and of the type to which I was making reference."

"Thank you for that explanation, Dr. Overby." Bud Sharp's remark brought forth another round of laughter. Bud looked at her. She was blushing and biting her lower lip. He regained the group's attention. "Colonel Jamie Rohrbach will be in overall charge of the technical examination of the weapon. Please refer any technical questions to him. Matters dealing with your comfort or support should be directed to me. Merv Collins and I will be leaving here in a few minutes and will return with the weapon within the hour. In the meanwhile, I've asked Dr. Bradley to describe the weapon to you and what we already know about it technically. I have provided him some photographs to use in briefing the warhead's characteristics until we return with the actual weapon for your detailed examination. Dr. Bradley, would you take over until I return?"

Bud Sharp was pleased that he had called Dr. Bradley early that morning asking him to brief the group. It would save time. He had handed him a few of the photographs that he had used earlier and suggested the group be given the same technical details he had briefed to the JCS the week before, without, however, divulging any details on the replica weapon.

Bud Sharp and Merv Collins arrived at Davison Army Airfield at the same time Bunson Burner Cochrane taxied the big C-130 to the ramp. Motioning the waiting van to follow, they moved out to the clamshell doors which had already been opened. Quick Draw assisted Bud and Merv in loading the styrofoam box into the body of the van. Bunson Burner said he wanted a few words in private with Bud Sharp. "Later, Bunson," said Bud Sharp. "Get some rest and I'll get back to you later today."

Joe Bradley had taken over for Bud Sharp and was waiting for Bernie Dunsfield to get the vu-graph machine set up. He remarked to the group that he and Dr. Dunsfield were happy to be back again working with old friends. They knew them all, with the exception of Dr. Overby and Leslie Overstreet, from previous associations.

When the first vu-graph was flashed onto the screen, he began describing what was known of the weapon, to be confirmed, he added, by the detailed examination about to take place. He was completing his final remarks when Bud Sharp and Merv Collins walked into the room carrying the styrofoam box.

Joe Bradley did a double-take. It was the same styrofoam box they had provided to house the replica weapon they had built. He watched eagerly as Merv Collins and Bud Sharp removed the lid and lifted the weapon from the container.

"Hell, it's the same weapon we built last week," he muttered under his breath. He walked over to take a closer look. Identical in every respect. Then he realized for the first time that there was a difference.

The small rectangular glass cover was a deeper red and a skull and crossbones were barely visible at the very top of the glass. Underneath appeared to be lettering of some type, but too indistinct to make out. Otherwise, the weapon was an exact duplicate of the one they so painstakingly manufactured less than a week before. He wondered what the relationship was to the one they had built and the real McCoy before them. To say the least, it was intriguing.

Merv Collins and Bud Sharp lifted the weapon and placed it on the large table which Jamie Rohrbach had pushed to the center of the group. Then like a drill sergeant, Jamie assigned each of them specific duties.

Jim Arnett and Rufus Hallsford would work with his two scientists in examining the warhead for size, weight, function, and yield. Marcell Halifax would lead a group to analyze the fusing mechanism. Dr. Overby would head the decoding effort with Jim McDonald and Overstreet assisting. Drs. Bradley and Dunsfield would be working with all the groups. He and Merv Collins would be linebackers and provide any help they could while concentrating on writing the technical evaluation as it was being produced.

"Let's get at it," he said, ending his instructions by warning them all again that as far as he knew, it was an armed nuclear weapon and they had better treat it that way until or unless they found out otherwise.

Bud Sharp left for the Pentagon after making sure that Merv Collins would take care of any support the group might need during his absence.

Jamie Rohrbach watched the various groups in animated conversation as they gathered around tables assigned as their working areas. One individual after another would walk over to the weapon, look at it carefully, then return to his group and renew the discussion.

Diagrams began appearing on the blackboards beside each working group table. At times, conversations became intense and wailing and flaying of arms to emphasize a point was common.

Rufus Hallsford made the first breakthrough. Using a spectro analysis technique, he found that the writing below the skull and crossbones in the rectangular glass-covered container was a warning.

He demonstrated how it worked. Much like a trouble light indicator in an automobile or airplane, he explained. A malfunction would illuminate a bulb which in turn would flash a warning signal. Using a small flat-headed flashlight, he pointed it into one side of the rectangular glass-covered box. The light reflecting against the container wall illuminated a skull and crossbones and underneath in large letters a warning: DANGER. EVACUATE AREA IMMEDIATELY. EXPLOSION IMMINENT. Obviously, Hallsford explained, a signal to crews that a major deficiency existed and for their safety, an order to get the hell out of the area. As far as he could tell, no other instructions to reset codes or switches. Only an order to clear the area.

Minutes later, Dr. Joe Bradley, using a fluoroscope viewing device, peered into the rectangular, glass-covered box and discovered a simple, but apparently effective, fusing device which was clock-driven by a small electronic watch-like instrument. Using a stethoscope, he determined that the pulsar type watch mechanism kept perfect time and with the second hand sweep on the stopwatch he held in his hand. He was fascinated as he listened with the stethoscope to the almost inaudible movement of the clock mechanism.

From photographs of the view reflected on the fluoroscope screen it was clear that the clock mechanism was driving a long thin pencil-like plunger forward. The plunger was inside a small clear plastic pipe. At the far end, a small hair-thin wire protruded from the pipe. Extending from the other end of the plastic pipe was a coated wire leading to a red bulb and a small bell.

As they looked at the system, all agreed that when the plunger reached the hair-thin wire it would complete a circuit, lighting up the bulb and activating a bell or buzzer. Obviously, a warning system to proclaim an imminent explosion.

Extending just beyond the hair-thin wire was another wire which the plunger would reach if it continued its forward movement. The wire protruded out of the other side of the pipe and into a small aperture which, they surmised, led to the fuse detonator.

However, they were far from sure. There was no perceptible movement of the plunger. At Dr. Bradley's insistence, a series of time-lapsed photographs were taken at fifteen-minute intervals. For over three hours, the photography continued over the objections of others in the group who complained to Jamie Rohrbach that the activity was obstructing their own work.

What caught Dr. Overby's attention in the fluoroscope examination was the small coding device at the extreme right side of the rectangular receptacle. Small revolving cylinders with evenly spaced numbers and letters much like the wheels on a slot machine. Line up the correct combination and the code was solved, and the jackpot hit. Thirteen cylinders in all.

The numbers were in sequence with each one interspersed with a letter. In five of the cylinders it was apparent that the numbers went from 0 to 9, then were repeated in that order. From the exposed portions of the cylinders, Wendy was able to count nine different letters which matched the letters on the small calculator-like board slightly recessed in the right side of the rectangular box.

Ten numbers, nine letters, she murmured. Simple but effective coding device. It shouldn't take her and Leslie long to come up with the codes.

She agreed with Dr. Bradley's observation that the code was apparently used to set the distance the plunger would travel before making contact with the warning device. She was adamant, however, in disagreeing with his observation that this was a self-destruct device, for whatever reason the Soviets had placed it on the weapon.

It was, she insisted, a device which had to be preset in connection with the firing of the intermediate range ballistic missile which would be timed to detonate at certain heights over the target. That way, the Soviets could obtain maximum damage to the selected target, rather than depending on impact for detonation. She went on to explain that impact detonation was the least efficient manner in which to achieve maximum destruction. Too much of the explosive power went into the ground or building when the weapon made contact. By setting the destruction mechanism to fire a pre-determined air bust, a ten-fold increase in damage would result.

Leslie Overstreet sat quietly while Dr. Overby and Dr. Bradley carried on their discussion. He was not overly impressed with either argument. Their job, as he understood it, was to deactivate the weapon, and breaking the code was the first order of business.

With his pencil, he placed the numbers 1 to 9 in sequence across the top of a sheet of paper. For a moment, he hesitated; then placed a zero before the one. Ten numbers in all. Then immediately below the zero, he placed the letter S, followed by F, B, P, M, R, U, X and Y; the same order in which they appeared on the calculator. Then taking his calculator, he began punching in letters and numbers and recording the results in the memory key. He continued punching in various combinations, recording the outcome on the legal size pads of paper on the table.

Finally, he walked over to the computer terminal and started punching in his recorded results. He scanned the screen to the terminal's immediate right. Then he punched in another set of figures and letters, each time looking only briefly at the answers appearing on the computer screen. Completely oblivious to the argument now raging between Dr. Bradley and Dr. Overby, he kept punching at the keyboard and without emotion, looked at the results being posted on the viewer at his side.

It was late afternoon before Bud Sharp put in the call to Dagger Donovan in Florida. General Taylor had kept him busy all day making arrangements for the United Nations meeting on Wednesday. Vu-graph equipment, the photographs, operators, communications links with the White House and elsewhere, the "hot-line" between Moscow and Washington extended to New York City, and a host of other details to include

THE COBRA TEAM

security forces from nearby Fort Dix to be on call.

The call to Donovan was his last item on the agenda before going to Belvoir to get a first-hand report on progress being made. Merv Collins had called him several times during the day giving him progress reports which he had immediately relayed to General Taylor, who in turn, kept the Secretary of Defense and the President informed. However, the break-through which they were so desperately seeking—the defusing of the weapon —still evaded them. Drs. Joe Bradley and Bernie Dunsfield had proven without a doubt that the weapon was armed. But how to disarm it still defied their best efforts.

"Dagger, hate to get you out of the sack, but duty first." Bud Sharp's opening comments to Dagger were always planned to needle him.

"I know exactly how much you hated waking me, you sorry bastard." Dagger's sleepy voice showed some trace of irritation. "What's up?"

"Here are the plans for tomorrow."

Bud Sharp then outlined the program for the following day. A plane would pick up Dagger and the team in Florida at noon, touching down briefly at Fort Belvoir where Dagger would get off. The remainder of the team would be flown to Fort Dix and remain on call. Sharp would meet Dagger and brief him on the exact duties General Taylor wanted him to perform. Then he would be flown to New York late tomorrow night, perhaps with his little baby along to keep him company.

"Bud, one request." Dagger's voice was almost pleading as he continued. "You know I've been told no outside contact. But, do me a favor, try calling Susan Ainsworth in Georgetown and tell her I miss her, love her, and will be calling her soon."

Bud Sharp was silent for a moment. Would this violate General Taylor's dictum of no outside contact by the COBRA Team until further orders? He decided it would not.

"Will do, Dagger." He hung up the phone and opened the top drawer of his desk searching for a small piece of paper he had put there some months before. Glancing at the number, he dialed it carefully and heard the telephone ringing.

"Susan Ainsworth."

"Miss Ainsworth, this is Colonel Sharp in the Pentagon. I have a message for you from Colonel Mike Donovan."

Susan Ainsworth trembled as she heard Mike's name. Her heart began to pound. Trying to control the emotions which were beginning to sweep over her, she spoke quietly into the phone.

"Yes, Colonel, what is the message?"

"Miss you, love you, will call soon."

"Is that all?"

"Yes, ma'am."

"Why didn't Colonel Donovan call me himself?"

"He's not in a position to do so."

"What do you mean? Is he hurt?"

"No, ma'am, he's just not in any position to call."

"Is he at Fort Bragg?"

"No."

"Where is he, then?"

"Sorry, I can't tell you."

"What kind of a game is this, anyway?"

"No game, ma'am. Colonel Donovan asked that I call and pass on his message. I can tell you nothing further."

"Just one thing, Colonel Sharp, has Colonel Donovan been at Fort Bragg recently?"

"No ma'am, he left there almost immediately after he saw you some months ago."

"Oh, my God!"

"What, ma'am?"

"Colonel Sharp, I need your help." Susan Ainsworth's voice was pleading as she continued. "There are some letters from me at Colonel Donovan's headquarters. Could you have them returned to me before he gets a chance to read them?"

"Ma'am, that would be highly irregular. I have no authority to delve into Colonel Donovan's mail and remove letters."

"Please, Colonel, *please*! It's so important to me that he not get my letters." Bud Sharp listened as he heard Susan Ainsworth's frantic voice. Obviously, there was something in her letters she did not want Mike Donovan to read, and he suspected he might know what.

"Miss Ainsworth," Bud Sharp's voice was official in tone, "I'm having Colonel Donovan's mail sent to me here today by courier from Fort Bragg. Is your name and return address shown on the letters so I could identify them?"

"Yes, sir, and thank you. Please return them to me at 6601 34th Street, Georgetown. My initials and that address appear on the upper left corner of each letter. Except for one of them."

Susan Ainsworth hesitated briefly before saying, "Rather than my initials and address, one will have only "3-F."

"3-F?"

"Yes, Colonel."

Bud Sharp grinned as he heard the 3-F. My God, what had Dagger told this girl, anyway? 3-F had a very precise meaning among members of the armed forces, but cripes, you didn't go around telling girls what it meant.

"Miss Ainsworth, I'll go through Colonel Donovan's mail and the letters which I can positively identify as coming from you I will put into a large brown envelope and mail them to you at the address you have given me. But I want to reconfirm the address. You see, Colonel Donovan had asked me to have the Pentagon florist send you some flowers months ago and the florist reported they were undeliverable. None of the neighbors had ever heard of you, according to his report. A call to the telephone company was also non-productive. They had no phone listed or unlisted for a Miss Susan Ainsworth. I know that Colonel Donovan tried calling you himself at this same number I've just used and received no answer."

"Please sir, tell Colonel Donovan that the apartment and telephone number were all listed under the name of Georgette Sylvester. She rented the apartment first and had the phone installed. I moved in with her, and when she left, I didn't make any effort to change the records to reflect that I was the new occupant. If Colonel Donovan tried calling me shortly after he last saw me, I can explain that. I was a crew chief on a flight that came up at the last minute and had to leave immediately for the far western states. I tried calling Fort Bragg to let Colonel Donovan know what happened but I was never able to reach him. His office kept telling me he was temporarily away but would leave my messages on his desk."

"Miss Ainsworth, I'm sorry about that. Colonel Donovan returned to Fort Bragg from Washington the last time you saw him. He stayed there overnight before leaving on a trip. He has not been back since. I'm sure he will be happy to know that you are still living in Georgetown. He had almost given up that there was a Susan Ainsworth living there."

"Thank you again, Colonel. Please tell Colonel Donovan that I'll be waiting for his call. Better yet, tell him I'm ready for another dinner at Banningan's." With a smile on her face, Susan Ainsworth hung up the telephone.

Chapter 17

IT WAS TEN minutes after 7 p.m. when Bernie Dunsfield stepped over to Colonel Jamie Rohrback and said, "Jamie, Joe Bradley and I have discovered something which we'd like to discuss with you."

"Sure thing, Bernie, I'll be right there."

Jamie Rohrback sat quietly as Joe Bradley explained what he and Bernie had found. Through the use of time-lapsed photography, they were positive that the clock-driven arming device was active.

"But," he hastened to add, "it won't detonate the weapon for another one hundred thirty seven days, four hours and fifty minutes. Contact will first be made with a warning device which will signal that an explosion is imminent and a beeper or bell will sound an alarm. After approximately a ten or fifteen-minute delay, the plunger will reach the second contact point which we surmise will cause the warhead to explode."

Bradley continued, "Bernie and I first determined that the clock mechanism driving the plunger is running on the same time as an ordinary watch. We measured the movement of the plunger for the past nine hours, first at fifteen-minute intervals, then at hourly intervals. We were thus able to measure the precise distance the plunger moved per minute. Extending this same rate of movement—and we're positive of this—the plunger will reach the warning device at the number of days and hours I've just mentioned. We are also certain that the coding device is directly related to the arming of the weapon and confident that through insertion of a code, the plunger can be pre-set at any distance, which translates into minutes, hours, and days to warning and weapon detonation. Further, we feel that the proper code can stop all movement, or retract the plunger. Now the big if. What's the code to do all this?"

Jamie Rohrbach looked at the date Bernie Dunsfield had laboriously written on a large, legal size pad. Page after page of formulas, diagrams, and notes explaining the function of each part. He was convinced that the supporting data proved conclusively the accuracy of the analysis.

But he wanted to be sure. He called Jim Arnett, Rufus Hallsford and Marcell Halifax to join them. They listened as Joe Bradley repeated what he and Bernie had found. Slowly, each man nodded his head in agreement. Jamie Rohrbach was satisfied. Walking to the stage, he asked for attention. Then he reported that the weapon was armed and the timing device was in an active mode. The sudden, hushed silence was followed by broad smiles as he announcd they had about one hundred and thirty-seven days left to clear the area. He explained how the code was the key and asked Dr. Overby for a report on the status of her work.

The Dr. Wendy Overby who walked slowly to center stage was a different girl than the cocky lady who had held forth earlier that day on her ability to break the code in nothing flat. She admitted that she and Leslie were having a difficult time. They had fed one set of data after another into the computers back at NSA headquarters at Ford Meade and still the secret eluded them. She also now agreed with Dr. Bradley's analysis about the purpose of the code. It was a self-destruct device for sure. She admitted grudgingly that her earlier assessment of its function had been wrong. However, she was confident that the code could be broken. She needed a bit more time.

Jamie Rorhbach conferred with Jim Arnett and Bud Sharp who agreed that breaking the code was the remaining obstacle to finishing the job. They were all convinced that no attempt should be made to dismantle the weapon without first breaking the code. No doubt in their minds that a disturbance device had been built into the warhead.

All other technical details were well in hand. Accordingly, the majority of the team could be dismissed. Dr. Overby, Leslie Overstreet and Jim McDonald would continue working the code problem. Drs. Bradley and Dunsfield would re-verify the data they had uncovered and give Dr. Overby a hand if she thought they could help. The rest of the team was excused. Bud Sharp and Merv Collins would spell each other off and provide any support those remaining might need.

As far as he was concerned, Jamie went on, he was going to take a nap. It looked as though it would be a long night.

Bud Sharp met Dagger as the C-130 touched down briefly at Davison Army Airfield at noon on Tuesday. After greeting the COBRA Team and congratulating them on a job well done, he and Dagger drove to Building 572 as the C-130 took off for McGuire Air Force Base, adjacent to Fort Dix, where Dagger's men would remain in seclusion until they were moved to New York City early the next morning.

As they wound their way through the Fort Belvoir reservation, Dagger gave Bud a rundown on their stay in Cuba. In turn, Bud gave him the details on the plan for the rest of the day and Dagger's role in the President's appearance before the United Nations. He also passed along his conversation with Susan Ainsworth. He didn't mention the letters he had so carefully extracted from the bundle of mail he handed Dagger as they got into the car. The letters by this time should be in Susan

Ainsworth's possession as he had sent his navy yeoman to personally deliver a package to Miss Ainsworth earlier that morning.

Dagger smiled when Bud mentioned Susan's comment about being ready for a repeat dinner at Bannigans.

"Bud, why can't I call Susan? Certainly Ben Taylor would understand." Dagger's request was rhetorical and he knew it. When General Taylor ordered no outside contact, that was exactly what he meant.

"Dagger, you know better than that." Bud Sharp looked at Dagger with small grin on his face. "She'll wait for you."

"It's easy for you to say that, Bud. After all, you've been able to get home to Jean every night. Remember, buddy, I've been in Cuba for over three months."

"Yes, Dagger, with Perfecto, pills and all."

Dagger winced. He decided he'd better change the subject. Dammit, Bud Sharp could really needle him, and this time he knew he couldn't win the argument. The PS for pills was a dead giveaway. And, try as he might, he'd never be able to convince Bud that he hadn't as much as touched Perfecto after that very first day. He wouldn't believe a story like that himself.

Bernie Dunsfield poked Joe Bradley and pointed to the far corner of the room. Sound asleep on two cots pushed close together were Dr. Wendy Overby and Leslie Overstreet. What had caught Bernie's attention was Dr. Overby's hand carefully holding Leslie's outstretched palm to her breast and just a twinge of a smile on her face. He wondered what was going through her mind as she lay dreaming.

"Joe, let's take a crack at breaking the code while those two love birds are in never-never land." Bernie Dunsfield had been getting impatient waiting for Dr. Overby to ask for help. He had suggested several times to her that they were available to assist as he and Joe had finished verifying the arming mechanism and were satisfied with the answers.

She rebuffed his offer each time with a comment that she and Leslie were doing just fine. Almost on the verge of cracking the code. They would do so after a short nap. After all, they had worked right on throughout the night without a break. A short rest would refresh their minds for the final attempt and she was confident it would be successful. She reminded Bernie that some eight or nine hours still remained before the deadline they had been given.

Joe Bradley looked over again at the love birds still sound asleep. He hated to be pushy, but dammit, they were part of the team charged with breaking the code. They couldn't wait forever for Dr. Overby and Leslie Overstreet to come up with the answers. "O.K., Bernie, but where do we begin?"

"As a starter, Joe, take a look at this." Bernie Dunsfield thrust the photograph of the nuclear weapon at Joe Bradley. "See that serial number SU 9 Y B 821 FR 934? Now, look at the serial number of the weapon on the table." Joe Bradley looked: SU 9 YB 821 FR 938.

"So what, Bernie?"

"See the last three digits on the picture—934. The last three digits on the weapon are 938. To me that would seem to indicate that we have two different weapons which were manufactured at about the same time, a four-digit difference. Now, if I were going to put a code into the machine, my first inclination would be to insert the serial number. Then, a specific code to pre-set the arming mechanism. Like any computer program, you must first put in a code to gain access to the data."

"Bernie, I'm inclined to agree with you. Do you think there is any danger if we insert the serial numbers? Damned if I want to be around if this blasted thing goes off. Remember Jim Arnett and his crew estimated the yield at 100 kilotons. And you remember what happened at Hiroshima from a 20 KT blast."

"Joe, the worst thing that could happen would be that

the machine would reject the code if it was wrong. No one in his right mind would have a weapon go off simply by pushing a wrong button. After all, even someone who knows the code well could accidentally push the wrong button when accessing it."

"You're right, as usual. Should we try?"

"I'm willing."

Joe Bradley and Bernie Dunsfield walked slowly toward the table. Bernie looked one more time at Joe who nodded his assent. Then cautiously he pushed the S. Immediately at the bottom of the rectangular glass tube, the letter S showed up brilliantly in dark red. He smiled. Then he punched the letter U, which simultaneously lit up to the right of the S. More confident than ever, he pushed each of the remaining numbers and letters corresponding to the serial number. When he pushed the last one, number 8, the entire sequence disappeared while the square remained lit.

"Joe, I believe we've accessed the computer correctly." Bernie Dunsfield's voice revealed the excitement which he felt as the numbers kept appearing as he had pushed each key.

"Damned if I don't agree with you." Joe Bradley's voice portrayed the excitement which gripped him as he watched Bernie punch in another number.

"Bernie, what if you had punched in a wrong number? For example, at the very end. Instead of punching in 938, you had punched 939."

"I expect the number 9 would have appeared on the console. But I suspect that the numbers would not have disappeared indicating that the minicomputer was ready to receive the next sequence of orders. You see, Joe, if the number did not appear, all one would have to do is sit here and take turns punching each letter or number until you hit the right one. No, the Soviets are smarter than that. Now, I'm more convinced than ever that we can break the code."

"Bernie, you're out of my element. But keep it up, I'll

sit here and keep you company."

"Elementary mathematics, my dear Watson. Nothing more." Bernie Dunsfield's sense of humor while literally monkeying around with a one hundred kiloton nuclear weapon amazed Joe. He knew his partner too well. He'd never risk his life or those of the group in the laboratory without being completely confident of what he was doing.

And Joe Bradley knew time was flying. Colonel Sharp had indicated that Tuesday evening was the deadline for a solution, or what they had been doing would be of no help whatsoever.

By now, too, Joe Bradley suspected the origin of the weapon and the purpose to which it was to be put. And he was certain that the replica which they had built a few days earlier was now somewhere in Cuba in place of the real one before them on the table. After all, the President had announced he had positive proof of Soviet nuclear weapons being introduced into Cuba and tomorrow, he had promised, he would present the evidence to the world during his speech at the United Nations. And Joe Bradley wanted to help. That's why he and Bernie had worked around the clock without a break.

"Joe, let's try another step. We may be cutting the time the weapon is set for detonation but not enough to cause us any immediate danger. For example, the weapon obviously is set on a passage of a certain number of hours and minutes. No different from any other detonating device which a madman might put into a bomb. A normal clock would handle twelve hours. The pulsar watch in this mechanism can handle almost any number of days up to a year. So, let's try and retard the plunger by say ten days or 240 hours. If, by accident, we advance it by that much, we'd still have one hundred and twenty seven days to get the hell out of here. But, I feel any attempt at less than ten days would be too insignificant to measure in a hurry. And, we are up against time."

"Go, Bernie, go." When Joe Bradley saw Bernie

Dunsfield this deeply involved in a problem and over the first hard hurdle, he felt confident that he was on the right track. While he couldn't contribute much to Bernie's thought processes in this business, he, too, was a nuclear physicist and a mathematician, and could keep abreast with Bernie most of the time, but not always. This time, though, they were in tandem.

Bernie Dunsfield then explained his theory of the code to Joe Bradley. A series of numbers or letters into the computer to deactivate the plunger. Another set to activate it. Others to advance the plunger toward the alarm and detonation. While another set would retract it. Increase the time interval between the time the code was put in and the elapsed time to detonation.

The purpose? His view, unsubstantiated, but still confident of its truth. To destroy the weapons automatically, should Castro become recalcitrant and order Soviet advisors out of the country without agreeing to return the weapons to the Soviet Union.

An insurance policy, so to speak, he continued, on the part of the Soviets to provide them with some measure of assurance that the weapons would not fall into the hands of a demented Castro and used against targets without Soviet Union concurrence or approval.

He continued his theory. A simple code, which could advance the automatic destruction date by Soviet technicians in the field, should Cuban and Soviet relations remain good. Or, a short reduction in the time before departure of Soviet technicians should they be ordered out. All circumstantial evidence, so to speak, Bernie concluded. But there seemed to be no other logical explanation. Joe Bradley agreed with the deductions advanced. After much thought, he nodded his head in agreement to Bernie's suggestion that they give it a try.

After first looking over to the far corner for reassurance that Wendy Overby and Leslie Overstreet were still sound alseep, Bernie, more cautiously than before, began punching numbers and letters on the keyboard.

As each one was punched, a simultaneous reproduction appeared on the lighted line at the bottom of the rectangular glass covered mechanism. Finally, the light lit up temporarily with the last letter, then the entire sequence disappeared from view and was replaced with a single set of zeroes.

Joe Bradley sat transfixed as he watched the plunger. He leaned forward in his chair with hands pressed hard down on the wooden sides, much like a boxer who was ready to spring from his corner at the sound of the bell to engage his opponent in combat. But, Joe's thoughts were on springing to safety if the plunger started moving. Finally, he realized how futile and silly his actions really were. Had the plunger moved rapidly forward, he might just as well relax and expect the worst. There was no escape. Nowhere to go.

"That's the first step." Bernie sat back to observe. No way to determine whether the plunger had stopped, was continuing to move forward, or had begun a backward movement. With Joe's help, he moved the camera into position and began taking a series of time-lapsed photography. They could do nothing more now than wait.

"Bernie, you've done it!" Joe's voice was exuberant as he showed Bernie Dunsfield the results of the time-lapsed photography. No doubt about it. The plunger had stopped moving.

A small grin was Bernie's only reaction as he again picked up his calculator and began banging away to check another formula he had written down some five hours before. Then, again, he cautiously punched letters and numbers into the machine, watching with grim satisfaction as each one was illuminated. Finally, he punched the last number.

Again, momentary lighting of the entire sequence, then it quickly disappeared to be replaced by another set of numbers, 240. He smiled. He had the key. No doubt about it now. Again, he started the time-lapsed photography and sat back and waited.

Looking over at Wendy and Leslie still lying side by side, he hoped that they wouldn't wake up until he had finished his experiment. If they did, he knew he was through. Wendy had resisted his every effort to help and she wasn't about to change her mind. Of that, he was sure.

As they waited for the results of the photography, Bernie Dunsfield went back to his calculator and his legal-sized pad still filled with formulas. Punching one set of numbers and letters after another into the keyboard, he rapidly recorded the results. He was still busily engaged when Joe dramatically announced that the plunger had moved rearward the equivalent of ten days. It was now one hundred forty-seven days to detonation, he said with a smile.

"Joe, we still have one more step to check out. And I want your consent because this one may be for keeps. I plan on advancing the plunger all the way to activate the warning light and the beeper, or siren. Then, we'll give it just a minute or so, and I'll punch in the code to retract the plunger back to the one hundred and forty-seven days it is now set on. But, to be sure, I want you prepared to punch in the code which I have written down here in the event that I faint when and if my theory works and we can do what I have just described."

Joe looked at Bernie. He knew that the weapon could be deactivated. He had just seen it for himself. Should he go along with Bernie's scheme to try out the alarm system and chance an explosion? By now, though, he was convinced that Bernie knew what he was doing. Taking the piece of paper in his hand, he nodded his agreement.

For once, Joe noticed, Bernie was not as confident as before. During the earlier tests, Bernie had punched away at the keyboard. Letters, numbers, followed by another set of letters and numbers. Now, Bernie seemed to hesitate.

Looking at Joe again, he returned to the weapon and started punching in a code and watching each letter being illuminated as before. Then he said, "This may be the end," and punched the last key.

Suddenly, the entire glass-enclosed rectangular mechanism lit up. The skull and crossbones stood out prominently. DANGER, EVACUATE AREA IMMEDIATELY, EXPLOSION IMMINENT, seemed to be in letters a foot high. But, it was the loud intermittent beeping of a siren that startled everyone in the room.

Dr. Wendy Overby was the first on her feet and rushed toward the weapon. Seeing the illuminated skull and crossbones and reading the warning sign below, she fled out the door dragging a still sleepy, reluctant Leslie with her.

Jamie Rohrbach had been sitting quietly in a chair at the other end of the room taking a snooze while he waited for Dr. Overby to awaken and resume work. There was nothing he could do but wait for her. He was not a code breaker. He was a technician who knew how nuclear weapons were built, armed, and the yield they would produce. But, codes were not his bag.

With one eye he had earlier watched Bernie and Joe poke around the weapon and their occasional hushed conversations, but nothing much of importance was happening that he could see. Only the camera recording the time-lapsed photography seemed to be in use. And Joe had used that earlier to prove his point. Just reverifying their conclusions as Jamie had requested earlier. Good men. While the others took catnaps, Joe and Bernie continued working. But, it was Wendy Overby who had to come up with the answers. She and Leslie were the code breakers. Not Joe and Bernie. They were nuclear scientists. Hell, he thought, they might not know a code from a monopoly set.

Leslie Overstreet covered his eyes with his right hand as Wendy Overby held on tightly to his left. Driving down Jefferson Davis Highway at sixty-five miles an hour and weaving in and out of traffic was not his idea of a good time. But Wendy kept reassuring him. If they could put five to eight miles between them and Fort Belvoir, they would be safe. The nuclear weapon was estimated to be one hundred kilotons. Dr. Bradley had earlier determined that there would be a time lapse of between ten and fifteen minutes between first alarm and detonation. Her quick reaction to flee the laboratory at the first sound of the alarm might turn out to be the difference between remaining alive and continuing their splendid relationship, or becoming the victims of the first nuclear holocaust in America.

She felt sorry for the others who had not reacted as rapidly as she had. Joe, Bernie, Jamie, Merv, Bud. They had all seemed hypnotized as they stood there looking at the weapon signal in bright letters, warning of danger and instructions to evacuate the area immediately. Then, the intermittent whine of the beeper. It was nerve-racking. But she had kept her wits.

Dragging Leslie by the hand, she had rushed to her car and was now well on the way to safety. Poor Leslie, if he didn't have her to watch over him, he'd be back there now, about to be pulverized by the full force of a nuclear bomb. The very thought caused goose pimples to break out on her skin. Her Leslie. They had so much in common. He would do anything she wanted.

And, he was such a wonderful lover now. Under her tutelage, Leslie had changed from an awkward, fumbling, indecisive youth, to a skilled, confident, passionate lover. All because of her. He would now be more considerate of her needs and wants than ever before after realizing that he owed his life to her quick thinking.

Bernie Dunsfield was the center of attention as he explained to Jamie Rohrbach and the others standing beside him how he could activate or disarm the weapon by the simple insertion of a code. As he talked louder and louder to overcome the intermittent whine of the beeper, Jamie Rohrbach, Jim Arnett, Bud Sharp and Merv Collins looked at each other. The anxiety each felt was reflected in their drawn, taut faces.

"Gentlemen, here is how we disarm the weapon." Bernie's confident voice was reassuring as he punched a series of numbers and letters into the weapon console.

Suddenly, the high-pitched whine of the beeper was silent and the warning light indicator disappeared, to be replaced by a piece of dull glass. A spontaneous clapping of hands applauded Bernie's performance. Jamie Rohrbach clasped Dunsfield's hand and at the same time gave him a bear hug. A slight grin lit Bernie Dunsfield's face. The inner satisfaction he felt caused a slight tremor in his voice. "Gentlemen," he said, "is there anything else we need to do before I hit the sack? I'm tired."

General Taylor was elated as he listened to Bud Sharp explain how Dr. Dunsfield had broken the code and disarmed the weapon.

"Have him stay there," Taylor said, "until I can get the Directors of NSA and CIA to join me there for a demonstration. I should be able to get the three of us together within the hour. Also, have Dagger present. I want to give him specific instructions on his role tomorrow. The President is enroute to New York now. I'll call him from Belvoir after we have seen Dr. Dunsfield perform. And, congratulate the team, Bud; you all have done an absolutely fantastic job."

Dr. Wendy Overby pulled her car into the gas station along the Jefferson Davis Highway. A frown had slowly replaced the look of horror on her face.

It had been over thirty minutes since she and Leslie had fled Fort Belvoir and still no sound of an explosion. She knew that by now they were well away from any danger, but still the sound of a one hundred kiloton nuclear bomb going off could easily be heard at that distance. In fact, she thought, it would have been heard in Richmond, some ninety-five miles south of Fort Belvoir.

And she was still sixty miles from Richmond according to the last road sign.

She looked over at Leslie who was sound asleep. Some miles back, he had pulled his hand from hers and folding his arms across his chest, had dozed off. Poor boy, she thought. After all, he had worked throughout the night and most of today. She had thought a few minutes earlier, as they passed a motel, that perhaps she ought to pull over and get them a room where they could get some uninterrupted rest. But only after Leslie had made love to her. They had missed the big evening they had planned together last night. It was only fair they catch up, as soon as possible.

She was still concerned about what had happened at Fort Belvoir as she told the gas station attendant to fill the tank. Seeing a pay telephone at the far end of the building, she reached into her pocketbook and pulled out a handful of change together with a small slip of paper on which she had written the building and telephone number of the lab at Fort Belvoir. She slipped a dime into the telephone and gave the operator the number. She heard the number being dialed and the receiver being lifted.

"Sharp speaking."

"Colonel Sharp, this is Wendy Overby. Are you all right?"

"Certainly. Where are you, anyway?"

"Leslie and I are having a bite to eat."

"Well, you'd better get back, your boss is enroute here from Fort Meade."

"You mean General Thompson, the Director of NSA?"

"None other. And, Wendy, you had better be prepared to brief him on how you broke the code. I'd suggest you get back as soon as possible so that Bernie Dunsfield can show you how he took your work and inserted it into the weapon to disarm the mechanism."

"We'll be back as soon as possible."

Bud Sharp smiled as he hung up the phone. A little white lie wouldn't hurt. After all, Bernie had told them that the data Wendy and Leslie had gotten out of the NSA computers was absolutely vital in breaking the code. All he had done was recast it into different matrices with one finally producing the winning combination. He had been laudatory about the work they had done. He had just put the finishing touches on their efforts, he said modestly.

Joe Bradley listened attentively as Jamie Rohrbach briefed Generals Taylor and Thompson, and John Askins, Director of CIA. Every facet of the warhead had been examined and they were confident of their findings. The work of every member of the group had been essential in getting the job done, he said in conclusion.

In particular, though, he wanted to single out Drs. Joe Bradley and Bernie Dunsfield, who had been so very helpful. The others on the team were government employees and it was their responsibility to work around the clock. But the two civilian scientists from Bradley, Dunsfield, and McDaniel, had also worked a twenty-four hour day and he wanted to recognize the important contribution they had made.

Wendy Overby nodded her head in silent agreement as Jamie continued. "This was a team effort, General Taylor, and I'm proud to have been a member, although my particular contribution was small compared to the others."

General Taylor complimented the team on their achievement and promised that their participation would be officially recognized. However, he was pressed for time. Would Colonel Sharp, Colonel Donovan, and Drs. Bradley and Dunsfield join him, General Thompson and Director Askins for just a few minutes in private while the others were excused.

Joe Bradley looked again at the officer who had been introduced to him as Colonel Mike Donovan when he arrived. He wondered who he was. Nothing but "This is Colonel Mike Donovan." No elaboration, no discussion as to his position and his role in what had transpired during the past week. But Joe Bradley knew there was some connection.

General Taylor had Dr. Dunsfield give Colonel Donovan instructions on how to arm and disarm the warhead. Then he had Donovan do it under Dunsfield's direction. After being satisfied that Donovan had the procedures well in hand, General Taylor thanked Joe and Bernie. They'd be hearing from him soon, he promised, as they picked up their calculators and other gear and left the building.

Taylor then instructed Donovan to accompany the warhead to LaGuardia where a security guard from Fort Dix would escort the weapon to the United Nations. He outlined in detail Donovan's role in support of the President's appearance before the United Nations and the importance of following the exact script. Donovan nodded his understanding.

Before departing, General Taylor asked General Thompson, with an assist from John Askins, to have their personnel reverify the codes and the arming and disarming procedures. He had to be certain that the President and the leaders of other nations attending the UN debate would not be exposed to danger. Absolute safety of the leaders would take precedence over any other action. If necessary, he would cancel Donovan's role and have the warhead removed to the middle of New Mexico's White Sands proving grounds if there were any question about the safety of the warhead and how it worked.

The first rays of the sun had begun peeking over the horizon as Bud Sharp and Mike Donovan pulled up to the C-130 at Davison Army Airfield. Bunson Burner Cochrane and Ted Tanley had filed their flight plan to LaGuardia and were ready to take off as soon as Dagger and his package were put aboard.

Quick Draw looked on in amazement as Colonel Sharp and Colonel Donovan lifted the styrofoam box from the van onto the rear ramp of the airplane.

"Good God, this again!" he exclaimed as he saw for the third time in less than four days the same load being put into the cabin of his plane. "What the hell are these guys hauling around, anyway?" he muttered under his breath.

PART THREE

Chapter 18

JACK KETNER ALWAYS enjoyed visiting New York City. He hoped this visit was going to be the best of all. Perhaps even the triumph of his presidency.

He began to savor the drama that was to unfold. His direct confrontation with Elonson Krenchev in the great assembly hall of the United Nations was only hours away. It was a stroke of luck that the leaders of the two most powerful nations on earth were about to meet face to face to debate the United States charge that the Soviet Union had introduced nuclear weapons into Cuba.

The Americans claimed that action directly threatened the security of the North American continent and, in particular, the United States of America. The President could thank the news media for a tremendous build-up in setting the stage. Their repeated stories and newscasts alleging that the Soviet Union had moved nuclear armed intermediate range ballistic missiles into Cuba had been the top news story for days. Krenchev's repeated denials only whetted the appetites of the news media, and ream after ream of copy explored every facet of the American charge and pursued all possible implications of the Soviet denials.

Yet, only forty-eight hours before did Jack Ketner have the hard evidence to convince him that the Soviets had armed Cuba with nuclear weapons that could wipe out a good part of the United States and much of the Western Hemisphere. His dramatic appearance on TV and radio announcing to the world that the United States had positive proof of this fact and that he had requested an emergency meeting of the United Nations kept the lights burning late into the night in most chancelleries of the world.

However, it was the President's offhand comment at the conclusion of his nationwide broadcast that really set the stage for today. He challenged Krenchev to come to the United Nations to see and hear for himself the evidence that the United States would make public at that time. Never for a moment had the President thought that Krenchev would come. But when the AP bulletin was flashed to the White House newsroom soon after his speech that Krenchev had accepted the U.S. challenge, it was almost as startling as the first view of the Soviet nuclear weapon that the COBRA Team had brought out of Cuba.

The President reflected again on that great achievement. What a tremendous bunch of guys. He would be forever grateful to Ben Taylor for suggesting their use.

As he gazed out the window watching the busy traffic below, he felt deep satisfaction at how things had developed. It seemed only yesterday that Ken Kern informed him privately that he had reliable information that the Soviet Union was about to arm Castro with intermediate range ballistic missiles. Then, the idea had seemed preposterous.

But knowing Ken as well as he did, he ordered photographic coverage of the island and directed the CIA to use its vast network of informants and agents to ferret out the truth. Their early reports remained vivid in his memory. No basis of proof for Kern's information. Then Taylor's suggestion to use the COBRA Team. His complete ignorance of its existence, then an appreciation of their capability after the team's first reports of possible sightings. The mixture of relief and worry when he saw their close-up pictures showing the Soviet weapons in every detail. But dammit, as he had said when first viewing them, they could have been taken anywhere.

Finally, the coup. The incredible operation that swapped a U.S. built look-alike weapon for the real thing, with the COBRA Team bringing it out complete with Soviet markings, serial number, and the baffling self-destruct device which the foreign technology group had uncovered in their detailed examination of the weapon. But the climax of it all to him was the round-the-clock operation by those remarkable consultants who had broken the code just hours before. Good God, would Krenchev ever get the shock of his life later on today! Jack Ketner could hardly wait.

Bobby's voice interrupted him. "Jack. Ben Taylor's on the phone. John Askins is also listening."

The President picked up the phone, now fully awake. "Ben, are we all set?"

"Yes, Mr. President." Ben's voice seemed a bit strained. Not having been to bed in the last forty-eight hours, Jack realized, would strain anyone's voice. But in this case for a good cause. Ben continued, "The plane with the baby has left Belvoir and will arrive at LaGuardia in about forty minutes. From there an army escort from Fort Dix will deliver it to the United Nations. It will be in place in plenty of time. Donovan is with it. I've instructed him on his role. He's ready. The hot line is in operation. We've made several test runs. All of our major commands have confirmed that their forces are on alert and ready for any developments. John, do you have anything to add?"

"Just one thing, Mr. President," said Askins. "We've double and triple checked the system with NSA and they assure me that the code is absolutely correct. Donovan is thoroughly trained in its use. And Good Luck!"

"I may need it. Thanks Ben, John. I'll be in touch."

Jack Ketner returned the phone to its cradle. Taking a long sip of coffee from the cup his brother had placed on the table, he said, "Bobby, I hope Krenchev is enjoying the presidential suite at the Waldorf Astoria because this may be his last day of luxurious living. If I read the tea leaves correctly, he'll be just as unpopular at home after today as he will be here before we're through with him this afternoon. I'm sure he's lording over his entourage—how he beat the President of the United States out of the presidential suite in the Waldorf, while I have to suffer in the mediocre surroundings of the Carlyle Hotel. If he only knew. This has been my favorite hotel for years and I've had some of the best times of my life here with several dollies whose names I had better keep to myself. By the way, flip on the TV. Let's see what's going on in the Big Apple."

Don Grimes, the nation's self-proclaimed greatest newscaster, appeared on the screen and with his usual dour face, intoned, "The greatest confrontation in history is now only hours away. When Elonson Krenchev, the erstwhile Premier of the Soviet Union, and Jack Ketner, the President of the United States meet face to face today in the great hall of the United Nations on the banks of the East River here in New York, the eyes and ears of most of the world will be focused on the great debate which will be taking place within this historic city. Not since the days of the Roman Empire have two such famous gladiators . . ."

"Turn the bastard off, Bobby. I can't stand any more of his puffery. He's full of shit. Why in hell the network keeps that pompous ass on its payroll is beyond me."

"Jack, you've never liked Don since he did that unflattering special on you after your first 100 days in office. He isn't that bad."

"Cripes sake, Bobby. Randy Johnson of ABC can run circles around him. If Randy was on either CBS or NBC, he'd be the top dog overnight. But, half of the United States can't even get ABC news and as a result, its newscasters seem to be forever doomed to play second fiddle to the likes of Grimes."

* * *

Susan Ainsworth was propped up in an easy chair as she watched the proceedings at the United Nations. She had been so happy the last few days. But in particular that morning. A call from Colonel Sharp informed her that Mike Donovan would be calling her later on that afternoon and asked her to keep the evening open. They were having a repeat of dinner at Bannigans.

Sharp's suggestion that she watch the UN debate today without fail aroused her interest. "Why?" she asked.

"I strongly encourage you to watch," Colonel Sharp replied. Then he added, "You may be pleasantly surprised."

After thanking him for the letters which had arrived yesterday, she hung up. A crash job at the nearest beauty parlor. A new dress from Jellef's, a bottle of perfume labeled "Forever Yours", from Woodies; and a new negligee. Yes, she was ready for Mike. She could hardly wait until his call. Now, though, she was settled back to watch the UN show, as the TV newscasters had begun to label the President's appearance today.

But a thought kept nagging her. What relationship did Mike Donovan have to the President's appearance at the United Nations today? Obviously, something. Colonel Sharp had as much as told her that Mike would call soon after the United Nations meeting that afternoon.

She thought back to months ago when she had first met Mike. Flown to Washington from Fort Bragg on a presidential plane: Was it for a visit with the President at the White House? But why back to Fort Bragg and out of her life? Now, somehow he was back with the President in New York, or at least would be in New York at the same time as the President. Try as she might, she couldn't figure out how they were related. But tonight, she'd ask Mike.

If only she had the power to move time forward; she set the clock for nine. She'd be in Mike's arms and would tell him how much she had missed him and loved him. Every minute between now and then would seem like days. But wait she must. And she might just as well be comfortable doing so as she slipped off her shoes, curled up in her wingback easy chair and, with a cold brew in hand, waited patiently for the big TV show to begin.

"Isn't it time Henry arrived?" the President asked.

"He's due in ten minutes," Bobby replied.

"God, we've got to go over our game plan. This is one time I'm going to be sure he and I are on the same frequency. You know, Bobby, when I appointed the Honorable Henry Stevenson as Ambassador to the United Nations, the *New York Times*, the *Washington Post* and the *Philadelphia Inquirer* all commended my acumen in naming this seasoned politician to this important post. Outstanding ex-Governor, distinguished United States Senator, Under Secretary of State, you name it. An Ivy leaguer, one of their own. Not a fault or blemish on his record. They recited chapter and verse of his accomplishments and how he would add luster, tone, and solid dimension to our UN effort. And what happens? Henry takes off on his own. Never mind those instructions from Foggy Bottom. Here's what the United States of America proposes to do. My first inkling of his latest position on UN issues is served up to me when I read the morning papers. Wham! The same *New York Times, Washington Post* and *Philadelphia Inquirer* rake me over the coals for failing to control Henry. When they talk about freedom of the press, it means only one thing to most of the media: an open license to criticize, blame, point, accuse, and second-guess. By God, today Henry is going to hew the line, or else. The stakes are too high, no drawing to fill an inside straight. We've got to win the pot."

The President's monologue was interrupted by an announcement from the secret service man at the door that Ambassador Stevenson had arrived. "Good morning, Mr. President, I hope you're enjoying our beautiful city." Jack Ketner thought he detected just a slight trace of rancor in Stevenson's voice.

"Henry," the President replied, "my only observation so far is that the mattress had several new lumps I hadn't noticed before, the traffic is more congested, and the people seem to be milling around more. But, enough of small talk for now. We've got a big day ahead of us. Now, here's the game plan."

The President was engrossed in deep conversation as Bobby softly tiptoed out the door and went down the hall to the elevator exit, turned at the next corridor and rapped on the door of a suite.

"Who is it?"

"It's me. Bobby."

The rasping sound of the dead bolt being opened echoed through the hall. Bobby glanced furtively in both directions. Not a soul in sight. He turned the knob, pushed open the door, entered hurriedly, and just as rapidly closed the door and returned the dead bolt to lock position.

He threw his arms around Carol and whispered softly, "I'm sorry I'm late but I had to keep the President company until Ambassador Stevenson arrived. God, how I've missed you." He pushed her slightly away and looked at her. She was even more beautiful than the last time he had seen her almost a month before in Miami. The light flickering in through the window blinds seemed to dance in minuet on her shoulder-length red hair. The sheer negligee she was wearing accented every curve of her body. He pulled her to him again. His lips met hers as his hands began caressing her eyebrows, ear lobes and shoulders. His hands cupped her breasts firmly. Her body quivered. He brushed his lips across her eyelids and throat. She clung to him, each of her kisses more demanding than before. God, how he loved this girl.

"Carol, I told the President I wanted to get a couple of chores done while he and Ambassador Stevenson had their meeting. I've got about an hour before getting back to see him off for the afternoon session at the UN. As soon as he leaves, I'll be back."

"I'll wait for you. I didn't think the plane would ever get here this morning. We were held in the landing pattern for what seemed like hours. Guess every head of state is coming to New York today. I got here about thirty minutes ago, showered and was having my first cup of coffee when you arrived. You know, you don't give a girl much time to get ready."

"I'm sorry about that, Carol, but it wasn't until late last night that I knew I'd be coming to New York with the President today. He wanted me along to keep him out of trouble, he said. I called you as soon as I could and am thankful that you made it on such short notice. I have often thought of those wonderful two days we had together in Miami after we met at Lansing Endicott's party. The President has asked me several times why it took me so long to check out a couple of leads in the Cuban community on what was to be a down and right back trip. I keep telling him it takes a while to get to the bottom of things."

She turned toward him again and began to unbutton his shirt. He untied his tie, and kicked off his shoes. She went to the window, drew the blinds and came back to him again. Her fingers moved in a slow, tender path across his back. He loosened the shoulder straps of her negligee and slipped it down her body until it lay crumpled on the floor. Bobby sat on the edge of the bed and pulled her toward him. He kissed her again and again, her lips, ears, neck, shoulders and breasts. Her fingers rumpled his hair and started to beat a slow tattoo on his shoulders. The hum of traffic many stories below provided an obligato to the tempo of their love.

As Robert Ketner walked by the secret service agent guarding the door leading to the President's suite, he asked, "How soon must the President leave to make a one o'clock arrival at the UN?"

"The chief just told me we are scheduled to leave at twenty minutes to one," the guard replied.

"Thanks, I'll have him all set to go in plenty of time." The President and Ambassador Stevenson were still engaged in conversation as Bobby entered the room.

Walking over to the far corner of the room he picked up the *New York Times*. The headline caught his attention "President and Premier To Meet in Shootout at UN." The headline in the *Washington Post* was a bit more subdued, "Krenchev and Ketner in Face-to-Face Debate at UN."

He quickly scanned the papers. Nothing more than a rehash of the accusations and denials which had been the lead stories for the past twenty-four hours.

Henry Stevenson said, "I'll see you there at one, then," and the meeting ended as he rose from the leather-covered chair and walked rapidly to the door into the hallway without a passing glance acknowledging Bobby Ketner's presence.

"Are you and Henry still at odds?" the President asked.

"Apparently," Bobby replied. "Ever since I gave him that ass-chewing—on your orders I might add—he has given me the cold shoulder."

"Well, for once I hope he sticks to the script we have just worked out," the President said, "or, by God, he'll be going back to Providence."

"I just checked with the Secret Service. They said you should plan on taking about twenty minutes for the trip to the UN. That means a 12:40 departure."

"I think I'll leave about 12:30 and do a bit of politicking on the way. I may need a few votes after today." It was obvious that the President was looking forward to his appearance at the UN. "Incidentally, Bobby, where did you go when Henry arrived? I really wanted to have you here while we went over our strategy, if for no other reason than to support my position should Henry screw this one up."

"Jack, I would have been a distraction. Henry would

have spent his time thinking of ways to harpoon me rather than concentrating on what you wanted him to do. I also had an urgent chore to take care of."

"Is the chore down the hall, Bobby?" the President asked mockingly.

"What do you mean by that?"

"Bobby, haven't you learned a thing while you've been my attorney general? Don't you know that there isn't anything going on within my official family that the Secret Service doesn't tell me? By the way, how is she?"

Bobby blushed. "Dammit, Jack, I never thought for a minute that you'd have the secret service reporting on me too."

"Especially you, Bobby," replied the President. "You've got to realize that I can't wake up some morning and find the roof caving in on me because of some indiscretion by any of my key people, especially my brother. However, in your case, I think I understand. Just be careful."

"Jack, do you understand?" Bobby replied. "Lucy has become a terrible drunk and unmanageable. If it weren't for my position in the government, and especially my relationship to you, she'd have been on every page of every newspaper every day. Truthfully, I'm more worried about Lucy's adventures making news than anything I do. I've had her dried out twice. It's no use. I can't tolerate her. You know I'll stick it out. I can't afford to be a party to a scandal so close to the presidency. I lost all feeling for Lucy several months ago when I caught her trying to seduce Mike Ahern when I stumbled across them in the rose garden at Janning's party. We have agreed to share the same house but it's been a platonic relationship since then."

"I'm sorry, Bobby. I had no idea things had deteriorated so badly. I knew you and Lucy were having a problem. I understand your position. But be careful. If the press ever gets wind of what's going on with your redhead from Miami, you will turn out to be the bum, not Lucy."

"I know that, Jack. I'm going to sort all of this out after this current crisis is over. I may even ask you to accept my resignation to avoid any possibility of embarrassing you. I'm not concerned with my own future. It's yours that counts now."

Bobby paused, then said briskly, "Let's have a sandwich and a beer before you dress to leave."

"Fine", the President replied.

Bobby summoned the White House steward from the adjoining room and placed the order.

"Let's see what's on the tube now," Bobby said and he flicked on the TV. "Soap operas—and the world's greatest show's about to take place!"

"A little patience, Bobby. The show doesn't begin for another hour."

Chapter 19

BLAND RAMSEY, CHIEF of the White House Secret Service detail was always punctual. Today was no different. He knocked softly on the door, opened it slightly and said, "Twelve-thirty, Mr. President. We should be leaving in a few minutes."

"O.K., Bland. I'm about ready." Jack Ketner looked at his brother and said, "Bobby, I wish you'd change your mind and come to see the show from the visitor's gallery."

"No, Jack, I've made other arrangements. I'm sure TV coverage will be complete. I don't want to distract from your performance. If I went along, the press would hound me for an interview."

"I'll see you back in Washington, then," the President said. "I'm going directly to the plane as soon as the afternoon's session is over."

The President picked up his pipe and with a glance into the large mirror to check his appearance, left the room. Within minutes, Robert Ketner walked down the hall and entered Carol's suite. He gave her a lingering kiss, flipped on the TV and said, "Let's watch the excitement."

Don Grimes' voice was clear and resonant. "The President has just left his hotel to begin the short ride to the United Nations. The crowds have been gathering since early morning to see history being made. We now take you to Ned Borman high atop the Waldorf Towers for an on-the-spot report."

"Thank you, Don. From this vantage point, you can see the huge crowds lining every square foot of the avenue. An air of anticipation is evident everywhere. Security is perhaps the tightest in the history of the city of New York." As the camera panned building after building showing guards with weapons at the ready scanning every window and doorway, Borman's commentary continued, "The President's car is moving slowly down the avenue. Secret Service agents surrounding the President are at least double the number which normally cover the President's motorcade. The President is raising his hand in what appears to be a V for Victory sign. That's it. You can see it clearly now. The crowd roars its approval. New York City mounted police are moving just ahead of the motorcade clearing the road and keeping the crowd back behind the barricades which have been strung the full length of Park Avenue."

"Ned, we've got to break away for a minute." Don Grimes' face appeared on the screen as he continued. "We have word that the Soviet Premier is about to leave his penthouse suite in the Waldorf. Rollie Jansen is there. Rollie, give us a summary on what is happening."

"Really nothing much from our viewpoint here in the corridor. Security has just told us that the Premier is about to leave for the United Nations. For the past hour, though, something certainly has been going on. One Russian official after another has entered the Premier's suite and few have come back out. It appears that a last-minute strategy conference is underway. A few minutes ago, a spokesman informed the press here that Premier Krenchev had been in contact with Mr. Castro. The Cuban dictator has confirmed Mr. Krenchev's repeated statements that the Soviet Union had not provided Cuba with intermediate range ballistic missiles armed with nuclear warheads. It is obvious that the Soviet Premier is going to make that point again in the debate which is only a half hour away."

Suddenly, the doors of the suite were opened and Mr. Krenchev, followed by a group of Soviet officials, came through the door. Two husky men flanking the Premier started elbowing their way through the cameramen and press crews who filled the hallway. It was obvious they were KGB agents, the dreaded Soviet secret police. As the group was about to enter the elevator, Mr. Krenchev turned and looked directly at the TV cameras.

"Mr. Krenchev, Neil Bowen of NBC News. Can we have a minute of your time?"

Krenchev's sharp "Nyet" was accompanied by a scowl. He and his party entered the elevator and as the doors closed cameramen and newsmen jostled each other as they hurried down to the lobby below.

The operations room deep inside the Kremlin was filled as General Boris Kartsalov led Mikhail Gretkov to his chair facing the large TV screen mounted on the far wall.

Mr. Gretkov, white-haired and stooped, walked slowly, stopping from time to time to catch his breath. The President of the Soviet Union was an old man, officially eighty-two. His brilliant, meteoric rise in the Communist party had come to a sudden stop years before when he suffered a massive stroke. In recognition of his long and faithful service, he had been named president, a largely ceremonial position. However, he was still the president, and first among other members of the Politburo also gathered in the operations room. They watched quietly as he made his way to his seat centered behind the large, oversized conference table.

Boris Kartsalov checked the list of names on the small, single sheet of paper cupped in his right hand. With Mr. Gretkov's arrival, all were present. He reflected back to the instructions he had received from General Sorge Llanmuth, Chief of Soviet Forces, just before his departure for New York to attend the emergency meeting of the United Nations.

"Boris," he said, "here is a list of personnel I want you to have assembled in our operations room while the United Nations debate is taking place. We may need some immediate decisions and I want key officials who can make those decisions immediately available at that time. Krenchev does not know of this arrangement. If everything goes well, he need never know. If not, we can respond to any unforeseen emergency we might encounter at the UN. And Boris, I'm counting on you to keep our group together and not go off half-cocked to support any whim or fancy that the Premier may indulge in while in New York. The stakes are too high."

Boris smiled as he accepted the list of personnel. For months, the two of them had been playing a dangerous game. He hoped today would see it end.

The nation sat glued to its TV sets as the big debate in the United Nations began to unfold. The build-up was familiar; interspersed with the running commentary were the now familiar maps showing the damage a nuclear weapon could inflict on the nation's cities.

Robert Ketner pulled Carol toward him as the picture faded. "Intermission time," he said laughingly as he kissed her. Her body pressed against his as she slid into his embrace. He caressed her breasts and ran his fingers through her hair.

"I'm planning on spending tonight and most of tomorrow in New York. Have only one appointment. With you. O.K.?" Her passionate kiss was the only answer he needed. He glanced at the TV as the station break ended.

The President was arriving at the UN building. Police were all over First Avenue holding back the crowd which surged toward his car. As the President stepped from his limousine, a spontaneous roar echoed across the city. The American people were going to show their President they were behind him all the way.

Kurt Mannheim, the Secretary General of the United Nations, who had been waiting at the entrance, moved forward and extended his hand.

"Welcome to the United Nations, Mr. President. We are deeply honored to have you here today. Mr. Longfellow, my under secretary, will accompany you inside. I must wait here for the arrival of Mr. Krenchev."

"Thank you, Mr. Mannheim. I'll see you later then."

Jack Ketner liked the portly Mannheim. He was the first UN Secretary General who was totally impartial in all his actions and never apologetic for his decisions. And, what John Ketner liked about him most of all was that he was discreet and truthful, never playing what he heard from one superpower against the other. Always factual, honest, and to the point. His big achievement in his first year in office was reducing the bloated UN staff, despite the wailing and objections of member nations claiming discrimination every time one of their nationals was selected for separation. The secretary general's decision to preside personally over today's debate had been welcomed by all the participants.

John Ketner walked through the main lobby and into the great hall of the United Nations. Television lights momentarily blinded him. He looked around. Every available seat in the visitors' gallery was filled. He spied Henry Stevenson waiting with the United States UN delegation. He walked rapidly toward the group.

Henry Stevenson was apologetic. "I'm sorry, Mr. President. I didn't see you arrive."

"That's all right, Henry. With this mob, it would be difficult to see anyone." John Ketner looked around again. The assembly hall was packed. On the floor itself, extra seats had been added to accommodate the large entourages of visiting heads of state.

"Mr. President. Everything is in order, exactly as you wanted it. This way to your seat, sir."

The President followed Ambassador Stevenson as he pushed his way through the delegates milling around the floor. John Ketner stopped briefly to shake hands with Mr. Gallois, the President of France, remarking that he was looking forward to their meeting in Washington later that week. Out of the corner of his eye, he saw the bearded Premier of Cuba, who took great pains to ignore his arrival.

As John Ketner took his seat behind the table marked "United States of America", Stevenson said, "Mr. President, here is the hotline phone," as he pointed to the brilliant red instrument on the right side of the desk. "This blue phone is connected directly to the White House switchboard. When you want to call, just lift the receiver. The operator will answer automatically. When a call for you comes in, this small bulb will glow.

"Mr. Krenchev has a similar arrangement," the ambassador continued. "His red phone is connected with the Kremlin, his blue phone to the Russian Embassy in Washington. Mr. President, when you push this white button here, all phones will be connected to the public address system permitting all delegates to hear what is being said. Mr. Krenchev cannot disconnect this system nor does he have a control to connect or disconnect the public address system. Finally, a Colonel Donovan is waiting in the small conference room just outside the exit door leading to the main hallway. He asked that I inform you that he has the baby with him. I don't understand his role or the meaning of the baby, but he said you would."

"Thank you, Henry. All the arrangements seem to be in order. Just follow our script and I'm sure everything will turn out to our advantage."

Henry Stevenson was perplexed and more than a little irritated. Why had the President ordered him to let an army colonel into the United Nations with the large cloth-covered push cart? Something was going on but he was not informed and he didn't like it. The four armed Green Berets with the colonel looked like a tough lot. Dammit, the President had appointed him as his United

Nations Ambassador. Why didn't he confide in him?

Jack Ketner looked at his watch, 12:48. Two minutes to go and Krenchev had not yet arrived. Just like the bastard. Showing the world it waits for him. Perhaps by the time the afternoon was over, things would be different.

He glanced around the room. Richard Cavanaugh, the British Prime Minister, was whispering with one of his advisors, nodding his head, then abruptly shaking it. Ketner finally caught his eye and the Prime Minister instinctively raised his hand. Jack Ketner smiled. He knew he could count on British support. The shape of his fingers outlined the figure V.

Siegbert Alber, the Chancellor of West Germany, walked over and gave the President a warm handclasp and exclaimed, "we're behind you in every way, Mr. President. You can count on our support." Jack Ketner acknowledged the greeting and said, "it's always nice to see an old friend. Especially today." Among all of the world's leaders, none had his admiration and respect more than the German chancellor. When Krenchev had threatened him in Vienna soon after taking office, the first one to publicly support the United Sates was Siegbert. They had been staunch friends ever since.

A sudden rise of excitement in voices signaled the arrival of the Soviet Premier. Jack Ketner watched him enter. Krenchev glanced up to the galleries and threw both arms high into the air waving them back and forth like a victorious gladiator. The two husky KGB guards were at his side. A half dozen Soviet officials stood quietly while the Premier continued bowing and waving. But what caught Jack Ketner's eye were the two men bringing up the rear. Both were in uniform and wearing the rank of Marshal of the Soviet Union.

The President quickly turned to Stevenson and asked, "Who are the marshals with Krenchev?"

"The one on the right is Marshal Bolinov, a member of the Soviet military committee to the United Nations.

I don't recognize the other."

Jack Ketner picked up his blue phone.

"Yes, Mr. President?"

"Anne, get me General Taylor immediately."

Jack Ketner heard one ring, then General Taylor's voice.

"Ben, are you watching the circus on TV?"

"Yes, Mr. President."

"Good. Who is the Soviet general with Krenchev? The one with the bushy eyebrows. I understand the other one is Marshal Bolinov."

"That's General Sorge Llanmuth, Chief of Staff of the Soviet High Command. I don't understand why you asked. When I heard late last night that Krenchev was bringing him along, I called Henry Stevenson and asked him to tell you the first thing this morning. I didn't want to awaken you with that bit of information. Felt you needed all the rest you could get."

"Ben, I may need some technical help from the military myself. Both Krenchev and I will be talking about a weapon neither one of us knows a damn thing about."

"I took care of that. When I called Henry, I told him Jerry Maxwell and Byron Peterson would both be available. In fact, they are standing by in the ambassador's office now, ready to provide any assistance you might need. They flew up early this morning. You know, of course, Byron is an army expert of rockets and nuclear weapons. Jerry Maxwell commanded all the Minutemen sites when he was commander of SAC and knows the missile business as well as anyone. I'm sure that between them, they can provide anything you might need in the way of technical information."

"Thanks, Ben. I knew I could count on you, but dammit, I don't understand why Henry didn't pass that information to me. I spent almost two hours with him this morning and not a clue that he had this information or had even spoken to you. Thanks again, and stand by in case I need you later."

As the President hung up his phone, he turned to Henry Stevenson with apparent irritation. "Henry, why didn't you pass on the information that Ben Taylor wanted relayed to me about General Llanmuth accompanying Krenchev? And how is it you didn't let me know that Jerry Maxwell and Byron Peterson would be here in the event we need their help?"

"That was trivia. I can handle this debate without any assistance from them. Frankly, I don't like Ben Taylor butting into areas of my responsibility. If and when I need his help, I'll ask for it."

"Henry," the President said, "we're playing for keeps today. I don't appreciate it one damn bit when a senior official in this government asks you to convey a message to me and you decide whether or not it should be done. Don't ever pull that crap on me again. I won't tolerate it."

As the Secretary General pounded his gavel, a silence grew in the packed hall. When he had the attention of all the delegates, he began speaking.

"Distinguished guests, delegates, this emergency session of the United Nations requested by the United States of America is now open. The usual procedures will be followed. However, in the light of the special character of this meeting and to avoid interruption while this meeting is going on, I have asked that all entrance doors be closed and guarded. There will be no further entrance or exit of delegates until the proceedings are ended. We have over fifty heads of state with us today and I have taken these unusual security precautions to avoid any act which might reflect adversely on this great body. I trust you understand my concern for their safety. At this time, the clerk will read the text of the resolution proposed by the United States."

A small, slightly bald, gray-haired, dark-skinned man moved to the microphone. He started reading in a quiet, deliberate manner.

"Resolution by the United States of America"

"The Union of Soviet Socialist Republics having introduced intermediate range ballistic missiles armed with nuclear warheads into Cuba poses a threat to the security of the United States of America and its sister republics of the Western Hemisphere.

1. The United Nations condemns such actions and demands the immediate withdrawal of such weapons from Cuba.
2. The United States and representatives of at least five other nations to be designated by this assembly will make on-the-spot inspections of Cuba, in concert with or without representatives of the Union of Soviet Socialist Republics, to verify that such withdrawals have been made.
3. That failure on the part of the Soviet Union and Cuba to immediately dismantle such missiles and remove them from Cuba, the United Nations authorizes and directs the United States of America, joined by such other countries who want to align themselves with this effort, to use such military force as necessary to remove this threat to world peace."

"That ends the resolution submitted by the United States of America."

Jack Ketner looked directly at Elonson Krenchev. Krenchev, with a sneer and a scowl on his face, looked quickly at Ketner then leaned over and whispered to one of his aides.

"Mr. Secretary," Henry Stevenson's voice could be heard throughout the great hall, "The United States delegation requests recognition."

Before Kurt Mannheim could respond, the voice of Mr. Krenchev came booming over the lousdpeaker. "Mr. Secretary, the Soviet Union will not tolerate these slanderous allegations by the prime imperialists of the world."

"Mr. Krenchev," the voice of Kurt Mannheim was firm, "The United States requested this emergency meeting. They have introduced a resolution. Under the rules of this body, they are entitled to recognition to present the opening arguments in support of their resolution. The Soviet Union will be given ample time to respond. If you would, sir, please reserve your comments until I recognize you after the United States representative has had an opportunity to present his statement."

The Soviet Premier jumped to his feet, waving his arms. "I will not sit idly by while the United States trumpets these ridiculous charges to the world. Neither Mr. Castro nor I are in New York as defendants. We are here to give the lie to imperialist propaganda. We deny that such weapons are in Cuba. I call on the President of the United States to renounce this resolution, and publicly apologize both to Comrade Castro and to me for this insulting attack on our integrity and honesty. We call upon the people of the United States to respect the motives and actions of the peoples of the Republic of Cuba and the Soviet Union. We stand firmly together with our Cuban friends. I warn Mr. Ketner and his aggressive militarists that should any attempt be made to use force against Cuba, the full weight of the power of the Soviet Union will be felt by all who assist them in carrying out this insidious and threadbare scheme to discredit the great Soviet and Cuban peoples."

"Carol, not now." Bobby Ketner, who had been stretched out on the bed watching the proceedings on TV, moved Carol's hand from his thigh and sat up on the edge of the bed where he could better see the TV screen. Unbelievable. There was Krenchev with clenched fist pounding on the top of his desk and furiously shouting a staccato outburst which, even in Russian, clearly sounded like epithets and vilification.

Don Grimes' voice confirmed his suspicions, "The leader of the Soviet Union has just blasted the U.S. resolution using language which for the benefit of our audience we will not translate. In earthy, peasant, barnyard four-letter words, he has accused the United States, which is supported and encouraged by the *revanchist* West German government—which he labelled as a band of detestable Nazis—of slandering the Soviet Union and its accomplishments since the great revolution. He claimed they are insanely jealous of Soviet success. The allegations about nuclear weapons in Cuba are a hair-brained scheme to divert attention from their own colossal failures, Krenchev explained."

The TV suddenly focused on the United States delegation. Momentarily, it caught the President pressing both hands tightly against the earphones as though not to miss a single word of the simultaneous translation. His face was grim.

The camera then showed Henry Stevenson, who, quickly recognizing that he was on camera, looked directly into the camera and smiled, exposing his even, gleaming teeth. "God," Bobby Ketner remarked, "that bastard plays to an audience, no matter what the circumstances."

The camera went back to the Soviet delegation. The Soviet Ambassador to the United Nations was tugging at Mr. Krenchev's arm. Krenchev turned, and with his other hand defiantly pushed the ambassador back into his seat.

Don Grimes' commentary continued, "it appears that there is some disagreement between Mr. Krenchev and Ambassador Petrov. As you have just seen, Mr. Krenchev physically shoved his own ambassador back into his seat. This whole sordid affair is being seen and heard around the world. What it will mean in the long run is hard to determine at this time.

"But one thing is certain. Mr. Krenchev did not come to this meeting to listen passively to the American charges levied against his nation. Instead, he has taken the offensive, and ignoring all rules of conduct normally governing United Nations proceedings, has accused the

United States of conspiring with its allies to denigrate the vast accomplishments of the Soviet Union.

"In all my years as a newsman, I have never seen such a display of rude and boorish behavior in any public forum. Looking at the delegates of the nations assembled here today, I believe it's clear that only the Cuban delegation headed by Mr. Castro is pleased. Even the delegates of the Iron Curtain countries appear taken back by the sudden vitriolic outburst by the Soviet Premier. They show no enthusiasm or support of the Soviet charges. On the contrary, they seem chagrined and embarrassed."

Bobby Ketner watched as the TV camera panned the East European delegations one after another. Not a smile could be seen. The Hungarian delegates actually squirmed in their chairs as the camera slowly panned their positions. The Romanian delegation sat stiff-lipped and silent, looking straight ahead.

The camera returned to Krenchev. With a final thumping of his clenched fist to emphasize a point, he abruptly sat down. The assembly suddenly fell silent. All eyes were focused on the Soviet Premier.

Chapter 20

THE OMINOUS SILENCE in the great hall of the United Nations was broken by the pounding of the gavel and Kurt Mannheim's announcement. "The Secretary General recognizes the United States Ambassador to the United Nations, the Honorable Henry Stevenson."

Henry Stevenson rose, walked stiffly down the aisle and up the platform steps to the dais carrying a small leather folder which he placed on the podium, and as he looked from one side of the hall to the other, removed the text of his prepared speech. Deliberately he began, "Mr. Secretary, fellow delegates. I hold here a well-documented, carefully prepared speech to deliver to this great assembly." He held aloft the thick sheaf of typewritten script.

Then in a strident, rasping tone he continued, "In view of the intemperate outburst of unsupported and unsubstantiated charges by the Soviet Premier, I intend to forego my formal, prepared speech in order to rebuff every one of Mr. Krenchev's utterances, line by line, item by item, word for word."

Jack Ketner cringed. After all the preparations they had made and rehearsed, Henry was going to abandon his role in the game plan and pursue his erratic political instinct. If he let him continue, the United States would come out second best for sure. Jack Ketner rose from his chair and walked toward Henry Stevenson who stopped talking and looked at the President with evident surprise.

"Henry, please be seated. I've decided that I will personally respond to the Premier's charges."

Henry Stevenson grimly returned to his chair. For the first time in his life he was to have been the focus of world-wide attention. Jack Ketner had humiliated him and by usurping that opportunity, denied him his great chance. He'd had enough. As soon as the session was over, he was going to have a showdown with Jack Ketner. Either he was going to be the UN Ambassador or else. He knew the President wouldn't dare fire him. Most influential newspapers in the country were solidly behind him and would support his position. Jack Ketner was not held in the highest esteem. Henry Stevenson knew why. Ketner listened to the Pentagon brass entirely too much in solving the affairs of state, rather than relying on seasoned diplomats like himself.

Jack Ketner stood silently looking at the assembled delegates. With a nod to the secretary general, he began: "Mr. Secretary, delegates, I had planned on having Ambassador Stevenson present the United States' position in support of our resolution. However, the Soviet Premier chose to open this great forum with a barrage of bald-faced lies. His vile propaganda and defamation of most of the representatives to this great body compels me personally to respond for the United States and on behalf of all freedom-loving peoples everywhere. As a start, I would like to ask the Soviet Premier a single question."

Facing in the direction of the Soviet delegation, the American President asked calmly, in measured tones, "Do you deny that the Soviet Union has deployed into Cuba medium range ballistic missiles and nuclear warheads for these missiles? I ask you, Mr. Krenchev, do you deny that statement?" Jack Ketner looked directly at Elonson Krenchev.

The Soviet Premier leaped to his feet. In a rage he retorted, "Who has appointed you prosecuting attorney? Who has appointed you to judge the action of the Soviet Union? However, for you and all the world to know, I say again, the Soviet Union has not placed nuclear weapons in Cuba. Anyone who doubts the truth of my denial is blind to the facts. I say again, and so does my comrade, the stalwart leader of the Cuban revolution, Fidel Castro, we absolutely deny these arrogant, provocative lies being spread by the United States and its lackeys."

"Thank you, Mr. Krenchev. You cannot imagine the great satisfaction your denial of these charges gives me."

Krenchev could hardly restrain himself and began to smile. Here was the President of the United States about to begin a public apology.

"See," he said to his ambassador sitting next to him, "I understand these Americans. Ketner is already apologizing. You've got to be tough with them. But, let's listen to the rest of his apology," he said as he settled back in his chair.

Jack Ketner was more confident than ever. "I know many of you must wonder what the United States has in the way of proof to support the resolution we have introduced in the United Nations to condemn the Soviet Union for providing Cuba with nuclear weapons and demanding their immediate withdrawal. These are serious charges and we recognize our responsibility to make every effort to ensure that such allegations be proven with clear, irrefutable evidence that will stand up in a court of law, and also be accepted by any objective, fair-minded individual or nation as constituting adequate and positive support of our resolution. No doubt must remain in any delegate's mind that what we present here today meets that standard of proof. If we fail to convince any one of you that the Soviet Union has provided Cuba with nuclear weapons, then you have every right, and indeed the responsibility, to vote against the resolution proposed by my government and deny us the actions we have requested."

The President paused for only a moment before continuing. "Mr. Krenchev, Mr. Castro, when these allegations were first brought to my attention several months ago, I not only did not accept them, I simply did not believe them.

"While I recognize that we have greatly different types of government, I felt certain that you would never risk the future of your nations nor court the danger of nuclear war by a direct challenge to the United States and the nations of the free world. A nuclear conflagration would destroy us all.

"But reports of the deployment of Soviet weapons in Cuba kept coming to me. At first, I was reluctant to commit the specialized resources necessary to attempt to ferret out whether the reports had any substance. It appeared beyond comprehension at the time that the Soviet Union would embark on such a dangerous course. However, reports of a continuing Soviet effort to put nuclear weapons in Cuba persisted and intensified.

"I then ordered the entire United States intelligence community to concentrate on determining the actual facts concerning these reports. I am now going to present what we consider to be absolute proof that Soviet nuclear weapons are in Cuba. Operator, if you would lower the screen and dim the lights, please."

A large white screen high over the speaker's lectern began to unfold. When it was fully open, the lights began to dim.

"Hold it there, please," the President said. "I think that is just about the right amount of light. Now the first slide, please."

The screen was filled with a large map of Cuba. The President's voice was clear as he said crisply, "You recognize the island of Cuba. In showing this map I ask you to focus attention on these areas here. Operator, the first overlay, please." The map of Cuba then appeared superimposed with bright red stars. The President continued. "As you can see, there are a number of stars shown to be concentrated on the north central areas of Cuba, all of them are located within one hundred and twenty-five miles of the United States. These stars pinpoint specific locations on the island of Cuba where the Soviet Union has emplaced intermediate range ballistic missiles armed with nuclear warheads. Now, please follow me step by step as I show you detailed photographs of these sites. First photo, please.

"This is Site A, near La Isabela, Cuba. This oblique, high altitude, high resolution photograph looks to the average viewer like a concentration of vehicles and trucks parked in a cleared area. This next photo shows the same area magnified over twenty times."

The screen filled with a clear picture showing trucks, weapons and men. "Ordnance experts and missile engineers tell me that this is a Soviet missile launching site." The President took a long pointer and indicated the large, weblike structure located in the left center of the photograph. "This is the launching mechanism for these missiles. They are placed for firing on this frame. This reinforced sandbagged building shown here is the command and control facility used to fire the missiles once they are armed. These long boxes, about thirty feet in length, six feet in width, and forty-eight inches in depth are the shipping containers in which the missiles are moved." Then the President brought a gasp from the audience when he said, "The smaller boxes, shown here, are the containers in which the nuclear warheads are shipped."

"Mr. President," the voice of Premier Krenchev quickly boomed over the public address system, "do you think that because you say these boxes contain missiles and nuclear weapons, anyone believes you? What you show are shipping crates routinely used in sending Soviet material and equipment to Cuba. These are much like those you use in shipping artillery and spare parts to your lackeys in NATO Europe and the Middle East."

"Mr. Krenchev, I have the floor, please let me continue." He paused. "I will now show you photographs of another Soviet site in Cuba, one we have designated as Site B. Operator, the next slide, please.

"This site looks very similar to the one I previously showed. However, there is one marked difference. I call your attention to this box." The President moved his pointer to a large container near the center of the picture. "Fortunately, our aircraft took this photo at an opportune time. The lid on the box had just been removed and was still being held by these two men. Both soldiers wear the uniform of the Soviet rocket forces. I call your attention to an enlargement of this in the next photo."

The screen then filled from end to end with a fully exposed missile. The President spoke quietly. "U.S. Army ordnance personnel have positively identified this missile as a Soviet-made SS-21, an intermediate range ballistic missile. This part of the missile contains the receptacle for the nuclear warhead when it is mated to the missile. You should understand that this missile without a nuclear warhead is essentially useless. That raises a question. Would the Soviet Union send missiles into Cuba which could not be used?"

The voice of the Soviet Premier again interrupted the President. "Mr. Ketner, we do not deny that your photos show the Soviet SS-21 missile. I would point out to you and to the world that the pictures must have been taken over Soviet territory, where we have every right to have such missiles. I suppose it was taken by one of those U-2 airplane pirates who you had flying over the Soviet Union until we shot one down. If that is your proof, the joke is on you. The photo is not of a Soviet missile in Cuba. The Soviet Union is prepared to accept your apology now, although it can never forget these slanderous allegations. What do you say to that, Mr. President?" the Premier said sarcastically.

"I say, Mr. Krenchev, that your statements are well put. What you say could be true."

"Thank you, Mr. President, but that is far from an apology," the Soviet Premier replied.

"You are very perceptive. But I did not intend that statement to serve as an apology. Please let me continue."

"Bobby, I don't think the President is proving his point very well. Krenchev's rebuttals cast doubt on the points the President is trying to get across. Unless I'm mistaken, the United States is going to come out of this second-best and with its reputation tarnished."

"You're right, Carol, from what you have seen and heard so far. But the President is following a well-rehearsed script. He's just building Krenchev up for a big letdown. Even Don Grimes and the rest of the reporters seem a bit confused. Be patient and you'll see."

"All right, Bobby, but I can think of more interesting things we could be doing."

"So can I, but it will even be sweeter when this comes to a climax."

"That's exactly what I have in mind."

"Shush, let's listen."

Don Grimes' face appeared on the screen momentarily. His voice bordered on sarcasm as he intoned, "It is this reporter's considered judgment that the President, after all the advance publicity on his charges against the Soviet Union, is on a weak reed. As I have said repeatedly during the two years since he assumed office, his administration lacks clear perceptions of the great issues this nation faces.

"Today, we witness another shallow, poorly prepared administration venture, with an almost callous approach to what was billed as a direct confrontation of the Soviet Union. The United States position was to provide 'positive proof', those are the administration's own words, 'positive proof', that the Soviets have armed Cuba with intermediate range ballistic missiles which have nuclear warheads.

"As presented by the President here today, the proof is neatly wrapped, but vapor-thin, without substance or anything smacking of evidence which would be admissible in any court of law, even a magistrate's court.

"The Soviet Premier, despite his vile and intemperate language, has every right to question the validity of our charges and the underlying motives in bringing them before this assembly. Apparently, the President has again been swayed by the top brass in the Pentagon. If their judgment on other matters is no better than that displayed here today, a shakeup in the Defense Department must be made, and is, in fact, long overdue.

"There have been rumors throughout the government in the past few days that the President is dissatisfied with the performance of his UN Ambassador, Henry Stevenson. If there is any substance to these rumors, I would advise the President to carefully review his actions. Henry Stevenson has been an able and valuable leader both in and out of government. The President should not attempt to cover up his own inadequacies by passing an unfavorable judgment on that outstanding and dedicated American, Ambassador Henry Stevenson."

"Dammit Carol, for the first time I'm beginning to see Grimes' true character. The President has been down on him for months. I've been defending him. I must have been blind. As soon as this is over, I'm going to get his network boss on the phone and give him a piece of my mind."

Grimes' commentary continued. "After a station break, I'll be back with additional coverage of this amazing UN session and the rather inept performance by the President."

Robert Ketner was livid. "Before the end of the day, that son of a bitch is going to eat those words." He turned the TV to ABC. The President was still speaking.

"Despite such pictures, until quite recently I was still not fully convinced that this was adequate proof that these Soviet missiles were in Cuba. On that point, I agree with the Soviet Premier."

The TV screen showed the Soviet Premier smiling and nodding vigorously.

The President continued, "However, I would have been negligent in my constitutional duties and my oath of office if I had taken no further action in the matter at that stage. So, I ordered agencies of our government to make a more deliberate effort to get a close-up photograph of a Soviet nuclear weapon with something in the background which would convincingly tie the weapon to Cuba. I believe this next photo does that. Operator, please show slide 19 A."

A sudden, uniform gasp reverberated through the assembly hall.

On the screen an enlargement of a nuclear warhead with Soviet markings was clearly visible. Two uniformed personnel were lifting the warhead from a box identical to the one shown by the President earlier. On each end was a uniformed soldier. On the left, a young Latin-looking individual in military fatigues. On the right, a figure of a slightly built Soviet officer who appeared to be straining to hold up his end of the warhead.

The President continued, "The next photograph is an enlargement of the one shown here. Operator, No. 19 B, please."

The large Soviet symbol in the center of the weapon filled two-thirds of the screen. The President's voice, which had become more confident with the showing of each photo, now echoed through the hall. "Mr. Krenchev, there is a Soviet nuclear weapon, serial number SU 9 YB FR 934. There, clearly visible, is a Cuban soldier. He is, Mr. Castro, a Sergeant Raul Gonzales by name. Mr. Krenchev, the Soviet officer in this photograph is Lieutenant Yuri Kerenkov, now serving as a member of the Soviet Advisory Group in Cuba. There, Mr. Krenchev, is your proof." Then after a pause, he said, "Lights, please." The President looked directly at the Soviet Premier. "Mr. Krenchev, now how do you plead? Mr. Castro, isn't Sergeant Gonzales one of your soldiers?"

The great assembly hall was quiet. Not a sound could be heard.

Elonson Krenchev was in a heated discussion with General Llanmuth as the President repeated his challenge, "How do you plead?"

For the first time, the Soviet Premier was subdued. He looked at Castro and scowled. He rose slowly from his chair and approached the dais. Jack Ketner stepped aside while completely ignoring the oncoming Premier.

Krenchev moved to the lectern and grasped each side. His knuckles were white, his face deeply flushed. He looked from one side of the assembly hall to the other. Not a sound. Tension filled the hall.

Jack Ketner turned his back on Krenchev and, with a slow, deliberate move, descended the steps and returned to his chair with the United States delegation. Every delegate was fixed on the movements of the two men. Like a chess game, the two opponents moved into position.

Bobby Ketner turned up the TV volume. He didn't want to miss a word. The camera focused on Krenchev who looked like a huge bear hugging the lectern with his paws pressed firmly against each side. Sweat was forming on his forehead. His scowl gave way to an intense, angry look.

Just as suddenly, Krenchev appeared to regain his composure. Looking directly at Jack Ketner, his voice rasping anger, he said, "So that's the proof you have. Photographs," he said sneeringly. "Incredible! Incredible that you would ever think that a photograph of a missile would be adequate proof that we have moved missiles into Cuba. These photographs could have been deliberately fabricated by the CIA, posing U.S. citizens as military personnel. These photographs could even have been taken in the Soviet Union by one of your sleazy, sneaking military attachés after entering one of our restricted missile areas and then surreptitiously taking a picture of one of our missiles being removed from a box by a Soviet Officer and a Cuban sergeant. I don't deny that is a Soviet missile; I might even acknowledge that the lieutenant is Kerenkov, as you allege. I can even assume the sergeant is a Cuban, Raul Gonzales, who is serving in the army. That all may be very true. We frequently have Cuban soldiers in the Soviet Union for training by the glorious Soviet Army.

"What you have shown, no doubt, is one of my commanders showing the Cuban soldiers Soviet weapons during one of their orientation periods. Yes, that must be it. While the Cuban soldiers were in the Soviet Union receiving training, they were given a general orientation on weapons systems which have been developed to defend us against the imperialist powers which continue to threaten Soviet progress in many areas of the world.

"One of your irresponsible attachés somehow entered the area illegally and took your photographs. You know, Mr. Ketner, your attachés are noted for violating the hospitality of the Soviet Union. I personally remember one I had to declare *persona non grata* several years ago. Misconduct. A rascal. He insulted the Socialist state. I banished him overnight. It was one of them. One of his ilk, who violated our posted restrictions imposed to insure our state security and took those pictures. Then you have the gall, the audacity, to attempt a great hoax here at the United Nations by saying it was taken in Cuba. But your statement is nothing but lies, lies."

Krenchev was white with rage. His arms flailed the air as he continued. "Mr. Ketner, your proof turns out to be nothing but a contrived Madison Avenue sugarcoated stage performance complete with slide show. I know every delegate in this room will agree with me that you have breached the code of conduct between nations by bringing these unwarranted and still unsupported charges before this great international body. I ask, no, I demand, an apology to the Soviet Union, the Cuban peoples, and the representatives of all the nations assembled here, for your maliciously calculated, mischievous attempts at slander. That I demand."

With a swish of his hand to Jack Ketner, the Soviet Premier concluded, "And now, Mr. Ketner, I turn this forum back to you in order that you may apologize to me, and the world."

Krenchev strode rapidly from the stage and returned to his seat. He looked at the delegates throughout the hall as if to acknowledge what he surely thought would be thunderous applause. Instead, he was greeted by a strained silence.

As Bobby Ketner continued watching the almost unbelievable telecast of the UN meeting, Don Grimes' face reappeared on the screen. His voice was confident. "Ladies and gentlemen, we have just witnessed one of the most impassioned debates in history. It hurts me deeply to admit that the United States had failed,—no, our President has failed—to convince me, and I'm sure the millions of viewers who have been watching these events, that the Soviet Union has indeed given Cuba nuclear armed intermediate range ballistic missiles.

"While the Premier of the Soviet Union has behaved crudely, I cannot fault him too greatly. The charges brought by President Ketner against the U.S.S.R., while serious, can be recognized to be provocative. The Premier was bound to become indignant, and perhaps throw a tantrum or two. The seriousness of these charges was certain to have had impact on the events that have unfolded here today. I see that the President is about to speak again. Let's return to the rostrum. Perhaps this is his apology."

Jack Ketner looked directly at the Soviet Premier. His

voice was choked with emotion, but while making an obvious attempt to control his anger, he began to speak in a quiet tone. "Mr. Krenchev, Mr. Castro, fellow delegates, you have heard the Premier of the Soviet Union for the third time this afternoon deny that his government has placed nuclear missiles in Cuba. I ask you to remember that he admitted that the photograph I presented here a few minutes ago was of a Soviet nuclear missile. I had hoped that I could spare any further embarrassment to the leadership of the Soviet Union by having their Premier admit what is patently evident—that Soviet missiles are in Cuba. But since I have thus far failed to achieve this purpose in a more rational manner, I have one last bit of evidence which I intend to show you at this time which I believe will remove any possible doubt in any delegate's mind that the charges presented here today by the United States are true. I call your attention to the doors to my immediate left."

Every delegate's eyes turned to the double doors which were slowly being opened. Bobby Ketner watched the camera focusing on the cart which was being pushed through the door by four soldiers all wearing Green Berets. A large black cloth was draped over the cart. Walking slowly, a pace behind the cart, was an army colonel wearing a Green Beret at a jaunty angle. Bobby Ketner immediately recognized Mike Donovan.

The President of the United States moved away from the podium and approached the cart as it was being pushed toward the dais. He turned it slightly and stopped it directly in front of the table occupied by the Soviet delegation.

Looking directly at Krenchev, he grasped one end of the cloth covering the cart and with a quick movement of his arm flung it to the floor. "Mr. Krenchev, deny if you can, that this is your weapon. We removed it from a Soviet missile site in Cuba located three kilometers from El Cuzo. That, I might add, is only one of some forty missiles you have already deployed in Cuba. If you will look closely, here is the Soviet Union serial number SU 9 YB 821 FR 938."

Krenchev's face went white. Turning to General Llanmuth, he shouted, "How did they get this? Who is responsible? Mr. Castro, did you give them this? How did they get it? I want answers. Now!"

The hushed quiet which gripped the hall made Krenchev's voice even louder as he kept asking questions of his advisors. Every delegate could hear his voice.

Suddenly, the whine of a siren permeated the air. Krenchev spun around. The small rectangular box was glowing a brilliant red. A skull and crossbones were prominently displayed. Underneath was the warning: DANGER: EVACUATE AREA IMMEDIATELY: EXPLOSION IMMINENT.

Krenchev's face turned ashen white. Turning rapidly toward General Llanmuth, he barked, "General, the code! Turn it off before it detonates and blows us all to kingdom come. You know it is set to detonate automatically in minutes unless we put in a code extending the timing device. Hurry—the code—*this nuclear weapon is due to explode in minutes.*"

Delegates sat in stunned silence as the simultaneous translation of Krenchev's remarks came through their earphones. The strident wailing of the missile's siren punctuated the air of the assembly hall.

Suddenly, almost in unison, the seated delegates and visitors began clawing their way to the nearest exits. Jack Ketner pushed the start button on the stopwatch he held in the palm of his hand. Colonel Mike Donovan did the same.

Bobby Ketner, eyes focused on the TV, was listening to every word being said by Krenchev. Suddenly the voice of Don Grimes was heard in the background. "Let's get the hell out of here! The damn thing is going to blow up any minute!"

Bobby Ketner watched in disbelief as the TV camera,

still focused on the podium, was abandoned. He reached up and flipped the set over to ABC.

The voice of Randy Johnson describing the scene taking place in the United Nations was calm, almost detached. "The Soviet Premier's statement that the nuclear weapon uncovered by President Ketner was about to explode has caused a mass stampede for every exit. Delegates are pushing, shoving, and clawing their way in every direction. There's chaos and bedlam in this assembly hall. What's going on is beyond description and comprehension. At the far end of the hall, literally the entire assembly—hundreds of delegates—are trying to get through the narrow doors. There is Henry Stevenson, our UN Ambassador. I believe I also see Don Grimes, the noted network correspondent, fighting his way forward attempting to reach the exit. Yes, it is Don."

The ominous ticking of the bomb and the wailing of the siren were heard clearly across the nation as millions watched the unbelievable drama being played out in the United Nations.

In New York City, people listened in hushed silence as the voice of the Soviet Premier was translated, stating that the bomb would go off in minutes. Then, watching the delegates in the United Nations scrambling and fighting their way out of the building, the entire city erupted in mass hysteria.

Office workers poured out of downtown buildings and started fleeing in every direction. Fathers grabbed their children and, pushing and shoving their way through the quickly gathering mob, fought their way forward. Streets quickly became jammed with automobiles and buses backed up by the jammed bridges and tunnels leading out of the city to the adjacent countryside and safety. Car radios encouraged them on to greater efforts to flee to safety as the announcers kept describing the scene taking place within the United Nations.

In Sacramento, Joan Anderson had been watching the proceedings at the United Nations while ironing. As the bomb's siren began wailing and with the announcement of an imminent explosion, she shrieked into the telephone, demanding that the long distance operator connect her immediately with her mother in New York City. The operator's reply that all lines were busy made no impression on Mrs. Anderson as she watched the mob scene on TV out of the corner of one eye. She kept insisting that the operator cut the others off and connect her at once. Her mother lived only four blocks from the UN and she had to be warned of the imminent explosion of the nuclear bomb.

Joan Anderson became more and more hysterical as the operator failed to complete her call. It wasn't until the fire on her ironing board which sent her husband's shirt up in flames that she dropped the phone and ran from the house, going up and down the street screaming that her mother was going to be cremated by an atomic bomb if someone didn't warn her.

A comment by a Chicago TV reporter that what was happening in New York City could as easily be happening in any city in Illinois convinced listeners that they had heard him say Chicago was to be next. Streets quickly filled with people fighting their way to the suburbs and freedom. Mayor Donely's almost instant appearance on TV by minicamera from city hall pleading for calm and asking citizens of Chicago to remain in their homes or offices went unheard and unheeded. Parents and children left their TVs and radios blaring as they fled the city.

ABC TV, which kept telecasting throughout, flashed from the UN to the streets of New York City. Utter chaos prevailed. Uniformed policemen, firemen and other city employees broke ranks to join the mobs shoving, pushing and clawing their way up and down streets, seeking safety. Abandoned cars and buses blocked all traffic as passengers fled the stalled vehicles and joined the rush of humanity toward the outlying areas of the city.

Men, women and children fought their way through the Holland Tunnel. Fire trucks, ladders thrust skyward, were in brilliant contrast to the flames shooting from the fires abandoned by firemen.

In Florida, TV and radio coverage was interrupted momentarily to announce that the governor had ordered a state of emergency. The National Guard had been called up and would defend Florida against an invasion of that state from nearby Cuba. The governor had also sent a telegram to the White House asking for the immediate dispatch of federal troops to assist in the defense of Florida.

In North Dakota and Montana, the covers on Minuteman silo sites were removed and the missiles readied for firing. Base commanders confirmed that they had been placed on full alert early that morning and were only waiting for a presidential order.

Vehicle traffic in Washington, D.C. became impossible almost immediately. The rush to freedom by thousands of government workers soon blocked every bridge leading to northern Virginia. The State Department switchboard could not handle the calls which flooded its overworked telephone exchange. Ambassadors and embassies were demanding assurances that their leaders attending the UN session would remain unharmed.

In South Korea, the Philippines, Chile, and in many nations in Africa, local military leaders seized the government and declared martial law, explaining that their heads of state were only minutes away from being destroyed in an atomic holocaust about to wreck the UN.

Ben Taylor sat quietly in the operations room of the Joint Chiefs of Staff in the Pentagon watching events unfold at the United Nations and across the nation.

Should he call the President and advise him to call it

off, or let events run their corse? He thought of the past month, the doubts cast upon the President's leadership and the fickleness of the population to understand what had been and what was about to happen. He knew the President and the other assembled heads of state were in no danger from an atomic explosion. The code to turn the bomb off had been broken and was in the hands of the President and Mike Donovan. But what about the mass hysteria that was sweeping the country?

Was the damage, destruction and perhaps death in the frenzied mob scenes being displayed worth the President's effort to get the Soviet Union to admit arming Cuba and effect the immediate withdrawal of their missiles and men from that Caribbean Island?

For the first time, Ben Taylor realized the tremendous impact the news media had had on the nation during the past month. Day after day, newscast after newscast showing the effects of atomic explosions and those damnable concentric circles of destruction had made an indelible impression on the people—now facing what they viewed as an almost immediate missile attack from Cuba. The instincts for survival had surfaced in men, women and children across the nation.

Should he call the President and inform him of what was happening and convince him to end the showdown? Or would backing down now only postpone the inevitable date when Soviet missiles were operationally ready in Cuba and set to fire? He wrung his hands and beads of sweat began rolling down his forehead as he thought over his decision.

He reached for his phone connected directly to the President's desk at the UN. Then he slowly pulled his hand away. Stopping this now would only cause a replay in living color, tomorrow, next week, next month. He was sure of that. No, the showdown had to come now. Tomorrow might be too late.

Chapter 21

JACK KETNER GLANCED down at the stopwatch he was holding in the palm of his hand. Three minutes had already gone by. He looked around the assembly hall. Over half of the delegates had fled. The visitors gallery was empty. On the floor, he was pleased to see the delegates and the leaders of the Western nations he had personally contacted on his game plan had remained.

His old friend, Yoma Hosimyka, the Prime Minister of Japan, and his delegation were still in place, although their faces revealed tension and uncertainty. He glanced at the Soviet delegation. Krenchev and General Llanmuth were struggling for the hot line connected directly to the Kremlin. Jack Ketner pushed the white button on his desk as Krenchev's almost incoherent voice shouted into the phone.

"General Kartsalov, give me the code to defuse our nuclear warhead No. SU 9 YB 821 FR 938. Quickly."

"Comrade, why would you want the code? You are at the United Nations. That nuclear weapon is in Cuba. The Cubans signed a receipt for it several days ago."

"Dammit, Kartsalov, somehow the Americans got the thing out of Cuba and now have it here at the United Nations. It's a live weapon! The warning device has just gone off. Can't you hear the siren? That means unless we insert a code it will explode and kill us all in minutes. Thirty minutes, isn't it?"

"No, Comrade, ten minutes."

"What idiot made it ten minutes?"

"You did, Comrade. Remember, we had it programmed for thirty minutes. You ordered me to reduce it to ten minutes, as you didn't care if the Cuban soldiers were able to get away or not. It will explode in ten minutes, unless the correct code is inserted before then."

As Krenchev's conversation was translated, the bearded Prime Minister of Cuba stood up and shook his fist at Krenchev and muttered an epithet. Jack Ketner smiled when he noticed Castro barking an order to his delegation and walking rapidly out the nearest exit. As soon as he disappeared from view, the Cuban delegation ran pell-mell in the opposite direction heading for another exit.

Jack Ketner glanced at his stopwatch again. Five minutes left. He pressed the earphones closely to his ears as he listened to the translation of Krenchev's conversation with the Kremlin.

"Please, General Kartsalov, the code, or we will all die here."

Kartsalov's reply was interrupted by another voice, "Comrade Krenchev, this is President Gretkov. You have brought us to the brink of war. The high command and the politburo have been sitting here watching your performance at the United Nations. We are unanimously agreed that your position as Premier must be terminated at once."

"Comrade Gretkov, please, the code. I don't want to die. I want to spend the rest of my days in my dacha with my wife, Nikitna. You can have my resignation. But I don't want to die. I must have the code."

"All right, Krenchev, the code for your resignation. And, an immediate order to the high command to get all of our nuclear weapons out of Cuba. Your adventurism must end. You will return immediately to the Soviet

Union. General Llanmuth is to go to Cuba immediately to oversee the dismantling and return of our weapons."

"Comrade Gretkov, I will do it—but hurry, the code!"

"Good. Here is Kartsalov. He will give it to you."

General Kartsalov spelled out the code. "Nine four L. B. two one three P."

As each letter and number came over the loudspeaker, General Llanmuth punched the number and letter into the console. As he pushed the final letter, the wail of the siren stopped as abruptly as it had begun and the brilliantly lit glass-enclosed rectangular box became nothing more than a piece of dull glass. Elonson Krenchev, who had become hysterical while General Llanmuth was getting the code over the hot line to defuse the warhead, fell exhausted into the nearest chair as the sound of the siren ended. He bowed his head and clasped his hands around his burly neck.

Jack Ketner looked at him and felt a twinge of compassion for the pathetic figure sitting alone, ignored by the Soviet delegation.

Jack Ketner glanced briefly at the President of France who rose from his seat and came over and shook his hand. The Prime Minister of Great Britain followed with a handshake and an enthusiastic embrace. Then the Chancellor of West Germany, the Prime Minister of Japan and other leaders of the free world came over to wish him well.

As Jack Ketner shook the hand of the last one in line, the President of Chile, he walked over to the Green Berets and with his voice still quivering said, "I can't thank you enough. I want you all in the White House Rose Garden tomorrow. Until then, my suite at the Carlyle Hotel is available to you for a short R and R. I'll have General Peterson make arrangements to provide you every service during your stay in New York. General Maxwell will arrange a flight for you to reach Washington in time to have you at the White House tomorrow afternoon. Colonel Donovan, I'd like you to return with me to Washington this afternoon."

With a final comment, "You're a great bunch of guys!" Jack Ketner walked to the exit where the secret service detail was waiting. Mike Donovan walked at his side.

Randy Johnson's voice was full of emotion. "I'm sure every viewer will remember this day. Nothing so dramatic has ever been telecast or filmed, nor could you stage a play with the drama that we have witnessed. The leaders of the two greatest nations on earth playing Russian roulette. But when the President uncovered an actual Soviet weapon, things began to happen.

"It seems inconceivable that President Ketner had any idea that the weapon brought into this great assembly hall might explode, yet that was the case. It was perhaps an accident of history which set this train of events into action. The live weapon sounding a warning that it was about to explode completely changed the complexion of the debate which has been underway here for hours. The Soviet Premier, who alone knew that the weapon's warning signal and lighted console conveyed a warning of an imminent explosion, used the hot line to the Kremlin to get a secret code to deactivate the weapon. Thereby he admitted to the world that the Soviets had introduced nuclear weapons into Cuba. That admission was itself a startling revelation.

"However, the real drama of the afternoon was the utter chaos and bedlam that broke loose on the floor when the delegates learned that the nuclear weapon was about to explode. Ambassadors, diplomats, generals, high government officials, and yes, even some newscasters, all fought to get out of the UN building here in New York trying to reach sanctuary on the outside. Even now, only a relative handful of people are here.

"A pitiable sight is now displayed on the floor for all of you to see: the Soviet Premier, Elonson Krenchev, who until a few hours ago was one of the great and powerful leaders of the world, reduced to a pathetic figure, his head bowed, sitting alone at the Soviet table.

"We close this telecast from the UN to take you to the airport where in a few minutes the President will be boarding Air Force One for his return to Washington."

Randy Johnson leaned back in his chair reflecting on the day's events. For the first time, he understood the meaning of the strange telephone call he had received from the President of the United States that morning. "Stick with the telecast at the United Nations today, Randy, no matter what you perceive is happening. It will be worthwhile." And Randy Johnson smiled as he sipped his coffee. It certainly had been.

The impromptu news conference at the bottom of the steps leading to the doors of the big jet above was hectic. Microphones of every type and description were thrust at the President and flashbulbs popped everywhere as photographers jockeyed for position to take that one shot which would win them a Pulitzer Prize. The whirring of TV cameras was barely audible as correspondents shoved and pushed each other to get within earshot of the President.

"Mr. President, Barry Sullivan of the *Washington Post*. Sir, I want to be sure I understand your last answer to Jack McManny's question. You did have a code in your pocket which you could have inserted into the nuclear bomb to defuse it, in the event the Soviet high command had not given Premier Krenchev the code over the hot line?"

"Your understanding is correct, Mr. Sullivan. I repeat, both Colonel Donovan, who was with the weapon at all times, and I had the code. Either one of us could have stepped up to the bomb and defused it in seconds. However, as I explained earlier, my purpose was to get Premier Krenchev to admit publicly that the weapon was his. He, of course, did not know that we had the code to defuse the bomb as he pleaded with his military command in Moscow to give it to him. Our National Security Agency personnel who did the decoding assure me it is a relatively simple code. I have time for one more question. Mr. Perkins, it's your turn."

"Mr. President, would you elaborate on Colonel Donovan's role in this affair? It seems rather strange that you would have a colonel come all the way from Fort Bragg, North Carolina to take charge of a four-man detail to guard a weapon." The *Los Angeles Times* reporter's voice could barely be heard as the engines of a nearby jet started up.

"Mr. Perkins, Colonel Donovan had been a military attaché in Moscow some years ago and had a good appreciation of how Premier Krenchev reacts in a stress situation. I had him stand by so he could advise me on that. In addition, I discussed ways of getting the Soviet Union to admit publicly that they had armed Cuba with nuclear missiles. His position as the officer in charge of the guard detail was used to avoid undue attention to Colonel Donovan's presence. In fact, I have been so impressed with his observations about Krenchev and his overall ability that I have arranged with General Taylor to have him assigned to a staff position in the Pentagon where he might be more readily available, should I have need for his services in the months ahead."

With a final "Thank you, gentlemen," President Ketner walked rapidly up the steps. He turned for a final wave to the large crowd which had gathered to see him depart. The doors of the aircraft closed as he entered. Moments later, the big presidential jet was airborne enroute back to Andrews Air Force Base.

Jean and Bud Sharp had been watching the UN proceedings intently. Jean let out a scream of delight when she first spied Dagger Donovan pushing a cart onto the stage. She was fascinated by it all as the great debate went on. However, it was the President's comment at his plane-side press conference that really got her attention.

"Bud, did you hear that? Dagger is being transferred to Washington. The President just said so. I wonder who will be taking his job?"

"Jean, I'd planned on telling you later tonight, but this is a good a time as any. Dagger and I are exchanging jobs."

"Back to Bragg for us? You're kidding. And you taking command of the 7th Speical Forces Group? You know that assignment isn't much during peacetime. Training exercises, run-of-the-mill details. Gee, Bud, I was hoping your next assignment might be to something more exciting. You know that all Dagger has been doing is going from one place to another checking up on the training of his special forces detachments. By the way, didn't you once tell me that the army assigned only single colonels as 7th Special Forces Group Commander?"

"You know the old story, Jean. You go where the army sends you. Maybe things won't be as dull as you seem to think. Yes, the army did have a policy requiring that a single officer be assigned as the commander of that group but General Peterson called me and said they had to change that policy—would you believe it? Because of the equal rights bit."

Bud Sharp smiled as he walked into the kitchen to get another beer before hitting the sack. He needed a couple of hours sleep and he'd be as good as new, he had reassured Jean. The last couple of days had been hectic but they were unusual. A staff job at the Pentagon was more or less an eight-hour-day affair. The personnel people had told him that some three years before when he was assigned to the Joint Staff as Chief of Special Operations. He'd have a delightful three-year tour and be able to lower his golf handicap to at least ten, as special operations was rather an inactive business during peacetime.

In their suburban home in McLean, Bernie and Anne

Marie Dunsfield had been watching the TV spectacular being broadcast from the United Nations. Anne Marie was particularly enthralled by the President's description of how agencies of the U.S. government had broken the code which armed and disarmed the Soviet nuclear weapon.

As the last scene of the President's press conference faded from the screen, she turned to her husband of twenty-five years and said, "Bernie, I wish you could get involved in something that exciting. All you ever get called on to do is go to Fort Belvoir and help the army work out another mathematics formula for some piece of equipment they are developing. You've got to get into something more challenging than that. Those math problems must be so dull by now."

"Yes, Anne Marie, I guess you're right." A slight smile crossed Bernie's face. "If you will excuse me, I'm going into the library and read a bit from a new book I've just picked up at the Tysons Corner book store."

"A new book. What is it?"

"Nothing that would interest you."

"Let me see." She took the book from Bernie's hands and looked at the title. *The New Science of Mathematics*.

"Oh, Bernie," she sighed wistfully as she handed the book back to him, "you'll never change."

Bobby Ketner watched the President's plane become airborne before he picked up the phone. "Operator, get me the White House."

"White House, may I help you?"

"Anne, this is Bob Ketner. Connect me with the President. He's airborne enroute back to Washington."

"Just a moment, Mr. Ketner. I'll put you through." Bob Ketner heard only a half a ring before his brother said, "Yes, Anne, put him right on."

"Jack, do you understand what you have done? Added twenty years to my short life, given me gray hairs, and I might add, made me your proudest constituent."

"Thanks, Bobby. I know what you mean. I had a few uneasy minutes myself."

"But, Jack, how could you dare take a chance on Krenchev getting the code in time to turn off that blasted nuke? Was your press conference comment about having the code in your pocket so much bull?"

"You know me better than that. I'd never leave so much to chance. I wouldn't put our fate in Krenchev's hands. I had the code all right. NSA, with an assist from some civilian scientists, had finally broken the code. Colonel Donovan also had a copy of the defusing code and was timing every second that passed. And, to be real honest with you, so was I. We were each prepared to step in the last thirty seconds and punch in the proper code. Donovan had actually inserted a code just before he wheeled out the weapon. We had to make sure it would activate the warning alarm at the proper time.

"We needed this gimmick to get a confession out of Krenchev. You must remember that was the only hole card I had left to play, after Krenchev's refusal to admit guilt based upon my presentation of the photographs. The photos were great, but not enough to make him crack. But, that's behind us now.

"I want a favor. Would you and that redhead with you take Donovan's men out to dinner and give me the bill? They can fill you in on some of the details. I've given them my suite at the hotel for tonight since you will be sacking out elsewhere.

"Incidentally, I expect to see you tomorrow afternoon when Donovan and his men are coming to the White House for a little ceremony. God, how I'd like to share their experiences with the American people, but I don't dare. We may need them again. Got another call, Bobby, see you tomorrow."

The President was relaxed as he invited Colonel Donovan to take a seat across from him in the small dining area at the rear of the huge presidential jet. Mike Donovan had never before been inside such a luxurious craft. Thick wall-to-wall carpeting, sound-proof rooms, and the presidential china on the table before him. Even oil paintings fastened to each bulkhead. It was a Cadillac compared to the Ford T-39 presidential flight detachment plane he had flown in, months before. He was pleased that he had been invited to accompany the President back to Washington. He'd get to see Susan that much sooner.

"Colonel Donovan, I can't tell you how pleased I have been with everything you and your team have done." The President was smiling as he looked at Donovan. "The nation owes you its gratitude, and I am personally indebted to you. There is nothing that can compete with success. I am certain that if we had not been able to get our hands on a Soviet nuclear weapon, my critics would have driven me from office. However, my political fate is not important. What is important was the ability to get the Soviets to withdraw their missiles from Cuba without going to war to get it done. Thanks to you, it was possible. Now, you must tell me about your operation. I have had a burning curiosity for the last week about the use you made of the laxatives you so urgently needed to pull off your operation."

Mike Donovan explained the operation in detail to the President, who burst out with a roar of laughter as he heard how the laxatives were essential to the success of the mission. Mike Donovan grinned as the President remarked, "I think I'll have General Taylor order in a new supply to keep on a standby basis. That's our secret weapon, if I've ever heard of one.

"Colonel Donovan, you may have some friends to call after being out of the country for so long. This telephone here is connected directly to the White House switchboard. Just tell the operator who you want to call. She'll connect you. While you're doing that, I'm going back to my office and make a few calls myself."

* * *

"Yes, Mr. President, this is Earl Wilson speaking."

"Mr. Wilson, please express my appreciation and thanks to Dr. Bradley and Dr. Dunsfield for their truly magnificent performance during the past few days. They have made a significant contribution to support this nation's security. Their manner of performance, as well, has been outstanding. Personally and officially, I am most grateful to them both.

"And, thank you, Mr. Wilson, for your firm's help. Please extend my thanks to all who have contributed, especially to Dr. Bradley and Dr. Dunsfield. Early next week I'm going to have them down to the White House. I intend to present them the nation's highest civilian award. And, of course, I'd like to have you there too when we honor their contribution to the nation's security. General Taylor will be making the arrangements and will be in touch with you later to set up a mutually acceptable time."

"Thank you, Mr. President. I'll pass your comments to them today. And congratulations to you, sir. Your performance in New York was superb, as well as being a spellbinder."

"Thank you. I'm sure you recognized the very important part your firm played in making it all possible."

"We did, sir, and thank you again for calling."

Earl Wilson pushed the intercom button connected to his secretary whose desk was located just outside his door.

"Yes, Mr. Wilson."

"Lorraine, you know those vu-graphs I just gave you to type up in final form for use in our annual management meeting next week?"

"Yes sir, I have them all completed."

"Bring in the one which lists the company's goals and objectives."

Lorraine searched through the stack of vu-graphs until she located the one wanted. She walked into Mr.

Wilson's office and handed him the vu-graph remarking, "I've already made your final corrections on that one."

"Sorry about that, Lorraine, but I have another slight change."

Taking a grease pencil, Earl Wilson inserted the words "Continue to make" before the very first objective listed on the slide.

"Mr. Wilson, do you want this to read . . . continue to make significant contributions to programs of national importance?"

"That's right."

"Gee, Mr. Wilson, I didn't realize we had already reached that goal, and now all we want to do is continue."

"That's right, Lorraine." Earl Wilson smiled. "We've reached that goal."

As she shrugged her shoulders and walked out, she said, "I hope this is the final change. I've retyped this one over twice before."

One more call. John Ketner had completed talking to each of the individuals listed on the sheet of paper given him by General Taylor. Each one, in his own individual way, had performed yeoman's work, as Taylor had described it, in helping bring the Cuban crisis to a successful conclusion. But one name was not on the list, and neither Ben Taylor nor his own brother would ever know the part that man had played.

The President picked up his phone again. "Anne, get me Senator Ken Kern."

"Yes, Mr. President, just a moment, please."

"Kern here."

"Ken, Jack Ketner."

"Good evening, Mr. President. My congratulations to you for the superb performance this afternoon. And, I might add, for the past several months."

"Ken, without your help it would never have happened. How about lunch and tennis tomorrow? I could fill you in on the gory details then."

"Sounds great to me. Incidentally, my minority leader has been pestering me about the frequency of my visits to the White House. After all, he reminded me, that's the enemy over there."

"What did you tell him?"

"Working on you to support my trade bill before Congress."

"I'll take it under consideration. See you tomorrow about noon then."

"I'll be there."

As John Ketner hung up the phone, his thoughts drifted back to that very first day many, many months ago when Ken Kern had first advised him about the possibility of the Soviet's arming Cuba with nuclear weapons. And the game plan they had devised. Ken to play the loyal opposition and keep the pressure on; John Ketner to do everything possible to smoke out the truth. But no secrets were to be kept from each other. And both of them had kept that promise.

John Ketner had debated with himself and had agonized over his decision before confiding in Ken Kern the knowledge of the COBRA Team and every detail they had been reporting from Cuba. Ken had continued to cater to every whim and wish of the Soviet Ambassador to the United States, who in the deepest confidence told him of the decision by Premier Krenchev to put offensive nuclear weapons into Cuba.

Outwardly, the ambassador had to deny all such allegations, including any conversations with the President of the United States. But to Ken Kern he would confide his deep concern, and as he expressed it, the misgivings of many of the senior generals of the Red Army, who on a clandestine basis were keeping him informed as to where and when the weapons were being deployed and the self-destruct system which Krenchev had ordered be placed on them. John Ketner knew that without the information he had been receiving from Ken Kern, he might be an ex-president by now rather than riding the wave of euphoria sweeping the nation since his dramatic confrontation today.

"Thank you, sir." Dr. Wendy Overby carefully replaced the receiver.

"Isn't that wonderful, Leslie?"

"What?"

"That call from General Thompson. We're invited down to the White House for an awards ceremony next week. For the outstanding work we did on the nuclear weapon program, he said."

"Oh."

"Leslie, you're not paying attention to what I'm saying. What are you doing, anyway?"

"Still trying to determine how Dr. Dunsfield broke the code."

"Leslie we figured out the code. Dr. Dunsfield said so himself. He used our work. All he did was put it into different matrices to come up with the answer. We could have done that ourselves in another hour or two. I'm certain of that."

"If you say so, Wendy, but I'm still curious."

"Let's change the subject. Come here, Leslie, and give your princess a big hug and a kiss. After all, we missed last night, remember."

"Not now."

Wendy Overby rose from her chair and reached over and grabbed Leslie Overstreet's hand. For the second time in twenty-four hours she dragged a reluctant man behind her. But this time, it was toward her bedroom.

It was already dark when the White House limousine pulled up to 6601 34th Street in Georgetown. Mike Donovan sprang from the car as the chauffeur held open the right rear door. He ran up the two steps leading to Susan Ainsworth's townhouse and was about to push the doorbell when the door was flung open. For a moment he stood there looking at the most beautiful girl in the world silhouetted against the dim light of the room. Her outstretched arms were the welcome he had hoped for so long.

Bobby and Carol had said goodnight to the COBRA Team members after a sumptuous dinner at Club 21. They had just returned to the hotel when the telephone rang. Bob Ketner picked up the phone and heard his brother's voice. "Bobby, thought I'd call, not to interrupt what you doing, but to suggest you might want to turn on the TV. I expect a news bulletin will be along any minute."

"Thank you, Mr. President, and good night. I'll see you tomorrow."

Bob Ketner turned on the TV. The "Streets of San Francisco" was on. He flipped the dials to the other channels, Johnny Carson, a late show and a good-looking chick giving the weather forecast. He set the channel on NBC and turned to Carol. "Obviously, something important has or is about to happen, to say nothing of what went on today. The President would not have called and alerted me for a routine news item."

"We interrupt this program to bring you several special news bulletins." Bobby Ketner quickly turned up the volume. The SPECIAL NEWS BULLETIN remained on the screen as the announcer continued, "The White House has just announced that Henry Stevenson, the United States Ambassador to the United Nations, has submitted his resignation which has been accepted by the President. In a curt letter to the President, Stevenson asked to be relieved of his United Nations duties immediately in order to return to Providence and take care of urgent personal business. The White House announcement did not indicate who would be taking his place, nor was there any reference to the ambassador's actions earlier today during the session at the United

Nations. Obviously, today's dramatic showdown with the Soviet Union played some part in Stevenson's decision. Also, the Associated Press is reporting that Don Grimes, considered by many as the nation's greatest TV anchorman, has been relieved of all duties. The network did not elaborate. We now return to the program in progress."

Bob Ketner looked at Carol and remarked, "What a day! Excitement, suspense, and having you here. However, there is one thing more which will make this day complete." Taking Carol's hand, he walked toward the bedroom. Silently, she looked up at him and smiled then squeezed his hand in hers.

It was three-thirty in the morning when Susan Ainsworth wondered what Mike was thinking about. He had been silent for over fifteen minutes. Yet she knew he was not asleep. His hands had been tenderly caressing her body, but he hadn't said a word.

"Mike, a penny for your thoughts." She remembered the last time she had posed that question, many months before. And she hoped she'd get the same answer.

"Thinking about everything I've got to do tomorrow."

"Tomorrow, darling, is a long way off. Tonight is what counts now."

"I know—but tomorrow is even more important for us."

"For us? What do you mean?"

"Must get to Fort Myer early in the morning, then the Arlington County Court House."

"Fort Myer! Arlington County! What have they to do with us?"

"Everything. Fort Myer to see the chaplain about a wedding, and Arlington County to get the license."

"Oh, Mike, you have the strangest ways to make a girl happy. And, I'll love you forever."

"I hope so. You know, we have a lot of catching up to do."

"Catching up?"

"Three months of it." And he took her once more in his arms and held her close.

Ross Latimer knocked softly on the Oval Office door and waited for the President's response. He was carrying a large box of telegrams and cablegrams to show the President the great outpouring of good wishes which had swamped the White House circuits in the past eight hours. The messages ranged from the world's greatest leaders to a chicken rancher from central Wyoming who was proud of the performance of his President. However, a message that Ross Latimer handed the President brought a smile to his face.

> "Am proud to be your representative in Congress. My best wishes as always.
> Harlington"

"You know, Ross," the President said, "politicians are a fickle lot!"

CHARTER BOOKS
SUSPENSE TO KEEP YOU ON THE EDGE OF YOUR SEAT

- **EAGLES FLY** by Sean Flannery — 18016-7 $2.75
  ODESSA is alive and making its final bid for world domination, in this chilling novel of international intrigue.

- **BARRACUDA** by Irving A. Greenfield — 04770-X $1.95
  The pride of the U.S. submarine fleet is in trouble...International suspense in the tradition of FAIL SAFE.

- **BLINDSIDE** by Dave Klein — 06735-2 $2.75
  An explosive, psycho-sexual suspense story, set against a background of professional football.

- **DECEIT AND DEADLY LIES** by Franklin Bandy — 06517-1 $2.25
  MacInnes and his Psychological Stress Evaluator could tell when anyone was lying but could he discover the lies he was telling to himself?

- **THE KREMLIN CONSPIRACY** by Sean Flannery — 45501-8 $2.75
  Detente espionage set in Moscow as two top agents find themselves as pawns in a game being played against the backdrop of a Presidential visit to the Kremlin.

- **THE BLACKSTOCK AFFAIR** by Franklin Bandy — 06650-X $2.50
  A small town, a deadly medical mystery, and the corruption of power provide the dangerous mix in this new KEVIN MACINNES thriller.

ACE CHARTER BOOKS C-03
P.O. Box 400, Kirkwood, N.Y. 13795

Please send me the titles checked above. I enclose _____
Include 75¢ for postage and handling if one book is ordered; 50¢ per book for two to five. If six or more are ordered, postage is free. California, Illinois, New York and Tennessee residents please add sales tax

NAME_____

ADDRESS_____

CITY_____STATE_____ZIP_____

Page-turning Suspense from
CHARTER BOOKS

THE MAN ON THE LEFT Gardiner 51891-5 $2.50
After Vietnam, David Mitchell finally made a new life for himself. But suddenly, Army Intelligence sends him a new assignment: assassination!

THE BEDFORD INCIDENT Rascovich 05290-0 $1.95
The commander of a U.S. destroyer brings two nations to the brink of World War III.

DEAD END OPTION Obstfeld 14125-0 $2.25
Harry Gould is on the run with more money than he knows what to do with—and everybody wants him!

THE GAME OF X Sheckley 27308-4 $1.95
William Nye, aka Secret Agent X, in a spy-tangled novel of suspense.

TALON Coltrane 79630-3 $1.95
Talon's attitude was bad, but his discovery was worse—now someone in the CIA wants him out... permanently.

THE CHURCHILL COMMANDO Willis 10672-2 $1.95
They organized to restore order and decency... then found out the cure was worse than the disease.

Available wherever paperbacks are sold or use this coupon.

ACE CHARTER BOOKS
P.O. Box 400, Kirkwood, N.Y. 13795

Please send me the titles checked above. I enclose _____.
Include 75¢ for postage and handling if one book is ordered; 50¢ per book for two to five. If six or more are ordered, postage is free. California, Illinois, New York and Tennessee residents please add sales tax.

NAME_____

ADDRESS_____

CITY_____ STATE_____ ZIP_____

C-04

CHARTER MYSTERIES

*Stunning Thrillers You
Won't Want to Miss*

VITAL STATISTICS Chastain 86530-5 $1.95
A missing body, several murders, and a fortune in diamonds lead J.T. Spanner through a mystery in which New York itself may be one of the suspects.

LOCATION SHOTS Burke 48765-3 $2.25
Hotel Detective Sam Kelley is cool, black—and upset, when the lady in 8A becomes a corpse!

THE PRINCESS STAKES MURDER Platt 67877-7 $2.25
Willie is a record-breaking jockey and everybody's friend. So why is he dead? A Max Roper mystery.

THE KISSING GOURAMI Platt 44717-1 $1.95
Max Roper is pitted against a bizarre murderer, a bitter designer, and a beautiful heiress.

FATHER DOWLING MYSTERIES
by Ralph McInerny

Bishop As Pawn	06286-5	$1.95
Her Death of Cold	32780-X	$1.95
The Seventh Station	75947-5	$1.95

Available wherever paperbacks are sold or use this coupon.

ACE CHARTER BOOKS
P.O. Box 400, Kirkwood, N.Y. 13795

Please send me the titles checked above. I enclose _____.
Include 75¢ for postage and handling if one book is ordered; 50¢ per book for two to five. If six or more are ordered, postage is free. California, Illinois, New York and Tennessee residents please add sales tax.

NAME_____

ADDRESS_____

CITY_____STATE_____ZIP_____

C-02

CHARTER BOOKS
—the best in mystery and suspense!

VICTOR CANNING

"One of the world's six best thriller writers."
— Reader's Digest

☐ THE PYTHON PROJECT   69250-8 $1.95
A Rex Carver mystery. British and Russian agents have Rex on their open contract lists, but he's the only one who can untangle a scheme gone wrong.

☐ THE DOOMSDAY CARRIER   15865-X $1.95
Rimster didn't have much time in which to find Charlie, a friendly chimp carrying a deadly plague bacillus. The problem was, he couldn't let anyone know he was looking!

☐ THE KINGSFORD MARK   44600-0 $1.95
A novel of murder and betrayal "in the best Canning manner," with a fortune as the prize.

☐ THE LIMBO LINE   48354-2 $1.95
The Russians are kidnapping Soviet defectors and brainwashing them.

☐ THE WHIP HAND   88400-8 $2.25
A stunning espionage novel whose twists and turns end at Hitler's corpse.

☐ DOUBLED IN DIAMONDS   16024-1 $2.25
Rex Carver returns in this brilliant novel of espionage and adventure.

☐ THE RAINBIRD PATTERN   70393-3 $1.95
Someone had already staged two kidnappings and the victims could remember nothing. The third target is the Archbishop of Canterbury!

Available wherever paperbacks are sold or use this coupon

C ACE CHARTER BOOKS
P.O. Box 400, Kirkwood, N.Y. 13795

Please send me the titles checked above. I enclose _____.
Include 75¢ for postage and handling if one book is ordered; 50¢ per book for two to five. If six or more are ordered, postage is free. California, Illinois, New York and Tennessee residents please add sales tax.

NAME_____

ADDRESS_____

CITY_____ STATE_____ ZIP_____

Gc

NICK CARTER

> "Nick Carter out-Bonds James Bond."
> —*Buffalo Evening News*

Exciting, international espionage adventure with Nick Carter, Killmaster N3 of AXE, the super-secret agency!

TRIPLE CROSS   82407-2 $1.95
It all began as a favor—a routine hit that explodes in Nick's face!

THE SATAN TRAP   75035-4 $1.95
Nick infiltrates a religious cult whose victims are the most powerful men in Europe.

THE REDOLMO AFFAIR   71133-2 $1.95
Nick must find and kill Redolmo—the mastermind behind a drug ring that is crippling the West!

THE GREEN WOLF CONNECTION   30328-5 $1.50
Middle-eastern oil is the name of the game, and the sheiks were masters of terror.

MACAO   51354-9 $1.95
Nick's partner is the ruthless and beautiful Princess da Gama—but is catching spies her game?

THE MIND KILLERS   53298-5 $1.95
They were human time bombs, programmed to assassinate. Their next target: the U.S. president!

THE OMEGA TERROR   64053-2 $1.95
A deadly man-made organism is about to be loosed on the U.S.

Available wherever paperbacks are sold or use this coupon.

ACE CHARTER BOOKS
P.O. Box 400, Kirkwood, N.Y. 13795

Please send me the titles checked above. I enclose _____
Include 75¢ for postage and handling if one book is ordered; 50¢ per book for two to five. If six or more are ordered, postage is free. California, Illinois, New York and Tennessee residents please add sales tax.

NAME_____

ADDRESS_____

CITY_____ STATE_____ ZIP_____